Mike

The
Channel of
Invasion

THOROGOOD

Thorogood Publishing Ltd
10-12 Rivington Street
London EC2A 3DU
Telephone: 020 7749 4748
Fax: 020 7729 6110
Email: info@thorogoodpublishing.co.uk
Web: www.thorogoodpublishing.co.uk

A CIP catalogue record for this book is available
from the British Library.

ISBN 978-185418 638-6

Book designed and typeset in the UK
by Driftdesign

Printed in the UK by Ashford Colour Press

Dedication

==============

To the people of the Isles of Scilly — especially those from Tresco — and to all those Allied servicemen and women whose courage made Operation Overlord the outstanding success that it was.

Author's note

====================

The story is based upon the fact that such a covert flotilla operated between Tresco island and Brittany, delivering and bringing back secret agents together with vital intelligence about German troop dispositions and coastal defences.

HMS Godolphin is pure imagination, included to provide the Tresco flotilla with a focal point and context for its shore-based activities.

Certain names have been inspired by the names of real people, but the characters are figments of my imagination — based upon Service experience. Any similarity between them and persons living or dead is purely coincidental.

Other novels by Mike Williams:
The Secret Channel
The Channel to Freedom (coming soon)

Contents

===============

Principal characters

======================================

In order of seniority of rank.

Character:	Referred to as:
Rear Admiral Hembury Director of Coastal Forces Operations	*Admiral,* *The Admiral*
Captain MacPherson Officer commanding HMS Godolphin, Tresco, Isles of Scilly	*The Commanding* *Officer*
Commander John Enever Senior Naval Intelligence Officer, HMS Godolphin	*Commander,* *SNIO/SIO*
Capitaine de Vaisseau **Nicholas Mercier** Head of the Breton Resistance group – *Confrèrie Bonaparte*	*Code name 'Lionel'*
Lieutenant Commander **Richard Tremayne** The central figure in this story – an RNVR officer transferred to Coastal Special Forces who commands the Tresco flotilla of MTBs and clandestine fishing vessels	*Flotilla Commander/* *Boat Captain*

Lieutenant David Willoughby-Brown *Number One, First*
Tremayne's First Lieutenant (Second- *Lieutenant, WB*
in-Command) – like Tremayne, an
RNVR officer

Sub-Lieutenant Pierre Quilghini *Sub, Pierre*
Former French naval officer, now with
RNVR commission, whose ideas and
initiative were fundamental to the
setting-up of the secret channels
between Tresco and Brittany

First Officer Emma Tremayne *Intelligence Officer*
Tremayne's wife and formerly Wren *(Navy) SIS*
Intelligence Officer on Enever's staff at
HMS Godolphin

Petty Officer Bill Irvine *Cox'n, 'Swain*
Tremayne's boat coxswain

Able Seaman Watkins *Pablo*
A key long-term member of
Tremayne's boat crew

**Leading Seaman John
'Brummie' Nicholls**
Close friend and from the same town as
Pablo Watkins

Lieutenant Hermann Fischer RNVR,
South African Boat Captain and close
friend of Tremayne's

Tresco island

Brittany and the Cotentin Peninsula

Cherbourg

Cotentin Peninsula

Guernsey

Sark

Jersey

Plateau
des
Minquiers

Granville

Roscoff

Ouessant

Carantee

St Malo

Morlaix

Dinan

Brest

Camarel
-sur-Mer

Carhaix Plouguer

Rennes

Quimper

Marlag
PoW □
Camp

Lorient

Vannes

St Nazaire

One

Time to finish what we started...

The impenetrable darkness, the dank, overpowering smell of rotting undergrowth and the icy rain dripping off the trees above his head, created a chilling sense of utter isolation. He had become separated from the rest of his group when they had plunged into the forest, rapidly moving ever deeper to escape their pursuers. Hoarse, urgently shouted commands followed by purposeful, stealthy rushes of movement, confirmed that those looking for Tremayne and his party of saboteurs were already into the forest, close behind them.

Never before had he felt so completely alone and afraid. Despite the cold and the chilling downpour, he was drenched in sweat and could feel droplets of perspiration running down his face and mingling with the rain dripping off the end of his nose. His sweat-soaked shirt stuck to his back as he shifted his body, pressing himself even closer to the sodden ground.

For several seconds he lay still, his mouth dry and his heart pounding, as he took stock of the situation, listening and straining to try to identify the number and whereabouts of those now closing in on him and his companions. At odds with the adrenaline rush and the overwhelming tension he was experiencing, was his sudden, detached recall of his instructor's words during battle training on Tresco in the Isles of Scilly more than eighteen months ago: "When you're listening, sir, and all is dead quiet – especially at night – keep your mouth open, sir, and you'll hear more."

The incessant patter of rain on leaves and branches frustratingly muffled the noise of more deliberate and cautious movement, but it was only too obvious that those stalking the saboteurs were closing in – too quickly for comfort. Instinctively, he checked that the short, ugly 'pig-sticker' bayonet was firmly fixed to the muzzle lug of his sub-machine gun. With his left hand, he made sure that the fifty-round magazine was firmly locked home in its brass housing – unique among modern British weapons – located to the rear of the Lanchester's well-ventilated steel barrel. Tremayne twisted his body round to ensure his webbing ammunition pouches were open and that the remaining full magazines were within quick, easy reach.

As he wriggled, soaking wet, into a comfortable firing position, silently clearing the undergrowth away from his gun muzzle to give himself sufficient arc of fire, a sudden, stifled oath confirmed that at least one of the Germans was only a matter of thirty yards or so away, directly to his front and heading right for him.

Controlling rising panic, his paramount concern at that moment was that he had no plan of action or means of coordinating the immediate defence and continuing escape of his team of six specialists. In a matter of seconds, the strictly timed and tightly organised operation had become fragmented as the group had scattered and raced for the nearby forest, following the successful destruction of the target and the unexpectedly rapid appearance on the scene of German troops.

Continued stealthy, measured rustling of wet undergrowth ahead of him – this time closer – gave immediacy to his need for survival. The leading pursuers were so near that he could hear frequent muffled grunts as they struggled to clear a way through.

An escape plan rapidly forming in his mind – born of desperation – was suddenly cut short by the distinctive metallic clunk of a Thompson gun being cocked about, he guessed, two yards or so to his left. The welcome, familiar sound prompted an urgently whispered password from Tremayne – 'Braiden'. The equally quiet, but clear response was instantaneous – 'Rock'.

With a sense of sheer relief, and checking that his gun's safety catch was on, Tremayne crawled noiselessly through the sodden vegetation, snaking his way on his elbows towards the speaker, his Lanchester cradled across the crook of each arm.

As he closed in, conscious in the dark of someone's presence, the calm, measured voice whispered again. "It's me, sir – Sergeant Kane. Corporal Cotterell and Marine Weaver are a few yards away to the left of us. I'm not sure, sir, where Major West, Mr Quilghini and Able Seaman Harberer are, but I think they may be way over to our left and possibly behind us, sir."

"Thanks, Sar'nt. Together, the four of us can probably put down enough hot metal and hold up the Germans to enable the others to make it back to the RV. Jerry will try to outflank us, so you take the left flank with Weaver and I'll look after the right with Corporal Cotterell." Tremayne paused to bring his Lanchester round to bear on their pursuers' line of advance, hugging the ground as he silently eased his way into a new firing position.

"Major West's escape is critical, Sar'nt. We *have* to get him back to SIS in London, as quickly as possible."

Still maintaining hushed tones, Sergeant Kane responded: "Understood, sir." He then added, "Each time we fire a short burst, we must immediately roll away, right or left. In the dark, return fire will be aimed at the point of our muzzle flashes. Our flash eliminators don't really work that well, sir."

"Sounds a bloody good idea – I'm all for self-preservation, Sar'nt!" whispered Tremayne.

"In about twenty seconds, sir, we should each lob two grenades, with a five-second interval between each volley. Corporal Cotterell and Weaver will do this automatically, on my command – it's a well-rehearsed drill with us, sir. Jerry will respond and give away some of his positions." Kane paused to lay two '36 grenades on the ground, immediately to his front.

"The command for the first volley of grenades will be a double hoot from an owl bird call – a training exchange souvenir that the Royals picked up from the Finnish army just before the war. The second volley follows automatically after five seconds, sir."

"Agreed. True to commando tradition, eh Sar'nt? When in doubt – use a grenade! It's now ten seconds to go – and counting," confirmed Tremayne, checking the luminous hands of his watch.

Right on time, Kane's bird call added an authentic, if somewhat eerie and melancholic, sound to the rain-drenched forest, with its hushed air of collective fear and tension.

In near unison, four arms went up and over and, seconds later, four Mills grenades exploded across a front of some forty yards breadth. For a brief moment, the flashes lit up the forest, revealing close to twenty hunched, well-deployed figures moving slowly and menacingly through the trees, the first of them now advancing less than twenty yards from Tremayne's group. Sickening screaming and an unearthly moaning followed the explosions, as Tremayne and the three marines poured in a sustained burst of automatic fire.

Recovering quickly, the Germans began to return fire with rifles and automatic weapons. With disciplined fire and movement, they aggressively used the ensuing blackness to begin to surge forward once more, closer towards the Franco-British party. Tremayne realised that close-quarter battle with such determined troops would be no pushover.

Then the second volley of grenades exploded amongst them, creating more bloody carnage and screaming as men fell dead or wounded.

This time the German response seemed to be more driven by sheer fury and a desire for revenge. In the depths of the darkened forest, the noise of the exchanges of fire was deafening at such close quarters and the acrid smell of cordite hung in the damp night air. A withering fire wildly swept the area occupied by Tremayne's group. Incoming rounds zipped and tore viciously through the trees, shredding branches and bark, immediately above their heads. Keeping low, Tremayne and the three marines replied coolly and selectively, pinpointing and firing at muzzle flashes, while rapidly shifting position, following each burst from their own weapons.

As they withdrew, beyond Kane's left flank position, Major West and the two French sailors were also desperately putting down a lot of hot metal over the advancing Germans, but were clearly following orders to reach safety as rapidly as possible.

Cries of both pain and shock told Tremayne and the marines that their disciplined, controlled shooting was hitting home and causing further casualties. Despite their mounting losses, the Germans continued to press forward. Laboured breathing and muttered obscenities confirmed that the leading ranks of the enemy were now only a few yards away, struggling to push through the increasingly dense, wet undergrowth. Firing two long, deliberately sprayed bursts from his Lanchester to keep heads down, Tremayne rolled over first to Cotterell and then to Kane, to tell them to throw their remaining two grenades, this time with only two seconds between volleys.

"Jerry is so close that we run the risk of being killed by our own grenades, so hit the deck and pray as soon as you've lobbed the bloody things," whispered Tremayne. Two short bursts of fire from him, separated by a gap of two seconds, would be the signal to throw. Kane rapidly slid away snake-like to the left, to inform Marine Weaver of the plan. Tremayne quickly fitted a new fifty-round magazine to the Lanchester, pushing it home with the palm of his hand, and squeezed off two bursts, each of five rounds.

As before, four grenades were lobbed at the advancing pursuers. Before they recovered sufficiently to resume hitting Tremayne's group with return fire, the second volley exploded amongst them. Tremayne and the three marines, with devastating, concentrated firing, emptied their weapons, hosepipe fashion, in the Germans' direction. Then, abandoning caution and cover, they raced back, deeper into the forest, crashing painfully into wet, clinging branches and plunging through the tangle of undergrowth, changing magazines as they ran.

The Germans reacted quickly, but not fast enough, and this time their return fire was neither controlled nor accurate. The RV, to which Tremayne and the marines now headed, was a small airfield some three hundred yards clear of the forest and behind a long row of poplar trees. Already waiting for them was their transport, a Lockheed Hudson bomber of RAF Coastal Command.

Tremayne stopped, briefly, at the edge of the forest.

"Right, lads – another couple of bursts to delay them, then split arse for the runway. We'll stop again beyond that line of poplar trees and give them a magazine-full if they come into range as they exit the forest."

He paused to check his magazine. "Thank God *they* didn't use grenades back there."

After two sustained bursts to keep the Germans' heads down, the group ran flat out, zigzagging across the open ground. Ahead of them, briefly flashed green lights – the agreed pick-up recognition signal – indicated that Major West and the smaller group were already at the line of poplars. At that point, the Hudson's twin Wright 'Cyclone' engines burst into life with a spluttering roar. With unsighted, unaimed rounds buzzing around them, they made it as a group to the shelter of the poplars. With their pursuers still not visible in the darkness and effectively out of the range of their sub-machine guns, Tremayne issued fresh orders: "Into the plane, everyone. Lively does it, lads!"

The group dashed through the line of poplar trees to the Hudson, scrambled up the short ladder, in through the open fuselage door and immediately joined Major West and the two French sailors, sitting inside on primitive, makeshift seating in the cramped area behind the pilot and navigator. The instantaneous high noise level of animated conversation reflected both the relief of escape and sense of triumph about what had turned out to be the group's biggest and toughest sabotage assignment yet.

After congratulating the group on what had been a highly successful raid into Brittany, with the major objective having been completely achieved, Tremayne quickly moved up to the cockpit to talk to the pilot.

"As we take off, we'll come into range of German rifle fire from our left. It would therefore be -"

The young RAF pilot smiled as he gently interrupted the begrimed, sweat-soaked naval officer. "Thank you, sir. Any moment now, as we clear the trees, our port beam and dorsal turret twin Brownings will open fire and start chamfering up the bastards. We'll thoroughly lace any area where we see muzzle flashes. You've done your share. We'll take over now, sir. Relax and enjoy the trip."

Just under two hours later, the Hudson touched down at an RAF airstrip in Wiltshire where Major West would be collected by car to take the intelligence gathered, together with his report on the raid, to British Secret Intelligence Service (SIS) headquarters in London. After quick but warm farewells to Major West, Tremayne and the rest of the party transferred aircraft and scrambled aboard an RAF Avro Anson transport, whose twin Armstrong-Siddeley 'Cheetah' engines were already revving as they arrived at the airstrip.

Within minutes, the Anson was heading west for the airfield on St Mary's in the Isles of Scilly. How different this raid had been, reflected Tremayne, from the similar, but abortive one, sixteen months earlier on the Ile d'Ouessant. Then, they had set out to investigate and destroy what was believed to be the Germans' main radio transmission – and intercept – station, covering the Western Approaches. The station was understood to be the principal source of radio communication, in the coordination of the deadly U-boat 'wolf packs' and their Luftwaffe counterparts, which were exacting an alarming toll of British and Allied shipping losses off the south of Ireland and the western entrance to the English Channel. It was also believed to be a key German listening post, in the monitoring of radio traffic for both intelligence and counter-intelligence operations in the area.

On that earlier raid, Major West and a colleague, who were both specialists in radio warfare, had, to their complete surprise, discovered that the set-up, which they had gone to destroy, was a very clever and elaborate ruse. Consisting of realistic but dummy radio aerials, it had been designed to divert the Allies' attention from the location of the real radio warfare station. The genuine article, Resistance intelligence had confirmed, was situated deep in a wooded area of outstanding natural beauty on the mainland, a few miles in from the coast and more difficult to access.

What Tremayne and his saboteurs had managed to achieve on that first, otherwise largely disappointing raid, was to seize, in an act of cool daring, one of the then latest German high-speed E-boats. Keeping camouflage finishes, flotilla insignia and pennant numbers up to date with current German Schnellboot practices, the captured E-boat had proved to be an invaluable addition to the Tresco flotilla's collection of boats for clandestine operations.

With the subsequent help of the forces of the Confrèrie Bonaparte, the new and most effective of the French Resistance groups operating in Brittany, Tremayne's Naval Special

Forces flotilla, operating out of Tresco island in the Scillies, had managed to locate – and now destroy – the Germans' real major radio transmission and reception centre.

Formed under two years previously and largely in response to Churchill's exhortation to 'set Europe ablaze', the covert flotilla operating out of HMS Godolphin, Tresco, was one of several such Naval Coastal Forces units based along the southern coast of England. With the appointment of Admiral Louis Mountbatten as Chief of Combined Operations, such 'maverick' flotillas had now begun to acquire the status and standing – even within some of the more staid Admiralty circles – that traditional, conventional thinking had, until recently, rejected out of hand.

Tremayne, as a young lieutenant, had established his reputation as the flotilla's leading boat captain and, subsequently, as the acting flotilla commander. In the latter role, he had been awarded the DSC for his leadership and gallantry in action. More recently, he had been promoted to the rank of Lieutenant Commander, RNVR.

Tresco flotilla's clandestine operations centred primarily on Brittany and their principal task was to keep open the sea lanes between the UK and France, in order to insert and extract secret agents – and military intelligence – and to maintain safe escape routes for downed Allied aircrews evading capture.

With its comparative remoteness and sheltered waters, Tresco provided an ideal base from which relatively shallow-draught boats could operate. Equally, because of its very small population, it was comparatively easy to maintain the degree of secrecy necessary for such covert operations to have any chance of success. Indeed, the rather bland cover adopted for the base was that of a small, typical coastal forces unit whose task was the routine patrolling of the waters around the Isles of Scilly.

The Tresco flotilla consisted of three very authentically disguised 'Breton' fishing boats, with powerful engines and cleverly reworked hulls, capable of over thirty knots. These were regularly repainted and numbered, in accordance with the prevailing fishermen's tastes and changing German regulations, according to the adopted Breton port of origin they purported to come from. To give the new paintwork a weathered and less-than-fresh look, iron filings were mixed in with the paint. To the islanders, these were universally known as 'the mystery boats'.

HMS Godolphin's flotilla also boasted a collection of three British Fairmile 'C' and one Camper & Nicholson motor gun-boats, plus the ex-German E-boat. On neighbouring St Mary's island – generally referred to by the ship's company as the islands' 'Metrollops' – was an airfield with a squadron of Hawker Hurricanes. Frequently, these provided much-needed air cover for the Tresco boats travelling to and from Brittany. When needed, longer-range air cover was provided by a squadron of Beaufighters, based at Bolt Head in South Devon.

The principal anchorage for the Tresco flotilla was off Braiden Rock, in New Grimsby Sound, on Tresco's western coast, opposite Hangman's Island, a rocky adjunct of the neighbouring island of Bryher. Its name had served as the operation's password.

Lieutenant Commander Richard Tremayne, who had recently celebrated his twenty-eighth birthday, reported to the station commander, the newly appointed Captain Hugo MacPherson. His other critical relationship – a close and well-established one – was with Commander John Enever, Godolphin's donnish, but highly capable senior intelligence officer.

As yet, Captain MacPherson was largely an unknown quantity, but he had already shown himself to be an austere, unapproachable disciplinarian, with not even the glimmer of a sense of humour. By contrast, John Enever was a sensitive, highly perceptive man, who concentrated far more on managing his relationships with people, than on trying to manage his people. As a consequence, he got far more out of his team than any other naval officer that Tremayne had ever encountered. What is more, he commanded their respect and willing loyalty, as well as their undoubted affection. Something of a scholarly eccentric, Commander Enever was often seen with an unlit pipe firmly clenched between his teeth. Much to everyone's amusement, except Captain MacPherson's, Enever would frequently return salutes with his left hand if his right arm happened to be full of confidential files – which it usually was.

The Avro Anson bringing in Tremayne and his party

approached the Scillies in the clear light of a bright, early December morning. The still somewhat watery sun cast its gentle, diffuse light on the shallow turquoise waters around the islands and the many stretches of near-white sand that were seen to advantage from the air.

Although he had been stationed on Tresco for almost two years, the Scillies had lost none of the beauty and magic that had captivated him from the outset. Tremayne had known both the pain of personal tragedy and the joy of a new love here on the islands – especially on Tresco – and, as a consequence, they continued to touch his emotions, as well as his senses, deeply.

After landing on St Mary's, the party was quickly transferred by naval motor launch to HMS Godolphin, two miles away across a stretch of windswept sea known as The Road, dotted with countless scattered rocks and the uninhabited, twin-humped island of Samson lying off their port beam.

Typical of his thoughtfulness, Commander Enever had organised breakfast for the six, followed by an order to 'get heads down and get some sleep' and then to attend an operational debriefing at a very civilised 14.00 hours.

Tremayne took the opportunity to telephone Emma, his wife, who was serving as a Wren officer in the Naval Section of SIS in London, but who had previously been a member of Enever's Intelligence team at Godolphin. The relief in her voice at his safe return was only too apparent, but quickly the warmth and laughter so typical of their close relationship took over from anxiety. Tremayne recognised just how deep his love for Emma had become and how central to his life she now was. They had been married a little over a year ago in St Nicholas, the parish church of Tresco.

He returned to his tiny quarters, to be greeted ecstatically by Bertie, his young black labrador, who was regularly looked after, in Tremayne's frequent absences, by the Oylers – the couple who ran the nearby New Inn. Within seconds, an exhausted Tremayne fell into a deep, untroubled sleep.

Just before 14.00 hours, Tremayne and Lieutenant Quilghini, the Breton-speaking French naval officer, joined John Enever in Hut 101, the 'Intelligence Centre', for the operation's debriefing. Hut 101 had more the appearance of a university professor's common room with its stacked-up papers and files and liberally covered notice boards screwed to the walls. Cupboards and other furniture had, at first sight, little in common with each other and clearly had been 'acquired', one way or another, from many different sources. The real unifying thread was one of old, well-worn quality, which reinforced the impression of 'Oxbridge' threadbare gentility.

The news of the complete destruction of the radio warfare station had already been signalled to Enever by SIS in London, who had given him a more or less chapter and verse account of the successful operation, based upon Major West's verbal report and feedback.

"Gentlemen, my warmest congratulations! Yours has been a major success and undoubtedly has set back Jerry in the clandestine war of intelligence. Of course, as I speak, they will no doubt be creating a new transmission and receiving station, but the collection of codes and other confidential material that West brought back has been of enormous value to Naval Intelligence." He paused, to remove the unlit pipe from between his teeth, and place it in the cut-off, highly polished base of a German 5.9 inch brass ship's cannon shell case on his desk.

"It has demonstrated to both the Germans – and, probably just as important, to our lords and masters of the Admiralty in Queen Anne's Mansions – that we can now hit Jerry, almost at will, and come off best!"

At that point, one of his Wren assistants appeared with mugs of tea and set them down on his leather-topped, ancient walnut desk.

"Many thanks, Jane. A lifesaver!" Gesturing to the mugs, Enever added, "Gentlemen, do help yourselves."

Tremayne and Quilghini gave their accounts of the operation, including the desperate firefight in the forest. Both officers were quick to give praise to the contributions of the men who had fought so effectively, with courage and professionalism, at their sides. Tremayne made special mention of Sergeant Kane's cool, disciplined leadership of his marines and his consummate competence in stamping his presence on the firefight in the forest. "Sergeant Kane gained us the fire initiative – and kept it, in extreme circumstances."

Nodding, he added, "And Pierre, here, along with Able Seaman Harberer, conducted an impressive, tactical withdrawal, with aggressive covering fire, so enabling us to extricate Major West safely with his vital intelligence intact."

Enever smiled and looked towards the young French sub-lieutenant.

"Well done, Sub. Getting Major West back to England in one piece was a most essential part of this whole operation. Please pass on my appreciation to Able Seaman Harberer and let him know that I am aware of the part he played too."

Enever paused for a moment, to take a drink of tea.

"Tell me about the demolition of the masts and destruction of the radio station, gentlemen. What happened, exactly?"

Tremayne began by describing the strangely deserted appearance of the station, with relatively few guards on duty – except at obvious points, such as the main entrance to the barbed-wire surrounded compound – and the absence of roaming guard dogs.

"We gained access to the side of the main building. Major West isolated and neutralised the electrics, without triggering the alarm, and Sergeant Kane's Royals cut out a section of the perimeter wire. That did take some time. The wire was complex and substantial and was obviously intended to deter all but the most serious attempts at infiltration. We posted a well-concealed Corporal Cotterell, complete with a Thompson gun and grenades, close to the entrance we'd created, to cover our return."

Enever could barely control his enthusiasm and need to ask more questions, but confined himself to asking, "How on earth, Richard, did you get around the place without being spotted?"

Tremayne continued: "The patrolling sentries each had comparatively large distances to cover and, at times, all were out of sight of us. It was, therefore, relatively easy for us to rush up to the main building and gain access through a back door. Pierre, Able Seaman Harberer and I each carried our single shot CO_2 pistols and these, for once, proved a real blessing. We disposed of the first guards we came across inside the building silently and even had time to reload our weapons."

Enever cut in, smiling, "So despite the usual criticism of this somewhat bizarre SOE invention as being a useless tactical weapon, it worked well for you on this occasion?"

"Exactly so, sir. Provided that you *can* get close enough, it will put somebody down permanently. Major West, Sergeant Kane and Marine Weaver formed the demolition party and secured charges with timer mechanisms to each of the radio masts, synchronised to detonate in twenty minutes."

"What happened then?"

"Unfortunately, one of the guards, deciding to grab a quick cigarette, suddenly appeared from round the corner of the stores and maintenance building and, quite literally, walked into Major West's party. He collided with Marine Weaver who despatched him silently, on the spot, with his fighting knife. Major West's group then joined us in the main building. We had to shoot three more guards with the CO2 pistols, and fire SMG bursts over a few heads, before we herded the radio operators, some Abwehr officers and the remaining guards away from the compound and through the main entrance, now obligingly opened for us by Jerry.

"The explosives group placed more synchronised, timed charges to destroy the cipher machines, radio transmitters and receivers and then grabbed as much intelligence information as possible. Major West, who speaks excellent German, clearly knew what he was looking for, found it and grabbed it."

Enever removed his spectacles, breathed exaggeratedly on the lenses, and then polished them with the end of his tie, much to Quilghini's ill-disguised amusement. "Almost a text-book operation, dear boy, apart from the unfortunate fellow going for what he thought was to be a quiet drag!"

"In general, it was sir. Harberer and Weaver collected all the guards' weapons and placed them close to the explosives in the main building, to make sure that they were destroyed. Corporal Cotterell rejoined us and, pretty well bang on time – if you'll forgive the pun, sir – masts and the radio station went up in a rapid succession of explosions. Thanks to Major

West, the base was completely destroyed – and with no casualties on our part."

"It sounds most impressive and clearly was very profess-ionally executed. My heartiest congratulations to you both, gentlemen. I will call Sergeant Kane in and thank him personally. Tell me, how did you then get away?"

"Sergeant Kane ordered all the prisoners to turn around, so they were not facing us, and then made them lie down – encouraging them with a couple of close overhead bursts from his Thompson to speed up compliance. To keep them down and terrified, we opened up with sustained bursts immediately over their heads – and I think that many believed a mass execution was under way. We then hightailed it, as fast as we could, into the surrounding forest, about a hundred yards distant. We assume, sir, that it was a group of Germans on routine patrol nearby who obviously reacted to the explosions and came after us so quickly."

"Richard, Pierre, thank you both. It's quite a story – and well done gentlemen."

After the debriefing, Enever then confirmed the emerging changing role of Godolphin, as the need arose to gather more intelligence, aimed at preparing for what was now the inevitable invasion of France and the opening of the anticipated 'second front'.

"The British and Americans are under enormous political pressure from the Russians to open a second front, to support the recent successes of the Red Army who have begun to turn the tide and roll the Germans westwards. Morally and politically, as well as militarily, we need to take some of the load off their shoulders – and add to Jerry's burden," added Enever.

"The new Confrèrie Bonaparte would appear to be somewhat more secure than our previous contacts in the Resistance and, as far as we can tell, this group has not been infiltrated by either the Germans or their local stooges. So, gentlemen, it seems that we have a reliable source of up-to-date intelligence, in Brittany and as far east as Cherbourg and the Cotentin Peninsula."

Retrieving his as yet unlit pipe from the ashtray – which came courtesy of the old German Imperial High Seas Fleet – Enever continued, "Our role remains that of inserting and extracting agents along the Brittany coast, and ensuring that the Confrèrie is supplied with weapons, ammunition and explosives to enable them to raise their game, as and whenever."

Getting up from his ancient 'captain's' swivel chair, Enever walked over to the wall behind him and released the rolled-up map of Brittany and western Normandy.

With a long wooden pointer in his hand, he continued, "What we are now also charged with, gentlemen, is the task of finding out exactly what Jerry's coastal defence systems are along these areas here –" as his 'magic wand', as he termed it, traced patterns around the north-west French coast.

"We need to know, especially, what underwater obstacles

are in place, where the locations and likely fields of fire of weapons emplacements are, and the extent of barbed wire, minefields and other hazards on the beaches themselves. In just over two weeks' time, gentlemen, it will be 1944 and if things go according to plan, my guess is that the invasion of France will take place some time next summer. That, by the way, is *not* for discussion outside this office."

As Enever paused briefly to finish drinking his tea, Tremayne asked, "Do we have access to COPPs teams to help us with this job, sir?" Quilghini's puzzled expression and quizzical, raised eyebrows, provided the cues for Enever to step in and clarify.

"What Richard is talking about, Pierre, are the Combined Operations Pilotage Parties. These guys are trained swimmer-canoeists, who wear waterproof suits, swim fins or rope-soled boots and buoyancy aids – but no oxygen breathing apparatus. They are dropped, or inserted, near to an enemy coast by a variety of means and then swim close inshore to observe, reconnoitre and bring back intelligence of the layout and location of enemy defences – and anything else that seems relevant to the preparation of a seaborne assault. Normally, they don't operate underwater, at least not for very long," he added with a wry grin.

"Back to your question, dear boy. We will be having attached to us, pretty soon, a couple of 'COPPists', courtesy of the Royal Marines, but the plan is for some of our people to be trained so that we fully understand the COPP role and know how best to give it support, whenever push comes to shove, in the invasion."

The kindly grey eyes twinkled behind the half-moon spectacles. "We shall shortly be calling for volunteers, Richard!"

"I already have two webbed feet, sir. If I grow flippers as well, Emma and I will be in danger of producing tadpoles," replied Tremayne.

Enever returned, laughing, to his chair, before continuing: "Though, undoubtedly, we shall be involved in more 'thud and blunder' across the Channel, one of our new tasks is to train up the members of the new Confrèrie into becoming a highly effective guerrilla force who can harass the Germans and carry out diversionary attacks, once the invasion of France takes place. Before that, they will carry out well-planned acts of sabotage, away from the coast to divert German forces' attention from the proposed landing areas – wherever they are to be."

After handling questions from Tremayne and Quilghini, Enever called the debriefing to a close, but asked Tremayne to stay for a moment.

"Richard, a brief word, please." Enever retrieved his pipe and studied it closely for a moment, closing the door after Quilghini had left. "Grab a pew, Richard, we're off parade now. Other than very briefly, I believe, you have not properly met Captain MacPherson yet?" Tremayne took a seat to face Enever, detecting a thinly veiled note of warning in his voice.

"No, not really, John, although that brief contact does rather confirm the reputation that he brings with him to Godolphin."

Enever smiled. "I know what you mean. We – and you, especially, Richard – have major, complex challenges facing us and it is vital that we meet those with the utmost professionalism. Such tasks, however, as we both well know, demand levels of initiative, adaptability and versatility that are way beyond conventional wisdom and quite outside naval standard operating procedures. From what I have already learned about our new commanding officer, he is a stickler for rules, regulations and keeping to the book. AFOs are his bible."

"And he's something of a zealot?" asked Tremayne with a grin.

"Absolutely, dear boy. Context and nuance don't exist for him. Everything is either 'right' or 'wrong', 'certain' and 'simple'. He has what he *knows* is the solution, before we've even decided exactly what the problem is. To make matters worse, the most excruciating detail and minutiae just don't escape his personal radar screen."

Enever paused and looked straight at Tremayne. "He *is* our skipper and his four gold rings must have our respect. But the demands of operational effectiveness and the intended outcomes of our role must remain the paramount arbiter of our, at times, very unconventional methods and activities. On that score, we have the wholehearted support of Rear Admiral Hembury. Thank God he too – as you well know – is a maverick operator. Tactically – and strategically – Admiral Hembury is our boss and mentor. If anything, Captain MacPherson is likely to be our *tormentor*!"

Enever placed his pipe back in the brass ashtray. "I will do all that I can to act as a buffer between you, your boat crews and Captain MacPherson's restrictive red tape, to enable you to continue the vital work that you and your men have done so impressively over the last eighteen months or so."

"Thank you, John. I appreciate that. Stifling bureaucracy and becoming a hostage to set procedures simply run counter to the spirit, intent – and whole ethos – of special operations."

Tremayne was glad to see that he had Enever's undivided attention.

"Working strictly according to the book would tie our hands to the point where our operational effectiveness would be severely limited. In any case, John, the definitive book, detailing Special Forces' activities in *absolute* terms, hasn't been written yet – and, I believe, never will be. While, inevitably, we *do* depend for success upon disciplined thinking and sound procedures – arrived at by direct experience – these are the bedrock, *not* the sole determinant, of our methods and actions."

Enever paused, reflectively, for a moment before responding to Tremayne.

"I agree, Richard. As I see it, we are likely to be involved in constant battles between what Captain MacPherson sees as regulatory 'efficiency' and what we consider to be *effective* practice and the achievement of necessary results. Make no mistake, he *is* intelligent – but in the channelled, excluding way of someone who has unquestioning self-belief and who believes in the divine right of rank and position. If ever there were an example of hubris out of control, then he is it.

"His approach appears to be driven by some narcissistic illusion of perfection – 'do it my way and you'll get it right'. The more he is convinced that he *is* right, the more he sees others as being wrong. Sad to say, he appears to gain much personal triumph from spotting flaws in others' efforts and rarely, if ever, does he give praise. Much of the time, he sees himself as the only one in step around here!"

Enever pointed with his pipe to three files, each marked 'Top Secret', that were lying on his desk and looked intently at Tremayne. "Critical intelligence such as that contained in these files is landing on my desk virtually every day now, Richard.

"We have a vital job to do and I'm bloody determined that we *will* do it – and do it well. Too many people – in France, as well as here – are depending upon us. Planning the intended invasion of France is already at an advanced stage and we will have a crucial part to play in both the preliminaries and the execution. Far too much, in both the immediate future *and* in the longer term, depends upon what our efforts – and those of others like us – achieve over the next twelve months. That – and *essentially* that – Richard, is our mandate."

TWO

A new menace in
the channel

Tremayne's motor gun-boat – MGB1315 – slipped her moorings at Braiden Rock anchorage at precisely 08.30 hours, accompanied by Lieutenant Hermann Fischer's Camper & Nicholson, to carry out a routine sweep of the seas south of Scilly. Recently increased and well coordinated U-boat, E-boat and Luftwaffe attacks on Allied shipping entering the English Channel from the west, were causing the Admiralty major concern. Although the Tresco flotilla's primary task remained that of keeping open the espionage sea lanes to and from Brittany, coastal forces based along the Channel and North Sea coasts had become increasingly involved of late in countering the new, highly effective German hit-and-run tactics of coordinated attack at sea.

The U-boat 'wolf packs' had recently suffered grievous losses and a severe strategic setback, since the British crypto-analysts and radio intercept specialists had mastered the German submarines' 'Enigma' code, used in their wireless transmissions. As a consequence, the locations of U-boats transmitting messages of their area of operations and targets were instantaneously picked up by SIS monitors. Both bombers and anti-submarine surface vessels were now quickly being sent to seek out and destroy the enemy submarines once they were located.

In what the German Naval High Command, the Oberkommando der Marine (OKM), had come to regard as 'Black May', forty-one U-boats had been sunk in that one month alone. In the period from January to May 1943, the Allies had sunk ninety-six German submarines. From May to December, another forty or so U-boats were sunk and the number of U-boat crews lost in action was running at around sixty per cent.

As a direct result of these unacceptable losses – compared with the rate of sinking of Allied naval and merchant ships – Admiral Dönitz had abandoned the large 'wolf pack' tactics in favour of small group, or single, U-boat attacks; with boats armed with special search receiver equipment, together with the new T5 Zaunkönig (Wren) acoustic homing torpedoes and up to eight 20mm anti-aircraft guns. These boats were now being supported in the Bay of Biscay and in Channel waters, almost as a matter of course, by E-boats, Focke-Wulf Condor reconnaissance aircraft and Heinkel He177s, the latter frequently launching Henschel Hs glider bombs at both Allied naval vessels and merchantmen – with alarming success.

Hermann Fischer was Tremayne's accompanying boat captain on the sweep. A tall, athletic, fair-haired South African of Anglo-German ancestry, he held a lieutenant's commission in the RNVR – as opposed to the regular Royal Navy – as did most of HMS Godolphin's naval officers.

Fischer's razor-like mind, ever-ready sharp wit and outspoken irreverence, complemented Tremayne's more reflective, but equally blistering criticism of the idiotic and unacceptable and his similarly penetrating, quick sense of humour. Whereas Fischer was outrageously extrovert, Tremayne was more inclined to sensitive introversion. In their twenty months of serving together as boat captains and sharing both the terror and elation of close-quarter battle on so many occasions, the two had become very firm friends and ideal foils for one another.

On this sweep, serving as the crew of MGB1315, were many of the personnel who had been with Tremayne since the formation of the flotilla almost two years previously.

Next to Tremayne, standing on the MGB's compact, open armoured bridge over the wheelhouse, was his First Lieutenant – David Willoughby-Brown – a language graduate, fluent in

French and German and well able to converse in several other European languages. Aged twenty-three, with a highly developed, enquiring mind, WB – as he was universally known – was blessed with an open, engaging approach to life, which drew – variously – affection, amusement and incredulous tolerance from others. Born into a wealthy family of generations of serving cavalry officers, Willoughby-Brown was socially well connected with powerful, influential friends. He had successfully overcome the initial resentment, ridicule and envy that knowledge of his privileged background had tended to generate, in certain quarters, during his early days at Godolphin.

His ingenuous, amiable approach, his willingness to listen and learn and also his personal courage in action, had won people's affection and admiration and he was considered to be an officer of high potential. Commander Enever described him as 'a touchingly eccentric and thoroughly likeable young Englishman'.

Tremayne and Willoughby-Brown had served together virtually from the day that the Tresco flotilla had been formed. The bond between them, based upon mutual respect and regard, was strong. When 'on parade', in front of others, they maintained a formal relationship of 'Number One' and 'Sir'. Off-duty, or in the company of Enever and the other boat captains and their First Lieutenants, they were always on close, first-name terms – and enjoyed what the imaginative Fischer colourfully described as a 'farting relationship'!

Occupying the position beside the First Lieutenant, hands on the wheel and eyes fixed on the horizon ahead, was Petty Officer Bill Irvine, MGB1315's coxswain. It would be difficult to find a more complete contrast to Willoughby-Brown than Bill Irvine.

Short, strongly built and in his forties, he was a long-serving regular in the Navy, from boy seaman to petty officer. Irvine hailed from east Belfast, close to the Shankhill Road, and frequently described himself as 'born within the sound of Harland and Wolff's riveters, so I was'. A taciturn man, who quickly made it only too obvious that he had zero tolerance for idiots, Irvine was an outstanding coxswain. The high mutual respect between him and Tremayne was immediately apparent. Underneath his tough, seemingly uncompromising exterior he was, as Tremayne had discovered on more than one occasion, a somewhat shy and sensitive person. But heaven help anyone who judged that to be a weakness and sought to take advantage of it. Irvine possessed the quick insight and wry, penetrating sense of humour of so many people from Northern Ireland and, while remaining deceptively poker-faced, he could quite unexpectedly reduce those around him to helpless laughter.

As her three Hall-Scott petrol engines, with their combined 2,700 horse power, roared into life, MGB1315 slid away effortlessly from her moorings, with Fischer's somewhat larger Camper & Nicholson keeping station thirty yards astern of her.

Turning to Irvine, Tremayne said, "We have the tide with us, Cox'n. Take her at half revolutions, south, if you please, with Great Rag Ledge to starboard and Hulman and Nut Rock to port. Once we're in The Road, clear of Nut Rock, open her up to maximum revolutions and take her south-east, between St Mary's and St Agnes."

"Aye aye, sir."

With the cold December morning wind freshening by the minute, white caps appeared on the rolling waves and boiling seas crashed up against and churned over the lower rocky promontories of Samson to starboard and those of St Mary's off the port beam. In The Road, black shag and the odd cormorant skimmed over the choppy wave crests to join those already drying their wings on the scattered surrounding rocks after diving into the shallow sea for fish. Keeping them company over the water — and on the rocky islets — were kittiwakes and both great and lesser black-backed and grey herring gulls. Along the shoreline, long-legged oyster catchers strutted importantly up and down the islands' many sandy beaches, their distinctive, long orange beaks clearly visible to those on the duty watch on deck.

East, south-east of Scilly by ten miles, Tremayne ordered "Test weapons" and both boats responded with measured thumps, of differing cadence, from their six-pounders and 40mm Bofors. The rapidly firing 20mm Oerlikons and 0.50 calibre

Brownings added a more frenetic beat to the noise until, ten seconds later, test firing ceased. Spent shell and cartridge cases were quickly cleared off the decks, as the two boats continued to plough a new course, south-east, through the now darker grey and steeper rolling waves of the English Channel.

A sudden off-key, catarrhal wail, emanating from the tiny galley below and just aft of the wheelhouse, announced to the world that Able Seaman 'Pablo' Watkins would shortly be coming round with a steaming hot cup of kye – the Navy's traditional, glutinous and cold-defeating hot drinking chocolate.

"Hmm, I wonder, Number One, which soul-inspiring aria accompanies our drink this morning?" asked a grinning Tremayne.

"Well, it's certainly not Mozart or Puccini, sir," responded Willoughby-Brown with one eyebrow assuming the distinctive, parabolic curve of mock horror. "If I *can* interpret the adenoidal vernacular, it sounds more like a Brummie rendering of *The Dockyard Cavalry* to me, sir!"

Seconds later, the stocky, powerful figure of the redoubtable Watkins appeared on the bridge, carrying a large, aluminium rum fanny full of the lifesaving, scorching hot brown liquid. Around his neck and barrel-like chest was a string of enamel drinking mugs, clanking noisily as he clambered over the ammunition and signal bunting lockers.

With an affable grin and a cheery, "Mornin' sir. It's a bit bleedin' parky up 'ere. I thought as 'ow an 'ot brew might 'elp, sir," he slipped off three mugs from around his neck and dipped each of them into the steaming, viscous sludge. Handing one to Tremayne, then the First Lieutenant and finally to the coxswain, Watkins quickly looked around for any more shivering duffel-coated figures. With the appreciative thanks of those on the cold, windswept bridge following him, Watkins made his way around the boat to the various gun crews, stood-to at defence stations and trying to keep themselves warm at their exposed, spray-drenched gun positions. Bursts of raucous laughter plotted his swaying, welcome tour as he joked with the shivering members of the duty watch on deck.

The two motor gun-boats continued to punch their way at twenty-seven knots through the wind-whipped sea, their churning, sparkling bow waves glistening frothily white, with the regular rising and falling of their purposeful hulls. On the bridge, Tremayne and his First Lieutenant continuously scanned the horizon through their powerful Bausch & Lomb naval binoculars, sweeping ahead, aft and to port and starboard.

After something like an hour of monotonous empty grey sea and sky, the rating watching the boat's radar screen in the wheelhouse below them called, "Sir, small blip on radar, about seven thousand yards, almost dead ahead". Two sets of binoculars immediately locked on to the horizon directly in front of the MGB.

"See anything, Number One?"

"Not yet, sir. In this running sea, I doubt if we'll see much until we're closer."

"OK. Maintain search, Number One."

Speaking into the bridge voice tube to Leading Yeoman of Signals 'Taff' Jenkins, Tremayne called, "Yeo, make to Lieutenant Fischer: *'Radar blip, dead ahead, seven thousand yards. Keep directly astern and in line to minimise profile. Maintain maximum revolutions to investigate contact'*." Calling to his engineering chief, Tremayne then yelled, "Chief, we have a probable contact. Squeeze me every last ounce out of those bloody engines please."

"Aye aye, sir. Well, I'll do my best." The bluff Glaswegian accent conveyed just the merest hint of parental outrage that his beloved, already overworked charges were now being pressured to deliver the impossible. The immaculately polished, gleaming brass and steel engines were tended and watched over by the chief as if they were his children and were known amongst the stoker mechanic ratings as 'Buchanan's bairns'.

In line astern, the two MGBs raced towards the contact picked up by radar, spray from their bow waves relentlessly cascading over their for'ard decks and gun crews.

Tremayne ordered: "Close up at action stations. Stand by all guns. Bring to bear on sight."

The tension began to mount as gun crews traversed weapons and checked magazines and cocking mechanisms — out of disciplined habit and a well-honed instinct for survival.

Suddenly, Willoughby-Brown pointed and called out, "Look, there she is! A submarine — about three thousand yards directly ahead. She appears to be dead in the water, sir."

Tremayne focused his binoculars on the boat. "She's stern on to us and on the surface. At this distance and angle, I can't see her ensign nor read her pennant number, but she appears to have guardrails and a gun platform immediately aft of her conning tower — and neither is British practice. But she might just be a Yankee."

Turning to his First Lieutenant, he said, "Quick, Number One, get the recognition book. Let's see if we can identify her."

The leading yeoman of signals was also now on the bridge and Tremayne snapped, "Yeo, make to 1517: *'Have confirmed contact, 2,500 yards dead ahead. Sub on surface'.*"

Closing the gap rapidly, the two MGBs were quickly within a thousand yards of the submarine, still regularly hidden by the heavy, swelling, white-capped waves.

Breathless, Willoughby-Brown reappeared on the bridge, grabbed his binoculars to look at the submarine once more and yelled, "She's a U-boat — a Type IX. She mounts a 37mm and a 20mm, aft and —"

Tremayne cut in, "All guns stand by, stand by — they've seen us."

"Yeo, make to 1517: '*Engage the enemy closely. Take her port side. We'll go starboard and divide her firepower*'."

"Thank you, Number One."

With his adrenaline running and controlled excitement in his voice, he yelled, "All guns. Commence firing, as you bear. SHOOT, SHOOT, SHOOT!"

Turning quickly to Irvine he said, "Right, Cox'n. Set course to pass her to starboard. Maintain maximum revolutions if you please."

The U-boat commander's reaction to the sudden appearance of the MGBs was quick and well directed. Almost simultaneously with the first six-pounder volleys from Tremayne and Fischer, the U-boat opened up with her after 37mm and 20mm automatic weapons.

"Cox'n. Ten degrees to starboard – we'll give our Bofors a chance to traverse and straddle her as well."

Fischer, seeing Tremayne's tactic, veered further to port to enable his after 40mm, similarly, to bring to bear on the U-boat.

Incoming 37mm shells suddenly began thudding into the MGB's hull and then, just as rapidly, turned her port Browning machine gun emplacement, immediately aft of the bridge, into a tumbled ruin of torn, twisted metal. The force of the shell-burst had torn the Browning off its mounting and the gunner, Able Seaman Bill Graham, decapitated in the explosion, lay in a grotesque bloodied heap, caught up in the tangled wreckage.

"Oh, God, no," murmured Tremayne, as he saw the obscene shambles no more than six feet away. He was brought back to immediate reality as, this time, his boat was raked by the U-boat's 20mm automatic cannon, which sent shrapnel and splinters flying in a lethal hail of jagged steel across the MGB's deck and armoured upper works.

The U-boat had recovered quickly from the unexpected arrival of the British and her controlled, well-aimed shooting had caused casualties and damage to both MGBs. But it was an unequal contest. Within a matter of minutes, her two after guns had been disabled and lay smashed and crumpled, their mountings up-ended and their barrels pointing at crazy angles. Several of her crew were dead and both her hull and riddled conning tower had sustained what was now certainly terminal damage for a submarine.

Unbelievably, to Tremayne and the others on deck, her captain had made a sudden decision to crash dive, despite her fatally holed hull and upper works.

"The bastard's diving! All guns! Keep firing," yelled Tremayne. At point-blank range, the two MGBs poured round after round into the disappearing submarine. Suddenly a huge flame, followed immediately by a deafening explosion and a towering pall of dense black smoke, signalled the dramatic end of the U-boat. Bow first, she began her final lonely, steep plunge into the cold, dark grey depths of the English Channel.

"Why the hell did he do that, sir? It makes no sense. He's just sacrificed himself and what must be more than fifty men."

"Heaven alone knows, Number One. Either he really believed that he had time to dive and escape us – or he was determined that his boat would not be taken by the enemy. Whatever the reason – sacrificial scuttle or desperation – it was a foolish, but very brave, thing to do."

Tremayne spoke to the leading yeoman of signals: "Yeo, make to Lieutenant Fischer please: *'Well done. Begin search for survivors. Please report casualties and damage'*."

Suddenly, Tremayne noticed blood seeping through Jenkins's left sleeve. "Yeo, you're hit. Into the wardroom with you man." Calling to Watkins, who had been gunner on the forrard six-pounder, Tremayne yelled, "Watkins! Quick as you like! The Leading Yeoman's been hit. Get him down to the wardroom. Check and dress his wound and give him a shot of morphine. Report back to me when you've done it, please."

As Watkins rushed over to help, Jenkins said quietly, his Valleys lilt even more pronounced, "It's a' right, Pablo, thanks, but just 'old fire while I get this signal off. It's a bit urgent, see."

Watkins hesitated and looked at Tremayne.

"OK, Watkins. Let him do that – but only that – and then look after his wound immediately."

"Aye aye, sir."

"Right Number One, let's see if we can find any survivors.

Release scrambling nets please and have lifebuoys and boathooks at the ready."

Turning to Irvine he said, "Slow ahead, Cox'n. Quarter the area up to where she went down. Lieutenant Fischer will cover the rest."

Picking up the loudhailer from the ledge in front of him, Tremayne called out, "All hands to look out for survivors."

Several bodies, looking pathetically harmless in death, were already floating in the sea amongst the debris and flotsam. Some of them were gun-crew members of the weapons astern of the conning tower, but others, mutilated by the explosion, were beginning to surface and float around sickeningly in the growing oil slick that confirmed the U-boat's dramatic demise.

The shocked silence that had descended on the MGB as a result of the emerging horrific carnage, was suddenly broken by a shout from a rating leaning over the port bow.

It was 'Brummie' Nicholls, the inseparable 'oppo' and 'townie' of 'Pablo' Watkins.

"'Ere, sir. There's one 'ere, but 'e's 'urt bad, sir."

"Stop all engines, Cox'n."

"Number One, take two men to help Leading Seaman Nicholls get the casualty on board please."

Taking two of the gun-crew members with him, Willoughby -Brown rapidly organised the retrieval of the oil-covered, injured German. Exhausted and shivering, he struggled to grasp the scrambling net with his one good hand and arm.

"Easy does it, lads. His right arm looks as if it's been broken. Help him up the nets and lay him out on the deck. Search him for any weapons." Turning to Nicholls, he added, "Get some hot sweet tea, laced with rum, down him as quickly as you can please. The poor bastard looks as if he's on his last gasp. Find a towel and a blanket for him. We need to be able to interrogate him later."

To the two seamen, slowly peeling off the German's sodden and oil-drenched clothes, he said, "Gently does it, lads. Morrison, check his arm, get a dressing on it and give him a shot of morphine once you've cleaned him up. See if he needs a splint. Then you, Roberts, take your Lanchester and stay with him. Make sure he remains in the wardroom. Jenkins should also be there, recovering from his wound."

"Aye aye, sir."

Willoughby-Brown, who spoke German fluently, turned to the shivering U-boat rating and asked him his name, rank and number. The prisoner gave his rating as Matrosengefreiter, or leading seaman, and his whole demeanour suggested to Willoughby-Brown that he expected to be thrown overboard once he had been questioned.

At the appearance of 'Brummie' Nicholls's well lived-in, good-natured face and the steaming brew, his eyes began to register less apprehension. Even the Englishman's quite incomprehensible,

"'Ere yo' am, our kid. Get this lot down yer pudding-chute," had a reassuringly genial ring to it. Nicholls himself had only recently returned to duty after hospitalisation following a severe wound and readily identified with the German seaman's plight.

Young to be a leading rate, the German volunteered that his U-boat was part of 10 Flotille, based in France, and that they had surfaced to give crew members some much-needed fresh air and daylight after several long periods underwater. He confirmed that they had been caught completely unawares by the speed of approach of the two British MGBs, undetected in the swelling seas until the last few minutes before the opening salvoes had straddled his boat. He indicated to Willoughby-Brown that their radar was 'kaput', which had limited their awareness of other craft in the area, and that they had been waiting for a replacement to be flown in by a Dornier flying boat.

He had received his wound and broken arm early on in the exchange of fire, when splinters from a Bofors 40mm high explosive shell ricocheted off the U-boat's conning tower and hit him, as he was directing fire of their after 37mm gun. The U-boat's sudden and unexpected steep dive had thrown him off the rear decking into the sea, where he had remained until rescued.

A search by both MGBs yielded just the one U-boat survivor and Tremayne ordered the resumption of their sweep into the western entrance to the English Channel, off the southern coast of Cornwall. After a further three uneventful hours of grey seas and grey skies, he ordered "Return to base".

Returning south of Land's End by fifteen miles, the keen-eyed port watchkeeper spotted three sleek, low profile vessels, travelling east, in line astern. Tremayne and his First Lieutenant swung their binoculars over to port and, even at over six thousand yards distance, identified them as E-boats, travelling at roughly half revolutions – possibly to conserve fuel.

Unnoticed at first – and heavily bandaged – Jenkins had returned to the bridge to resume his role as yeoman of signals. Tremayne momentarily broke off visual contact with the E-boats and saw Jenkins.

"What the hell are you doing up here. Get below, Yeo, back to the wardroom. Tell Watkins to make you a brew of tea with plenty of sugar in it."

"Let me stay yer', sir – at least until you've decided what to do about those E-boats."

"Thank you, Yeo. Much appreciated. Just one signal – then away with you below and, this time, bloody well stay there."

"Aye aye, sir." The triumphant grin was barely perceptible.

"So, Yeo, make to Lieutenant Fischer: *'We have company, fine on the port beam, six thousand yards. Tally-ho!'*"

With his binoculars still tracking the E-boats, Tremayne ordered Irvine to alter course to intercept the enemy, at maximum revolutions.

"Well Number One, let's see if we can add to the day's score."

The boat's radar screen, temporarily unmanned, was

registering the three small blips as the rating monitoring the
set returned from the heads. The two MGBs sought to close
the gap between themselves and the E-boats as rapidly as their
maximum speeds of twenty-seven knots would allow. At a
distance of just over five thousand yards, it was clear that the
two MGBs had been spotted and, within seconds, the three
E-boats had accelerated to over forty knots.

"Shit and bloody derision — we'll never catch those
bastards," Tremayne fumed, but ordered the bow six-pounder
to fire ranging shots at the fast-departing Germans. He called
the boat's company back to action stations with the order,
"Stand by all guns. Fire as you bear when we're in range."

To the radio operator he called down, "Signal RAF St Mary's
giving coordinates, and an approximate speed of forty knots,
of three E-boats travelling east."

A triple thump from the forrard six-pounder, followed
by a fall of shot still at least five hundred yards short of the
target, left him even more frustrated.

"We might just as well throw a bloody fanny full of kye
at the bastards, Number One. I'm afraid we've got to leave
this one to St Mary's Hurricanes, but I'd like to know just what
Jerry is up to in these waters."

Turning to Irvine, he snapped, "Damn the bastards. Cox'n,
resume our original course, if you please. Take us home!"

"Aye aye, sir. That was bloody galling, sir. We badly need
a few more 'horses', so we do."

Tremayne, angry as he was, smiled at what was one of the longest sentences he had heard the taciturn Ulsterman utter in a long time.

Willoughby-Brown, ever the reasoning philosopher and anxious to apply balm, added, "On this occasion, sir, we'll let St Mary's have the glory. Or, as I believe Leading Seaman Watkins is wont to say, 'there are more ways of killing the cat than stuffing its arse full of cream buns!' though personally, I doubt many would be more pleasurable, sir."

Tremayne exploded with laughter. "Thank you, Number One – you've just restored my sense of humour! Tell me, is your illustrious family's motto by any chance *'Adapt, improvise and overcome'*?"

About ninety minutes later, Tremayne, followed by Fischer, arrived at Braiden Rock anchorage. After boats were secured, their prisoner was led ashore, blindfolded and under armed escort, for treatment by Godolphin's ship's doctor. Further interrogation by Enever and the Intelligence Section – or the 'I' as it was generally known – would follow, and then subsequent transfer to a PoW camp on the mainland.

Graham's remains were also carried ashore to await subsequent funeral arrangements, privately or at HMS Godolphin. Still protesting – "Look, lads, I'm fine, *really*. I don't need no MO buggering me about, isn't it" -Leading Yeoman of Signals 'Taff' Jenkins was led to Godolphin's tiny sick bay for examination and Surgeon Lieutenant Hegarty's professional ministrations.

Tremayne and Fischer, having thanked, debriefed and dismissed their boat crews, made their way up the steep, narrow, rocky exit from the anchorage and onto the shoreside shrub and flower-lined path leading to HMS Godolphin.

The shock of Bill Graham's appalling death remained with them as they walked together, their conversation uncharacteristically forced and awkward, talking about disconnected banalities and trivia. For both, it was a temporary, but much needed, relief to be able to escape to the privacy and solitude of their cabins – even for the normally ebullient Fischer.

They had returned more or less in time for dinner, in one of the First World War's former seaplane base buildings, which now served as a somewhat cramped and spartan wardroom. Dinner itself was a convivial affair with Enever, Willoughby-Brown, Mick Taylor – one of the boat captains, and two Wren officers from Intelligence. Enever, ever sensitive and alert to people's moods, allowed Tremayne and Fischer to rehabilitate themselves gradually into the wardroom's normal level of noisy sociability with its customary badinage and lighthearted escapism. In all officers' messes, the golden rule about conversation is 'we never discuss religion, politics, or other men's wives' and that was, thankfully, the rule meticulously observed in Godolphin's wardroom.

The two Wren officers – friends and former colleagues of First Officer Emma Tremayne – had hired a sailing dinghy from one of the local fishermen and had spent a day's leave sailing around the fascinating Eastern Isles and St Martin's island, with its beautiful long, deserted white beaches.

Theirs had been one of the few bright, sunny December days and they were bubbling over with the spectacular sights, so typical of the Scillies, which they had seen. Luckily, both Tremayne and Fischer were keen, experienced small boat sailors. Their amusing accounts, childlike in their earnestness and sense of wonder, quickly lifted Tremayne and the others out of their mood of sombre introspection. As dinner ended on a high, lively note, Enever judged that he might usefully take a few minutes to review the day with Tremayne and Fischer, informally over a glass of brandy.

The three disappeared to Enever's quarters and went through the day's action with the U-boat and the sighting of the three E-boats south of Land's End. Enever's principal concern was that the E-boats might have been in the area specifically to sniff around Godolphin and, if so, why exactly? Were the Germans onto Godolphin's true role at what was emerging as a critical period in the base's short history?

"Obviously, Jerry knows of HMS Godolphin's existence. As part of our radio intelligence and counter-intelligence, we have been deliberately transmitting both the normal routine WT traffic associated with a small naval base, as well as regular low-level misinformation."

He leaned forward to retrieve his empty pipe from an elaborately ornate 'Golden Hart' ashtray, clearly 'liberated' on some run ashore to Portsmouth in his distant past.

"I hope, gentlemen, that acute paranoia is not accompanying the onset of senility," the grey eyes twinkled affably behind the steel-rimmed spectacles, "but I'm more than a little curious about our visitors and the reason for their presence in our waters. We picked them up on our radar here but, unfortunately, St Mary's Hurricane squadron was otherwise engaged so we had no means of getting to grips with the blighters."

He carefully filled his pipe from a packet of RN-issue 'Blue Liner' tobacco and placed it, unlit, between his teeth before continuing. "The radar plot rather disconcertingly showed the three blips to be moving quite unhurriedly and in what appeared to be possible reconnaissance mode, keeping to the south of the Bishop, Crebinicks, Gilstone and the main group of the Western Rocks, yet, it would appear, close enough to observe a good deal of detail of those rocks and islands.

"My principal concern, gentlemen, is that they were right in – and cutting across – the out and return routes of our disguised courier fishing boats. The sea lane that we have established between Tresco and Brittany is, in effect, our 'secret channel' to France and it is critical that we keep it as such. It would only need one of our phoney 'Breton' fishing vessels, with a largely British crew dressed in French fishermen's rig, to be caught as far north as these waters and our cover would be permanently blown. What's *your* reading of this?"

Tremayne was the first to respond.

"I'm curious, too, John about their intentions. It could have been, quite simply, that they were looking for easy pickings, such as the odd freighter or cargo vessel. However, the pattern of their movement that you picked up on the radar screen could possibly suggest a much more threatening reason from Godolphin's point of view. For example, they may have been laying mines, which increasingly seems to be a major E-boat role, in this end of the Channel."

"That could well be so, Richard, though, curiously, radio intercept has picked up nothing yet to confirm our suspicions. What do you think Hermann?"

"I agree, sir, that it's important to find out what Jerry is up to in our waters. It could be that it was a small flotilla out marauding in what are new hunting grounds for them. It's also possible that they had been guided, by radio using code, onto a surface target further south and to the immediate west of the Scillies, sir, and were returning from that mission."

"Those are certainly possible solutions, Hermann, but somehow – and I can't, for the life of me, explain why – my instinct tells me otherwise. So, gentlemen, for one week I'm going to go along with my nagging gut feeling. If, after seven days, we haven't cracked it, I'll take it that Jerry's was a less sinister agenda and that either routine, or happenstance, were at the root of it."

At this point, Tremayne came back into the discussion. "You said a moment ago, John, that intercepted German radio traffic gave no clues about anything other than routine patrol work."

"Absolutely. I've been through the 'I' Section's intercept transcripts and could find nothing untoward in any of them."

"It is, of course, inevitable that German Intelligence, our friends in the Abwehr, play a very similar game to us, putting out apparently bland, routine stuff, plus misinformation, as part of a very different hidden agenda. That could lull us into thinking that there was nothing seriously untoward in their activities — just as we attempt to do with them."

"Well, Richard, we do have verbatim transcripts of every message transmitted and I will get Lucy and Jane, who are currently our two top 'Y' Service analysts, to go through the stuff we picked up by radio with a fine-tooth comb.

"Current feedback about the Abwehr from SIS does suggest that we might have overestimated the imagination, resourcefulness and effectiveness of the German Intelligence Service, so I might just be worrying unnecessarily. Though, it seems, they may lack creativity, they *are* thorough, gentlemen. We'll no doubt see."

Enever rang for the steward to replenish their empty brandy glasses.

"I shan't keep you much longer, gentlemen — you must be all in. I want us to come up with a plan first thing tomorrow to out-guile the bastards and find out exactly what they *are* up to in this area. Sleep on it, both of you, and at 08.30 hours tomorrow we'll meet in Hut 101 and give pure genius free rein and see what answers we can generate between us. Ah, Higgs — good man! Thank you. On *my* mess bill, if you will."

Raising the full glass in his hand, Enever said, "Gentlemen, I give you a toast: 'Confusion to our enemies!'"

Three

We'll out-guile the bastards

Breakfast the following morning had been a quiet, subdued occasion for Tremayne. He had risen early and was first into the wardroom, as he had intended, in order to be alone with his thoughts for as long as possible before the inevitable, noisy conversational push and shove began.

Late the previous evening, after Enever's debriefing, he had written a personal letter to Graham's young widow who, he had learned from Nicholls, had a baby son less than twelve months old. In the peaceful solitude of the empty wardroom, he found that his thoughts were still returning to Able Seaman Graham and his now suddenly bereaved family.

He had rung Emma, whose sensitivity and infinite capacity for empathy had helped him to articulate his condolences in the letter in ways that focused his concern and thinking on Bill Graham, his wife and their baby son, rather than on his own grief.

As he spoke with Emma, Tremayne recalled the depth of her feelings and the caring she had shown him when he had told her that he had lost his first wife so tragically, in a blitz on Plymouth, while he was away at sea. Her patience, her listening and her supportive presence had, he knew beyond any doubt, slowly brought him back into the living world again. Motivated neither by indulgent personal gratification nor morbid curiosity, Emma's support came from her head, as well as her heart. Tremayne knew, from personal experience, that her ability to help others to see context – and recognise fresh hope – went way beyond mere pious platitudes.

Her perceptive yet gentle sense of humour could inject necessary smiles and laughter and add perspective to people's sorrow, without demeaning their grief – and their need to grieve. Emma, too, had already known full well the desperate sense of personal tragedy in the loss of the young subaltern she was about to become engaged to at the beginning of the war. He had been a second lieutenant, serving with the Seaforth Highlanders, when he fell near St Valery during the retreat to Dunkirk. Her own untimely bereavement added the depth of personal pain to her natural empathy and spontaneous concern for others.

Tremayne broke out of his reverie as Quilghini, followed by three other officers, joined him for breakfast. Very soon, serious personal reflection was replaced by lighthearted banter and laughter and the noise level began to rise to its usual boisterous heights. Captain Waring, the officer commanding Godolphin's small detachment of Royal Marines, immediately became the butt of the latest round of uncharitable stories that sailors can't wait to tell about their bootneck colleagues. Though heavily outnumbered, as more naval officers joined the breakfast table, the ever eloquent Waring acquitted himself admirably as the badinage began to take on a somewhat more Rabelaisian tone and the Navy, in turn, came in for a hilarious verbal drubbing from the urbane marine.

Now engaged in the boisterous laughter, Tremayne, conscious of the time, looked at his watch and made excuses for himself and Quilghini to attend Enever's morning meeting in Hut 101.

Pierre Quilghini, as the longest serving and most senior of the French RNVR officers – although still a sub-lieutenant – had done much to pioneer and open up the sea lanes between the Scillies and Brittany. Though an excellent young sea-going officer, he was – as Enever had discovered – a natural for intelligence work. He spoke fluent English and Breton, as well as French, and could get by quite well in German, albeit with a disarmingly exaggerated Breton fisherman's accent.

"He is that rare breed of bird, Richard — a thorough professional with passion as well as consummate ability," was how Enever had described him to Tremayne.

A beaming Enever was sitting at his uncharacteristically clear and tidy desk as they entered and saluted.

"Gentlemen. Good morning. Do seize a pew."

He waved them to sit down and take one of the freshly poured cups of coffee.

"Before we begin, gentlemen, I have a most pleasant duty to perform."

Addressing an increasingly puzzled Quilghini, he said with mock solemnity, "Sub, put your arms out over the table towards me, please."

Clearly wondering just what was going on, a now quite bewildered Quilghini hesitatingly complied.

"My warmest congratulations, *Lieutenant*," laughed Enever, as he placed one badge showing the golden wavy double rings of a lieutenant, RNVR, on each lower arm of the now surprised and delighted Frenchman.

"Those, Pierre, are richly deserved — and long overdue."

"Thank you, sir, I am so pleased. I don't know quite what to say. I —"

Tremayne stepped in. "Congratulations and well done, Pierre! I am — we *all* are — so pleased for you. You've earned your promotion many times over. The bad news is, of course, that the drinks are on you tonight over at the New Inn! The good news is – I'm sure that you have Commander Enever's permission to find the prettiest Wren to sew those lieutenant's rings on for you!"

Over laughter and coffee, Enever returned to his concerns about yesterday's first known appearance of E-boats so close to the islands.

"I've given the issue a lot of thought – as you can probably guess!" The thoughtful grey eyes softened and smiled over his half-moon spectacles.

"I've already put Rear Admiral Hembury in the picture and he's offered one possible tactic to deal with the problem, should our trio of friends decide to visit us again." Tremayne and Quilghini perceptibly leaned forward, closer to Enever.

"As you know, the admiral is known in senior naval circles as 'the Artful Dodger' and 'the Body Snatcher' because of his infinite ability to filch, permanently 'borrow', or otherwise expropriate others' property and equipment for the benefit of RN Coastal Forces."

"What has he managed to 'rescue' for us this time?" asked Tremayne, as he looked with a knowing grin at Enever's imposing, carved, Georgian walnut desk and early Victorian 'captain's' chair, both of which had come courtesy of Hembury's genteel wheedling and pillaging.

"Ah, dear boy, you've guessed it!" Enever reached for his

pipe before continuing, "Our gallant admiral has excelled himself this time. By some miracle — perhaps that earnest, infallible 'I-really-do-*need*-your-help' stratagem that he sometimes uses on me — he has managed to convince a Bristol trading company to lend him one of their fleet of small coastal freighters."

"Now that's expropriation on a grand scale. I hope that she's not to be on your slop-chit, sir!"

"Ah, Richard, I'm too wily an old bird to be caught napping with something like that! She's a single-funnel steamer, 1912 vintage, displacing some 1,300 tons and approximately 220 feet in length. She's powered by a single-shaft triple expansion engine and her service speed is around ten knots. She was built in Helsinki by Maskin & Brobygnade AB apparently, and, up until around 1928, she served as a Baltic trader carrying timber. She is the *SS Karelia* and still bears the original Finnish name she was launched with."

"I imagine, sir, that she looks the part — ideally rust-stained and well used. Is the ploy to use her as a decoy?"

"Hole in one, Richard — and more!" Enever nodded and smiled conspiratorially.

"From her timber-carrying days, she has retained her masts and various winches, at the end of her bridge deck as well as on her fo'c's'le and poop. Because of the well decks between these structures, Admiral Hembury has managed to fit a couple of six-pounders on powered mountings — one fore and one aft — to her now reinforced decking. With tarpaulins draped over them, set between all those derricks and winches, they look just like some rather anonymous deck cargo."

"She's really a Q-ship, then, sir. Lure the enemy close in and then – off with the tarpaulins and thump the bastards?"

"Just so. Admiral Hembury had borrowed her primarily to tempt U-boats to surface in order to try to sink her by gun-fire since, as a small freighter carrying cargo, she's worth sinking but obviously not with a costly torpedo. As soon as the sub surfaced to attack her with gunfire, the freighter would radio St Mary's for air support. They would be with her in minutes to sink the sub. She would have whipped the tarpaulins off her six-pounders and joined in the sub's destruction. He believes that we could possibly make similar use of her as a decoy with these three E-boats. What do you both think?"

Quilghini responded first: "In principle, sir, I think this is a clever idea and a tactic that could possibly work. But – and it is an important but – she would need to be protected very quickly by, ideally, MGBs *and* aircraft working in collaboration. To do that successfully, the location of the action is critical to ensure that the necessary support arrives in time and in sufficient strength. Three E-boats would, typically, have the firepower of, at least, three 37mm and up to six 20mm cannon."

Enever filled his pipe with his inevitable aromatic 'Blue Liner' tobacco and looked at Quilghini. "Thank you, Pierre. You've given us a lot to think about."

Turning to Tremayne, he asked, "What say you, Richard?"

"I think that Pierre is right. Three E-boats could deploy rapidly to the Q-ship's fatal disadvantage and, with concentrated shooting, shred her in sixty seconds flat, sir."

"Hmm. As quickly as *that?*"

"I'm afraid so, sir — assuming that she is unarmoured — especially around her lower hull, engine room and bridge."

"No, she carries no armour whatsoever — except for her six-pounder gun shields."

"As we discovered recently from the Confrèrie, sir, some French-based E-boat flotillas are taking delivery this month of the new Type S139-150 series of boats. These can easily top forty-two knots — with a seven hundred-mile radius of action — and it is possible that the three E-boats we saw were of this type. The new S139-150 boats are lower and more streamlined than their predecessors and those we saw were very sleek, menacing boats indeed. They are understood to be equipped with the new FuMB-24 radar, which is capable of picking up enemy aircraft and surface vessels to a radius of about ten miles."

"They sound formidable, Richard, and we've nothing at Tresco that can approach anywhere near their top speed, but we can certainly match their firepower with our boats."

"I think, however," said Tremayne, "that I can see a possible way to use this Q-ship."

He paused to drink the remains of his now cold coffee.

"Dear boy, we'll get a fresh brew 'toot sweet' — *and* 'toot hot' – as it were." Enever rang Jane Topping for more coffee.

"Timing and coordination are paramount, sir – and so, too, are the location and proximity of help, as Pierre has already emphasised. We *must* have prior notice of Jerry's movements in order to set this operation up and to be in place, in time, already prepared for his arrival."

"That makes sense to me, Richard. We can track the Germans' manoeuvrings by reconnaissance aircraft, way ahead of his ability to monitor the movement of our boats."

Tremayne took the cup of coffee that one of Jane Topping's Wrens handed him, before continuing.

"What I believe would work is this. Provided that we can entice Jerry relatively close to the southernmost tip of the Western Rocks – Pednathise Head – by, say, up to seven miles maximum, we could set up an apparent capture of the Q-ship by our own E-boat, S53. Well timed, 'staged' gunfire should be heard by the Germans who, we hope, will come across to investigate, confident in their strength of three vessels. Meanwhile, lurking out of sight, close to Corregan, Daisy and/or Rosevean in the Western Rocks themselves, will be our three MGBs, revving up and ready to close with the Germans, at maximum revolutions. Additionally, we will need Squadron Leader Tim Stanley's Hurricanes on standby, ready to leave St Mary's immediately to support us from the air.

"On a point of detail – but a crucial one – we will need to check up on current E-boat flotilla pennant numbers, wheelhouse insignia and camouflage paint schemes, to make sure we know who we're dealing with and how best to disguise our own E-boat – should you decide to use her in such a role."

"Thank you, Richard – an interesting proposal. Pierre?"

"I like Richard's plan, sir. Given the constraints we've identified, that tactic has a good chance of success, sir. What we then have to do is to capture at least two, or maybe three, officers, and preferably a radio operator, to find out exactly why they are in the area. Then, possibly, we need to 'allow' others to escape, with a suitably banal story about Godolphin, that we *want* them to take back. That, I think, will be the really tricky bit, sir."

"Gentlemen, thank you. I believe we have the bones of something here that might just work. You are both giving me a lot to think about, but I have three concerns. One, I want to keep the operation as simple as possible – and yet give ourselves sufficient back-up options if things go haywire. Two, I don't want to arouse – or increase – German interest in the islands and what they think might be going on here. Three, why don't we just call up Beaufighters from RAF Bolt Head if and when the trio appear again and simply destroy them?

If we had our MGBs in the area, coordinating with the Beaufighters, we could look for possible survivors for interrogation."

Enever stopped to return his pipe to what he proudly termed his '*SMS Von der Tann*' ashtray in front of him.

"Let me work on this and make some telephone calls –

oh, and I'll also check what Lucy and Jane have made of the radio intercept transcripts. I suggest that we meet here at 17.00 hours to see how much further we can take this idea. By the way, I shall need to involve Captain MacPherson at that meeting or all three of us are likely to be keelhauled for conspiracy to mutiny. I will see you then, gentlemen."

On his way to an early lunch in the wardroom, looking out at the stunning views across to the island of Bryher, Tremayne remembered that, in just one day's time, he was due for a thirty-six-hour leave, starting at 18.00 on the Friday and returning to duty by 06.00 hours on the Sunday morning. To his utter frustration and chagrin, Emma was on duty watch in London for that weekend and he now had to resign himself to an enforced bachelor Friday night and Saturday.

"At least Bertie and I can tramp the hills of St Martin's or St Agnes and escape from the stone frigate for a while," had been his rationalised musing about the situation and its restrictions on his precious and all-too-infrequent time with Emma. They had been married sixteen months and, in that time, had only been able to spend less than thirty days and nights together – though he ruefully acknowledged that they had been luckier than many young Service couples.

After lunch with WB and several of the other officers, Tremayne left with his First Lieutenant to check with the 'I' Section to find out the latest information about the current E-boat identification markings.

"Identifying which flotilla the three E-boats belong to — and where they are based — might add a few key pieces to the jigsaw puzzle. It's also vital that we repaint S53 in current operational colours and markings if we decide to use her in this operation. In any case, David, working in 'I' Section gives you a chance to see Lucy!"

"Thank you Richard. By the way, Lucy and I are planning to get engaged next month and I believe she is ringing Emma tomorrow to let her know."

"David, I'm delighted for you both and I know that Emma will be too. Let's celebrate as a foursome in the New Year when you announce your engagement."

The ever knowledgeable and enthusiastic 'I' Section staff produced copies of the latest E-boat flotilla pennant numbers, insignia and camouflage paint finishes, which had been sent by courier from the Confrèrie Bonaparte as part of the regular updating of intelligence about German activities in Brittany and the Channel.

Tremayne noted that most of the insignia — generally painted port and starboard of the hull or wheelhouse — consisted of wild animals, various forms of the Baltic cross on a shield background, or simply a large ace of spades. Camouflage paint schemes ranged from all-over light grey to various mottled finishes including mixtures of blues, greens, dark greys and browns, over-sprayed on the original grey. The camouflage of the latest S139-150 E-boats was somewhat different from that of previous boats he had learned. They were finished in light grey, but over-painted with large, irregular patches of sea green, and their insignia appeared to be primarily either playing-card ace designs or a stylised version of the German eagle surmounting a swastika.

"Swotting up on this artistic collection will be this week's homework for officers and crews," said Tremayne, as he and Willoughby-Brown left 'I' Section. "I want boat captains, their First Lieutenants and all watchkeepers to be thoroughly familiar with E-boat flotilla recognition by Friday."

"David, will you please make sure that we have sufficient copies of the 'I' Section artwork available to boat crews and check with Commander Enever that it would be sensible to let Squadron Leader Stanley have copies. I'm sure that Lucy will be delighted to help you with this," Tremayne added, with a gentle grin.

The meeting with Enever at 17.00 hours was a tenser, formal affair as Captain MacPherson made his stifling, hypercritical presence felt.

Neither for the destruction of the U-boat, nor for the capture of one of its crew, were any congratulations forthcoming from MacPherson. Rather, his style was to explore detail – much of it tedious minutiae – of little or no consequence to the operation. Tremayne felt that most of it was designed to impress his captive audience with his grasp of chapter and verse, however irrelevant. He positively gloated, with ill-disguised triumph, whenever he spotted an error – however minor – in others' reports and proposals. Never once, noted Tremayne, did MacPherson take up others' ideas and build upon them.

On the matter of the three E-boats and the closeness of their monitored route to the Scillies and, of more importance, to the espionage sea lanes between Tresco and Brittany, his focus on detail was excruciating. On no occasion, despite the opportunities to do so, did he demonstrate the conceptual professionalism of a trained mind. What he lacked in relevant interpretive understanding, he made up for with arrogant confidence.

Clearly aware of MacPherson's presence – though in no way outwardly fazed by it – Enever presented his plan of action for finding out just what German E-boats were doing so close to Scilly.

He began by restating his three principal criteria for the form – and conduct – of the operation: simplicity – for ease and speed of execution; low key – to avoid arousing unwelcome German interest in the Scillies and Godolphin; and operational impact – by making high use of available, coordinated air and sea power.

More out of intellectual narcissism than relevance, MacPherson explored the detail – rather than the context and qualification of each of the criteria and Tremayne was impressed by Enever's cool handling of the captain's nit-picking.

Deliberately holding MacPherson's eyes, Enever stated, "I value the experience — and perspective — that Lieutenant Commander Tremayne and Lieutenant Quilghini have given me in arriving at my proposal."

Enever, largely to get his plan past MacPherson, then elaborated each stage of his proposed strategy to a degree of thoroughness and detail that cleverly pre-empted many of the unnecessary questions that he had wisely anticipated from his superior.

He then summarised his proposal in the form that he knew Tremayne and Quilghini would welcome and enthusiastically engage with. "So, gentlemen, to summarise our proposal at this stage. The *SS Karelia* will be on operational standby in St Mary's Sound, ready to steam south-west to the outer Western Rocks if and when we have aircraft radar reports of the E-boat trio and their intended route. Alongside her — and on the E-boats' blind side until they decide to split forces — will be our E-boat in support. Her unexpected presence will confuse the Germans, albeit temporarily, and give us the fire initiative. We discovered some time ago that, occasionally, E-boats are transferred from bases in Norway and Holland to the Bay of Biscay flotillas and their pennant numbers and paint schemes are not always instantly known to all the Brittany-based units."

Enever paused to let MacPherson comment but there was no response — other than a rather contrived, bored expression. Whatever his private thoughts, Enever continued.

"On immediate call, will be Squadron Leader Stanley's flight of Hurricanes, each armed with four 20mm cannon and one 150-pound bomb. To give further support at sea will be our three MGBs, out of sight – and radar contact, concealed within the Western Rocks. Apart from adding firepower, their role is to pick up any survivors for interrogation. We shall, of course, be monitoring the Germans' radio signals to see what intelligence we can gather from them about the operation and, more importantly, anything that they happen to transmit about Godolphin."

Enever addressed MacPherson specifically, "I have, obviously sir, analysed the transcripts of the radio messages from the three E-boats which we decoded yesterday."

"And just what, pray, Commander, *have* you found out?"

Tremayne looked across at MacPherson's cold, supercilious face and unashamedly felt an overwhelming desire to smash his fist into it. By way of contrast, he was full of admiration for Enever's calm, controlled response.

"Essentially this, sir – the E-boat transmissions indicated that they viewed the islands as a possible area for shelter in stormy weather for merchant vessels plying the Channel routes and, therefore, a potentially rich source of easy pickings at anchor."

Enever paused for a reaction from MacPherson, who merely raised his eyebrows questioningly but otherwise maintained his arrogant silence.

Tremayne, sitting observing, again felt his anger rising at MacPherson's affected indifference towards a very talented, capable man whom he admired and respected.

Seemingly unperturbed, Enever retrieved his pipe, clamped it firmly between his teeth, and went on.

"The only specific reference to Godolphin was that a small flotilla of patrol boats protected the waters around the islands –" There was a slight, but deliberate pause before he added an obviously perfunctory "sir".

"Very well, Commander, I shall leave you to finalise your plans. Keep me informed of what you are doing." MacPherson's final words were characteristically aloof and lacking in warmth – and showed how little genuine engagement he had in the proposed operation.

As the door closed behind MacPherson, Tremayne, unable to contain his anger any longer, snapped, "What an utter arsehole that bloody man is." Quilghini, with a broad grin spreading across his normally composed face and clearly relishing what he was about to say, added, "He is what we call, sir, a typical *Rosbif* – of the stupidest kind!"

Enever roared with laughter. "I hope, Pierre, that you don't consider us all to be tarred with the brush of *la perfide Albion*. A few of us *are* relatively normal and genuine, you know! At least, gentlemen, he hasn't put the kybosh on our proposal and I interpret that as having permission to go ahead with our plans – or any variation of them – that further discussion recommends. Had we not, I should have brought our gallant Admiral Hembury into the fray!"

Enever gathered together his papers from the meeting and said, "Gentlemen, thank you for your presence today. Though, of necessity, this evening's meeting was predominantly my show, I sensed your support most strongly. This operation is now beginning to *feel* right to me – both in my head and in my gut. There are loose ends that we still need to tidy up and tomorrow, at 14.00 hours, I should like you both to join me when I brief the *Karelia's* skipper and ship's company. A launch will leave New Grimsby quay at 13.15 hours to take us to the *Karelia*. She will be anchored in deep water in St Mary's Sound, off Woolpack Point. After serving in smart frigates and regularly scrubbed-up MGBs, I think that you'll find her quite an intriguing proposition!"

The meeting broke up and Tremayne and Quilghini made their way back to their respective cabins and, later, to dinner in the wardroom.

Tremayne spent the following morning briefing boat captains, their First Lieutenants and coxswains on the proposed operation stage by stage, emphasising the importance of speed of response and coordination of action. He stressed, too, the likely need for adaptive individual initiative and resource-fulness of the highest order, when the unforeseen, rather than the predicted or expected, dictated the course of the operation. Squadron Leader Stanley joined the briefing at 10.30 hours to confirm and amplify the RAF's support, having earlier been brought up to speed, in overall terms, by Commander Enever.

"If you're going to use that E-boat of yours, gentlemen, please paint a large RAF roundel on her deck and ensure that she's flying a white ensign by the time we arrive. We don't want to blow her out of the water by mistake."

"I'll probably be skippering her, so I'll make bloody sure that she's carrying British identification. We'll hoist our battle ensign – which is the biggest flag that we have," replied Tremayne, amidst laughter.

After his boat crews' briefing and questions and a quick lunch at the New Inn, Tremayne – together with Quilghini – joined Enever in the motor launch to visit the *Karelia*. With the incoming tide and sufficient depth of water they were able to go through Tresco Flats and then on into The Road at maximum revolutions in the shallow draught boat, until they secured alongside the freighter some twenty minutes later.

Tremayne looked at her with a mixture of amusement and amazement. She was, more or less, as he had imagined her – ancient yet full of character, rusting, and displaying – as trophies of her countless sea miles – the scars and dents of years of minor collisions with jetties and quaysides. She also possessed a certain charm with her corrosion-streaked black hull, white upper works, yellow ochre derricks and masts and her tall, elegant black funnel with two light blue rings painted on it. Every inch of her appeared to be what she had been originally built as – a typical Baltic timber carrier.

As they scrambled up the gangway, Tremayne saw the deceptively innocuous-looking tarpaulin covers concealing her two six-pounders. Her captain, like Tremayne, was an RNVR lieutenant commander. A short, stocky man, he smiled as he saluted Enever and then held out his hand to welcome the three visiting officers onboard. His Number One was a slim, neat, grizzled lieutenant RN in his late forties, who had obviously served many years as a rating and petty officer before his wartime commission. His friendly, open face broke into a grin as Enever remembered, somewhat belatedly, to salute what passed as the *Karelia's* quarterdeck – now that she had been given temporary RN status – and with his left hand. Tremayne caught the old lieutenant's eye and knowingly smiled back before he too saluted the quarterdeck in the time-honoured tradition of navies throughout the world.

Over tea, served in exquisite fine china cups and saucers – so out of keeping with the battered, utilitarian appearance of much of the ship, Lieutenant Commander Hardy introduced the rest of his officers to Enever's party and gave a brief background to the *Karelia's* recent conversion to a Royal Navy Q-ship.

Hardy had already assembled the ship's company of over forty chiefs, petty officers and ratings in the main mess deck, which bore the stamp of orderliness and operational efficiency typical of a Royal Navy ship.

Enever, relaxed and clearly at ease in such an environment yet, at the same time, authoritative and professional, had the crew's full attention as he outlined the expected forthcoming operation and *Karelia*'s dangerous part in it.

Most of her new crew had already seen action in the Atlantic, the Channel, or off Norway, but he drove home the need for rapid, but accurate shooting when facing such fast, manoeuvrable and hard-hitting targets as E-boats. He emphasised the speed at which both air and surface vessel support would be on hand and stressed the need for *Karelia*'s radio operators to communicate rapidly and accurately her bearings, as well as all radar contact with the enemy.

Tremayne was impressed by the number and relevance of the questions raised by ratings as well as by the ship's officers and, clearly, Enever was delighted by the degree to which his audience had already engaged with both the spirit and intent of his unorthodox plans.

He was even more obviously popular – especially with the members of the lower deck – when he ended the meeting, showing a sensitive feel for timing, and announced, "Thank you for your questions – they have been most helpful. It is time, though, that we finish. I'm conscious that many of you, too, are due for a thirty-six-hour leave and that liberty men will need time to get ready to go ashore. I look forward to working with you. Good luck and enjoy your leave."

Hardy called the ship's company to attention, while he and his officers saluted the departing Enever, before he dismissed his assembled crew.

On arrival back at HMS Godolphin, Enever bade farewell to Tremayne and Quilghini before leaving for Devonport and a Coastal Forces strategy meeting and update with Rear Admiral Hembury.

Tremayne returned to his cabin — and an ecstatic Bertie — to plan his bachelor weekend's leave.

After taking his ever-eager black labrador for a long walk in the dark along Appletree Bay beach, Tremayne showered, dressed and got ready to have supper at the New Inn. He was settling his dog down for the evening when there was a knock on his cabin door and an indistinct female voice said, "Lieutenant Commander Tremayne, sir."

More irritated than puzzled, as he was just about to go out, Tremayne opened his door — and there stood Emma, her Wren officer's holdall in her hand.

Exaggerating her normal gentle West Highland accent to broad Glaswegian, she said, "Och, hello sailor. Wuid ye be wantin' anythin' frae a bad wee gerrl?"

"Emma — dearest Emma — I don't believe it. It really *is* you.

But I thought that you were on wretched duty this weekend!"

"I was, but at the last minute one of the junior officers asked if she could swap duty watch with me, so that she could have my thirty-six-hour leave in two weeks' time for her engagement party." Smiling, they fell into each other's arms and seeing Tremayne briefly look with grimacing disappointment at his narrow bunk, Emma laughed and said, "Don't worry. I've booked a room for the two of us, for two nights, at the New Inn. Dick and Aileen are already expecting us – and they've made sure that we have our old room back."

Giving an equally welcoming Bertie an affectionate hug, Emma said to Tremayne, "I'll help you pack some kit and then we'll go for supper. Aileen's quite happy that Bertie comes with us. He can have the kennel he uses there when you're away."

Supper was a heady mixture of their shared sense of joy at being with one another again after so many weeks apart and their similar – at times outrageous – humour. Their room – not that initially, at least, they took much time to look at it – was, as they later saw, just as they remembered it. So typical of an old English country cottage bedroom, it was pretty, in a chintzy way, although tastefully so. Aileen had made sure that a huge floral china vase, full of winter-blooming Scilly narcissi just cut from nearby fields, had been placed on the ancient mahogany dressing table opposite the foot of their large old oak bed.

Aileen, the wife of Dick Oyler, the proprietor of the New

Inn, came from the small, rural village of Kilmoganny in County Kilkenny and had a great deal of affection for both Tremayne and Emma. In an almost maternal way, she had come to regard them as members of her own family. In real terms, it meant that they were always assured of the best possible treatment and care whenever they managed to stay at the inn. It was a place that already held so many shared poignant and precious memories for them.

Just past three o'clock in the morning, Tremayne stirred in his sleep and Emma woke to find the pale moon shining through their window. With a sense of wonder at being together once more, they made love again and then fell into a deep, exhausted sleep. Around nine o'clock, still sleepy but laughing and catching up with each other, they went down to one of Aileen's 'real Irish' breakfasts.

With eggs, home-cured bacon, Aileen's 'secret recipe' sausages and both Kilkenny 'tater' bread and soda bread fried to a golden brown, they breakfasted like royalty.

"What an improvement on those dreadful wardroom 'snorkers' of questionable origin and content – and that awful reconstituted powdered egg!" laughed Tremayne.

They had already decided, the evening before, that they would hire a dinghy, complete with outboard motor, and make for St Martin's – and then, if time and weather allowed, visit St Agnes. The station met officer had forecast a cold, clear and fine day and, for once, his prediction turned out to be accurate. After breakfast they walked up through Dolphin Town, stopping to look in at the church of St Nicholas where they were married – one year ago the previous August, and then meandered on to Old Grimsby quay to collect their dinghy. Clinker built, of clear varnished hardwood, with an old British Seagull outboard attached to her transom stern, Tremayne and Emma – both experienced sailors – were delighted with her, although Tremayne rightly anticipated that "those Seagulls can be an absolute beast to start".

Arriving at Lower Town quay on St Martin's about twenty minutes later, they secured the dinghy and then walked together under a bright, cold wintry sky up the long road through Middle Town and on up to Higher Town – and to the little green painted wooden hut which served as the island's post office. There they wrote and mailed postcards to their parents – Emma's in the Western Highlands at Achiltibuie and to Tremayne's near Newton Ferrers in Devon.

At a nearby tea shop at the top of Signal Row, usually closed at this time of year, they managed to persuade the owners to provide them with a makeshift lunch of home-baked bread, meat paste sandwiches and a pot of tea – much to Emma's amusement.

"It may not be the Ritz, but these are so good and, right now, I could eat a horse – despite Aileen's unbelievable breakfast!" laughed Tremayne.

After lunch, during which they spent a good deal of time

studying an old, cloth-backed 1933 edition Ordnance Survey map of the Scillies – that Margaret Bond, the tea shop proprietor insisted they keep, they set off to walk the length of the completely deserted Parr Beach and Higher Town Bay. They followed the long curving stretch of glorious pale golden sand, backed by low dunes, round to English Island Point, before cutting inland up to the gentle hill of Chapel Down. Together they looked out from the top of the hill, across Chimney Rocks, to pick out the various Eastern Isles which they had sailed around during the weekend leave that had become the moment of truth – and new beginning – for both of them, during the summer in which they later married.

"I'd hoped that we would also get across to St Agnes but at this time of year, Emma, winter darkness is going to close in on us before we've even landed there. Let's start wandering slowly back and we should time it well to arrive home on Tresco in the light. We'll save St Agnes for another day. I do want to find some of those glass beads that were washed ashore from the seventeenth century Venetian galley which went down off the island all those years ago. Apparently, they can still be found in a place called Beady Pool on the south coast of the island."

"I shall expect at least enough beads for a handmade necklace from you!" laughed Emma.

Walking hand in hand down the long winding road which eventually leads to Lower Town, they suddenly saw a familiar, sturdy figure striding towards them, with his rolling sailor's gait, coming up from Middle Town. As he drew closer, a broad grin of recognition lit up his amiable face.

"Watkins! What on earth are you doing here? Don't tell me you're planning to set up a kye-making plant for the locals!"

"Afternoon, sir, ma'am," he responded, saluting Tremayne. "No sir – no such luck, but what I 'ave been doing, sir, is looking at a cottage down there in Middle Town that's up for sale. If I can persuade my missus to come over, we might turn it into a small bed and breakfast place and tea room, sir. When this lot's over, sir, I don't think I could face going back to the Austin at Longbridge. Prices are cheap over here, sir – and this one's freehold."

"What an amazing and enterprising idea. I feel quite envious and I hope this comes off for you both. It'll be one hell of a change from Birmingham though!"

"Thank you, sir. The big test will be persuading my missus to leave the little 'ouse she in'erited from her mom and dad, but I 'ope that it 'appens too, sir, and that eventually we can pass it on, as a thriving business, to our daughter."

"That sounds fantastic – and we wish you luck. By the way, how are you getting back to Tresco, Watkins – can we give you a lift?"

"That's very kind of you, sir, but the bloke I 'ope to buy this place from 'as laid on transport from and back to Tresco, sir." Watkins grimaced in mock despair. "It's a leaky sailing dinghy, sir. 'E's the sailor and I'm the baler, sir!"

"Well Watkins, if you haven't arrived back by midnight, I'll instruct the master-at-arms to send out a search party for you, led by Leading Seaman Nicholls!"

"Thank you sir, but 'e'd never let me live it down and I'd never be able to face Coxswain again, neither, sir!"

With another affable grin to accompany his salute, 'Pablo' Watkins went on his way as Tremayne and Emma left to return to their dinghy, moored on Lower Town beach.

"You know, Emma, having people like Watkins, Nicholls, Jenkins and Petty Officer Irvine – plus an outstanding Number One like David, makes me realise just how lucky I am – apart from you being drafted to London."

"I know – I feel exactly the same. Those few months I had at HMS Godolphin, when I could see you and talk with you every day you were at the base, were a heaven that disappeared all too soon. We have to part company again at six o'clock tomorrow morning darling – so let's make the most of every moment we still have in the islands before you return to duty and I go back to London."

Four

Success and disaster

Tremayne knew that the only way he could hope to fill some of the physical and emotional void left by Emma's departure was to immerse himself fully in his role at HMS Godolphin. At 05.30 hours on a cold, black December morning, Tremayne had walked with his arm around a shivering Emma from the New Inn to New Grimsby quay, from where the launch would take her to St Mary's – the first stage of her long journey up to London. The sadness of their impending parting added to the bleakness of the morning and almost engulfed Emma, who tried desperately to hide her tears from

Tremayne. The dark blue and white motor launch, manned by two naval ratings, was already secured alongside the quay. It was there and then, on the quay, that she broke her happy news, which she had reserved for this moment: whilst still not one hundred per cent certain, she was most likely pregnant.

Tremayne took her in his arms and held her close. Almost lost for words, all he could manage to say was, "Oh, Emma – fantastic! What *wonderful* news – just bloody wonderful!"

As the launch cast off and rapidly drew away, her waving figure was all too soon swallowed up in the blackness of the chilly wintry dawn. For a few moments longer, all he could see in the darkness was the sparkling phosphorescence of the boat's wake as she surged through the choppy sea. The deep sense of loss that he felt – as the sound of the launch's engine faded in the distance – alternated with overwhelming feelings of elation at the unexpected news that he was to become a father.

A bewildering range of emotions washed over him as he walked back to the New Inn for an early breakfast, prior to rejoining HMS Godolphin. He experienced, successively, desolation, joy, anxiety about the war – now he was to become a parent, and also a calming sense of hope for his future with Emma and their child.

He had telephoned the master-at-arms' office at 05.15 hours to announce his return following breakfast and to check that there were no emergencies awaiting him.

At 07.00 hours, Aileen Oyler presented him with his pre-ordered breakfast. Hovering like an anxious mother hen over her brood, she watched his face – trying to choose her words carefully to express her sadness at Emma's departure, but also to acknowledge the steel edge in Tremayne that she knew hated any sort of fuss.

Tremayne, sensing her unusual shyness, said – with a grin bordering on the ridiculous, "Guess what my news is, Aileen." With barely a pause for reflection, Aileen looked at him – a warm smile spreading across her face. "Well now, Mr Tremayne, if I think of young Emma alannah's lovely complexion this weekend, sure I'd say that you're going to be a dad. Am I right now, Mr Tremayne?"

"Aileen, wherever do you park your broomstick – or are you gifted with second sight?" laughed Tremayne.

"Sure and I'm so happy for the two of you and I know Dick will be too. God keep you, when you do those things that you get up to – and always come back safely home now."

After breakfast, Tremayne walked with his overnight bag back to Godolphin, returning the sentry's salute as he strode through the main gate and on to his quarters.

At 08.30, he attended a specially convened meeting for boat captains and First Lieutenants in Hut 101, run by Commander Enever.

The purpose of the meeting was to plan the deployment of the flotilla's boats and crews to meet two urgent operational priorities – one of which, directed by SOE, had just arisen. The other, the visit to Scillonian waters by the three E-boats, remained an issue to be dealt with and Enever, overnight, had been forced to divide his limited resources to meet the two demands. He had decided to deploy Lieutenants Mick Taylor, Maurice Simmonds and Jean-Paul Trenet to support the *Karelia*, should the E-boats reappear within the next three days, and to put Tremayne in charge of the SOE operation, backed up by Lieutenants Hermann Fischer and Pierre Quilghini.

Talk of the intended invasion of France and the opening of a 'second front' was now a question of 'when', *not* 'if'. Both SOE and SIS were now increasing the numbers of trained agents being parachuted into France, or landed on her coastline by small boats.

SOE had requested that the Tresco flotilla ensured the insertion of six highly trained French nationals into eastern Brittany, to the east of St Malo, within the next forty-eight hours. Their role was to intensify and focus the gathering of information about German coastal defences and troop dispositions in the areas of north-east Brittany and the west coastline of the Cotentin Peninsula. The six were to liaise with the recently established Confrèrie Bonaparte, but their principal mandate from SOE was to operate independently on key issues of intelligence gathering. Their brief specifically excluded any acts of sabotage, which would draw unwelcome attention to them, since the emphasis of their role was anonymity and clandestine work, under cover, with minimum risk of detection. They would also continue to work, via wireless transmission, with German-speaking radio intercept specialists operating within the UK, who would feed them with intelligence picked up by monitoring German radio traffic in their particular areas.

The agreed plan was to use the three Tresco-based disguised fishing boats, each carrying two agents, and to land them, in the early hours of the morning, on three separate beaches south of Granville in the Baie du Mont St Michel. The agents consisted of four women and two men, all of whom could speak Breton convincingly, as well as their native French.

All naval crew would wear Royal Navy Coastal Forces uniforms, consisting of white woollen sea-going jerseys and Service trousers under duffel coats. RN caps, appropriate to rank, would also be worn. This was to give them some protection – albeit barely adequate – against Hitler's Kommandobefehl, the Commando Execution Order of October 1942*. This Order, to hand over all captured members of raiding parties for interrogation and execution by the German security authorities, was largely in retaliation for the killing of German soldiers, whose bodies had been found with their hands bound following an earlier British Special Services raid on the Channel island of Sark. Carried out by a small group of men from Number 12 Army Commando, Operation Basalt had been a successful raid but, to keep the German prisoners quiet

See Appendix

and passive while the operation progressed, their mouths had been stuffed with grass and their hands had been tied behind their backs. One prisoner spat out the grass and started shouting loudly. He was shot dead and two others who tried to make a break for it were also shot, or killed with a fighting knife. The commandos had been faced with German responses that could have jeopardised the outcomes of the raid and, in the tense situation that had arisen so quickly, they believed that their brutally expedient actions had been necessary.

Details of Hitler's Commando Order had been filtering through to British Intelligence via many sources, including feedback from French Resistance groups, and the deadly gravity of it was becoming increasingly apparent. Following two recent raids – including Operation Frankton, conducted in Bordeaux docks by Royal Marine swimmer-canoeists – several captured commandos may, it appeared, have already been summarily executed by the Germans.

The British authorities were still waiting to learn of the fate of the missing marines. Apart from Major 'Blondie' Hasler and Marine Bill Sparkes, who had managed to get back home after a long, tortuous journey through Spain, the remaining frogmen-canoeists had failed to return from France and nothing more had been heard of them since the raid. One bizarre twist to the Sark incident, which had possibly triggered the fury behind the issuing of the Order, was the publicised indignity inflicted upon the bound prisoners by the commandos. To reduce the captured Germans' chances of escaping, the commandos had removed any belts and braces worn by their prisoners and then ripped open their trouser flies and cut off their fly-hole

buttons. Such a sensible and practical – if somewhat grotesque – expedient had, unfortunately, received full propaganda treatment in the German press, with consequent – and intended – public outrage and international coverage.

Enever's wry perspective on life and very visual sense of humour temporarily got the better of him as he pictured this particular stage of the raid. He could well imagine the sheer terror and alarm felt by the Germans as, with flies wide open and hands tied, they were forced to stand still while the commandos, faces streaked black with burnt cork, savagely hacked away with fighting knives so perilously close to their vulnerable private parts.

The Order, personally signed by Hitler, was aimed specifically at members of small raiding parties, rather than at those troops involved in major seaborne assaults or large-scale parachute drops, who were subsequently taken prisoner by the Germans. Although illegal under the terms of the Geneva Convention, Hitler had justified his Order on the grounds that he considered commando behaviour had, itself, been contrary to the rules of the Geneva code governing the conduct of warfare. How he could justify the reasoning behind the Order, in light of the repeated massacres of prisoners of war and civilians by his own troops in occupied territories, beggared belief, mused Enever.

He had long agonised over this threat and it had caused him a great deal of anguish and soul searching. He knew that, ultimately, he could only resolve the dilemma by allowing his sense of duty to assume precedence over his personal obligations to Tremayne and the boat-crew members. Even so, he did not sleep any more easily, despite what he saw as the only professional and realistic outcome of such a moral conflict in the responsible and aggressive conduct of a war.

Enever was only too aware that the continuing insertion of groups of saboteurs or agents and the small raiding party operations conducted by personnel from HMS Godolphin would, most likely, now justify summary execution of such captives in the eyes of the Germans.

In his briefing, he concentrated on the practical measures and attention to detail that so often make the difference between success and failure – and life or death – in covert operations. He had emphasised the need for each of the boat crews to agree cover stories appropriate to the circumstances, if they were captured. One common factor was that no mention of Tresco must be made under interrogation. Rather, they would confirm Plymouth as their base.

Tremayne supported Enever on the issue and added that all members of the unit were, after all, volunteers and that, as such, the option to withdraw from the flotilla was open to each and every individual. However, as Tremayne already knew, no one present would think of opting out, but all agreed to offer the option to their crew members during their pre-operation briefings.

The agents would wear COPP surface-swimming water-proof suits equipped with small buoyancy aids, together with swim fins, and all carried large waterproof bags for their French civilian clothing, ready to exit the fishing boats rapidly in an emergency. Otherwise, the plan was to row them ashore from the fishing boats in inflatable rubber dinghies.

Members of the Confrèrie were organised to meet them at each location and update them on the state of play locally. The Resistance would also provide the means of regular radio contact with SOE in England.

Operation Guz, as Enever had termed it, was, subject to weather conditions, due to commence at 23.00 hours the following night, so that the three fishing vessels would reach their respective RVs on the French coast by 03.00 hours, the ETA agreed with the Confrèrie.

When asked by Fischer why the operation was given the name 'Guz', Enever replied, his eyes twinkling above his half-moon spectacles, "Because Hermann, it's got bugger-all to do with the place where you're going should the name leak out beforehand and," he added more seriously, "I wanted to keep it 'Navy', with no suggestion of commando or espionage activity. Since we've agreed that under interrogation, if captured, you will state that your base is HMS Drake at Devonport, the Navy's nickname for that venerable place seemed a good cover for the operation."

More detailed briefing, accompanied by questions and answers, followed for a further forty minutes or so before Enever finished his part in the proceedings.

As flotilla commander, Tremayne then took over the meeting and briefed the group on the critical issue of regular communication, by maintaining radio contact between the boats and with base during the operation.

"As you know, gentlemen, with the help of the RAF we shall be using aircraft frequencies already known to the Germans, but using new codes which they will not be able to crack – most certainly not in the short term at least. So hopefully, we shall fool their radio monitors into thinking that some new activity is afoot, involving aircraft only. To allay their suspicions about possible parachute drops – and, therefore, the insertion of agents, which could possibly compromise our operation – we will be transmitting and receiving on frequencies routinely used, to date, solely by fighter aircraft.

"As you have already been told, further radio contact with and between the agents we land, will be courtesy of the Confrèrie – and SOE. Our role, gentlemen, is primarily to act as 'bus drivers'. SOE will keep us posted on progress through Commander Enever."

Quilghini raised the question of fishing boat authenticity

and cover, to which Tremayne replied, "A barrel of fresh fish, caught locally in waters around the Scillies, plus some Breton caps and fishermen's smocks, are all we'll take for possible close-up emergencies. Since we hope to complete everything in the dark, making full use of our boats' high speed, I want to keep anything likely to be considered to be 'espionage kit' to a practical and rapidly disposable minimum."

He paused, as Quilghini nodded his thanks and then continued. "We shall, of course, be carrying our operations boxes on deck, but under casually draped spare fishing nets and full of whatever weapons you decide to take. For example, WB and I will be taking a couple of Brens, enough Lanchesters for everyone, two .38 Webley revolvers, one Winchester pump-action twelve-bore – with a six-shot mag, a Very pistol for signalling and emergencies and a dozen '36 grenades."

Tremayne paused and looked around the group, to lend emphasis to his message, before adding,

"Oh – and plenty of mags, gentlemen, for the automatic weapons. If we *do* get into a firefight, we want enough clout to win it – or at least gain and maintain the fire initiative!"

Twenty minutes later, the briefing broke up and boat captains and their First Lieutenants went to bring their crews up to speed on the two respective operations – Guz for the fishing boats and Operation Nimrod for the MGBs hunting the E-boats.

Later that night, Tremayne telephoned Emma to relive

together something of the leave they had just shared and to talk so much more about her joyful news. He then finished his call with that deceptively innocuous phrase – or variations of it – used by a whole generation of Special Forces personnel: "I've got a little job to do, but I'll be back with you just as soon as I can." He heard Emma's sharp intake of breath and knew immediately that she had seen through his attempt to reassure her.

"Don't worry, darling. I'll be back before you know it and then we can bemoan the fact together that neither of us has Christmas leave and that we have to wait until January before we see one another again."

Tremayne and the other boat captains spent the following day making their final preparations for Operation Guz: checking engines, fuel levels, equipment and weapons, as well as finalising the details of the planned landings. Passwords were rehearsed until they became second nature and signals were also practised. It was agreed with the French reception groups that three white flashes, followed by a pause of three seconds and then one green flash of light, would be repeated, identically, by the welcoming parties on shore. It had also been agreed that any crew member who had gone ashore and not returned to the fishing boat within twenty minutes would be left, and his subsequent rescue organised with the help of the Confrèrie. Anyone going ashore must carry one of the white, green and red lens torches and make every effort to flash a red light back to the boat, hove-to offshore. A red light signalled: 'Get out of here as rapidly as possible'. Follow-up rescue would be organised via Confrèrie assistance. All members of boat crews had earlier been given training in counter-interrogation techniques, under realistic and rigorous conditions, simulating – as closely as possible – the likely circumstances that they could expect if taken prisoner. Necessarily, very rough handling was substituted for extreme physical torture and, as Tremayne ruefully pointed out, it was impossible for their instructors to simulate execution with any degree of reality! The SOE staff who conducted the training had emphasised the increasing degree to which the Germans were coming to rely on psychological torture, as well as on the harsh physical abuse of prisoners. It could obviously only be in the shape of mental torture that they were able to achieve the degree of realism needed to make the training stick. Tremayne and the others were all aware that, however realistic the training in counter-interrogation had been, nothing could ever completely prepare them for the real thing – should it ever happen. At best, the training reinforced the dictum 'to be forewarned is to be forearmed'.

At 23.00 hours precisely, the three fishing boats – each painted in typical Breton colours of blues, browns and white and bearing current identification demanded by the Germans – slipped their moorings at Braiden Rock and headed out to sea.

As flotilla commander, Tremayne skippered the vessel *Muguette*, while Fischer was in charge of *Vas-y-Voir* and

Quilghini commanded *Les Trois Anges*. Clear of St Mary's, the group formed into arrowhead formation, with Tremayne leading, and set course for the Golfe de St Malo, bearing west of the Channel Islands. This particular route spared them the danger of navigating their way, in the pitch dark, through the many dangerous small islands that make up the Plateau des Minquiers and, to the east, Les Iles Chausey.

The north Brittany coast, generally, is a jagged, indented, forbidding area of islands, reefs and rocks and in the Bay of St Malo the tide, which tends to sweep in like a huge battering ram, has been known to reach heights of around forty feet. The beaches of their planned landings lay in the less rugged Baie du St Michel, at the eastern edge of the Golfe de St Malo.

North of the Cote d'Emeraude and St Malo itself – and once south of Les Iles Chausey – the small flotilla would need to alter course to port, to sail eastwards to their respective RVs on the coast between Granville and Avranches.

As the tiny, but sturdy vessels punched their way south through the black, swelling wintry seas, Tremayne, Willoughby-Brown, Petty Officer Irvine and Leading Telegraphist Hatfield, the radio operator, were together in the tall, spacious wooden wheelhouse, studying charts and constantly monitoring the compass bearings.

Littering the tiny makeshift chart table were the paraphernalia typically used by sea-going navigators – parallel rulers, dividers, pencils and note pads, constantly in use by Tremayne and his First Lieutenant. Cramped, but dry and warm below decks, were the two agents – women recruited by the formidable Vera Atkins of SOE's French Section, Petty Officer McDonald as chief engineer, and two seamen – both Frenchmen – who acted, variously, as deckhands, cooks or engineering assistants to McDonald.

At 02.30 hours the two agents came up on deck, clad in their COPP suits as a precaution against any last minute mishaps and carrying swim fins and waterproof bags containing their clothing and personal effects.

Willoughby-Brown made ready the dinghy and oars and, to reduce engine noise, Tremayne ordered half revolutions, even though there was now considerable wind blowing and the constant churning and breaking of the white-capped waves significantly muffled any sounds coming from *Muguette*.

Operations boxes were opened up, weapons were distributed, and boat's company stood to at defence stations. The night was still pitch black and low cloud covered the area, blocking out stars and the moon. In the wheelhouse, eyes strained to see the coastline ahead, looking for any sign of surf breaking on the shore. It was Irvine who was the first to see it: "Enemy coast – dead ahead, sir. About five hundred yards, so it is."

"Thank you, Cox'n. Take her in slowly, if you please, for another two hundred yards – then we'll launch our guests and row them ashore, once we receive the proper signal."

Tremayne immediately called for action stations and placed

the two seamen to port and starboard of *Muguette's* bluff bow, each with a Bren gun and spare magazines close to hand. Lanchesters were issued to everyone in the wheelhouse.

At that point, Petty Officer McDonald appeared on deck from the engine room to speak to Tremayne.

"Sir, the fuel gauge could be wrong but it suggests that we might be losing fuel. I've checked pipes and valves for leaks but, so far, I can't see anything wrong, sir."

"If it goes on like this, will we have enough to get home, Chief?"

"Possibly, sir, but it'll be touch and go and I'd be happier with another few gallons spare, sir, in order to be sure."

"OK, Chief. You know what you need. You and I will paddle the agents ashore and see if the reception party can help us. We'll each take a .38 revolver in our pockets. I'd feel naked there without at least a side arm."

Turning to Willoughby-Brown, Tremayne said, "Right Number One, you're in charge. Give them the signal now please and see if we receive the correct response."

Right on cue, the identical signal came back from the barely discernible shore – three white flashes, a pause of three seconds and then a green flash.

"Give us a hand, Number One, with the dinghy please and we'll be off." Then, realising the severe limitation of the twenty-minute ruling if they were to try to obtain fuel, Tremayne added, "David, since Chief and I are going for fuel, we'd better make it a *maximum* delay of ninety minutes before we signal. If all is well, we'll use the white and green flashes. If the balloon goes up and you *are* discovered, then get the hell out of here as quickly as possible. Should anything go wrong with us ashore, we'll do our best to get a red light signal to you. Have some hot kye with rum ready for us on our return, please, David."

The rubber dinghy was quickly lowered over the fishing boat's transom stern and secured by Willoughby-Brown and Irvine, while Tremayne, together with McDonald – clutching an empty five-gallon fuel can, scrambled aboard. Each grabbed a paddle and then held on to the fishing boat's side fenders to steady the dinghy for the two agents.

As they quickly pushed off, Willoughby-Brown whispered, "Good luck, Richard, see you soon," and Irvine added a murmured, "A safe home, sir, and you Mac."

The strong incoming tide made paddling to the shore a relatively easy task, apart from the constant need to counteract the yawing – and frequent loss of direction – created by McDonald's lack of paddling experience.

Once ashore on the sandy beach, willing hands reached out to steady the boat, welcome Tremayne and the others and then pull the dinghy well up on to the sand, clear of the incoming tide reach. The leader of the reception committee introduced himself as 'Jean-Paul' and quickly organised the agents' safe departure and onward journey from the beach, accompanied by two members of the Confrèrie armed with Sten guns.

Turning to Tremayne and McDonald he asked, "Messieurs, you have a can for petrol? Is there a problem? Can I help you?"

"Yes, please. We may have a fuel leak and, if possible, we should like to find enough petrol to make sure that we get home. Ideally, we would like about thirty litres of fuel. Consequently, we would also need another container. Unfortunately, we only have British money to pay for this. Can you help us, please?"

"I will do my best. As I am sure you must know, Messieurs, petrol is rationed here – as in England – and *les Boches* keep strict control over such matters. But, come with me please. I will take you to a local petrol station run by a friend in a nearby village, less than two kilometres from here. We'll see what we can do – and please keep your money. You bring us weapons and supplies. This is the least we can do in return."

"Thank you, Jean-Paul. We're grateful for your help."

The three set off in the dark along the mercifully unlit winding coast road. After about thirty-five minutes, they came to a collection of whitewashed low stone buildings, which appeared to Tremayne to serve as an agricultural and marine general repair and engineering facility. The petrol and diesel station was situated more or less in the centre of the small service complex, which gave off a rather run-down impression – although one of a business which was in regular use by the local, largely rural population of farmers, fishermen and – until war broke out – holiday accommodation owners.

Jean-Paul went up to a light blue wooden door at the front of a building, which looked like a self-contained single-storey residence with a dormer roof. He knocked repeatedly until he heard a gruff voice, speaking somewhat aggrieved and irritated French: "Merde! Qu'est ce que tu veux?"

The owner of the voice, a stocky, powerfully built man in his fifties with a shock of tousled grey hair, opened the door and looked suspiciously, first at McDonald with his fuel can and then at Tremayne who smiled reassuringly in return. The man broke into rapid French with Jean-Paul, simultaneously shaking hands with him.

Beckoning everyone inside, the proprietor, who introduced himself as Louison, quickly prepared coffee while, at the same time, confirming in strongly Breton-accented French, through Jean-Paul, that he could 'lose' a maximum of thirty litres of petrol, including a spare can. Keeping his fairly fluent French simple, Tremayne thanked Louison profusely for his welcome, hospitality and the promise of fuel and apologised as graciously as his French would allow for waking him up at such an ungodly hour of the morning.

"Ah, Monsieur, de rien. Je vous en prie."

Louison unlocked one of his regulated 'For Agricultural Use' pumps and filled two cans for Tremayne and McDonald.

Speaking through Jean-Paul, Tremayne told Louison that he *must* telephone the local gendarmerie, after a delay of about forty-five minutes, to tell them that he had been held up, at gunpoint, by British naval personnel at just before four o'clock in the morning. They had demanded fuel for their motor gun-boat — and transport to carry it away down to the beach. He should say his captors had not hit him, but had pushed him around and threatened him with pistols and then tied him to his kitchen chair — hence his delay in telephoning the gendarmes — before they disappeared into the night. To reaffirm his message, Tremayne and his engineer pulled their revolvers out and showed them to the much-relieved Frenchman so that he could describe the weapons stuck under his nose. Louison's bovine face broke into a grateful smile and welcome acknowledgement of Tremayne's thoughtfulness as Jean-Paul interpreted for him.

Louison showed them an ancient two-wheeled rustic cart, made of weather-faded elm, in which they could transport the heavy fuel cans more easily — if with considerably more noise, with its rusting, well-worn axle bearings.

Tremayne thanked him again and added, through Jean-Paul, "Louison, leave a length of rope or electric flex dropped on the floor by your chair, as if you had rushed to the telephone in panic and, remember, rub your wrists with a rough towel to redden them. Mark the end spindles on the chair back, just sufficiently to show where the tight ropes had made an impression on the already worn waxed finish, but let the *police* discover that. With a wolfish grin, and one of the most naturally devious expressions that Tremayne had ever seen, Louison said, through Jean-Paul, "Thank you, Monsieur, I shall enjoy playing a role of terrified indignation with *les Flics*."

Shaking hands, they parted company, as Jean-Paul disappeared into the darkness and a still smiling Louison closed and re-bolted his door.

Tremayne and McDonald set off at a fair pace, pushing the squeaking cart, hoping that the increasing wind noise would help to drown out the sound. They were so close to the coast that the sound of the incoming waves, breaking on the shore, also helped to hide the noise of the tortured, oil-starved metal.

On the way out, Tremayne had noted recognisable land-marks, despite the darkness, which would help them to orientate themselves on the return journey to the RV. The first of these was a long line of poplar trees along the roadside, which indicated that they still had about six hundred yards to walk to where they should leave the road and move down onto the beach. Just after the end of the row of trees, Tremayne saw the tubular bus stop, which marked the actual turn-off point.

He and McDonald struggled to drag the heavy cart over tussocks of grass that separated the road from the sandy beach. Then, removing the fuel cans to carry them by hand, they left the cart, to appear as if it had been carelessly abandoned in a rush and only partly concealed. Finally, they remembered to drop – with equal apparent 'British amateurism' – a 'Blue Liner' cigarette packet into one of the many clumps of sea thrift close by, to give some credence to Louison's story of terror, in the middle of the night, when all honest folk were in bed.

As quickly as they were able, and with just over five minutes to go before their ninety-minute deadline expired, they struggled with their jerry cans to the small cluster of rocks, now considerably closer to the incoming tide, where the members of the Resistance group had stashed and secured their rubber dinghy. Tremayne and McDonald stepped behind the rocks to collect their boat when suddenly a voice yelled

"Tiens! Hausez les mains!" accompanied by a torch shone directly into their faces and the metallic clicks of several weapons being cocked.

"Oh shit," muttered Tremayne, "bloody shit!" – more in utter disbelief than fury. Raising his hands, he quickly told McDonald to do the same. The voice demanded to know who they were and what they were doing with an inflatable boat on the beach at that time of the morning. Replying in French, Tremayne explained that he and his engineer had come ashore to find fuel for their MGB to get back to Plymouth. To protect Louison, he told them that eventually they had found a petrol station 'of sorts' where the owner had been most bloody-minded and uncooperative.

Still speaking in French, Tremayne said, "I thought you were supposed to be our Allies and would help us, but that miserable bastard wouldn't give us any help at all, until we threatened to shoot him."

What turned out to be a party of five gendarmes, all armed

with ungainly looking but menacing 7.65mm MAS38 sub-machine guns, quickly surrounded the two Britons and jabbed them with their weapons, indicating the direction in which they were to walk. The voice continued, "You will tell us more at the gendarmerie my friends." The word 'friends' seemed pretty incongruous to Tremayne at that very moment.

Within seconds, they were searched and their revolvers were taken from them. To a now desperate Tremayne, escape looked to be an impossibility. At that point, so too did the opportunity to signal 'red' to his boat, hove-to off shore but as yet still invisible in the featureless blackness of the cold, early dawn.

Suddenly, right on the ninety-minute deadline – and as if to confirm his story that he and McDonald were members of a motor gun-boat boat crew, *Muguette*'s specially-fitted powerful engines burst into life and, churning up an impressive phosphorescent wake behind her, she departed at speed on her course northwards.

"Well, Englishmen, it seems your crew have deserted you – does that amount to mutiny in your navy?" he added with a sneer.

Turning to McDonald, Tremayne murmured, "Keep your spirits up, Chief, we'll –"

"Silence! No talking!" The command was reinforced with a painful jab in the region of Tremayne's kidneys with the muzzle of a MAS38.

They were led to a large gendarmerie van, parked between

two spreading trees on the edge of the road, fifty yards beyond the bus stop. Following gruff orders to get in and repeated prodding by sub-machine guns, Tremayne and McDonald climbed aboard. Within twenty minutes and with the van's klaxon blaring noisily all the way, they arrived at the gendarmerie in a nearby town. Tremayne had been prevented from identifying the precise location by guards who deliberately blocked his view through the van's tiny windows.

Roughly pushed out into a paved courtyard and surrounded by the austere brick walls of the police building, they were manhandled through the massive oak door and along a bleak corridor lit by bare electric light bulbs and pushed into hard wooden seats in what obviously served as an interrogation room. How different, thought Tremayne, from John Enever's Hut 101, with the kindly intelligence officer's personality stamped all over it in so many subtle ways.

Three of the guards stood watching over them, while the two, more senior, gendarmes disappeared.

Tremayne thought he heard a rapid, but unintelligible telephone conversation taking place in an office some distance away, virtually beyond earshot. Moments later, one of the more senior gendarmes returned, together with a thin, fair-haired man of slight build, dressed in civilian clothes. He had the most impersonal, yet penetrating and unblinking eyes that coldly looked right through Tremayne and completely ignored McDonald.

The man spoke in accented, but faultless English. Still looking at Tremayne he said, "Take off your coats – both of you." Before leaving *Muguette,* largely as a precaution against the cold but also to confirm their essentially naval identity, the two had slipped on uniform jackets over their sea-going white sweaters, before donning their duffel coats.

"So, we have a lieutenant commander, RNVR and a petty officer engineer – what we would probably call a Kapitänleutnant and, I believe, an Obermechaniksmaat. How very interesting. I may be wrong in the preciseness of my translation, but then I am a member of the Gestapo – not the Kriegsmarine."

Tremayne's heart had begun to sink at the accent and the use of German nomenclature, but his sense of foreboding increased a hundredfold at the mention of the Gestapo. All at once, *Muguette,* Tresco and, above all, Emma, seemed so very far away. He found he needed all his reserves to fight down the feeling of utter hopelessness that threatened to overwhelm him.

"So, gentlemen, what is your reason for being in this part of France?" The unblinking fish-like eyes held Tremayne's as he continued, "I want the real reason – not some cover story that you have fabricated."

Instinctively – which he immediately regretted – Tremayne glanced at McDonald to see how he was bearing up in the increasingly threatening atmosphere that the Gestapo man was deliberately creating.

The observant German pounced on Tremayne's concern.

"Ah, how touching, Lieutenant Commander. I see you are perhaps anxious about your petty officer's ability to cope with our little talk. But, come now, isn't that more sentimental than professional for an officer of the much-feared British commandos?"

"Commandos? We're not bloody commandos. I am the commander – and he is the chief engineer – of a Royal Navy motor gun-boat. He discovered a possible fuel leak and we decided to come ashore, under cover of darkness, to try and find some petrol. We calculated that we didn't have sufficient fuel to get back to our base in Plymouth. We regularly patrol the waters close to the French coast at night, just as your S-boats come into our waters looking for prey."

Tremayne was deliberately exceeding the amount of information he was obliged to give under the rules of the Geneva Convention, to ensure that McDonald had enough leads to make his story tally with his own. He knew, only too well, that the real interrogation would begin once they had been separated. Although McDonald was not Tremayne's regular chief engineer, he had served in that role on board MGB1315 and so was well aware of the type of patrol sweeps that Tremayne had alluded to.

The meeting was interrupted by a gendarme who spoke briefly to the Gestapo agent.

"So, now we shall soon see what the truth is. Transport to take you to Gestapo headquarters has just arrived."

Tremayne felt a cold chill run through his body and he shivered involuntarily, as he and McDonald were bundled through the door into the courtyard and into a waiting black Citroën Traction Avant with a driver and a guard armed with a machine pistol.

The journey took about fifty minutes, during which, at a traffic hold-up that momentarily preoccupied both driver and guard, Tremayne was able to whisper, "Stick to that story Chief. Make it MGB1315 for consistency." The generally dour, calm McDonald nodded silently in agreement.

Gestapo headquarters was another ugly, sombre building, situated close to the centre of what appeared to be quite a large – again anonymous – town. At pistol point, Tremayne and McDonald were directed up a flight of stone steps and in through the huge, stained wooden doors, flanked by stone columns and topped by an embellished pediment of the same material. Above that, hung a large red, white and black swastika flag.

Inside the building, they were roughly pushed through a wide reception hall, along a corridor and then down two fights of stairs to a series of cells. Several armed guards, wearing black uniforms with swastika armbands, stood around outside the cells and one, with keys, violently pushed Tremayne through an open cell door and then quickly closed and locked it. Several yards away, Tremayne heard shouting and another cell door slammed shut and locked.

He took stock of his surroundings and shuddered in horror.

The cell was about eight feet by six feet. There were no windows, simply the locked, steel door and a small ventilation hole above it, through which it was possible to hear noises from the wide corridor outside. On the stone flagged floor, against the right hand wall, was a filthy straw palliasse and, in the rear corner opposite, was a large cylindrical metal receptacle that served as a lavatory. There was no washbasin and a single electric light bulb hung on the end of a short flex from the centre of the ceiling. It appeared to be switched on permanently. There was a strong, pervasive stench of urine and faeces. Things looked bleak, beyond despair, to Tremayne, as he took in the details of his new accommodation.

The bare stone walls were covered in scratched messages in French — some of defiance, some of utter desperation and others of hope. Tremayne's duffel coat had been returned to him and he placed this over the palliasse, to give him some insulation from the filth and stench of the straw pad. He took off his uniform jacket, sat down on his makeshift bed and tried to get his head together by recalling the counter-interrogation training that he had been given on courses at Godolphin.

"Be prepared for isolation and separation from colleagues. Your captors will set out to divide the group, with mis-information and rumours about your fellow prisoners. They will work on — and exploit — people's perceived weak-nesses and vulnerabilities. Keep cover stories as simple as you can, but be ready to go into sufficient authenticating detail to reinforce their plausibility. Remember what you tell people, so that you can repeat it accurately. Listen carefully to what is said to you. Watch out for tricks and constantly be on your guard. They will try to disorientate you by waking you up at, say, 03.00 hours and tell you that you've overslept and that it's now midday. They will substitute new, unfamiliar routines to disconcert and confuse you."

Tremayne's watch had been taken from him, but he guessed that it must now be breakfast time.

No breakfast and no one appeared and what must have been several hours passed. Fighting down a growing sense of isolation and helplessness, Tremayne went back mentally to his training and drew once more on the guidance of his SOE instructors.

"One antidote to the misery and despair that can so easily invade hearts and minds in enforced isolation, is to recall — and to *sustain concentration* on — happier times. Think about a place or an event where you were particularly happy and draw on that for strength and energy. But think about it *in great detail* — that is essential — become *involved* in your description. Recall, as graphically as you can, sights that you enjoy or love there. Visualise the *detail* of the beauty. Do the same with sounds — especially music. Try to hear them again, in your mind, and bring them back to life for yourself. Recall smells that you've enjoyed and that bring back happy memories for you. Do the same with touch and tactile experiences."

Tremayne began with a detailed recall of places where he loved to be, beginning with sailing trips around the Inner Hebrides, reliving the detail of the magnificent backcloth scenery of the Ardnamurchan peninsula and the white sandy beaches of the islands, such as Kiloran Bay on the island of Colonsay, which he had sailed along in his university days.

After what had probably been an hour concentrating on the Scottish islands, Tremayne had just shifted south, in his mind's eye, to the magical beauty of the Scillies, when his cell door was flung open. With harsh, barked commands, he was alternately dragged and pushed out by two black-clad guards and forced along the corridor, up a flight of stairs and into a large room.

Seated at a scrubbed wooden table and writing what appeared to be notes on sheets of lined paper, was the pale-eyed interrogator who had questioned him at the gendarmerie.

At a nod from the Gestapo official, the two guards brutally forced Tremayne into the chair facing him across the table. Quickly and expertly they bound his hands and feet to the chair.

"Ah, so we meet again, Lieutenant Commander. Well now, your engineer petty officer has given us his story. I would now like to hear yours. What, precisely, was your mission?"

Tremayne began, "I've already told you. We were returning from a Channel sweep when our engineer petty officer suspected that we were losing fuel, but he could not really trace from where."

"I don't believe you, Tremayne. Try again — and make it the truth this time. We know you are British commandos. Do not waste my time." The cold eyes looked directly into Tremayne's, seeking any indication — however small — that Tremayne was lying.

"I have also already told you, that we are not — repeat NOT — commandos. We —"

At another nod from the interrogator, one of the guards swiftly moved round in front of the seated Tremayne and punched him hard in the mouth, knocking him and the chair backwards onto the wooden floor. Tremayne felt a numbing pain across his jaw and the taste of blood from his rapidly swelling split lip. The two guards then heaved him and his chair upright and the questioning began again.

"Spare yourself this unpleasant treatment and just tell me the truth — not a pack of stupid lies. So, why *were* you in these waters, so close to the French coast?"

Finding it difficult to speak because of the acute pain and swelling, Tremayne responded as before. As he repeated his story, almost word for word, another nod brought a second massive punch — this time to his jaw — and he quickly lost consciousness.

Some time later, he knew not how much, he came to in excruciating pain, lying on his palliasse where he had obviously been flung. He was no longer bound hand and foot and, despite the agony from his facial injuries, he felt intense hunger — but wondered how well he would be able to eat should any food come his way.

Much later on what he assumed was the same day, he was dragged out again for further interrogation. Once more, the process was repeated and, after another beating, he lost consciousness for a second time.

He awoke in his cell at some completely unidentifiable time, under the bright light, in pain that seemed to reach into all parts of his being from his waist to his head. Next to the palliasse was a mug of drinking water, which he gulped down despite the agony of his brutally injured mouth and jaw.

He tried once again to rise above the increasing hell he found himself in by falling back on his SOE training. This time, he concentrated on a visit, during a leave shared with Emma, to a wonderfully atmospheric performance of *A Midsummer Night's Dream* that they had seen together. To focus on the detail necessary to take away at least his mind from the sheer hideousness of his current circumstances, he tried to recall lines and even complete passages from the play. One of his favourites was the speech of Oberon's, which began:

'I know a bank where the wild thyme blows

Where oxlips and the nodding violet grows…'

Tremayne finally gave up the struggle to recall the passage accurately, but instead concentrated on identifying all the flowers quoted and how they were portrayed. He focused, too, on the laughter he had shared with Emma during and after the performance and the supper that they had enjoyed at a nearby small restaurant. Her smiling deep blue eyes, her soft dark brown hair with its many natural chestnut coloured highlights, and her gentle West Highland voice all dominated his concentration. The temporary escape from his present reality, together with his complete exhaustion, resulted in him falling into a deep sleep.

He awoke suddenly to his door being flung open again. With neither any idea of the time of day, nor even what day it now was, he was forcibly dragged off his bed and pushed along the corridor but, this time, past the windowless interrogation room, up another short flight of steps and out into a large tree-surrounded grass clearing behind the building. It was daylight, but a freezing cold, grey, overcast day. His eyes took a moment to adjust to the light and then, to his utter horror, he saw two bullet-scarred execution posts about five feet high, six feet or so apart, driven into the ground some twenty yards in front of him. Emerging from another door, with his hands bound behind him and being propelled along by two guards, one on either side, staggered McDonald, barely able to walk on his obviously severely injured legs. His face, like Tremayne's, was also badly bruised and covered in blood. He looked up and, seeing Tremayne, smiled bleakly through the intense pain he must be feeling. Moved almost to tears by McDonald's distressing appearance and now in a state of shock himself, Tremayne smiled back and called out, "Hello Chief —"

Before he could say more, he was viciously punched in

the back and fell forward, only to be grabbed and hauled back onto his feet.

Following McDonald, five soldiers carrying rifles, led by an officer and all wearing SS insignia, marched out into the clearing, forming up into a line in front of the further of the two wooden posts. Tremayne was held by his two guards and watched in growing horror as McDonald's hands and feet were now tied to the post. Forced to look on as a spectator to the unbelievable and surreal scene unfolding before him, Tremayne had never known such total and overwhelming helplessness.

A hoarse, shouted word of command brought the firing squad's rifles up to their shoulders and, on another sharp command, the five fired in volley. Completely distraught, Tremayne saw McDonald stretch up and arch his back in a sudden jerking movement and then he slumped forward, his chin on the bloody mess that was his chest and his legs buckling at the knees.

The officer in command of the firing party, with drawn pistol, strode up to the body and fired one shot at close range into McDonald's head.

Prompted by utter anguish and grief – rather more than anger, Tremayne shouted at the top of his voice: "Oh, you bastards. You fucking bastards."

A cold voice, devoid of any feeling, said, "Now it is your turn, Lieutenant Commander," and emerging at his side was the pale-eyed interrogator.

Tremayne's arms were immediately pinioned and tied behind his back, as he was savagely pushed forward to the nearer stake. As McDonald had been, Tremayne was rapidly and securely tied to a deeply pitted wooden post. Like McDonald, he too refused the blindfold that was offered and forced himself to stand as upright as he could. The firing party was marched opposite him and, as one, turned to face him. On command, their rifles came up to their shoulders into the firing position. Tremayne closed his eyes, struggling to calm his urgent, rapid breathing as he sought to concentrate – not on King and country but on Emma and the child he would now never know.

He softly murmured, "Oh Emma, dearest Emma," and then braced his body to receive the sudden sledgehammer blow that would end his life.

And tomorrow would be Christmas Eve...

Five

PoW – 'In the bag'...

Another harsh, guttural command rang out over the clearing and Tremayne gave a sudden involuntary shiver, his eyes still firmly closed, as he waited for death. Several seconds passed – but as an agonising, mocking eternity – as he stood tied to the wooden post. Still trying to remain braced, to receive the expected volley of shots into his taut body, he finally opened his eyes in utter disbelief. The firing party were standing at attention with shouldered arms, then, on command, turned right and marched back into the main building.

Tremayne, already covered in an icy cold sweat, began to shake. To regain mental, as much as physical, control, he deliberately forced himself tightly back against the post to steady his shivering body and limbs, telling himself that, against all hope, he was still alive.

Was this some cruel turn in the sadistic game that the twisted, evil little bastard was playing? What was going to happen now? What else had the sadist in store for him? The reality of the terrible moments preceding his anticipated execution came back agonisingly as, overcome with utter distress, he turned to look at the pathetic, crumpled body of McDonald just a few feet away to his left. The terror and helplessness that Tremayne had been fighting down only moments before were suddenly replaced by a burning rage, the like of which he had never known before. His previous shocked despair had now been taken over by a physical, destructive hatred of the interrogator and his sick, perverse enjoyment of others' fear and distress.

Tremayne's churning emotions were suddenly interrupted as he was quickly untied by the two guards and led by his arms, back down the flight of steps, along the corridor past the interrogation room and finally flung into his cell.

He dropped down onto the straw palliasse, still covered by his naval duffel coat, utterly drained and, for the moment, in what amounted to a complete emotional vacuum. The temporary insulation from the horror of the previous thirty minutes allowed him to fall exhausted into an immediate and deep sleep.

Sometime later, he was woken up by shouting voices and a hand shaking him violently. Suddenly, the temporary escape and oblivion were over and he was once more thrown back into the hell which sleep had shielded him from. The same two guards dragged him to his feet and propelled him forward, stumbling, as he tried to get his legs moving and find his balance.

Pushed along the corridor, he was roughly thrust into the familiar seat with its horrific memories, but this time he was not tied to it. Sitting opposite him was the interrogator whose attempts at a smile were even more chilling than his pale, cold eyes. Fixing Tremayne with his unblinking stare, he pulled a slim, solid gold case out of his jacket and offered him a cigarette —"Lieutenant Commander?"

Tremayne's reply was terse, as he fought to control his hatred and loathing of the man: "I don't smoke."

"You are a brave man, Tremayne, but I still don't believe that you are telling me the truth. We shall see, however," he added ominously.

"You have a visitor coming to see you today. You will be taken back to your cell where you will take off all your clothes." He deliberately hesitated, looking for anticipated signs of alarm in Tremayne's eyes, but now there were none — only cold contempt.

"They will be washed and dried while you are taken to the washroom showers. You will be given food when you have washed yourself."

The interrogator nodded and Tremayne was seized and roughly hauled out of the chair and returned to his cell.

He stripped off all his now lice-infested clothing and was marched unceremoniously – naked under his duffel coat – to the washroom on the same floor, along a narrow, bleak corridor painted pale 'institutional' green.

He was given a completely inadequate hand towel and a bar of coarse red soap, similar, he recalled, to the ones with which his mother used to scrub the kitchen floor. The shower was turned on and he was pushed under it. The icy cold water hit him, causing him to gasp with shock. He began to rub the crude soap vigorously all over his body and head – the energy being put into it was as much to warm him up and get his circulation moving as to rid himself of dirt, sweat and lice.

Of just above average height, but lean, strongly built and muscular, Tremayne felt his physical strength returning, despite the fact that he hadn't eaten in over forty-eight hours. He dried himself as well as he could with the thin little towel, taking care to avoid rubbing his desperately painful face. With no comb, he ran his fingers through his thick, short dark hair in an attempt to tidy himself up. He noticed a small, badly cracked mirror on the wall, which was to the side of the three showers. Far greater than the shock of the freezing water was that of his appallingly bloodied and bruised appearance. For a moment, he hardly recognised himself. "Shee-it," he muttered — and then his now ice-cold anger returned. Addressing no one other than the battered image in the mirror, he breathed, rather than spoke, "I'd enjoy ripping that little bastard's fucking head off."

As soon as he put his duffel coat back on, he was seized once more and marched back to his cell. All his clothes—apart from his naval officer's uniform jacket and cap—had disappeared. In their place was a plate with a chunk of coarse rye bread and a piece of sausage made from some indeterminate meat. A mug of ersatz coffee — no doubt made from acorns, mused Tremayne — had also been placed on the floor by his bed.

Both the intense cold and the horrendous experience of the execution had left him numb and empty — physically, mentally, but even more so, spiritually. Despite his badly swollen mouth and the unremitting pain of his jaw, he found much-needed solace in the food and warm drink.

How impossibly distant and remote he felt from the people and things that meant so very much to him —Emma, John Enever, WB and his crew. Pulling his duffel coat close around his body and legs to try to keep warm, Tremayne ravenously wolfed down the bread and heavily spiced sausage and then drank the dark coffee with its curiously earthy flavour. At least it was still hot. With his spirits slowly starting to rise once more, he smiled to himself briefly as he began thinking longingly of Leading Seaman 'Pablo' Watkins's rum-laced kye and the wonderful sausage, egg and bacon breakfasts that he miraculously managed to produce on the ridiculously inadequate stove in the motor gun-boat's tiny galley. No wonder the man was thinking of opening a guest house, when the war was over – it could well prove to be a triumph of Navy blue over Cordon Bleu!

As an excuse to practise his SOE training, Tremayne began to concentrate on the unique aroma and taste of kye with rum and then switched back to Watkins's unbelievable breakfasts, which Willoughby-Brown frequently referred to as 'culinary miracles'. He smiled again, as far as his swollen mouth allowed, as he remembered the marvellous smells wafting up from the galley whenever Watkins was in charge of their makeshift catering – and the outrageous banter with Nicholls, his fellow Brummie, as Watkins served the food.

Just letting his mind run free and concentrating selectively on members of his crew, with recalled amusement and affection, was helping to restore his sanity – and his soul.

For what he estimated must have been at least another hour, he ranged over so many sources of happiness, joy and fulfilment and was comforted to discover just how frequently Emma figured in his thoughts.

His concentration and reflections were rudely interrupted when the key turned in his lock and his cell door was flung open by one of the guards, who placed Tremayne's cleaned and pressed clothes on his bed. Accompanying him, the interrogator said, "Get dressed, Lieutenant Commander. Your visitor will be here in fifteen minutes. The guards will bring you to meet him."

With a deliberate display of indifference, Tremayne asked no questions and made no comment whatsoever in response to the questioning look from the interrogator at his continuing silence. Sheer cold murder remained in Tremayne's heart, for what the man had done to him and McDonald. Turning his back on his tormentor, Tremayne dressed and put on his uniform jacket and naval officer's cap and, as carefully as he was able, brushed off both by hand.

"Ready," was all he said before marching out between his guards with 'that bastard', as Tremayne mentally called him in the absence of any name, walking in front of the trio.

Tremayne was aware of just how much more he was now back in command of himself — whatever lay in store along the corridor. He began to recognise, too, the focused power of cold, controlled anger and the directed impetus it gave to thought and action, as he concentrated on the back of 'that bastard's' head. Remembering one of the lethal headlocks that Sergeant Kane had shown him in close-quarter battle training, he indulged his consuming need for personal vengeance: "Will I choke the little fucker to death, or simply snap his skinny neck like a dry stick?"

The interrogator opened the door and directed Tremayne to the chair he had already occupied so painfully and nodded to the guards to release their prisoner. Sitting in the chair usually occupied by the interrogator, was a naval officer wearing the rank insignia of a Kapitän-zur-See. In his buttonhole, he wore the red, white and black ribbon of the Iron Cross, Second Class and a Knight's Cross was pinned on the left breast of his jacket, immediately above a metal Schnellboots-Kriegsabzeichen, indicating that he was a senior E-boat flotilla officer. Instinctively, Tremayne came to attention and saluted the German officer who significantly outranked him. The officer returned Tremayne's impeccable salute and indicated that he should sit down. Studying Tremayne's badly distorted face with undisguised disgust, he said, "Are you responsible for this, Neumann?" Tremayne's knowledge of German was sufficient for him to understand the question and — most important of all — to learn the interrogator's real name for future reference.

"We wanted to get the truth out of him, so we —"

"You can go Neumann. I'll tell you when *I* want you to return." The captain's cold dismissal of the interrogator — and the undisguised contempt in which he held the man, were only too apparent to Tremayne. He was, however, alert to the possibility that this could all be an elaborate, calculated ploy to soften him up, as the brutal treatment had failed to produce the answers the Germans wanted from him, and so he remained on his guard.

For a moment the German officer studied Tremayne, mentally noting the ribbon of the DSC and the oak leaves, denoting a mention in despatches, worn on the left breast of

138

his uniform. Speaking slowly, in almost faultless English, he said, "I deplore the use of such brutality, it makes us all look like barbarians. I am sorry this happened Tremayne and I regret the death of your engineer."

Tremayne replied with a rather perfunctory, "Thank you sir."

"Neumann believes that you are really a commando and that you were here in France to commit acts of sabotage. What is your answer Tremayne?"

"Neither my engineer nor I are – or ever were – commandos, sir. We were most certainly *not* here to engage in acts of sabotage or initiate them through others. McDonald was – and I am – members of the Royal Navy. His was a regular engagement and mine is an RNVR commission, sir. I protest, most strongly, at our treatment here."

The captain said nothing but looked at Tremayne and nodded, in a not unfriendly way.

Tremayne then referred to the engineer's reported fuel loss and the increasingly desperate need to obtain enough fuel to get back to England. Tremayne preserved the logic and consistency of his original story, but deliberately varied the wording to avoid an over-rehearsed version, seeing that the captain was constantly referring to typed notes on the table in front of him.

The interrogation continued for at least a further hour, during which more 'acorn' coffee was served on demand from the captain. Tremayne remained alert to the possible implications of questions and remembered to feed in relatively low level information and, in some instances, plausibly presented misinformation. He also, from time to time, judiciously used the time-honoured military captive's response – "I can't answer that question" – legitimate under the conditions of the Geneva Convention to questions which sought classified information from him.

"I am going to talk with Neumann now, Tremayne, and I am afraid that you will be returned to your cell while we decide what to do with you." He hesitated, his expression softening as he added, somewhat ruefully, "I wish that we could have met in happier circumstances, Lieutenant Commander."

"So do I sir." Tremayne came to attention and saluted. Returning Tremayne's salute, the captain called through the door for the two guards to reappear. This time, after what was clearly an order barked at them by the captain, both simply walked either side of Tremayne as they escorted him back to his cell.

Left alone again, Tremayne reflected on what had been more of a professionally conducted, searching interview, rather than an interrogation. He found himself actually liking the captain – who appeared to be 'Navy' through and through – and, on that, they had related to one another spontaneously and naturally. Tremayne similarly felt somewhat reassured by the captain's demonstrable repugnance towards Neumann and his methods – assuming that it *was* authentic and not staged distaste.

As he reviewed the interview, he recalled how although the German captain had been in a position of almost complete power, holding all the cards, not once had he abused that power. That too, admitted Tremayne to himself, could also have been a clever stratagem yet, in his gut, it just didn't feel so.

After what must have been another hour alone in his foul-smelling, cramped cell, Tremayne was ordered to his feet by the two guards who indicated that he should take his duffel coat with him. He was led into the interrogation office where Neumann and the captain sat side by side facing him. Tremayne saluted the captain, studiously ignoring Neumann.

The captain addressed him: "Tremayne, we have decided that you should be transferred immediately to a prisoner-of-war camp for naval personnel. You will therefore be taken in about ten minutes by Kriegsmarine transport to Marlag 9B, near to our naval base at Lorient. I hardly need warn you that we take a very serious view of prisoners' attempts to escape. Punishment of those caught and found guilty is severe."

"Sir." The response was minimal because Tremayne felt that the rhetoric had been principally for Neumann's benefit and possibly to ensure his release as rapidly as possible.

"Do you have any questions, Lieutenant Commander?"

"Will my murdered," Tremayne deliberately held

Neumann's eyes with stony contempt, "engineer's identity disc be sent on to the appropriate international authorities, sir?"

"Yes, of course, Tremayne."

"Thank you, sir. One final question, sir. Having arrived here, out of necessity, with no intention of staying – the irony was not lost on the captain – I have no washing gear or razor."

"Details like that will be dealt with at the camp, Tremayne."

"Thank you, sir."

"I will escort you to your transport. I don't believe that I shall need this," smiled the captain, as he tapped his pistol holster with his hand.

"I hope not, sir."

Outside, drawn up by the main entrance, a grey-green Horch 4x4, 108 heavy vehicle, with a driver and two armed guards, awaited Tremayne. The naval personnel were dressed in standard field-grey Wehrmacht uniforms, but with distinguishing metal 'U-Boot' or 'S-Boot' naval badges pinned on their left breast. Well out of sight of Neumann, the captain returned Tremayne's faultless salute and then warmly shook his hand.

"Good luck, Lieutenant Commander. We're not all like that bastard Neumann, you know."

"No, I can see that, sir – I wish you good luck too, sir."

Seated between the two impassive Kriegsmarine guards, Tremayne sat back and relaxed in sheer, blessed relief as the Horch roared away from Gestapo headquarters, somewhere in the town of Rennes he estimated. The outlandish horror of the day slowly began to ebb away, as complete exhaustion started to take over...

Some four hours later, Tremayne woke from a fitful sleep as one of the guards — the equivalent of a leading seaman — shook his shoulder and indicated, with the barrel of his MP40, that it was time to follow his colleague towards a collection of single-storey stone and brick buildings. Beyond them, floodlit in the darkness, was a huge barbed wire fence about fifteen feet high, within which were rows of wooden huts and more single-storey buildings.

Tremayne was ushered at gunpoint into what appeared to be the camp administrative office. The first guard, who seemed to be of petty officer rate, knocked on a door marked 'Kommandant' and waited until a clear-cut voice barked "Herein". About five minutes later the guard reappeared and Tremayne was firmly guided through the door by his two watchdogs.

In front of him stood a naval officer, of a similar rank to himself, with the ribbon of an Iron Cross, Second Class in his buttonhole and an Iron Cross, First Class on his left breast above a bronze U-Boot war badge, indicating his branch of the navy.

The German officer saluted first and, obviously shocked at Tremayne's appearance, welcomed him to Marlag 9B camp in good, but strongly-accented English, announcing that he — Kapitänleutnant Reinhard Lehmann — was second-in-command and that Korvettenkapitän Schneider, the CO, was away at present.

He ended his carefully rehearsed – and, no doubt, much used speech – by adding, "Kapitän-zur-See Petersen telephoned us to say that you should receive treatment in the camp hospital for your injuries." Once again, he winced as he studied Tremayne's bloodied misshapen features.

"Thank you – I appreciate that."

Lehmann continued, "We were also told that as yours was an enforced stay – not a planned one – you naturally have no razor and soap and so on. We shall provide those things for you and also one set of spare underwear. Your presence here will be registered with the Red Cross authorities, so that you will then be able to send and receive mail shortly."

Tremayne thanked Lehmann and, this time, was the first to salute, before he was led to the camp Medical Centre for examination and treatment.

Too late for official camp supper, he was given hastily improvised food and a drink at the Medical Centre after his injuries had been attended to. Tremayne was then led by two guards to Hut 14, his billet at Marlag 9B.

As he was ushered in through the door of the long wooden hut, with its rows of double bunks, people – about a dozen of them – stopped whatever they were doing and came forward to meet him and to introduce themselves. Quickly he was surrounded by smiling, friendly officers of various Common-wealth navies, who also voiced shock and outrage at his appearance. Once the introductions had been made all round and as the buzz of conversation quietened a little, he was led to the top bunk of a pair, close to a window.

His guide, Eric Thorne, an Australian lieutenant who occupied the lower bunk, took time to brief him on the camp routines and schedules. A mine of information, and a man with a wry 'Aussie' irreverent sense of humour, Thorne seemed to use the same phrase – "'Kin 'ell, mate" – to express disgust, disapproval, amazement and pure joy. Only the varying inflection in his voice gave any clues as to the true nature of his reaction.

Tremayne took to Thorne instinctively and was both amused and flattered to be called 'mate', which he took to be a sure sign of approval.

Minutes later, the large, sturdy figure of an elderly commander, wearing the dark blue stripes of the Engineering Branch between the three gold rings on his sleeves, came up and said, "Hello, Richard, I'm 'Pop' Tongue, the hut leader. I'm here, in the role of a naval divisional officer, looking after people's welfare – as far as I am able. Is there anything I can do to help you settle in and acclimatise?"

Tremayne replied with a grin, "My wife will obviously be wondering whether it's safe to cash in the insurance and, before she does, I'd like to send mail to her asap to let her know that I'm *still* around!"

"Lehmann is a pretty good chap – for a Jerry," Tongue replied with a throaty chuckle, "and he moves things as quickly as he can. But it may help if I chivvy him up."

Tremayne was concerned about Emma's anxiety — especially in the absence of any concrete news of his fate. He was also anxious to let Enever know of the state of play of events, following the landing of *Muguette*'s two agents and her return to Tresco.

Over the days that followed — which included an incredibly camp Christmas panto in true naval 'Sods' Opera' tradition — Tremayne rapidly integrated himself into the group and soon adapted to the somewhat unreal existence of a PoW. One development that did wonders for his recovery was the eventual regular exchange of letters between him and Emma. Clearly, her gradually advancing pregnancy was of concern and he desperately wanted to be back in England, closer to her. She wrote to say that she would have to resign her commission in the Wrens in about a month's time, but was so pleased to be retained in the role of civilian NAAFI canteen manageress, much to Tremayne's amusement. "Hmm, a true Intelligence Branch professional, and what a convincing 'cover' to pick for those censoring incoming and outgoing prisoners' letters," laughed Tremayne to himself.

He was delighted, too, to receive regular letters — always postmarked 'Truro, Cornwall', from his 'Uncle' — a certain 'retired vicar', the 'Reverend' John Enever — whose agile, versatile mind skilfully conveyed snippets of intelligence information, brilliantly disguised as the most tedious domestic trivia and mind-numbing minutiae of 'Parish Council' proceedings. Using a simple, but very secure code, which had figured in training at Tresco, Tremayne readily deciphered Enever's cleverly encoded messages.

Underneath his collaborative, energetic and sociable exterior, however, Tremayne experienced intense frustration at the irksome tedium of repetitive camp life routines and distance from the job at which he excelled. Within a day of arriving at Marlag 9B, he had broached the subject of escape — only to be met with a collective, resigned, "We're built mostly on bloody rock. Tunnelling's out. We've tried it several times — and got absolutely nobloodywhere at all."

'Pop' Tongue elaborated on the story for Tremayne when just the two of them were together one day:

"The 'Goons' patrol the compound with dogs outside the wire every night and the watch towers are able to cover the whole of the camp with searchlights and those damned lethal MG42s. We too are frustrated beyond belief and the only way out is to seize the moment whenever an opportunity presents itself. But therein lies the rub. If you are going to go on the run, you already need prepared kit and a disguise, ready to hand when you actually make your break. And that, Richard, is the tricky bit."

The older man's kindly eyes expressed a degree of sensitivity similar to Enever's, thought Tremayne, as he said, "As you're no doubt aware, Richard, we don't discuss one another's Service roles — beyond superficialities — especially if they happen to be members of Special Forces, so that any classified information about them can't be beaten, teased – or tricked – out of their colleagues. But I somehow feel that your agenda on escape is professional, as much as it is personal. I believe, too, that yours *is* a background in SF. Am I right?"

"I can't answer that question," replied Tremayne unhesitatingly – accompanying his response with a broad grin.

"Ah, my dear fellow. The mark of Cain *is* upon you!" Tongue smiled, knowingly, at Tremayne's standard interrogation response.

"Right Richard, if that's the case, we'll do all we can to make you a priority for exiting this God-forsaken place and give you what help we can. In Hut 17 – known as 'Frogs' Hollow' – there is a French naval lieutenant from the Intelligence Branch of their Marine Nationale. His name is Jean-François Dupont. He's a bit older than you, although junior in rank. He's a great guy and is probably the most experienced and – compulsive – escapee in the place, having broken out twice before from other PoW camps before he was sent here. I'll organise a meeting with him – if you would like that."

Later that evening – before curfew –Tongue introduced Tremayne to Dupont. They hit it off immediately. Tremayne possessed the advantages of speaking good, reasonably fluent French, as well as his background in Naval Intelligence and Coastal Special Forces. For two people who had only just met, their shared professional backgrounds – and complementary roles in Intelligence – took their dialogue and increasing mutual trust rapidly forward. Just as important were the common regard and personal chemistry that grew between them over the following week.

Tremayne recognised and acknowledged the older man's considerable experience as a seasoned escapee, recognising that he, as a beginner, had much to learn.

One day, when the two of them were apparently preoccupied with a ridiculously harmless game of fivestones outside in the compound – and right under the guards' noses, Tremayne raised the question of the Confrèrie Bonaparte.

"I know of it, of course, mon cher Richard, but it was formed after I was captured." Then, seemingly concentrating on capturing at least four stones and yelling, "Aha, les voila!" he added, "I retain contact with someone outside who keeps me informed. Why do you ask, Richard?"

Before Tremayne's quiet reply, another noisy outburst, feigning indignation – "Oh, la la. Merde!" – lent more emphasis to their apparent intense involvement in the game.

Tremayne offered two reasons in response to Dupont's question. One was the likely need for Confrèrie assistance in getting them to the north Brittany coast – 'the Reverend' John Enever's 'Parish Council minutes' indicated that a Tresco-based fishing boat would collect them from an agreed pick-up point, should they need it. The second reason was that of bringing Neumann to justice and Tremayne wanted to sound out the possibility of back-up and help.

After another noisy, very Gallic outburst for the benefit of the watching guards, in which perfidious Albion came in for some serious stick, Dupont muttered, "That arsehole – he's known as the 'Butcher of Rennes'. The Confrèrie have forbidden attempts on his life because of the very real risk of major reprisals against the civilian population. But, if he could be lifted – or killed – *obviously* by British or American Special Forces, they might agree but it will, I'm afraid, be a matter for negotiation, mon cher Richard."

"OK – point taken, but thank you."

"On the other matter, I know that the Confrèrie would be only too happy to help us. My contact can make the initial local arrangements here in Lorient and set up the immediate best options and routes. How we break out of the camp is the real problem." Dupont casually glanced up, with a broad smile, to see that one of the guards was watching them closely and hissed "your turn to shout".

"Oh, you bloody crafty, cunning Frog," yelled Tremayne, struggling to gather up the scattered fivestones.

Casually they finished the game and wandered off separately to rejoin others at recreation in the grass- covered sports area of the prison compound.

Over the course of the next few days, Tremayne and Dupont explored several options for making a getaway – however wild and improbable.

Idly kicking a football between them, Dupont looked up to see the local *blanchisserie* van come to collect and return the camp's laundry and the German officers' dry cleaning. Watching the complete process in an apparently bored, disinterested way, Dupont said, "Kick the ball away from the wire and let's stroll – don't hurry."

Wrapped up against the early February bitter cold, with his hands in his pockets and casually kicking at scattered stones, Tremayne walked slowly alongside Dupont.

"Richard, I think I have a solution – the laundry van."

"But surely, they check the washing and dry cleaning bags carefully and prod them with their bayonets."

"Of course they do, Richard – and with such impressive German thoroughness and efficiency! In fact, they concentrate on the large bags and the underneath of the van, to the virtual exclusion of everything else. Which is ideal for us, don't you see?"

"Because, presumably, they don't really check the driver and his mate – except for their paperwork to make sure that totals tally. And, in this bloody awful weather, the two in the van are usually muffled up to the ears."

"Absolument!"

"Brilliant, Jean-François! Let's get the detail right and then go for it."

"Agreed!"

To reduce the boredom, Tremayne, like Dupont and several

others, had volunteered for various routine roles, such as manning the camp library, chairing the writers' group – and helping to collect laundry bags from the many huts and bring them to an empty office within the compound which served as the returns and pick-up point.

In time for the next delivery and collection, Tremayne and Dupont made sure that they were nominated as the appointed duty helpers.

Together in the compound, nonchalantly leaning on one of the accommodation hut walls, they developed their plan. They would make sure that they were together in the room when the two laundrymen started to bring in the returned washing and cleaning to the delivery and pick-up point.

When the laundrymen had both completely cleared their van of the returned laundry and fully loaded it up with the dirty clothing, there was a delay while the paperwork was checked, initially by the duty prisoners in the room. The papers were then returned to the driver and his mate, still within the building, and the driver subsequently handed these to the guards – who had checked bags out and in, and who remained standing at the van rear doors – for the final scrutiny. It was during this stage that extra large bags – one for each hut – were prodded by the guards with bayonets if anything looked suspicious. What concentrated the guards' attention on this particular stage of the proceedings was that, over the last eighteen months, two failed attempts to escape had been made by prisoners burying themselves amongst the dirty washing within the huge hut bags.

The driver and his mate sat in the van, with their engine off, until the guards finally returned copies of their carefully checked paperwork. At no time were prisoners allowed outside the office while the van was present within the compound. The guards then gave permission for the van to leave and waved the driver off.

Dupont emphasised the critical importance of timing, speed and attention to detail in removing the laundrymen's outer clothing, quickly getting dressed in it themselves, tying them up and gagging them before hiding them under a few, deliberately delayed, remaining bags awaiting final dispersal to the huts.

"That sounds fine, Jean-François, but how the hell do we keep them quiet *before* we are able to gag them?"

Dupont gave one of those uniquely French gestures that graphically convey what is the obvious logical answer, "We threaten to shoot them." For a moment, Tremayne looked aghast and then, slowly, his face broke into a huge grin as Dupont produced from his overcoat pocket a perfect replica pistol — complete with dummy silencer — beautifully made from carefully carved wood, stained black and given a realistic metallic sheen with black boot polish.

"However did you get that? It's unbelievably realistic."

"Ah mon cher Richard, I indulge a hobby of mine as a modelmaker, working whenever I can in the carpenter's shop. Every so often, I smuggle out a small piece of wood, a little glue – or whatever else – and slowly shape the pieces I need whenever I can and then – voila!"

In what would be rather poor electric lighting, on a dark February late afternoon, Dupont's very accurate replica Walther P38 would be indistinguishable from the real thing, felt Tremayne. The silencer – instantly recognisable as such – lent further menacing authenticity to the gun and emphasised the capability and likely intention of being used by a desperate escapee, especially one so fluent in gutter French.

With two days to go before the laundry van was due, Tremayne and Dupont went over their plan, in detail, several times – constantly raising and seeking ways to prevent or counter the many 'what-ifs' of the unexpected and unwanted. They collected and hid baling twine and any pieces of string, cord or rope that they could lay their hands on, as well as scraps of material torn off old shirts and underwear, to act as gags.

Tremayne put 'Pop' Tongue in the picture and asked that the members of Hut 14 covered him for pre-breakfast *Appel*, if his absence hadn't been picked up before early morning roll-call. Tongue offered Tremayne a packet of French francs – both as notes and coins – sufficient to buy food and drink and, if needed, a short distance rail fare. Dupont had done likewise with his hut leader in 'Frogs' Hollow'.

In the interests of security, and genuine ignorance under

inevitable subsequent interrogation, neither hut leader had informed the escapees' colleagues.

The day of the planned break-out arrived and at recreation breaks in the compound, Tremayne and Dupont checked and rechecked the sequence and realism of their intended actions, as well as their contingency plans to attempt to deal with the sudden and unexpected.

It was already dark and bitterly cold – with a slight fall of snow – when the van arrived.

Tremayne and Dupont, with hearts pounding and mouths dry, tried to look suitably bored and indifferent at the prospect of another irksome routine task.

They were both on grunting acquaintance with the laundrymen and consciously maintained that casual, uninvolved level of relationship as they stacked the incoming bags in the far corner of the room, seemingly in order to check them against the list before organising their dispersal within the camp. They then helped the laundrymen stack all the outgoing sacks, prior to loading them in the van.

Tremayne had pointed out to Dupont the rough similarity in respective heights between the laundrymen and themselves – one being taller like Tremayne, whereas the other was shorter and more thickset like Dupont. Because of that, it was decided that the cold weather clothing, pulled-down hats and mufflers of the laundrymen would be sufficient disguise to enable Tremayne and Dupont to do the actual loading of the van, while the crew were gagged and tied up under the returned bags.

Just as the two were about to start loading their van, Dupont produced his wooden pistol and put it close to the temple of the larger of the laundrymen. The commands, hissed in particularly threatening gutter French, had an immediate effect and two pairs of hands went up as the pair began to shake uncontrollably.

Having first removed their hats, scarves and long thick overcoats, Tremayne swiftly tied their hands tightly behind them and forced the cloth gags into their mouths, securing them with lengthy strips torn off some unfortunate inmate's Service shirt. Dupont maintained a suitably evil expression as he periodically thrust his pistol into the bellies of the two sweating laundrymen, swearing obscenely and creating near bowel-evacuating reactions.

Waving his pistol and muttering threateningly, he prodded the two over to the pile of incoming bags on the floor. He ordered them to lie down, whereupon Tremayne quickly tied their ankles together securely, making sure that there were enough of the large bags between them, as well as on top of them, to delay the opportunity to untie each other's hands. Speedily putting on the laundrymen's outer clothes, Tremayne and Dupont set about loading the van. Dupont, with a particularly savage whispered oath, threatened to shoot anyone who attempted to move while the bags were being loaded into the van. Tremayne felt his pulse quicken and his breath shorten as he walked past the guards – who cradled the machine pistols slung over their right shoulders – to heave the first bag into the back of the van. He managed a convincing "Merde!" and suitably French gesture of hopelessness as his foot skidded on a patch of compacted snow. One guard laughed while the other watched the approaching Dupont, who was quietly whistling the song *J'attendrai* as he carried out his first bag.

Inside the room, collecting the next two bags, Tremayne whispered a relieved, "So far, so good."

"Maintain the nonchalance, mon ami," grinned Dupont, then hissed in French at the still figures buried under the mound of bags, "You two. Lie perfectly still or you're dead men and the Boche won't hear a damn thing with this silencer," as he winked broadly at Tremayne.

They carried on loading the bags under the watchful eye of the two guards. If they suspected a bag was particularly heavy – watching the degree to which Tremayne or Dupont appeared to struggle with the weight – they insisted on prodding it to make sure no one was concealed. The bags loaded tallied with the paperwork and the guards raised the steel barrier as Dupont put the van in gear and began to drive away unhurriedly, audibly muttering French banalities to Tremayne with his window deliberately still fully wound down.

Tremayne was sweating profusely, despite the bitter cold,

but the sensation of utter relief and feeling of overwhelming joy as they passed through the barrier and under the stone arch of the camp exit was exhilarating.

"Jean-François, you amaze me. Quelle panache!" He smiled as he settled back into the worn cloth-covered seat of the old, rusting Renault van.

"I must admit, there were times when I really wondered if we'd —"

"Halt — HALT!!" The shouted, peremptory command cut through Tremayne's words with a chilling suddenness. For one moment, as he froze, Tremayne felt gut-wrenching despair and then, as Dupont braked and put the vehicle into neutral, he rapidly recovered and whispered, "Let's appear as helpful to the bastards as we can — and use humour."

Exaggerating his French accent and making his attempts at German sound suitably Breton and rustic, despite his fluency in the language, Dupont said, "Sorry, mein Herr. What is wrong, please?"

"Idiot! You have given us *both* copies of the paperwork. *You* need one or your boss will most likely accuse us of fiddling the records and that fat bastard will try to overcharge us!"

"Mein Herr, I'm so sorry. Please excuse us." Indicating Tremayne with his thumb, he said, "Er hat eine Schraube los!" At the mention of a 'screw loose', a term which, thankfully, he understood, Tremayne rolled his eyes heavenwards with a typically Gallic 'both hands' gesture — which could have meant almost anything – as the two German guards roared with laughter at his convincing display of embarrassment.

A marvellously contrite Dupont apologised again, glowering theatrically at Tremayne, and asked if they could go since they had another collection to make and were already running behind schedule. Still giving full vent to their Schadenfreude sense of humour, the Germans cheerfully waved them on again.

"God help us – we don't need many more moments like that," said Tremayne, as Dupont gently accelerated away from the camp. Once well clear of Lorient and on the road north to the small town of Carhaix-Plouguer, which lay some six kilometres beyond Les Montaignes Noires, he floored the throttle.

Dupont had devised a plan for the first stage of their escape route in conjunction with his local Resistance contacts outside the camp. This involved travelling, as quickly as possible, in order to reach the first of a succession of potential safe houses, scattered throughout north-west Brittany, before the inevitable hue and cry following their discovered escape closed all surrounding road and rail routes.

Dupont was well aware that the closer to the coast they were, the far greater risks they ran of meeting surprise German road blocks and more thorough checks. At their first safe house, a small, remote farmhouse at the edge of a tiny hamlet, a little over a kilometre north of Carhaix-Plouguer, they would be given false identification papers to help them get through local spot checks by sentries guarding key points in and around towns, at river crossings and, especially, at the entrance to all seaports. Until they had the necessary papers they were particularly vulnerable and, without even side arms, they had no viable means of fighting their way through a road block if they were stopped.

At around 7.30 in the evening, they arrived close to the farmhouse and stopped. Dupont switched off their lights and they waited for several minutes to allow their eyes to adjust to the complete darkness.

Once they were able to see the outlines of the farm buildings, trees and other features more clearly, Tremayne suggested that, just to make sure, they should wait and observe the location for another fifteen minutes for any signs of activity. Wartime blackout restrictions made it more difficult to distinguish between rooms with lights switched on, where there was likely to be normal, everyday activity, and those in darkness, where someone could well be lying in wait.

Silently approaching one window, where Dupont had spotted the merest chink of light in the bottom left-hand corner, they stopped and listened, their ears pressed against the cold glass. After a few minutes someone spoke in French and this was answered by a loud laugh. Dupont immediately tapped Tremayne on the shoulder, gave him a 'thumbs up' sign and whispered, "It's OK Richard. I heard what he said. It's time to introduce ourselves, mon ami!"

The door was slowly opened in response to Dupont's obviously pre-arranged three raps, followed by a wait of three or four seconds and then two more raps. A large man, aged about fifty, stood in the doorway with a woman of a similar age close behind him. Both were dressed in typical Breton farmers' clothes. They welcomed Tremayne and Dupont, warmly shaking their hands, and, once inside, introduced them to another man and woman sitting around a large, scrubbed wooden table.

The aromatic smell of meat and vegetables being cooked as a stew, with added herbs and wine, filled the big, homely Breton farmhouse kitchen and Tremayne realised that he had not eaten a decent meal, which he had really enjoyed, in almost two months. The large man, who turned out to be the owner of the farm, saw Tremayne's obvious relish and, smiling, said in French, "We shall eat in about five minutes, Monsieur. But, please, first join us in a glass of wine." It may have been only plain *vin ordinaire*, but at that moment, to Tremayne, its taste and nose were better than those of the finest claret.

Over supper, the six talked through the preparations that had already been made to move Tremayne and Dupont progressively towards Roscoff, their planned point of departure. After five nights lying low at the farm, they would move, with the relatively busy early morning traffic, in an anonymous-looking ancient farm lorry, as itinerant farmhands going to work on the land just north of Morlaix, about twenty kilometres south-east of Roscoff. Daniel, the farm owner and a member of the Confrèrie, explained that though it must seem frustrating – especially for Tremayne – not to be moving on immediately, the German authorities would put in maximum effort to recapture the two fugitives within the next few days. Their hiding place for the following five days would be one of two old cellars beneath the house. One cellar – left obvious for searching troops to investigate – was accessible from the family room.

The other 'secret' one was accessible by a trap door, set in the floor of the first cellar under an old worn rug and long-disused, broken furniture. Ventilation had been cleverly concealed via the house drainpipes.

"Nobody ever thinks to look *below* a cellar," laughed Daniel's wife, Monique.

Deliberately, the Confrèrie had been built up essentially as a cellular organisation, to confine knowledge of other members to a necessary minimum. It did, however, have a strong infrastructure and well-regulated system of networking, which would be put to use later that night in disposing of the laundry's elderly Renault van. This would be the job of the other couple, also Confrèrie members, who were to meet up with others – for necessary muscle power – at a deep reservoir well to the west, the van's intended resting place.

Tremayne and Dupont took every opportunity for exercise over the next five days, including working to help out on the farm whenever it was safe to do so. The farm was visited twice during that period by German search parties, while Tremayne and Dupont spent two very tense hours in their subterranean hideaway. The searches of the cellar above their heads seemed to take for ever and both expected the trap door to be lifted at any moment and a stick grenade thrown in.

Moving throughout the area, making dairy deliveries, Monique's trained eye noted a good deal of activity by German troop transporters and armoured SdKfz 251 half-tracks on the roads around Carhaix-Plouguer.

On the fifth day, they were taken to the second farmhouse. Generally, their journey in the farm lorry, with other – genuine – farm workers, was relatively uneventful. At the one road block and checking of identification papers that they did encounter, Tremayne came in for worryingly close scrutiny because of the smooth condition of his hands. Thinking quickly and speaking in French, he explained that he had been ill for some considerable time and had just resumed work. After a second, agonising examination of Tremayne's fingers, the German grunted something unintelligible and nodded them through. Similar in general layout and architectural style to the first one, the second farm was set close to woods, which formed its northern and western boundaries. This time, their hideout was in a large barn, above a false ceiling, the entrance to which was ingeniously hidden by crude, typically rustic carvings. There, too, their 'host' – Alain – was a Confrérie member, who was in touch by radio with SOE and, therefore, indirectly with Enever. The plan, he explained, was to move them that same night to a deserted point on the coast, about seven kilometres west of Roscoff, and row them out by dinghy to the fishing boat sent from Tresco.

Lying up during the day, Tremayne and Dupont were forced to endure another search while hidden above the false ceiling in the barn. At one point, both were alarmed when one of the search party took it into his head to tap the ceiling, which formed the floor of their hideout, with the handle of a large wooden rake. Luckily, the responding sound was very solid and didn't suggest the presence of a significant empty space.

At around 01.45, Alain woke up Tremayne and Dupont and announced that it was time to move. Driving a rather nondescript, battered old Simca van, he took them north-west via twisting minor roads and narrow, meandering lanes towards the coast. One heart-stopping moment occurred just as they emerged from a local village road onto the main highway connecting Roscoff to Brest. Coming towards them at high speed were several large, German, eight-wheeled armoured cars. Luckily, Alain had had the presence of mind to approach the crossing with his headlights off and he reversed rapidly back into the narrow road which they had been about to exit. The tension in the little car mounted unbearably as the armoured cars drew near. The only weapon they had between them was Alain's Luger. With lights off, they remained back from the highway, hoping that the trees along the narrow road would hide them. Once again their luck held and the Germans went racing past, obviously after some other unfortunate quarry.

By 02.45, just one hour since they had left the farm, they were within a kilometre of their RV — and the rubber dinghy.

At one point on the road along the jagged, deeply fissured coast, Alain stopped the car, ensuring that it was sheltered as far as possible by the thick twisted branches of several large bushes.

"So, now we must start walking, Messieurs. Follow me closely — the rocks down to the shore are dangerous. Use your hands, as well as your feet, to find your way and keep your balance. They are also wet and very slippery."

Taking a torch — and handing another to Tremayne 'just in case' — Alain confirmed the signal to the Tresco fishing boat as two flashes of light, a pause of three seconds, then another two flashes. They should then wait for the identical response before pushing off and paddling over. Alain continued:

"The man with the dinghy will have seen our lights and will make the boat ready as soon as he sees the answering signal from the sea. But first, I must signal him, to make sure *he* is there. I shall need him to help me paddle back to the shore."

One long flash from Alain's torch was answered immediately by a similar one from about fifty yards away. By now, Tremayne could clearly hear the breakers pouring in over the rocks ahead of them. He had already welcomed the familiar smell of the sea and breathed it in, deeply, to clear his lungs of the lifeless air of the cellar and the barn.

Tremayne's heart leapt as Alain's signal to the still invisible fishing boat was answered, seemingly from the depths of the black, starless night. The darkness of the sea was relieved only by the phosphorescent progress of the incoming waves and out there, only about three hundred yards offshore, was a Tresco boat. Tremayne could feel his hopes rise, the adrenaline coursing through his veins as he moved towards the shoreline. The scramble over the rocks was every bit as difficult as Alain had warned them and, several times, all three of them fell and rose, cursing quietly.

At long last, they reached the rubber dinghy and Louis, the Confrèrie member who guarded it. Shaking hands with him, they grabbed the single-blade paddles he offered them, walked out into the icy water up to their knees and, one by one, climbed in carefully so as not to capsize the precariously bobbing craft.

Quickly establishing a good, unified rhythm, the four of them struck out for the fishing vessel, paddling with deep, long strokes into the choppy sea. Someone in the bows of the fishing boat repeated the earlier signal to guide them directly on to their rescuers.

At that moment, a throaty roar opened up from a fast launch that had clearly been alerted, while on patrol, by the succession of signals passing between the sea and the shore. It had obviously been quietly cruising along at minimum revolutions on the look out for people trying to slip away from the Brittany coast.

"Oh, mon Dieu, les Boches!" shouted Louis. "Paddle hard everybody. We are almost there."

A small but powerful searchlight, switched on from the wheelhouse of the approaching launch, lit up the fishing boat, which Tremayne immediately recognised as the *Muguette*, as well as their flimsy, unprotected dinghy. The launch was about two hundred yards away when it opened fire on the dinghy with a machine gun. With a sharp gasp and then an agonised groan, Dupont let go his paddle and rolled over into the sea.

As Tremayne cried out "Jean-François" in anguish, the Frenchman's bullet-riddled body slowly slipped beneath the waves. Almost simultaneously, the familiar 'knock' of a Bren gun spelled the destruction of the launch's searchlight. Seconds later, another Bren gun, together with several Lanchesters, joined in — shredding the wooden wheelhouse of the launch and most of those sheltering within it.

In shock, at the loss of the man who had been his closest friend over these last seven weeks, Tremayne instinctively seized the line thrown out to him. Freezing cold and close to collapse, he felt strong hands grab his arms as Willoughby-Brown's familiar voice yelled an ecstatic, "Welcome aboard, sir."

Six

Operation nimrod – the hunters hunted

Tremayne was pulled up gently, but quickly, onto *Muguette*'s crowded deck while Leading Seaman Nicholls, the port bow Bren gunner, continued to empty successive magazines into the launch, which was now stopped, dead in the water. Mercifully, the launch's machine gun had also been put out of action by Nicholls's accurate shooting.

Grabbing the rigging of the for'ard mast, Tremayne rapidly hauled himself to his feet and warmly shook Willoughby-Brown's outstretched hand.

"Am I bloody glad to be back, David. It seems a whole lifetime away since we set out together for the Baie du Mont St Michel."

"It's so good to see you again – how are you, Richard? We've been hearing some terrible stories about your capture from Commander Enever through SOE's encrypted messages. We wondered if we'd ever see you again. Emma, of course, has been spared any details. Lucy has been keeping in constant touch with her while you've been a PoW."

"Thank God for that – there are some things that Emma need never know."

Tremayne smiled, as he put on what he termed his 'on parade face', and turned to his First Lieutenant, having quickly taken in the situation. "Right, Number One, get us out of this bloody unholy mess and take us home!"

"Aye aye, sir" – the immediate response was accompanied by the happiest of grins.

Willoughby-Brown called to Irvine: "Set course for Tresco, if you please, Cox'n. Maximum revolutions."

Turning to Nicholls and his impressively mounting pile of spent cartridge cases, he yelled, "Cease fire! Check, check, check."

He then called, "Maintain action stations," as a smiling Tremayne said quietly, "Hmm, Number One, I think it's high time you had your own command!"

"Thank you, sir. By the way, where *is* McDonald? Whatever has happened to him? Commander Enever told us that, from what information he had managed to get out of SOE, it looked as if Mac might have been shot – although he said their message could possibly be supposition rather than fact. There was no official confirmation and, apparently, their information was based on contact from the Confrèrie. Surely that can't be true, sir – they wouldn't have *executed* him?"

"That is exactly what the bastards *did* do." Tremayne recounted, in outline, the events leading up to McDonald's completely unjustified, merciless killing, to a horrified Willoughby-Brown.

"When we get back, I'll put everybody in the picture, once I've cleared it with Commander Enever.

If it's the last thing I do, David, I'll bring the scum who killed Mac to justice."

Tremayne's anger was that which is perhaps the deepest and least forgiving of all – the rage of things still unsaid and of actions as yet untaken.

He then slipped into the wheelhouse in order to speak to Irvine, the redoubtable Ulsterman. "Glad to see you, 'Swain. As ever, your navigation was spot on and it was one hell of a relief to see *Muguette* right on station. Thank you for that."

"Thank you, sir. If I might say, sir, we were all glad to see you, too. Every one of us – so we were."

With his First Lieutenant taking over the logistics and routines of command, Tremayne was temporarily free to reflect on the events leading up to being hauled on board – but especially the shockingly sudden death of Jean-François Dupont. The speed of his rescue — and the brief, but intense firefight — had demanded intuitive response and immediacy of action on his part. Now that routine had taken over once more, inevitably, considered thought had succeeded gut response and the instinct for survival. He felt again the intense pain of the cruel loss of a dear friend, with whom he had shared so much in so short a time, and the strangely paradoxical feeling of survivor's guilt. Briefly, Tremayne put his hand to his forehead — first McDonald, then Dupont…

A timely interruption to his deep sense of bereavement came in the form of the dry Midlands wit of Leading Seaman Watkins.

"Excuse me, sir. I remembered, about two months ago, that you asked the First Lieutenant to have a cup of kye, with rum, ready for your return, sir. Well, I've bin keeping it 'ot for you, sir!" Watkins handed over the steaming enamel mug with a broad wink to the taciturn coxswain, whose eyes remained firmly fixed on the darkness ahead.

"Watkins! Thank you. It's good to see you. D'you know, I even found myself thinking about you while I was in prison!"

"Blimey, sir. Yo' *must* have bin lonely!"

Under cover of the continuing darkness and in Irvine's capable, experienced hands, the sturdy fishing boat pushed her way through the rolling seas, at a consistent thirty-two knots, her twin powerful engines maintaining maximum revolutions.

Looking around her deck, as he gratefully sipped the Navy's own unique nectar, Tremayne was impressed to see how Willoughby-Brown had imposed his quiet, authoritative presence on the boat and her crew. Everything was shipshape, cleared away and in place. Meticulous attention to detail was apparent in the barrels of freshly-caught fish, the fishing nets at hand to cover the operations boxes in an emergency, the tightly furled sails — and the professional manner in which *Muguette* was being handled.

With the Channel Islands some seventy miles to the east, they headed directly for the Scillies. It was still dark, with the barest hint of early dawn in the eastern sky as they approached St Agnes to port, with St Mary's fine on their starboard beam. Tremayne confidently left the last, trickier stage of navigating the final entrance to Tresco's New Grimsby harbour and Braiden Rock to his now equally assured First Lieutenant.

Quickly gathering the small crew around him on the rocks bordering the anchorage, Tremayne thanked them all for their impressive rescue operation and their rapid, effective destruction of the motor patrol launch. Had it not been for their disciplined, well-directed fire, the patrol launch could have completely wiped out all hope of escape. He repeated his promise, made earlier to Willoughby-Brown, that he would put crew members in the picture as soon as he was able.

Willoughby-Brown had already ordered Sparks to radio ahead to Godolphin and Enever's lean, agile figure appeared at the top of the short, steep rocky path leading up from the makeshift quay.

"Richard, my dear boy – thank God! Welcome home!" Enever vigorously pumped Tremayne's hand, beaming all over his face.

"It is so good to be home again, John – or should I say Reverend Uncle?!"

Enever burst out laughing.

"Y' know, the greatest fear I have, is that I'll now never make it up 'topsides' when I finally depart this mortal coil, after so profaning the cloth! I can just imagine the reception I'll get from a very disapproving St Peter – 'Vicar, my arse, Enever'..."

Amidst more laughter, Enever touched Tremayne's arm, "Richard, please grab a quick breakfast in the wardroom with me. Bring me up to speed and then, dear boy, go and disappear and have some time for yourself. Ring Emma and grab some shut-eye."

"Thank you, John. I'd like to do both very much."

Together they walked back to Godolphin, talking animatedly all the way. Even so, Tremayne found time to take in the welcoming familiar smells and sounds that he would always associate with Tresco – and the shapes of the rocks and islands, which he so loved, now gradually emerging and taking form under the slowly lightening sky. This magical place, he recognised, had now become a special — and permanent — part of his very being.

Over a cooked English breakfast, which to Tremayne seemed like long-absent gastronomic bliss, he recounted his story to Enever, from the time he and McDonald paddled ashore to the time when he was hauled back onboard *Muguette* only hours ago.

Enever's attentive face and sensitive eyes registered the many reactions he felt as Tremayne gave chapter and verse of events during the last eight weeks or so.

"I need to put SOE in the picture and it's possible that both they and SIS in London may wish to interview and debrief you. Right now, you must be utterly banjaxed. Thank you for updating me, Richard — yours is a most harrowing story. But you've been an enormous help and I'll be on the blower to SOE and SIS within the hour. By the way, dear boy, you have a rare — but quite unnecessary — talent for self-effacement. There's so much more about your part in this horrendous saga that I'll wheedle out of you one day. Now, make the time your own until 14.00 hours when we'll meet in 101 — and I will bring you up to speed on events here. I think that you'll be interested, to say the least!"

Enever rose to take his leave of Tremayne and said, with some obvious discomfort, "Richard, I'm so sorry, but when you speak to Emma please don't plan any specific dates just yet for your much-needed and well-deserved leave. I'm afraid we have another job for you, which is urgent – as well as essential. Once that's over, you *will* be able to disappear for a couple of weeks, I hope. I'll tell you more about it at 14.00. Please do give Emma my very best!"

Tremayne rang Emma from the telephone in the officers' quarters and his heart leapt as her soft West Highland voice answered his call.

Putting on his best institutional sing-song accent and imitating the style adopted by many boy entrants into the Navy, he asked, "Mornin' luv. Is that the NAAFI canteen manageress? I want two Nelson slices, quick as yer like, luv – and a large cuppa tea please!"

There was the briefest of puzzled silences, then he heard a sharp intake of breath and an excited "RICHARD!" followed by uncontrolled tears of sheer relief – and joy.

They talked, as they had always done, with laughter, feeling and so many shared interests – and especially the child that they were expecting.

Tremayne told her of Enever's need to delay their leave together for as short a time as possible, but that they would be with one another again just as soon as circumstances allowed. Resuming his boy-entrant voice at the end of his call, he added, "'Ere, luv. 'Ave them Nelson slices and that tea ready for me when I see you!"

Laughing, she replied, adopting her exaggerated 'Glaswegian', "Och, dinna fash yersel', sailor — ye'll get a lot more than Nelson slices and a cuppa tea when I get ma hands on ye!"

Tremayne roared with laughter. "Oh, Emma. Just roll on my leave!"

His meeting with Enever turned out to be more than he had been promised and it went way beyond merely being 'interesting'. Anxious to know what had been happening with the rest of the flotilla, he enquired about the outcomes of the planned Operation Nimrod.

"That, Richard, is the main agenda issue of this meeting and what I want to talk through with you. It has not yet taken place and the flotilla has been on standby for almost two months." Enever reached for his empty pipe from his treasured brass ashtray.

"But," he continued, "from the most recent decoded radio intercepts, it now looks as if it's imminent.

The *Karelia* has plied up and down the approaches to the Channel but neither she, nor anyone else it appears, has received any radar surface vessel contacts. Knowing that the 'eyes of the Kriegsmarine' — Arado 196 reconnaissance floatplanes — are constantly watching those waters, we decided that regular sightings of the *Karelia* might excite Jerry's curiosity and bring him looking. To make the *Karelia*'s regular sorties suggest something important, Hermann's Camper & Nicholson has accompanied her as a dummy escort vessel on each of her short voyages. This tactic has emerged as a result of Jerry's undisguised interest in her and is something that we didn't plan with you a couple of months ago. The Germans' sightings of her will, we hope, suggest to them that whatever she *is* up to is worth a closer look."

Enever paused to fill his pipe with 'Blue Liner' tobacco – though, characteristically, it remained unlit – then continued, "Decoded radio traffic, received only yesterday, suggests that they have finally taken the bait. We have now discovered what the E-boats are mostly about. They are laying strings of mines – magnetic, sea-bed acoustic, direct contact, you name it – from just west of Scilly to as far east as Lyme Bay. The recent dramatically increased U-boat losses and consequent demise of the dreaded 'wolf packs' has led, we know, to regular rethinking of Kriegsmarine strategies and tactics in the English Channel but, frustratingly, Jerry remains a scourge in our waters."

Enever paused again and, to Tremayne's amusement, actually lit his pipe – from a cigarette lighter ingeniously fashioned from a First World War .303 cartridge case.

"The E-boats," he continued, "make excellent mine layers unfortunately and their activities are posing a new serious threat in some areas of the Channel. I want you, Richard, to take command of the flotilla and destroy them."

Enever paused to check the sheaf of notes on the table in front of him.

"Typically, each E-boat can carry up to fifteen mines. Just this one small flotilla, on its successive missions, spread over convoy and local cargo routes, is laying enough to do punishing damage to shipping in these waters. Well-coordinated mine laying, in conjunction with other E-boat flotillas, is making the English Channel as a whole — and its approaches — a dangerous place to be. What is more, E-boat surface attacks, in strength, appear to be on the increase." Enever looked directly at Tremayne.

"Hermann has done an excellent job in your absence, on standby, but this time — at long last — it looks like the real thing and Operation Nimrod needs *you* to make it a success."

The following morning, at 08.15 hours, Enever called an urgent meeting of all boat captains and their First Lieutenants. Beaming broadly at the assembled officers, he announced, "Gentlemen. Operation Nimrod is on! Decoded radio intercepts, received at 01.15 this morning, indicate that the E-boat flotilla we've been monitoring will certainly be heading our way on a major mine-laying spree in our waters and, at the same time, will try to seize and investigate the *Karelia*. Their ETA, off the Western Rocks, is 13.00 hours. It seems they are confident that, around here, they don't need the cover of darkness. The arrogant bastards are in for a bit of a surprise, gentlemen!" he added, smiling, almost saint-like, in the manner of a benign country parson addressing his flock, thought an amused Tremayne.

Tremayne, delighted to be back once more with his boat

crews, briefed them on the final details of the already well-rehearsed plans and confirmed that he wanted all four MGBs – including the former E-boat that he would command – in position, among the Western Rocks, by 11.00 hours.

"Crews will be at defence stations and will take early lunch while we wait for the E-boats to appear. Following the revised plan that you have developed in my enforced absence," he smiled ruefully, "Hermann will be stationed, alongside the *Karelia*, seemingly 'riding shotgun' to her in the pattern we have already established for our German monitors."

He looked at each face in turn before concluding, "I'll be hove-to off the Gilstone, out of sight, while Leading Telegraphist Westwood will be in Bishop Rock lighthouse to confirm visual contact to us by radio. "We will all be monitoring their progress by radar. I will signal 'go' by radio. Speed will be critical to support Hermann who will, most likely, be the first of us to come under fire. The sudden appearance of my E-boat, now suitably disguised as a transfer from an Ijmuiden-based flotilla, should throw them into temporary confusion as you speed to the scene in close support. Squadron Leader Stanley's Hurricanes are on standby, ready for our call. Good hunting gentlemen – and good luck!"

Well north of the Brittany coast and maintaining course for the Isles of Scilly, were three of the Kriegsmarine's latest sleek, low-profile S-boats — the 'greyhounds of the seas' — under the command of Kapitänleutnant Freiherr Johannes von Reichenau. Born into the German aristocracy and the son of a senior naval officer, who had served with distinction in the Kaiser's High Seas Fleet, von Reichenau had, as a relatively junior officer, established a formidable reputation within the S-boat arm.

A colourful, yet chivalrous and sophisticated man, he had developed apparent languor to an art form of subtle arrogance. His reputation amongst his fellow S-boat officers had gone sky-high when a hectoring senior victualling officer arrived onboard his boat, pompously demanding to see von Reichenau *immediately* over the amount of fine wines being ordered into the boat's stores.

The blustering officer in charge of supplies and stores was met at the top of the S-boat's companionway by a well-briefed junior orderly officer to be told that, "Freiherr von Reichenau sends his compliments but is rather too busy relaxing and, therefore, regrettably unable to see you, Herr Kapitän."

He was adored by his crews for his panache — and his fierce loyalty to them — and respected for his courage and daring in battle. At the age of twenty-seven, he held the Iron Cross, First Class and the Knight's Cross for gallantry in action. Although of aristocratic birth and upbringing, von Reichenau would frequently switch into Plattdeutsch dialect with those of his crew who hailed from the coastal regions of northern Germany – which further endeared him to his men.

Punching through the heavy, rolling seas in line astern – each driven at over forty knots by three 2,500hp DaimlerBenz MB 511 engines, and with their bow waves cascading white water over their for'ard gun emplacements – the S-boats created an impression of purposeful power. Devoid of the currently favoured mottle camouflage finishes, all three boats were uniformly painted light grey, emphasising their sleekness and rakish lines.

Typically, von Reichenau had his loudspeakers switched on, playing stirring naval marching songs at full volume. At this point, it was *Das Lied der S-Bootfahrer* that officers and men alike were singing along to as they raced north by north-east, enjoying the cold but clear, bright February sky. Under his deceptively lighthearted attitude, von Reichenau recognised the critical importance of strong, mutually supportive relationships and close teamwork among his boats' crews. A strict but professional disciplinarian, he nevertheless showed imagination, humour and understanding as necessary means of lifting – and maintaining – the spirits of his officers and men.

He stood on the decking of the open-topped armoured steel bridge of the S-boat's low-set forecastle, along with his First Lieutenant – Oberleutnant zur See Wilhelm Steinhauer, his coxswain, and a rating acting as watchkeeper. All were dressed in their leather sea-going coats, lined with thick blanket material, as protection against the strong wind. While the two officers and the watchkeeper constantly swept the clear horizon with their powerful Zeiss binoculars, the coxswain — a large, raw-boned man from Schleswig-Holstein — concentrated on his gyrocompass and the sea immediately ahead. Close to his left hand was the Chadburn engine transmitter box and bridge throttles, capable of lifting the 110-ton boat's speed to almost forty-four knots, in short bursts. By the coxswain's right hand was the boat's magnetic compass in its protective housing.

As an aside to his First Lieutenant, von Reichenau said — a broad grin on his otherwise composed, aristocratic features, "Willi, the song is finished. As we're about to go trespassing in the Kanal*, put on for us *Rüber über den Kanal!* Then, as a special treat for the Tommies, we'll have *Wir ziehen nach Engeland* — that should put us all in the right mood to deal with them."

Turning to the petty officer on standby at the stern depth-charge racks, which also served as mine-chutes, von Reichenau shouted, "Start sowing the seeds, Volkmar. Minen los!**" On command from the flotilla leader, the other two boats also began sowing their mines and, within minutes, another mixed batch of forty-five magnetic and acoustic mines had been laid in position, right on the vital coastal trade and supply routes.

"So, Willi, with that little lot we might just catch the odd

*English Channel
***Let go the mines!*

local freighter or cargo vessel," he grinned wolfishly. "If we're really in luck, we might even blow the arse off one of our British Coastal Forces friends' MTBs, patrolling the waters here off Scilly!"

Anticipating that, by now, his small flotilla must already be gracing some British radar screens, he pressed on confidently, loudspeakers blaring out strident martial music, on towards the outlying Western Rocks – and destiny...

=====O=====

Von Reichenau's prediction proved to be only too accurate. Tremayne's flotilla had indeed picked up the three E-boats on their radar sets. Leading Telegraphist Westwood, in the Bishop Rock lighthouse, confirmed visual contact through his binoculars, at a range of seven thousand yards, shortly after.

Fischer's Camper & Nicholson had gone about with her bow pointing out to sea, slightly to port, so that her powerful six-pounder and after 40mm Bofors would be his first guns to engage the enemy once they were within range. With her engines slowly turning over, she would be able to maintain station until she needed to move. Fischer had so positioned her that the *Karelia* also had a free arc of fire for her two, still hidden, six-pounders.

Tremayne ordered the other three MGBs – including the

fast, former E-boat which he commanded – to warm up their engines, in readiness for a fast sortie from their places of concealment among the Western Rocks to come to Fischer's aid and that of the well-armed, but unprotected *Karelia*.

On von Reichenau's boat, his First Lieutenant lifted his binoculars from his eyes and, pointing excitedly, yelled, "There sir, there they are, the first of the Isles of Scilly, ahead and ten degrees to starboard."

"Thank you – well spotted! As ever, Willi, you've eyes like a gannet searching for herring in the Wattenmeer!"

With all three S-boats closed up at action stations, von Reichenau ordered arrowhead formation and 'Volldampf voraus'*. With their elegant, deeply-flared bows raised clear of the water, the black anti-fouling paint covering their lower hulls was clearly visible through the cascading silvery white spray.

Within minutes, the watchkeeper on the port bow picked out the *Karelia*, hove-to with Fischer's MGB in close attendance, off Pednathise Head by about fifteen hundred metres.

"There she is, Willi. There's our quarry, with just the usual motor gun-boat guarding her." Von Reichenau turned to Meier, his NCO signaller. "Signal Müller and Künzel: *'Enemy directly ahead. Auf dem Anstand!'***"

Standing on the signal platform abaft the bridge, the Signal-meister used his Scotte projector to send the messages in Morse

*Full speed ahead
**Commence attack

code to the other two boats.

"Break out the old Imperial Navy ensign, Willi. Stick that bloody butcher's apron with the swastika on it in the bunting locker. We're going in as the Kaiserliche Marine*—not as some floating whorehouse full of Nazi psychopaths. That'll be one up the arse of the 'Bohemian Corporal', eh Willi?!"

Giving the order "stand by all guns", he turned back to his First Lieutenant: "Let's give the Tommies a rousing musical finale before we hit 'em! So, Willi, put on for us *Heut' stechen wir uns blaue Meer!*"

To some of his more staid and conventional Kriegsmarine colleagues, von Reichenau's showman-like approach seemed rather over the top. From experience in action however — many times over — he *knew* just what charge of emotion and adrenaline thirty men singing such songs together could release in battle.

It had long been a tradition of the German military—both in training and in action — that their soldiers should march, singing together, as a means of emphasising collective identity and reinforcing *esprit de corps*. Like the escalating collective 'rebel yell' of the Confederate soldiers in the American Civil War, singing the marching songs had a deeply unifying impact upon the boat's crew. He understood the primeval power of the bonding — and the morale — that it developed, transforming a boat's crew from a collection of individuals into a tightly-

*The navy of the former Imperial Germany

knit team. At its most primitive, it inspired the raw emotional energy so necessary for sudden, concerted action.

=====O=====

Some fifteen hundred yards away, monitoring the rapid approach of the three E-boats, Tremayne signalled the order to those hidden within the Western Rocks: *'Engage the enemy closely. Maximum revolutions!'* Turning quickly to Willoughby-Brown, he ordered, "Right Number One — hoist the battle ensign. This calls for some style! Flying this may cost us the advantage of complete surprise, but unexpectedly confronted by the Ijmuiden camouflage and the familiar E-boat profile, they may be confused just long enough for us to gain the fire initiative."

Fischer, now directly in the path of the Germans, opened fire with ranging shots, as the three E-boats approached at speed in tight arrowhead formation. Rapidly dispersing, they attacked him from three different angles in order to break the aimed concentration of his fire.

Known to the E-boat arm as 'Stichtaktik' — 'sting tactic' — it was a manoeuvre designed to inflict maximum damage in as short a time as possible, often followed by high-speed breakaway under cover of smoke. It was, too, a tactic that demanded concentration, close collaboration and seamanship of a very high order.

Almost simultaneously, *Karelia*'s gunners whipped away the covers concealing their guns and opened fire with their power-mounted six-pounders.

In less than two minutes, Tremayne had appeared from behind Gilstone Rock, firing at the E-boat nearest to him with his 40mm Bofors, at a range closing on his target from twelve hundred yards. Concurrently emerging at maximum revolutions from first the jagged Daisy Rock and then from behind the grey granite mass of Gorregan, were the MGBs of Lieutenants Simmonds and Taylor – positioning themselves ahead of the Germans as ambush cut-off boats. Firing their six-pounders – and any other weapons that they could bring to bear – they began to straddle the two leading E-boats with both high explosive and armour-piercing shot.

On von Reichenau's E-boat, nearest to Tremayne, Fischer and the *Karelia,* there were already several casualties and significant damage to both his boat's upper works – including the wheelhouse – and to her hull. Her twin 20mm cannon, sited amidships, had taken direct hits and had been destroyed. Both the gunner and his gun-layer lay dead amidst the twisted, blood-drenched shambles of the smoking wreckage. Ever defiant, she was still crashing onwards through the rough seas, martial music blaring from her speakers. The strident sounds carried across the water to Tremayne, commanding the previously captured E-boat, and it was Willoughby-Brown who reacted first.

"Good heavens, sir. Perhaps a *little* outré, as Mama would say. They rather sound like a bunch of water-borne Valkyries! Perhaps I should have brought my Gilbert and Sullivan records along — 'A British tar is a soaring soul…' would have been *so* appropriate!"

Even in the fraught urgency, acrid stench and increasing din of closely fought battle, Tremayne couldn't help but laugh at his urbane First Lieutenant's summing-up of their flamboyant opponent's élan.

Tremayne's boat was taking hits in return, but only from von Reichenau's 20mm for'ard cannon, which made comparatively little impression on the captured E-boat's vital areas, although two ratings, manning weapons on deck, had been wounded — one seriously. Both had been carried below for treatment and had been replaced by fresh gun crews.

The noise of the engagement, using automatic weapons at such close quarters, was now both deafening and unrelenting. Because of the clever, well-rehearsed tactical manoeuvring of the British boats, von Reichenau, experienced though he was, was finding it almost impossible to bring his heavier 37mm stern cannon into position for accurate, sustained firing. The one gun that he could consistently use was his bow-mounted 20mm automatic and this lacked the stopping power necessary to sink the British MGBs, unless it happened to strike lucky. Throughout the Kriegsmarine, this weapon was contemptuously referred to as the 'door knocker'. Adding to his firepower and sweeping the British decks though, were two awesome MG42s, with their cyclical rate of fire of 1,200 rounds per minute and characteristic sound of tearing linoleum.

Fighting the battle with skill, determination and extreme gallantry, von Reichenau was, nevertheless, soon hopelessly out-gunned and taking severe punishment, along with mounting casualties. By some miracle, he had survived – unscathed – repeated hits to his bridge, but his First Lieutenant and coxswain had been wounded, although both had remained at their posts. On his deck, several ratings and petty officers lay dead or wounded. Von Reichenau glanced round, visibly shaken, as he saw blood already beginning to run down the scuppers, aft of the wheelhouse.

Seeing Fischer swing the large Camper & Nicholson around to engage von Reichenau's already badly damaged boat, still closely backed up by the *Karelia,* Tremayne turned sharply to port to give support to Simmonds and Taylor. Racing to join the fray at over forty-two knots, Tremayne's E-boat was soon in the thick of it – exchanging shots at point-blank range with the enemy boats – as were Simmonds and Taylor.

As the first burst of 37mm shells struck her, Tremayne's boat shuddered, the impact transmitting the shock throughout her hull. Immediately she began to take in water, up for'ard on her port side.

The Fairmile 'C's of Simmonds and Taylor were inflicting heavy damage and casualties on the two German E-boats with their six-pounders, equipped with the latest Molins auto-loaders. They were just beginning to win the brutal close-quarter engagement when, with a huge sheet of flame accompanied by a loud explosion, Taylor's boat blew up.

Shocked by the suddenness of the destruction of Taylor's boat, Tremayne murmured, "Oh my God." Aware of the need to help Simmonds to deal with the second E-boat, he had to make the split-second decision to race on, leave the survivors and resume the attack to prevent the chance of another British MGB 'brewing up'.

Under a dense, towering pall of smoke, Taylor's boat began to settle in the water, her back broken. With no time to launch their rubber dinghies or Carley floats, her surviving crew members, wearing life jackets, began to jump into the cold, grey churning sea. As Simmonds continued to pound the remaining E-boats, Tremayne ordered Irvine to head directly for the nearer of the two enemy vessels.

Yelling, "Stand by to ram!" he then shouted to Irvine, "Hit her amidships, 'Swain — *all* engines, maximum revolutions!"

Ordering fire to be concentrated on her bridge — and on anyone else on deck, manning weapons — to reduce the E-boat captain's options for defending his vessel against the impending ramming, Tremayne directed his boat right onto the target.

At a speed burst of almost forty-four knots, Tremayne smashed his bow into the E-boat's starboard side, slightly astern of her amidships gun emplacement.

The shock of the violent impact flung those on the bridge off their feet, hurling items of equipment not already lashed down onto the German boat's deck or overboard into the sea. With his port and starboard machine guns giving covering fire, concentrating on any visible movement from the German crew, Tremayne, leading his blue-jacket boarding party from the front, stormed onto the E-boat's deck. Their Lanchesters and grenades quickly cut down what was largely token resistance from a crew in a state of shock following the ramming of their boat. Quickly, Tremayne forced the surrender of the surviving officers and crew after a firefight lasting no more than three minutes – such had been the effect of the sudden violent collision. Prisoners were rounded up and placed under guard while he called to his telegraphist to signal Fischer to pick up any survivors from Taylor's boat still struggling in the sea and to rescue his own crew and the E-boat survivors. Both boats were beginning to settle in the cold, inhospitable seas following the ramming and Tremayne knew that many people would not survive more than about fifteen or twenty minutes in the icy water.

Two hundred yards away, Simmonds's Fairmile, with her superior armament, had finally bested the E-boat after a particularly bloody and bruising engagement. Under the sudden cover of smoke and using her greater speed, the badly damaged E-boat rapidly turned westwards and began to make good her escape. Seeing this, Tremayne directed his Sparker to request immediate air support from RAF St Mary's to finish her off. What he hoped was that, before her own destruction, she would manage to signal her base and let them know of the outcome of the engagement — as a partial deterrent to future similar incursions into the waters around Scilly.

He then set about organising the rescue of the survivors of the battle. Simmonds's boat quickly came alongside and, though damaged herself, was well able to take off the crews of both Tremayne's now severely listing boat and those from the sinking German E-boat. Fischer, who had picked up von Reichenau and his remaining crew and already transferred them to the *Karelia*, was now engaged in retrieving the survivors of Taylor's boat.

Suddenly, Fischer's distinctive South African accent, accentuated by his loudhailer, was heard across the still turbulent waters as he shouted, "We've found him! — he's safe and well. Lieutenant Taylor is here with me!" A spontaneous, ragged cheer went up from those already packed tightly into Simmonds's boat. Tremayne, overjoyed, yelled back his thanks to Fischer. Then, reflectively, he murmured to himself, "And how many good men have we *lost* today?"

Quickly, Tremayne transferred the survivors of his boat from Simmonds's overcrowded decks onto Fischer's Camper & Nicholson and scrambled onboard himself, shaking the South African's welcoming hand. He left the rescued prisoners, under guard, on Simmonds's Fairmile.

"Thanks a million, Hermann — am I glad to see you. Get

us back to the *Karelia* asap if you will. We'll take stock of casualties and damage once onboard."

At that moment, the approaching roar of aircraft engines announced the arrival of the Hurricane squadron from St Mary's. Waggling their wings in salute, they raced over the two MGBs in the direction of the fleeing E-boat. Minutes after that, several loud detonations – and the staccato noise of prolonged bursts of 20mm cannon fire – shattered the now eerie quiet of the afternoon. A large plume of rapidly rising dark smoke on the otherwise clear horizon, graphically announced the destruction of the cornered E-boat.

Fischer confirmed that he had picked up von Reichenau, together with his wounded First Lieutenant and several members of the E-boat's former crew.

"Von Reichenau is an incredible character, Richard. He's a Freiherr – a baron – who detests the Nazis. He's a very entertaining man who is almost as well-versed in English ways and literature as he is in those of his own country."

"Hmm. Sounds interesting, Hermann – thank you. I'll have young Willoughby-Brown with me to interview him in some depth – they can exchange pedigrees and compare their respective 'blue blood' counts!"

Within minutes they were alongside *Karelia*'s companionway and onboard her main deck. The pockmarks of bullet holes and those created by cannon shells on her upper works and bridge, reminded Tremayne of a giant, irregular colander. Despite her extensive damage, she remained completely seaworthy and was now serving, simultaneously, as flotilla HQ, temporary hospital ship and floating PoW camp.

Briefing *Karelia*'s captain, Tremayne confirmed that he and Willoughby-Brown would interrogate the prisoners on behalf of Commander Enever, before they were taken on to RN Coastal Forces base at Dartmouth. His second priority, he announced, was to get back to HMS Godolphin as quickly as possible to bring Enever up to speed on events and their outcomes.

Willoughby-Brown acted as interpreter — quite unnecessarily as it turned out. Accompanied by two naval ratings armed with Lanchesters, von Reichenau confidently strode, rather than walked, into the room set aside for the interrogation.

Tall, fair-haired, athletically built — in a relaxed way — and with piercing blue eyes, he looked, thought Tremayne, like some idealised Aryan hero from the *Götterdämmerung*.

He came to attention, clicked his heels and gave a barely perceptible nod of his head before saluting Tremayne.

"Gentlemen, Kapitänleutnant von Reichenau at your service."

Tremayne returned his salute and quickly introduced himself and his First Lieutenant.

"It is a pleasure, Baron von Reichenau. Please do sit down. Some coffee perhaps?"

The German's brief nod of acknowledgement saw coffee arrive five minutes later, with the interrogation under way.

With a few exceptions, the Kriegsmarine remained the least politicised branch of the German armed services. Hitler was never really happy at sea, or on board a ship, and the Navy, generally, had little time for the 'Bohemian Corporal' and his predilection for waging warfare by horoscope.

"I believe," said von Reichenau, "that the British military also studies von Clausewitz's theories and writings on the art of war. Nowhere in his classical treatise *Vom Kriege* do I recall seeing that astrology and the rantings of a junior NCO are essential to successful battle strategy – particularly so in the conduct of naval warfare!"

To Tremayne, still emotionally scarred by his treatment at the hands of the Nazis in France, it was obvious that the aristocratic von Reichenau shared his contempt for the deranged upstart and his unbridled barbarity. However, apart from making his political standpoint crystal clear, von Reichenau, professional to the end, gave away no more than his name, rank and service number. Tremayne merely raised his eyebrows when the German refused to answer questions about his mission in the Channel.

He was, however, unstinting in his professional approval of what he termed Tremayne's 'brilliant Lauertaktik'*.

"It was intelligently conceived and superbly executed. I assume, Lieutenant Commander, that that was in the best traditions of Nelson, Drake and Frobisher?" Tremayne smiled at von

* *The use of a well-coordinated hit-and-run ambush, where surprise is the key element of success.*

Reichenau's comment, which came across as a matter-of-fact observation and not mere flattery.

"We were stupidly quite unprepared and suffered badly as a consequence. Usually, we have come off best in our encounters with your MTBs or MGBs, but your tactics and seamanship came as a bad surprise."

For a moment, the fine patrician face softened and he looked closely at Tremayne.

"I take it that, in your hands, my wounded will be well taken care of. I am especially concerned about my First Lieutenant, Oberleutnant Steinhauer."

Tremayne gestured towards his own First Lieutenant — "Number One?"

"Of course, Kapitänleutnant. Willi and I —" Willoughby-Brown paused for effect and then resumed in effortless, fluent German, "spent some considerable time together. His wounds have been cleaned and dressed. He was given a shot of morphine and will be transferred to a Royal Naval hospital — along with your other wounded crew members — when we reach land. Your First Lieutenant's wounds are not life-threatening. He will make a complete recovery."

In his deceptively low-key and disarming way, Willoughby-Brown had managed to garner a good deal of freely given intelligence while looking after the wounded, but considerably relieved Steinhauer. His non-threatening, gentlemanly approach and old-world courtesy had subtly elicited the main answers that Enever was anxious to have confirmed about the real reasons for the Germans' presence so close to a clandestine operations base.

Tremayne had long recognised that his First Lieutenant had also learned the most important lesson any gentleman learns – which is to know when to *stop* being one. Underneath Willoughby-Brown's genteel exterior – and, for most of the time, well masked – was the steel of a finely-honed professional 'edge'.

Ready to move on, Tremayne nodded his thanks to Willoughby-Brown.

"My First Lieutenant and I were impressed by your stirring music, but we should so like to have heard *Grüss an Kiel* – such a fine tune and so 'Navy', don't you think?"

Tremayne held out his hand to the clearly surprised von Reichenau as he wished him luck and nodded to the guards to return him to his locked and guarded quarters.

He and Willoughby-Brown interrogated the remaining prisoners – one at a time to verify facts and information and check for inconsistencies – before leaving *Karelia* to rejoin Fischer and return to Tresco. Cold, apprehensive and uncertain, many of them gave away far more useful intelligence than their urbane, supremely confident captain, without their interrogators having to infringe the codes of the Geneva Convention.

Building up the jigsaw of intelligence gathered, Tremayne, Fischer and Willoughby-Brown began to establish a coherent and consistent picture of the E-boats' role that had emerged, partly piecemeal, during interrogation. Of considerable comfort was the fact that the Scilly Isles simply did not feature in the E-boat flotilla's strategy and tactics — other than being relatively close to coastal cargo routes and therefore an area for possible easy mercantile prey.

Essentially, it seemed, the E-boat flotillas had been tasked with making the English Channel — and its exit and entrance — a very costly place for Allied shipping to be.

Working as very small flotillas — but closely coordinated, and often at night — the E-boats' roles were essentially predatory, based upon systematic mine laying and roving, opportune 'sting' tactics. So far, no Tresco 'Breton' fishing boats on covert operations had been encountered by the marauding E-boats and interrogation yielded no evidence that the Germans were aware of such activity coming specifically from the Scillies. The fact that HMS Godolphin's clandestine role was not under close scrutiny was a major relief to Tremayne.

It would appear, he reflected, that their 'secret channel' was, in fact, still secret.

What did emerge — and what Enever would be especially interested in, thought Tremayne — was that the Germans *did* believe that the invasion of France was imminent and were seeking evidence of amphibious warfare training in Channel waters. What the Germans clearly did not know, was that Tresco flotilla's 'secret channel' represented the beginnings of what would soon become an essential element of the 'channel of invasion'.

Large numbers of lightly armed landing craft, packed with troops undergoing training in beach assaults, would be the sort of vulnerable target that E-boat crews dreamed of. Moreover, they believed that such encounters might give them a clearer picture of the form of any such invasion and where its likely main landing areas might possibly be.

At around 20.30 hours, on what had become a spectacularly beautiful, calm night with moonlight casting shadows over a gently rising and falling sea, the two MGBs glided quietly into New Grimsby harbour and secured off Braiden Rock. Tremayne had signalled ahead so that the wounded would be taken care of and sent across, by launch, to the hospital on St Mary's.

News sent on ahead that there were prisoners to be interrogated and then rapidly transferred to the mainland, saw armed guard detachments of HMS Godolphin's marines and ship's company ready and waiting to escort the blindfolded Germans to a temporary holding compound at the naval base.

After thanking officers and men of the boats' companies for their outstanding achievement, followed by a quick debriefing at the anchorage, Tremayne led the way back to Godolphin. Conversation was subdued and most of those slowly walking back to their quarters were using the opportunity to be alone with their own thoughts and feelings. Some good shipmates had been lost, several more had been wounded and two of the flotilla's precious boats had gone to the bottom of the Channel.

After supper together, during which an attentive Enever eagerly listened, asking open questions at this stage and exploring implications, rather than probing in detail, he turned to Tremayne and the boat captains with a smile, "That was a vital job, bloody well done, gentlemen. Thank you — each and every one of you."

He beamed amiably over the top of his steel-rimmed spectacles. "Debriefing, gentlemen, at 08.00 hours tomorrow — Hut 101."

The kindly grey eyes twinkled, "Oh and I'll make sure that coffee is ready and waiting! Goodnight gentlemen."

As he turned to go to his cabin, Enever paused. "Senility almost got the better of me again — one week's leave, gentlemen, commencing 17.30 hours the day after tomorrow. The rest of the ship's company will do turn and turn about as duty watch and liberty men."

The noise level and pace of conversation soared as Tremayne and the others raced for the one telephone to let their loved ones know of impending leave.

Tremayne waited until the others had rung home before calling Emma...

Seven

Some catching up...

I n Hut 101, furnished overnight with several of Admiral Hembury's mysteriously acquired leather club armchairs, Enever led the early morning debriefing of the Tresco flotilla's participation in Operation Nimrod.

Tremayne, Fischer, Taylor and Simmonds each gave their own accounts of the engagement and its immediate outcomes. Enever listened attentively, his kindly, expressive face registering his various reactions to the boat captains' reports; his inevitable, unlit pipe either clamped between his teeth or resting in his polished brass ashtray.

The flotilla's encounter with the E-boats had been costly

– and bloody. Two of Tresco's MGBs had gone down, but of more importance were the casualty figures for so small a complement of officers and men. Taylor's First Lieutenant, his coxswain and two of his boat crew were dead and five petty officers and ratings had been wounded, three of them suffering severe wounds in the explosion which had destroyed his boat. Added to these were the casualties suffered by the other Tresco boat crews, giving a total of six dead and nine wounded. Of the latter, Enever had thankfully learned that four would be back on duty within two weeks at the most. Nevertheless, he acknowledged that so many casualties were disproportionately high for a ship's company the size of HMS Godolphin's.

Though clearly distressed by so grievous a casualty rate, Enever recognised that Operation Nimrod was by no means a pyrrhic victory. The Tresco flotilla's contribution to a carefully planned, coordinated operation -involving several coastal MTB flotillas from the Scillies to as far east as Kent—had been highly successful. As part of a far larger, overall strategy, aimed at inflicting sufficient severe damage to deter E-boats from systematically laying mines wherever they chose in the Channel, the Tresco flotilla had achieved its objectives. That the Germans would continue to attempt to do so, as opportunities arose, Enever was in no doubt, but Operation Nimrod as a whole had been a major success. It represented a serious setback to their current tactics and would force them to rethink their mine-laying operations in the English Channel.

Of immediate, critical importance to Enever was confirmation that the Germans had not been trying to identify and uncover the clandestine activities of the Tresco flotilla, but had operated close to the Scillies in order to destroy local traffic heading to and from the mainland.

Enever was particularly pleased about the undoubted success of Tremayne's ambush tactics and the clever ruse, involving a tempting target – the *Karelia* – as a decoy.

"Even allowing for the carefully managed element of surprise, gentlemen, your conduct of the engagement – and individual slogging matches boat to boat – with such a flotilla as von Reichenau's was impressive to say the least." Enever looked round the group taking in each face in turn.

"Von Reichenau has long been recognised by Coastal Forces Command as a formidable opponent, whose competence as a flotilla commander is matched by his daring and readiness to use unorthodox tactics." Turning to Tremayne, Enever asked, "Because of his own preference for the unexpected, he must have been impressed by your tactics. But tell me, Richard, what sort of a man is he?"

"I think that your word 'opponent' best sums him up for me, sir. I would find it impossible to regard such a man as my 'enemy'. He is, by any standards, the consummate coastal forces professional – but his is a professionalism with a very human face. He is, without doubt, regarded as a great leader by his crew who would follow him to hell and back. What is more, he demonstrates that he believes in *them*. During interrogation, their admiration and affection for him were very apparent. There is a depth and compassion in the man, way beyond his acquired social skills and natural charm. I should dearly like to have him in my flotilla. Perhaps that's the simplest way to sum him up for you, sir."

"Thank you, Richard. I must say, though, that I'm glad to have him out of our waters. Such a talented and daring maverick would, I believe, eventually come nosing around these islands out of curiosity, as well as on the hunt for easy pickings."

Moving the agenda of the meeting forward, Enever confirmed that both the Tresco and Helford fishing boats would be increasing the frequency with which they would be transporting agents – and intelligence – to and from Brittany in the lead up to the planned invasion of Europe. "The next few months are going to be some of the busiest and most challenging that we have experienced at HMS Godolphin." Enever paused to refer to a sheaf of typed Admiralty papers on his desk. "As I speak, gentlemen, our chippies are refurbishing our fishing boats in their workshops in readiness for numerous planned, or expected, trips across to Brittany.

Rear Admiral Hembury has confirmed that, as a matter of urgency, he wants us to become familiar with the role and tactics of COPP beach reconnaissance teams as it is likely that part of our role will be to work in close collaboration with them during the invasion.

"So, gentlemen, following your well-earned leave, all boat captains and their First Lieutenants will be spending some intriguing days — and nights — at Lieutenant Commander Clogstoun-Willmott's Beach Pilotage School at the Commando Training Centre in the West Kyle of Bute. To keep Godolphin manned, port and starboard watches will attend consecutive courses."

Enever took a quick drink of the coffee that one of his Wrens had placed in front of each of the participants.

"Sergeant Kane and about a half a dozen carefully selected Royal Marines will be up there with you, undergoing training as COPP swimmer-canoeists. They are likely to be there, learning the skills of navigation, reconnaissance, night drills and escape and evasion, for a very minimum of four weeks' intensive training.

"Hitler's Kommandobefehl does not, of course, apply to commandos and related personnel landing in a major assault or full-scale invasion. It *does*, however, apply to small groups of people who land from the sea or by parachute and so much of the COPP's training will be aimed at developing the skills and 'do-how' of *avoiding* capture and the torture and execution which automatically follow. The probable fate of those Royal Marine canoeists who were captured in Operation Frankton is a constant reminder of just how skilled and proficient we must become in escape and evasion, as well as doing our jobs with the utmost professionalism and impact."

Tremayne felt a deadly chill envelop him, as his mind went back to his own experiences at Neumann's hands in Brittany.

Enever continued, "I'm told the chief instructor there makes our own fearsome Colour-Sergeant McGrory look – and sound – like an auditor's clerk. His motto seems to reflect that of the Russian Field-Marshal Suvorov – 'Hard on the parade ground: easy in battle'."

He beamed affably as he scraped his pipe clean of what Fischer had once termed an 'improbable mixture of mouse droppings and old burnt tram tickets'.

"You will learn all about the use of infra-red homing devices, augurs for obtaining beach samples, swimming in waterproof suits and swim fins, and handling the currently operational COPP's Mk 1** canoe – or 'Cockle' as the Royals know it. After a couple of weeks in Scotland you come south again and return to civilisation" – the humorous grey eyes twinkled once more – "for, we hope, a final five days' COPP training at Hayling Island Sailing Club." He paused, smiling. "Ah, I thought *that* might grab your attention, Richard! At this stage, gentlemen, the Hayling Island course is only a possibility – not a copper-bottomed certainty."

After taking questions from his boat captains, Enever drew the meeting to a close.

"I have already informed Admiral Hembury of the loss of two of our boats and our currently depleted battle strength and I'm very pleased to tell you that, as always, he has come up trumps. Going through official channels would have got us nowhere. We would have been up against far too many 'armchair admirals' with thumb up bum and mind in bloody neutral."

Like a small boy with an exciting new toy, Enever beamed enthusiastically and then, with an air of undisguised conspiracy, added, "He's managed to lift – heaven knows how – two of the new seventy-three- foot Vosper MTBs for us. And those little beauties are capable of forty-two knots!"

With the briefest of pauses, in order to relish the impact of his announcement, he smiled and said,

"Enjoy your leave, gentlemen. Oh, as always – but now more important than ever, please ensure that Jane Topping has your addresses and any contact telephone numbers before you depart."

With a buzz of noisy, animated conversation, the officers slowly dispersed and went their separate ways to resume duties.

Tremayne caught the Navy's combined liberty and mail boat to Penzance and then travelled on, by bus, to a small, pretty hotel in Mousehole where Emma was waiting for him, packed and ready for their onward journey together.

Tremayne and Emma had planned their leave in outline only. They had, however, made the decision to travel to the north-western Highlands, to see her parents in Achiltibuie, despite the distance and, therefore, amount of travelling time involved from Tresco. After two or three days in the Highlands, they would return south to spend two days in Devon with Richard's folks and then take two final days together on Tresco – now, more than ever, their spiritual home.

After what seemed interminable train journeys, leaving Penzance on the Friday evening, they reached Inverness late on the Saturday to be picked up by Iain Fraser, Emma's father. As manager of a vast, now relatively productive, agricultural estate, he qualified for a special petrol ration to enable him to get around the seven or so thousand scattered acres of the ducal land and livestock that he looked after. In the clear moonlit night, travelling north-west from Inverness, Tremayne was conscious of the huge, indeterminate, yet awesome landmass surrounding them, but still found it possible to give some definition to the many mountains that Emma was identifying for him. To their right, the steep slopes of Cul Beag, with glimpses of the great moonlit mass of Cul Mor behind, followed by the distinctive shape of Stac Pollaidh, made a deep impression on Tremayne with their remote, primeval grandeur. On their left, the black waters of Loch Lurgainn and Loch Bad a'Ghaill dramatically reflected the pale spring moon on their still, smooth surfaces. Both Fraser and his rather battered 1938 Hillman Minx seemed perfectly at ease as they made their way slowly along the narrow, winding and bumpy road. Passing Aird of Coigach on their right, they soon came upon a third lake – Loch Osgaig – and then onto the sharp left-hand bend in the road that was to lead them to Achiltibuie, another five miles further on.

Mhairi Fraser, a warm, welcoming lady with curling chestnut hair, threw her arms around Emma, hugging her and speaking softly in Gaelic – a passionate, expressive language which can so readily convey depth of feeling, even to those who don't understand it. Showing Tremayne great affection, she led him by the hand into their quaint, beamed sitting room.

"Ye'll take a wee dram, Richard, after a long journey like that? Iain here has a wonderful Glen Rothes single malt. Ye'll take one, too, Emma?"

"Thank you, Mhairi. Right now, that sounds like heaven to me," said Tremayne.

So obviously delighted to see his only daughter again after many months apart, Iain Fraser's craggy face, shaped so much by the outdoor life that he led, split into a broad smile as he poured what he termed 'a proper dram – not a parsimonious Sassenach measure'.

"I believe I can say that Richard, without fear of insulting you, since we know your mother is a Hieland Lassie – born a McIntyre from near Oban, I understand?"

"She is indeed – and proud of her Jacobite leanings. When I was a child, she taught me to sing *Hey, Johnnie Cope* and *Come O'er the Stream Charlie* – though she never made me wear the white cockade in my school cap," laughed Tremayne.

"Aye, and she has the Gaelic too. We spoke together at your

wedding and what a wonderful, wonderful surprise that was for me," added Emma's mother with a gentle smile — so like her daughter's, thought Tremayne.

Emma feigned shock and said, with mock outrage, "I never realised *you* were a Jacobite rebel, Richard. You'll be telling me next that you toast 'the King across the water'!"

"Well, I don't — at least not when I'm sober — but my mother certainly still does! Even now, I don't believe that my father has really understood why, for the loyal toast, my mother always insists that there is a glass of water directly below her raised glass as she says 'to the King' with a secretive, knowing smile on her face!"

"So, you toast Charlie only when you're drunk then, Richard," laughed Iain Fraser. "Och well, in vino veritas, but right now, let's drink to you two and to the wee bairn that you're expecting!"

With the weather cold, but clear and unusually dry for late March, the next two days passed blissfully for Tremayne and Emma. Iain Fraser, knowing of their shared love of sailing, had carefully restored the small dinghy that Emma used as a teenager and university student before she joined the WRNS.

Pushing out into the chilly, grey choppy waters of Baden-tarbat Bay, they sailed round the Summer Isles, taking their time to explore the different rugged — and softer — shorelines of the many smaller islands. Having sailed close to and around the rocky, indented western coastline of Tanera Beg, facing the Isle of Lewis, they eventually landed close to the pier on Tanera Mor, the largest island, with its small settlements and three little lochs. Wandering hand in hand over the island's rugged, heather-covered landscape and enjoying their shared love of islands, they compared and contrasted the Summer Isles and their flora, birdlife and atmosphere with those of the Scillies. Walking and talking together had been one of the principal — yet simple — shared things that had brought them together and slowly developed their relationship at a time when Tremayne had been grieving over the loss of his first wife. It had become an essential part of their deepening relationship — and something that each so desperately missed during the many times that they had to be apart.

Picnicking in the shelter of the hilly ground above the hamlet of Ardnagoine, Emma reminded Tremayne of their first picnic together, "twenty-one months, one week and six days ago!" as she laughingly recalled, on Gun Hill at the northern end of Tresco — an occasion when they had first realised that they were falling irrevocably in love with one another. Smiling, Emma asked, "Do you think anyone has discovered those coins that we buried under that funny triangular stone — including my old 'crookit bawbie'?"

"Not unless some wily local had us under observation with his telescope! But, yes, it *was* a wonderful day — and one I'll never forget dearest Emma. You know, we should ask your mother, or mine, to remind us of all the words to that delightful song *The Crookit Bawbie* so that we can sing it in the bath together!"

"It's one of those many little things, Richard, which now hold such very happy memories for both of us."

That evening, Mhairi and Iain Fraser, with more than a little coaxing, were finally persuaded to sing the beautifully moving song with its haunting melody, accompanied by Tremayne on the piano. With fine, clear voices they sang both the solo male and female parts and then the poignant concluding duet. "Thank you both," said a delighted and appreciative Tremayne who turned, smiling, to Emma and saw tears of happiness rolling down her cheeks. "I think you can now see just how important that lovely song is to us."

On the Tuesday, they set out to travel south to Plymouth, where Tremayne's father would collect them from the station and take them to the family home at around lunchtime the following day.

As Tremayne and Emma stepped out of the forecourt of Plymouth station into a cold, biting wind, a slim, distinguished-looking, grey-haired man emerged, waving, from behind a cigarette kiosk. Tremayne and his father shook hands and then embraced, before John Tremayne held Emma's hands, kissing her on both cheeks.

"You don't know how good it is to see you both – and Emma, dear, are you keeping well? Sheena, I'm afraid, will want to know chapter and verse about your baby – so be warned! Now, into the car both of you – out of this freezing breath of Siberia, while I stow your luggage in the boot!"

Smoothly, the immaculate cream and burgundy Riley 1500 Six Light Saloon, with its powerful twin cam engine and pre-selector gearbox, pulled away from the station. Some forty minutes later, it was on the drive of the Tremaynes' large Victorian house, overlooking the River Yealm and part of Newton Creek at Noss Mayo, near Newton Ferrers.

Sheena Tremayne was out on to the drive in a trice, embracing her son and Emma alternately and addressing everyone, it seemed, including a bewildered Tremayne and his father, in excited, unstoppable Gaelic. She and Emma were in their element, judging by the animated but – to the others – totally incomprehensible exchanges.

"They should have kept the barbarians north of Hadrian's Wall. The Romans have a lot to answer for!" laughed the elder Tremayne. "Come on in Richard, we'll get the kettle on and get a brew going asap."

Along with tea, Sheena Tremayne had prepared the most delicious Dundee cake and, much to the relief of father and son, conversation was now in English once more. "How civilised people used to a proper, decent language can ever hope to learn a primitive tongue like that, with its mute consonants and unpronounceable vowel combinations, heaven alone knows." Then, turning to Emma and Richard and playing the role of indulgent host, John Tremayne, still laughing, said, "Here, both of you, do have some more of this marvellous Dundee cake, you must be starving!"

Tremayne smiled ruefully to himself, as he suddenly felt the immense discontinuity between the worlds of their respective parents and the one in which he and Emma had been operating during the last eighteen months.

"To answer your question Dad, quite impossible. You're absolutely right – they *are* barbarians!" and then, smiling at Emma, added a quiet "Thank goodness!" As much as anything, Tremayne's response was to bring himself back into what, temporarily, had become an unfamiliar, almost alien world compared with the one he now lived in. "Which one," he found himself reflecting, "represents normality, since each of these worlds has its own very different values and reality?"

He knew he could never – and would never – talk to his parents about people like Neumann and share with them the utter horror of his experiences in France. Even to his father and uncle, who had been naval officers in the First World War, such experiences had no reference points and would be way beyond their comprehension and belief.

He and Emma had talked about the problems of readjusting to a world that had yet to acknowledge that some of the things they had known as children – and taken for granted – would be eroded away for ever and replaced by a new order. Those with more direct personal experience of the war and its horrors – in the blitzes, on the battlefield and in the hospitals and prison camps – would have, he already knew, different hopes, aspirations and expectations from those of a more complacent, less involved Establishment.

Over his mother's delicious roast dinner, Tremayne's mood lightened considerably as lively, humorous conversation took over and his father regaled them with tales of his work at Devonport. A solicitor by profession – and with several years' commissioned service in the Royal Navy – John Tremayne had been given a post, as a civilian, in the Navy's Legal Department. Some of the stories he told of trying to extricate both the Navy – and individual ratings or officers – from legal entanglements with the police and local magistrates were hilarious.

On one occasion, he had managed to persuade the local police to drop their case against a Royal Marine commando, arrested as he started to 'fill in' the black marketeer whom he'd just caught in bed with his wife on returning home early for leave. He then convinced the police sergeant in charge of the case – luckily, a former Royal himself – that the aggrieved commando should be allowed to go back and finish the job and give 'lover boy' a real good thumping – and *then* have him arrested for his black market shenanigans!

The pretty bedroom that Sheena had prepared for them was at the end of a lengthy, winding landing, with long-distance views over the Yealm Estuary and part of Wembury Bay beyond — "if you stand on the chest of drawers and hang on to the curtain rail," said Tremayne with a grin. The moon was shining on the dark, treacly sea, with its glistening, decorative trails of silver phosphorescence at the entrance to the estuary and onto the Yealm itself, casting long black shadows across both land and water.

"How often have we made love by moonlight just lately?" asked Tremayne, taking Emma in his arms.

"Not nearly enough," laughed Emma, "and let's just hope that we're not due for an eclipse of the moon while you're on leave!"

"You shameless young hussy!"

The next morning — a cold, but clear and sunny one — Sheena organised a rucksack of packed lunches for Tremayne and Emma who had said that they would like to walk some of the coastal path that stretched for many miles, east and west of Newton Ferrers.

"One of the most beautiful stretches — with glorious views of the coastline — is that which leads from the village of Hope through to Salcombe. Scattered along it are some of the most enchanting coves and rocky inlets that you'll ever see in the British Isles," explained John Tremayne.

"In places the path is pretty steep, with some long uphill drags in it, Emma, and I just wonder if young Tremayne-to-be will allow you to walk that far without tiring you unnecessarily?"

"Thank you for the thought, John, but I would really like to try it. Richard has often told me about the coastal path and described its breathtaking beauty. While we're here, it would be a pity not to see some of it at least."

"OK. What I'll do is run you both to Hope, to the start of this stretch, and plan to meet you on the edge of Salcombe, below Sharpitor on the little road between Splatcove Point and Stink Cove at, say, four o'clock – if that would be fine for you. That would give you about five hours or so. Richard knows exactly where the suggested pick-up point is." At this stage, Tremayne stepped in.

"Nearly halfway along the route, Emma, there is a marvellously located small hotel – the Soar Mill Cove* – which has its own idyllic beach, set in what has to be one of the prettiest coves along this magnificent coast. It has been temporarily commandeered by the RAF as an officers' mess and I reckon that, if we carry our ID with us, we should be able to take a break there and get a drink at least. You never know – they might even let us eat mother's meat paste sandwiches and reconstituted egg custards there!"

"We know it well, Emma dear, from at least fifteen years ago when it was originally called the Sea View guest house. It really is in the most heavenly spot and has grown some since it became the Soar Mill Cove Hotel in recent years. When this

*Now a superb 4-Star AA and RAC hotel run by the hospitable and ever-welcoming Makepeace family.

wretched war is over and it eventually becomes a proper hotel once more, it will certainly be *the* ideal place to stay around here I promise you," added Sheena.

Walking up the long incline out of Inner Hope, through fields of grazing cattle and sheep, Tremayne and Emma soon came onto the coastal path with its mind-blowing views of the sea and the sweeping coastline, stretching westwards to Plymouth and beyond. To the east lay Bolt Head and Salcombe, as yet well out of their line of sight.

They walked along the coastal path, the precipitous cliffs and sea to their right, passing above rocky indentations and promontories with evocative names like Graystone Ledge, Hugh's Hole, Slippery Point and Saltern Pike. After about two and a half miles they reached Cathole Point and, looking inland, Tremayne pointed out a low, single-storey, rectangular building nestling in the hills and looking out to sea. "There, Emma, that is Soar Mill Cove Hotel. Think you can make it down from here and then up the other side?"

"Neither wild horses, nor Tremayne-to-be, could keep me away. Follow me, sir, I'm right behind you!" she laughed, quoting Hermann Fischer's customary response whenever Tremayne signalled the flotilla to slip moorings at Braiden Rock anchorage.

After a further fifteen minutes they reached the hotel, now signposted RAF Bolt Head Officers' Mess, and it was approaching noon as Tremayne and Emma walked in and entered the bar area. The bar steward, wearing a smart, short white coat over his blue RAF-issue shirt and black Service tie, snapped – rather too brusquely and without so much as a "good morning, can I help you?" – "I'm sorry, sir, civilians are not allowed in here. I'm afraid I must ask you to leave. This is Royal Air Force property."

"RAF property, eh? Then, steward, we should be assured of the very best of hospitality as guests. We should like something to drink please."

He felt Emma stiffen by his side as she sensed her husband bridling at the steward's officious lack of welcome.

Producing his own ID and Emma's he added, his voice quieter and even more authoritative, "Tremayne, Richard Tremayne, Lt Commander RNVR, and this is my wife – formerly First Officer, WRNS, now a Government Civilian Intelligence Officer." The steward went bright red and stammered an apology. "S-sorry, sir and m-ma'am... I'd no idea, sir. W-what can I get you both?"

"A pint of draught bitter for me and a half of bitter shandy for my wife, please." Seeing the confused embarrassment on the now deflated bar steward's face, he said, with the merest hint of a smile, "Oh, and steward, put yourself down for a drink on us since we're on leave and not in uniform."

"T-thank you, sir. Most kind, sir."

"I take it that you've no objection to us eating our sand-wiches here?"

"N-no sir. You're most welcome, sir."

"Good, thank you."

The spectacular view down the wide coomb to the surging, white-capped sea beyond, provided a delightful setting for their lunch, during which several RAF officers wandered in, most of them nodding to Tremayne and Emma. One young, fair-haired flight lieutenant caught Tremayne's eye because of an elusive familiarity about his face and the set of his shoulders. Turning and catching the interest in Tremayne's expression, he commented, "Isn't it a stunning location – and that wonderful view? I've been here almost a year and I never get bored with it." Taking in Tremayne and Emma's civilian clothes and rucksack, he asked, "Are you RAF, on leave?"

"No, we are both Royal Navy – at least I am and my wife was until a few weeks ago. Do please forgive my staring, but you remind me so very much of someone and I'm trying to make the connection."

"Oh, I'm sure it will happen – like a bolt out of the blue! By the way, my name's Ken Stanley." Tremayne shook the proffered hand. "I'm Richard Tremayne and this is Emma, my wife. Please do join us and let me get you a drink." He paused, smiling at the younger man, and said, "Your surname is Stanley? May I ask – do you have a brother, Tim, who is a wing commander based on St Mary's in the Isles of Scilly?"

Stanley's fresh, youthful features split into a wide, surprised grin. "Yes I do! Good heavens! How come you know Tim?"

"I command the Tresco flotilla and your brother frequently

provides fighter escort and air cover for us on our missions. On one occasion I actually fished him out of the drink off Cornwall, when he'd been shot down!"

"It's your name, of course, that rings bells with me rather than your face. I do recall Tim talking about a Richard Tremayne. You've actually been in Brittany together on some cloak and dagger mission or other and I do remember Tim telling me about that. If you'll forgive me that awful cliché, it really is an unbelievably small world!"

Tremayne and Emma passed a very enjoyable and considerably more bacchanalian lunch hour than they had intended, but found Ken Stanley a most delightful and congenial companion. Tremayne and Ken Stanley's elder brother, Tim, had become increasingly close as a result of combined operations in the Channel off Ushant and on the mainland of France.

Leaving the Soar Mill Cove Hotel at around 2.45pm, they made their way back up to the coastal path, after a short, steep scramble over the uneven, gorse-covered hillside, littered with empty 20mm cannon-shell cases from RAF Spitfire training strafing runs. Passing the rocky promontory of Bolt Head, they skirted Starehole Bay and passed through the jagged rocks of Sharp Tor, before making their way along the narrow path to John Tremayne's waiting Riley.

The following day, together with Tremayne's parents, they went for a long, breezy walk around the steep, rocky headland south of the Yealm estuary, facing a strong, blustery headwind on the return journey.

In the early evening, having made their thanks and reluctant farewells, they caught the train to Penzance where, courtesy of John Enever, a motor launch met them and took them back to Tresco – and to Dick and Aileen Oyler at the New Inn. Happy, but weary from the amount of travelling that they had done during the preceding five days, they tumbled into bed at around midnight – but not before a wildly happy welcome from Bertie.

During the night, the strong winds appeared to have blown themselves out and the morning was bright, with a light offshore breeze and clear skies apart from a few scudding white clouds. In readiness for their final three days of leave, Dick Oyler had persuaded Tommy Goddard, his cousin on Bryher, to lend the Tremaynes a beamy, sea-kindly sixteen-foot inshore fishing boat, with inboard diesel engine and a narrow, but tall wheelhouse. She had a very short foredeck with guardrails and an open cockpit, with bench seating aft of the wheelhouse.

Painted white, apart from the navy blue strakes emphasising her pronounced 'S' sheerline and curving chine, Tremayne fell for her immediately when he laid eyes on her, tied up near New Grimsby quay.

He and Emma familiarised themselves with her engine, her controls and her ingenious stowage spaces while they waited a final hour for the incoming tide. Bryher-built, she was a well-designed, strongly constructed and handsome craft. Emma examined her with the critical eye of an experienced sailor and confidently took the wheel when there was sufficient water beneath her keel.

As they headed south through The Road, on a course for Porth Conger – the main quay for landing on St Agnes, Tremayne looked at Emma's exquisite facial profile, still unable to believe that she really was his wife and, now, the mother-to-be of their first child. So used to standing on the bridge or the wheelhouse of MGBs and Breton fishing boats next to the redoubtable Irvine, he said with a smile, "Well Coxswain, you're a damn sight more beautiful than the last one I sailed with!"

"So I am," added Emma, feigning a very passable Ulster accent and with a happy grin that lit up her face.

She skilfully navigated round the 'Cow and Calf' at the entrance to Porth Conger and drew alongside the quay for Tremayne to leap ashore and secure their boat. With a borrowed RM commando bergen over his shoulder, carrying waterproofs and just-in-case drinks, Tremayne took Emma's hand and set off for the island's only real pub, The Turk's Head, just over half a mile away behind the island's post office in Middle Town*.

Situated a few hundred yards from the old disused lighthouse – a white painted structure that dominates much

---

* Visitors to St Agnes in recent years will know the present location of The Turk's Head. This fine pub is now situated much closer to the landing and departure quay near to Porth Conger.

of the St Agnes skyline – the pub was able to offer some tasty meat and vegetable pasties and Cornish beer for their lunch. Tremayne had previously told Emma about Beady Pool and the possibility of still finding coloured glass beads washed ashore from a Venetian galley, which had foundered off St Agnes in the seventeenth century. Emma, who had been intrigued by the story, asked the landlord about the chances of finding any of the beads and exactly where to look.

"Yes, my dear, you can certainly still find 'em and a lot of people here have them on display in their homes. Many of them are little terracotta-coloured long beads – like tiny sausages – about half an inch in length. There are also some lovely sapphire blue glass beads and some deep red ones too. Mind you, you've got to be prepared to spend some time looking for 'em. You can find 'em if you're patient almost anywhere on Beady Pool beach. As far as I'm aware, there's no special spot. Scrape away the surface sand, sift it carefully, keep scratching and scraping and I reckon, my dear, that you'll find some!"

After some more stories about the history and folklore of St Agnes, they set off down Barnaby's Lane, with St Warna's holy Celtic well to their right, and then across Wingletang Down and onto the beach at Beady Pool.

Emma's childlike enthusiasm amused Tremayne as she threw herself wholeheartedly into the task of looking for the beads. He also recognised that these would become the happy memories he would gratefully and frequently draw upon in the future, on the long nights of watchkeeping at sea. Using his ancient Brownie box camera and his remaining precious film, he took several snapshots of her to reinforce the pictures he knew would now forever be in his heart.

He joined in, scraping, collecting the sand in his hands and carefully sifting through it. Suddenly, an excited cry broke his concentration.

"Look, Richard! Just come and see this!" Emma was holding up, between her finger and thumb, a beautiful blue glass bead about an inch long. It was pendant shaped, multi-faceted and in near perfect condition, despite having been three hundred years in sea and sand.

Tremayne kissed her. "I'm so glad that you found one of the more spectacular beads – this one is a real beauty." For another hour and a half they continued to search and, between them, found four of the little terracotta-coloured ones – two of which were broken, together with a fragment of one of the sapphire blue beads.

On the way back to their boat, they stopped at a house offering teas and refreshments. Emma washed out her collection of beads in a saucer of water obligingly provided by the owner's wife, who clearly had become very know-ledgeable about the beads and their most likely origin – the island of Murano in the Venetian Lagoon.

Back at the New Inn, Emma, full of her afternoon on the beach at Beady Pool, showed the ever-attentive and indulgent

Aileen her collection of beads. Quickly caught up in Emma's sense of wonder, Aileen excused herself for a moment and returned with another blue glass bead, identical to the one Emma had found, and a red one which sparkled like fire in the electric light of the inn's bar.

"There, Emma. alannah, that makes a more complete set for you. You keep those now. Dick and I have collected quite a few of those beads over the years!"

The following day was to be the last of their leave together. Emma decided that she would like to spend some of it on St Mary's, leaving the late afternoon to walk around their favourite haunts on Tresco, with the many happy and precious memories those places held for them.

Much of the morning was spent browsing round the shops and their sadly depleted stocks due to wartime rationing. Far more important to both of them was the time that they were still able to share together. After lunch at one of the pubs in Hugh Town, close to the harbour, they returned to Tresco by one of the few inter-island boats still running, landing at Carn Near – the quay at the very south of the island. Instead of heading straight back to the New Inn, they walked in the direction of the Abbey and the spectacular gardens and then bore right, across to Pentle Bay. It was there that Tremayne and Emma had decided that it was time to stop grieving, break with the past and for each of them to make a new beginning.

As they walked together, hand in hand, along the beautiful

deserted bay, the memories of the decision they had made almost two years ago came flooding back.

Emma looked up, her earnest blue eyes searching his face, "Do you have any regrets, Richard?"

Tremayne held her close and then kissed her. "None, dearest Emma. Except that we have too many partings – but that won't always be so. I love you more than ever – even though you have me on my hands and knees, sand in my mouth, down my shirtfront and in my shoes, as we look for confounded glass beads!"

Laughing and talking, their arms around one another's waists, and looking out across the shallow green-blue water, taking in the wonderful seascape cross to St Martin's and the Eastern Isles, they made their way through Rushy Porth and Cradle Point.

Eventually, passing below the ancient blockhouse, they reached Old Grimsby and cut off left for Dolphin Town and the New Inn.

After one of Aileen's magnificent suppers and Dick's superb, carefully hoarded clarets, they slipped out, wrapped up against the cold evening wind, to wander around New Grimsby harbour to the long quay.

"Next time we have leave together, let's spend some time on Bryher and take a closer look at that beautiful island – we still don't know it well enough."

"Agreed, so long as young TTB allows me enough mobility!"

Tremayne looked puzzled for just a moment, then he grinned. "TTB – of course – 'Tremayne-to-be'! We did settle on Catriona if it's a girl and David if it's a boy but, in the meantime, TTB will do just fine!"

They returned to the New Inn as the moon broke through the clouds. "Hmm, Emma, right on cue," laughed Tremayne. The exaggerated 'Glaswegian' response left him laughing as they went upstairs: "Och you sailor boys are a' the same. Always after ma poor wee body and never ma brains!"

The next morning saw another of their heartbreaking departures, as Emma left by fast motor launch to Penzance for her onward train journey through to London. They continued to wave to one another until the launch carrying Emma finally disappeared from view. Tremayne felt empty – almost bereaved – as he collected his gear, said his farewells to the Oylers and, now back in uniform, made his way to HMS Godolphin.

A typed note from Enever awaited him, placed on the tiny chest of drawers in his cabin.

The key lines stated:

'WEF 17.00 hours tomorrow, you will be attending a COPP Familiarisation Course for Officers (duration fourteen days) based at the Beach Pilotage School, CTC, West Kyle of Bute, Scotland.

Assemble at New Grimsby quay 07.00 hours for the harbour motor launch for St Mary's. The RAF transport aircraft will leave St Mary's for an RAF airfield close to the CTC and the School.

RN transport, to take you to CTC, will meet you at the airfield.
Lt Commander Clogstoun-Willmott will brief you on arrival, setting out
the fourteen-day programme. Due to unforeseen circumstances, the continuation
familiarisation training at Hayling Island has been cancelled.
(signed) Commander J. T. Enever, SIO

Eight

Beach reconnaissance

By both instinct and training, sailors have a high respect for unfamiliar and uncharted coastal waters. Naturally occurring hazards such as submerged rocks, seabed contours and unknown tides and currents, represent formidable navigational challenges to those operating at sea. These difficulties and dangers are increased dramatically by the presence of enemy onshore coastal defences, underwater obstacles, mines and the threats posed by regular inshore patrols. This is especially the case where there may be limited opportunities or options for manoeuvre by the attacking or invading naval forces.

A costly example of this had occurred four years earlier, in 1940, when more than half of the Allied naval vessels lost in Norwegian waters foundered on submerged rocks, shoals and sandbanks – and not directly as the result of enemy action.

First-hand experience of such hazards – and hence the need for thorough surveillance and reconnaissance prior to undertaking a raid or invasion – had led to Lt Commander Nigel Clogstoun-Willmott's setting up of a Pilotage Training School in the west of Scotland.

His attempts to survey the coastal waters and beaches of Rhodes through a submarine periscope during operations in Greek waters, had convinced him of the severe limitations of such reconnaissance methods. Together with Captain Roger Courtney of the SBS (Special Boat Section), Clogstoun-Willmott began to establish the Combined Operations Pilotage Parties and develop their systematic training.

A man of great personal drive and commitment, Clogstoun-Willmott had assembled an impressive tutorial staff of navigators and hydrographers, as well as specialists capable of giving professional instruction in canoeing techniques, rock climbing, weapons handling and beach reconnaissance. He drove his students and his instructors but, above all, he drove himself.

Admiral Lord Louis Mountbatten, as Chief of Combined Operations, had given his full enthusiastic support to Clogstoun-Willmott – and also to the establishment of several other Commando Training Centres close by including HMS

Armadillo at Ardentinny, HMS Dundonald at Troon, and CTC Inverary. Such bases possessed the advantage of being in comparatively remote areas and offered ideal coastal waters for realistic training in inshore reconnaissance and beach assault. Like the main Commando Training Centre further north at Achnacarry Castle, these locations also offered ideal terrain for battle training inland, as well as on the beaches.

By early 1944, COPP training had become both rigorous and sophisticated, based upon techniques of direct observation and the detailed analysis of acquired data on obstacle locations, tides, currents and samples of sand and gravel taken method-ically from beaches and shorelines.

Tall, slim, impeccably turned out and meticulous in his approach to his role, Lt Commander Clogstoun-Willmott, together with several of his instructors, met the party from Tresco as they arrived by RN lorry in the late afternoon. With Tremayne were Fischer, Simmonds, Quilghini and their First Lieutenants, including Willoughby-Brown.

After Clogstoun-Willmott's welcome and endless cups of fresh hot tea, Lieutenant Graham Cole, RNVR, one of the School's training officers, led the Tresco officers to the ship's stores to collect their khaki battledress work uniforms, rank insignia, commando-sole boots, bergens and other operational kit. He then took them to their spartan cabins — pointing out on the way the communal heads, washing facilities, classrooms, mess hall and canoe sheds.

"Dinner, gentlemen, will be at 19.30 hours in the mess – not the wardroom," he announced, "where a

table has been set aside for the eight of you. Please be kitted up, with rank insignia sewn on your issue BDs, and be wearing your new SV boots – but you won't need your bergens."

"It sounds as if dinner itself might be rather more than a mere gastronomic adventure – shall we need entrenching tools and bolt cutters rather than knives and forks?" commented Fischer.

Cole grinned in reply, "No – not tonight, at least, but immediately after dinner we will assemble outside the canoe sheds at 20.15 hours for a night navigation exercise."

"Hmm," murmured an unusually pensive Willoughby-Brown, "it looks as if we're in for a riotous evening of good natured fun!"

After a dinner of roast lamb and vegetables, followed by an unexpectedly marvellous treacle tart, Cole led the Tresco officers out to the School canoe sheds where four Cockle Mk 1**s, complete with life jackets, waterproof hooded anoraks, paddles and spray covers, were lined up outside and close to the edge of the loch. Nearby, stood an RN three-ton lorry, in which the khaki battledress-clad driver and his mate, wearing seamen's caps, were already sitting and waiting.

Halting the group outside the canoe shed door, Cole addressed them: "Right, gentlemen, 'O' Group time." He began to read from the papers on the clipboard he was holding.

"Operating as four two-man canoe teams, your task is to reach the Hollywood Hotel, Largs by 24.00 hours, where an umpire will check you in. Hot kye will be available. The distance from Dunan, your point of departure, is eight miles, but be aware, gentlemen, there are tides to contend with. A motor launch will pick up you and your canoes from the jetty at Largs and bring you back to the School quay. If you fail to make the hotel by 00.01 hours at the latest, the launch will have left and you will have to make your own way back to Dunan, which, by then, will be largely against the tide, gentlemen." He looked at the group and then, clearly for effect, added, "Morning parade will be here at 08.00 hours."

Cole paused to distribute waterproof blue-lens signalling torches, luminous compasses and maps of the area to the four pairs of paddlers, each of which had been teamed up as boat captain and First Lieutenant.

"The three-tonner will take you and your canoes to Dunan for the launching, gentlemen. Are there any questions?"

"I take it that we are free to plan how we get there, for example as all eight together, or as four separate teams?" asked Tremayne.

"On this occasion, yes sir. It is entirely up to you to decide how you will complete the task."

With no further questions, Cole told the group to stow the canoes onto the lorry and to climb aboard, ready for the off. Tremayne used the time in the lorry to work out a plan with his boat captains – to paddle and navigate the crossing all together. Using their muffled torches to read the maps, they first checked, then set – and checked again – their common compass bearings. They settled on a simple signalling code should canoes start to become separated in the dark. In the event of capsize, they agreed that they would 'raft up' on either side of the upturned canoe using their paddles, braced across its hull, to give added stability while the paddlers in the water climbed back into their well-supported boat.

"Between us, we already have some experience of handling canoes in the sea. So Hermann, Pierre and I will be on hand to help." Turning to Simmonds, who had the least experience of such craft, Tremayne said, "I'll lead, with your canoe immediately astern of me Maurice, while Hermann and Pierre will maintain station to port and starboard of you, so we'll paddle across in arrowhead formation."

At Dunan, they unloaded their canoes and carried them down to the water's edge. Cole confirmed that the on-shore recognition signal to the canoeists at Largs would be five flashes of white light, in response to five blue ones from them.

The outer Firth of Clyde was relatively calm, but with a strong swell running. The night was pitch dark, the moon being completely hidden by dense low clouds, and a drizzling rain had just started as they silently paddled away to Cole's "Good luck, gentlemen. I'll see you – I hope – in the hotel!"

Tremayne had already pointed out to the group that the

exercise was essentially a long, hard arm- and shoulder-aching slog, as well as a challenge in navigation – even to experienced sea-going officers.

"We'll need to maintain our bearings strictly and will have to correct our course regularly to check that we are not straying. If WB and I wander at the front and don't correct fast enough, then call us back on course please."

Tremayne was confident that he and his First Lieutenant would not stray off their bearings. He was, however, concerned to keep the others closely involved in navigation, as an essential lesson in the value of constant directional monitoring in a canoe at sea – and in complete darkness.

At 22.15 hours, after one hour's hard paddling, with regular corrections to maintain course, Tremayne called for a gratefully received five-minute break. Bodies and arms were aching and already some hands were showing blisters. With paddles held flat across each other's canoes, the eight 'rafted up' to maintain stability and station as a complete group, as they bobbed gently up and down in the noticeably rising swell.

Tremayne had previously briefed the group to take their nutty ration and water bottles with them and they now made the most of half of each in their short break.

After paddling for another hour, Tremayne called for a second five-minute break, while all eyes scanned the barely perceptible North Ayrshire coastline. The wartime blackout had completely obliterated any evidence of human presence along the coast, so that it was not possible to identify coastal villages marked on their maps.

"After a further fifteen minutes' paddling, I'll use my torch to signal the shore," Tremayne told the others, "and we'll maintain course until then. Keep closed up on my canoe please."

At 23.35 hours, Tremayne gave the agreed signal of five blue flashes, while Willoughby-Brown continued to paddle. There was no reply. Tremayne smiled as he heard several disappointed muttered oaths and a distinctly South African "'kin' 'ell" and pushed his paddle into the sea once more. Continuing on their original bearing for another ten minutes, the outlines of buildings just discernible on the otherwise indeterminate dark skyline indicated that they were close to the shore – and what looked like a fair-sized town. Tremayne once more flashed the pre-determined recognition signal. After a pause, which seemed to last for ever to the tired, soaking wet paddlers, five white flashes ahead and three hundred yards to the right signalled the anticipated response. "Right lads," called Tremayne, "one final effort – flat out for the spot where the light was." Seven minutes and several blisters later, the four canoes beached and both they and the kit were secured as Cole emerged from the darkness with a welcoming grin.

"Well done, gentlemen, the hotel – and hot kye reinforced with pusser's rum – await you. The umpire will check in each pair in the hotel foyer."

Cold, aching and stiff from the effort of paddling eight miles across the Firth, but with a sense of triumphant achievement, the eight checked in with the umpire – with just six minutes to spare. He turned out to be the humourless, taciturn Sergeant Major McKay of the Cameronians. Temporarily attached to the School pending the arrival of a permanent instructor, his reputation had already preceded him at HMS Godolphin.

McKay's deliberately unwelcoming silence and body language conveyed nothing but derision and were totally at odds with the often outrageous, but good-natured irreverence of the petty officers and Royal Marine instructors whom they had been used to as officer cadets at HMS King Alfred and then, operationally, at HMS Godolphin. Several of Tremayne's officers looked with questioning expressions of surprise, or mock resignation, at McKay's obvious and uncalled-for disdain.

"Goodness, I never thought that pusser's kye could taste this good. I'm absolutely perished," said a still shivering Simmonds, as he and the others gathered around Tremayne.

Instinct made Tremayne suddenly turn to look at the sergeant major whose face showed a contemptuous sneer, which he made no attempt to hide, as he stood, hands on hips, arrogantly facing the group.

Quickly moving over to the sergeant major, whose coarse face continued to display obvious derision and disrespect, Tremayne snarled, his lowered voice full of cold menace, "Sar'nt Major. A word – NOW!"

Addressing their chief instructor and still speaking quietly, as chilly, matter-of-fact professionalism replaced the ice-cold fury of seconds ago, he said, "Lieutenant Cole. A moment please."

In Cole's anxious presence, Tremayne directed his tautly controlled anger onto McKay. "Sar'nt Major. Whatever you approve – or disapprove – of, you will show my officers the respect to which they are entitled. *All* of them have had far more battle experience with the enemy than I know you have."

Tremayne moved threateningly close to McKay, his face inches away from that of the sergeant major's. "Any recurrence of the blatant, dumb insubordination that I have just witnessed and, I promise you, your feet won't touch the ground. Make no mistake, you *will* be on the next captain's defaulters' parade. In front of *anyone* from my flotilla, you will conduct yourself with the utmost professionalism, as befits your rank and role at this School. Do I make myself perfectly clear?"

Used to riding roughshod over what he considered to be young, naïve, inexperienced officers with no balls, McKay flushed bright scarlet at being so forcefully taken to task. He came to attention and snapped "Sar!" He instinctively probed Tremayne's face for any sign of weakness – but there was none. The instant authoritative command in Tremayne's voice, the set of his strong, muscular body and the unblinking steel in his eyes warned McKay that he would regret trying anything on with this officer.

"Right, carry on Sar'nt Major." Tremayne dismissively held the other man's eyes, forcing McKay to look away. Then he spoke quietly to a clearly shaken Cole, to explain what had happened and why he had gripped the situation, showing zero tolerance from the outset of the relationship for the warrant officer's unprofessional – and inappropriate – conduct.

"I know that he has a job to do, Graham, but so do we all. That man has got away with murder for too long in showing disrespect to young officers. Mine may be young, but they are experienced, battle-hardened men – not a bunch of midshipmen or cadets. Several of this group have been mentioned in despatches for gallantry in action. McKay, as one of your instructors, reports directly to you. Set the example Graham, don't collude with his insolence by turning a blind eye to it. Take control of him and make it an official reprimand before I do. Any more unprofessional nonsense involving my people and I'll personally deal with it through the CO."

Ashen-faced, Cole stammered profuse apologies. "I'm most sorry, sir. You're right, I have gone along with his disrespect, sir, because I believed that it introduced an unexpected element of 'edge' – fear even – that kept people on their toes."

"Remember the Navy's way, Graham – and that would also be Lt Commander Clogstoun-Willmott's way. We earn respect through competence, professionalism and toughness – plus the *appropriate* use of humour – not undisguised contempt for those we are training and who are learning from us. We encourage and build people up. We don't humiliate and despise them, or attempt to break them. We also show *them* respect."

Before dashing for the waiting launch, Tremayne briefly addressed his officers and told them what he had said to McKay and to Cole.

"We'll start as we intend to conduct ourselves throughout the programme. We have a lot to learn at what is an excellent school. That is exactly what we're going to do, gentlemen." Tremayne paused to take in each pair of eyes whose undivided attention he already had.

"But I will not tolerate behaviour like that from anyone, especially from some deranged egomaniac with an identity crisis who thinks he's the Almighty."

"Although we couldn't hear, we realised from your stance that you were giving McKay a right roasting. We've already made our minds up to give the bastard no quarter if he tries anything like that with us again," said Fischer.

"I rather had in mind a good dose of the lash – followed by keelhauling," drawled the ever urbane Willoughby-Brown.

"Just so, Captain Bligh – then hang the bastard from the highest yardarm in Chatham dockyard – to quote Charles Laughton!" added Fischer amidst laughter, as they piled through the door and onto the jetty and the waiting launch.

The next day was spent with introductions to COPP typical standard equipment, followed by repeated practice in using the kit in the loch. The 'dry' suit, with its watertight fit around the face, reinforced knees and elbows, buoyancy control and rope-soled boots proved to be a source of amused excitement – with a marked impatience to get into the treacly black water to try it out. Quilghini was the first to fall for the NCO instructor's standard joke – "Fasten all those pockets and pouches before you get in the water, sir, otherwise you'll have a wet run!"

Conscious of their trainees' superior rank, the instructors spared the officers the other old chestnut regularly inflicted on marines kitting up in their COPP, or frogman, suits for the first time – "Blimey, Royal, you've got no hairs on your arse. Oh well, I suppose grass never grows on a busy street!"

Having familiarised themselves with the wetsuits, boots and alternative swim fins by extensive swimming in Loch Striven, the eight were then given exercises in using a weighted line to gauge differing water depths. Following that, by the end of the day, they were using fishing lines on reels to measure various distances from shore. They then were given matt white slates and, using the chinagraph pencil attached to their wetsuits by a line, they were able to practise writing down and recording measurements and topographical features. This they learned to do while floating on the loch surface, largely submerged, with only their heads showing above the water.

By the end of the first week they had mastered the techniques of 'quartering' a beach with a fishing line, beaded every twenty-five yards or more. As they reached each bead, slowly swimming the length of the fishing line, they measured the depth of the seabed, at that point, using their other, weighted line to determine its changing contours with a high degree of accuracy.

On the second day – and destined to continue for one and a half hours on each of the remaining days – was a session on unarmed combat. Almost two years previously, all the officers – with the exception of Simmonds who joined the flotilla more recently – had undergone intensive unarmed combat at HMS Godolphin, prior to taking part in several commando raids. Tremayne and Fischer had demonstrated a particularly high level of proficiency in what was essentially a deliberately lethal form of ju-jitsu and Tremayne had used such close-quarter battle techniques in action 'with extreme prejudice'.

Similarly, they had received training in the use of the Fairbairn-Sykes commando fighting knife which, Tremayne had noted, was also on the curriculum at the School. Much to the amusement of the others, the genteel, sensitive Willoughby-Brown, brought up in a family of generations of cavalry officers, was horrified at the prospect of silently knifing someone from behind. "So unsporting," he drawled – his right eyebrow assuming its cultivated curve of mock horror, "and quite without the nobility of a sabre slash!"

Their unarmed combat instructor was no less than the sour-faced Sergeant Major McKay, accompanied by two tough looking soldiers wearing commando flashes. With his eyes studiously avoiding Tremayne's, he introduced the topic to the group with a short, but clear lecture and then the two soldiers gave demonstrations of various chops, headlocks, strangleholds and throws – culminating in a simulated, terminal boot to the nape of the neck of the downed opponent.

"Now, gentlemen, it's your turn. I need a volunteer." Some of the previous night's malice, which appeared to be McKay's essential stock-in-trade, was again apparent as he looked meaningfully at each face in turn – but still avoiding eye contact with Tremayne.

"Count me in Sarn't Major," called an ebullient Fischer, as he strode forward to where McKay and the two commandos stood. "Is it you I'm going to flatten?" He looked directly at McKay, who flushed an angry scarlet and muttered, "No sir, these are your instructors, sir."

After some personal instruction in applying one of the previously demonstrated strangleholds, Fischer was invited to practise on one of the commandos who quickly broke the officer's hold and, in a split second, put a very surprised Fischer flat on his back. The group were then shown how to prevent the intended victim from turning the tables on his attacker. Following Fischer, each of the others readily volunteered in turn with Tremayne, as last to volunteer, deliberately raising the stakes by inviting McKay to demonstrate throws with him.

All eyes turned expectantly on McKay as the group, remembering the night before and sensing blood, eagerly awaited his response. Something in Tremayne's obvious confidence and challenging eyes, implied an unexpected level of competence in close-quarter fighting that was disconcerting, even to a tough, experienced soldier like McKay. Though his eyes clearly betrayed his doubts to the group about taking on Tremayne, he recovered sufficiently to say, "That's a pleasure, sir, that unfortunately I'm denied on this course."

"A great pity, Sar'nt Major. The pleasure would have been all mine," said Tremayne tersely, promptly flooring the instructor he was offered before eventually being laid flat himself by a very swift, sweeping hip throw from one of the commandos.

In order to use the COPP's infra-red signalling lamps, close to enemy beaches, time was also set aside to bring the officers' ability to use Morse code back up to speed. All had become so accustomed to using signallers and telegraphists to transmit and receive messages on operations, that their personal transmitting and receiving skills were now in need of considerable polishing.

As the course progressed, with navigational and reconnaissance exercises taking the lion's share of both day and night-time training, so the involvement of more equipment – and lessons in how to use it – shaped the nature and content of their two-week programme.

To learn how to locate canoes or swimmers at sea, the group were introduced to both infra-red homing beacons and to what the Navy termed 'bong sticks'. These consisted of a metal box containing a fixed mechanical hammer, which was operated by turning a handle attached to a rod that projected outside the box. When the rod was placed in the water, the sound of the hammer could be picked up by ASDIC from a distance of up to twelve miles. Though primitive, 'bong sticks' proved to be more reliable as a homing device than the more sophisticated infra-red beacons, which could become obscured by the constant movement of the waves.

The group also learned how to use steel augurs, with inbuilt hollow tubes, to collect samples of beach sand and other materials in order to test a beach's suitability for assault landing craft. The samples, taken from different pre-determined locations using the beaded line technique, were kept separate and brought back in bandoliers with a pouch for each different sample.

Although previous commando training at HMS Godolphin had included rock climbing and abseiling techniques, four half-days were devoted to cliff assault. Included in their roping-down experiences was abseiling from the lofty battlements of Achnacarry Castle – which Willoughby-Brown described as 'an awesome, bowel-liquefying descent into oblivion'.

Here, at the seat of Clan Cameron, close to Spean Bridge, the group met up with Sergeant Kane and some of the Royal Marines from Godolphin, who were refining their already impressive cliff assault and rock climbing skills as part of their COPP training, in preparation for the invasion of France.

Tremayne and Kane had served together for two years in many actions – both on land and at sea – and a strong bond, based upon high mutual respect and considerable affection, had developed between them. Within moments of meeting, Tremayne took time to talk with Kane, each bringing the other up to speed on events both at the Pilotage School and at Godolphin.

Unfortunately – simply because of the differing timetables and syllabuses, Tremayne's programme and Kane's course had paralleled, but not converged on, each other and they had seen nothing of one another down in The Kyles of Bute or on Loch Striven.

As the last stage of the course rolled round, time was devoted to the officers' role in supervising and liaising with COPP teams prior to – and during – a commando beach assault. The last two days were devoted almost entirely to such an exercise, to use the skills and knowledge gained. Highly experienced umpires gave immediate feedback, as well as detailed debriefings, to identify what went well – and what lessons needed to be drawn from any disasters. Cole reported to Tremayne that the directing staff of the School rated the Tresco group as one of the most effective and positive that they had encountered.

One bonus outcome for Tremayne was that the already tightly-knit group of boat captains and their First Lieutenants was even more interdependent as a team following the intense and challenging experiences of the course. Even more so than before, they had reinforced their close bond by developing disciplined, collaborative responses to danger. The training had been well conceived and delivered and even McKay had provided thoroughly prepared instruction, once he had recognised that this was a group that simply would not tolerate his unacceptable and misplaced arrogance.

Having returned to HMS Godolphin, Tremayne, the boat captains and Enever spent most of the first day back debriefing and, from their joint analysis of their experiences, began to shape, in detail, the supportive, supervisory role of boat captains working with COPP teams along the French coast when 'D-Day' – as it was now being termed – finally arrived. In his usual thoughtful, thorough way, Enever concentrated upon the outcomes of their training experiences in Scotland in order to avoid or minimise mistakes at the critical start of the invasion.

Enever then turned his attention to his other main agenda item – diversionary activities and the laying of false trails – to deceive the enemy into thinking that the invasion would be somewhere other than where it was planned to take place.

"Because much of the coastline of Brittany, as you well know gentlemen, is unsuitable for large-scale invasion such as that envisaged by the D-Day planners, our diversionary tactics will have to be clever enough to keep the Germans guessing." Enever reached for his empty pipe, studied it thoughtfully and then clamped it between his teeth as knowing smiles crossed the faces of his audience.

"So, gentlemen, we're back in the business of out-guiling their Intelligence Services. The area that SOE and SIS have allocated to us to work on is the western coast of the Cotentin Peninsula, from Cherbourg south, while obviously the invasion, for real, is planned to take place to the east of it." He paused to ring for tea and open up a large file marked 'Top Secret' on the desk in front of him.

"Our task will be to leave subtle," he smiled benignly at the group over the top of his half-moon spectacles, "yes, *subtle* evidence, with one major exception – but more about that later, gentlemen – of extensive COPP activity along the beaches or in the sea, ready to be swept ashore by incoming tides between St Malo and Cherbourg. We shall also – with a degree of apparently careless, inefficient 'British amateurism' in such matters – leave evidence that we are inserting significantly increasing numbers of agents into the same area."

He paused once more as a Wren came in with tea and a plate of some of Aileen Oyler's hot, buttered Irish potato bread. "Thank you, Anne. Gentlemen, do tuck in please." Removing his pipe he continued, looking with obvious concern at Tremayne, "The people that we need to fool immediately are the local gendarmerie and their masters, the Gestapo at Rennes. If *they* are convinced that they are dealing with the genuine article, as it were, then we're in with a chance of duping the Abwehr and the OKW. Richard, Rennes must be ever present in at least the back of your mind, dear boy, after your appalling experiences there."

For a moment, Tremayne was silent and an involuntary shudder ran through him as the image of McDonald's badly beaten, sagging body, tied to the execution post, flashed across his mind. In an instant, he also recalled the terror of the moments awaiting his own execution as he stood helpless and freezing cold, tied to another post, in that bleak grass-covered clearing.

Conscious that the group had fallen silent – some looking at him with obvious concern, others looking down as if seeking an answer to the moment's shared anguish, Tremayne responded: "Life has moved on, sir – and so have I."

Tremayne's disciplined self-control was obvious to Enever and the others as he continued, "Even if I have to wait until the war is over, I will personally see that Neumann is brought to justice. However, the drive to avenge Mac will not interfere with whatever job I have to do back in that locality and, even if the opportunity to kill Neumann did arise, I would do nothing whilst the area around Rennes was still occupied and reprisals against the civilian population were likely. My intended future career as a barrister would be made a mockery of if I let a personal vendetta rule my feelings, my handling of them and my conduct of an operation against the enemy." He looked at Enever, whose expression was one of concerned concentration, "Have I anticipated what you were going to say, sir, or am I way off course?"

"You're right on course, Richard – completely so. However, only if captured while on an operation, God forbid – and under the illegal criteria of the Commando Order – are you likely to be in the area of Rennes. Your mission – and that of each of you, gentlemen – is to give the impression of pre-invasion preparation in eastern Brittany and the peninsula immediately to the south of Cherbourg."

Enever stopped to remove his still unlit pipe and place it on his desk. "The chances of capture *are*, inevitably, a major risk and so, with your hideous experience in mind Richard, I am calling for volunteers for the upcoming operations, which must precede D-Day and so will commence with effect from tomorrow night."

Tremayne quickly looked around the room at the other boat captains, registering their expressions of surprise at Enever's words.

"I think, sir, we all know – and appreciate – why you said what you did, but I believe I'm right in saying that each one of us here would automatically *expect* to be involved in these planned operations."

Vigorously nodded assent from all, several comments of "most certainly", "yes, definitely", and a strong "too bloody right" from Fischer, set a positive, committed tone to the meeting as Enever beamed a very happy, "Thank you gentlemen – each and every one of you."

Ringing for more tea, he looked up at the group and continued, "Tomorrow night's operation will involve all four MGBs – including our two new Vospers, which arrived while you were in Scotland and have now completed commissioning trials with us. They are absolute crackers, both faster and more manoeuvrable than anything else we've used – other than our late, lamented E-boat." Enever smiled and added, "Richard, I'm afraid that it falls to you to decide who should have these splendid toys, but whoever takes them over will need to familiarise themselves with the boats tomorrow before the operation begins. They are, incidentally, MTBs, mounting two twenty-one-inch torpedo tubes – the other pair having been stripped away for the sake of lightness."

Tea arrived and Enever stopped briefly, as the young Communication Branch Wren handed round cups to each member of the group. As she left the room, he continued, "Tomorrow night's exercise is to convince the Germans that extensive COPP activity has been taking place to the immediate west and to the south of Cherbourg. While you were away, several items of COPP kit and equipment – including a Cockle Mk 1** – were delivered to us from the Pilotage School for our planned deceptions. One major task – and I'd like you to take this on, Richard – is to deliver a body, already dressed in a COPP suit, close to the shore off Granville, north of the Baie du Mont St Michel – waters which you already know."

Enever paused briefly to drink his tea and then went on: "We estimate that the incoming tide will carry the body – with a suitably convincing, marked-up white observation slate attached to the suit – from about 03.30 hours onward. Two of you will scatter other items of kit that will wash up on the beaches north of Granville and obviously east of the Channel Islands, while one will leave hints of COPP activity south of Richard, closer to St Malo. Since Cherbourg happens to be a main E-boat base, their patrols are likely to be very active, unfortunately, in your selected areas. I don't doubt for one minute that Jerry's radar will pick you up as soon as you approach your designated target zones.

"However air cover, in the form of Beaufighters from bases along the south coast, will be on standby should you need them. In any case, all four boats are now equipped with six-pounders, with Molins auto-loaders for'ard, so that, if push comes to shove, you have the firepower to fight yourselves out of trouble – so long as the odds are one-to-one or less."

Enever handed out typewritten notes, taken from his 'Top Secret' folder.

"These, gentlemen, are detailed operation instructions which I need you to inwardly digest – and then discuss amongst yourselves – tonight, ready for operational briefing with your First Lieutenants at 08.15 hours tomorrow, here in Hut 101. Thank you, gentlemen, I wish you all a very good night!"

Nine

Laying some false trails

It was an unusually subdued group that made its way back to quarters to study the new operational brief. Everyone appeared preoccupied with his own thoughts and, for once, conversation was minimal. Typically, when together – and especially after one of Enever's meetings – they were in a happy, ebullient frame of mind, with a good deal of lively banter and laughter going on.

Enever's latest *ruse de guerre* – his planned use of a corpse – had introduced an unexpected element in the operation that didn't sit comfortably and had generated a mood of uneasy reflection within the group. Before going their separate ways, the decision was made that Tremayne would take one of the new Vospers and Taylor would have the other as a replacement for his Fairmile, blown up in the flotilla's most recent engagement with the E-boats. Because of the Vosper's superior speed, it was agreed that Taylor would undertake the operation planned for the coast near to St Malo, where there were likely to be extensive Kriegsmarine E-boat patrols. Operating so close to a large town and busy enemy sea lanes, a fast boat would be needed to have any chance of evading capture. Because of the similar maximum speeds of the Camper & Nicholson and Fairmile MGBs, Fischer and Simmonds agreed to work the waters as a pair close to the Cotentin Peninsula, south of Cherbourg and north of both Tremayne and Taylor.

Assuming that all went well with the various operations, the Vospers' speed would allow them to catch up with Simmonds and Fischer in the slower boats and rendezvous some twenty-five miles west by north-west of Alderney. The RV was deliberately chosen to leave the Germans with the impression that the flotilla would be returning to a base at either Dartmouth or Devonport. Only once well out of German radar range, would they then swing to port and set course for Tresco.

The following morning, Tremayne and Taylor and their crews took out the powerful and manoeuvrable seventy-three-foot Vospers to familiarise themselves with the new boats and the differences in their handling and seaworthiness when compared with the 110-foot long, slower Fairmiles.

Standing next to Irvine on the MTB's armoured bridge, Tremayne was amused to see the undisguised expression of pleasure on his dour coxswain's otherwise serious, poker face. Clearly, the usually taciturn Ulsterman was pleased as he enthused over his new toy: "Oh, but she's a wee beauty, sir, so she is."

To Tremayne's left, Willoughby-Brown was similarly impressed by the boat's handling: "Especially at maximum revolutions, she's a sea-kindly boat and not as wet as a Fairmile. She's also more manoeuvrable and turns more easily. When we're clear of the islands and test weapons, I'll be interested to see how stable a gun platform she is at speed."

Indicating the two torpedo firing levers on the bridge bulkhead, close to the coxswain's arm, Tremayne said with obvious regret, "Unfortunately, all the torpedoes that Godolphin possesses at the moment are the four that Mick Taylor and we have between us, so testing those is out I'm afraid. We'll test the other weapons ten miles south of St Agnes and see how that latest version of the six-pounder, quick firer, and the new twin Mk XII Oerlikons affect the boat's stability at speed."

Turning round to face the MTB's stern and indicating the engine room companionway aft, Tremayne added, "Petty Officer Buchanan should be pretty happy with those three twelve-cylinder 5M-2500 engines. Between them, they deliver 4,500 horse power. Built in Detroit by the Packard Motor Company, they give a boat of this size one hell of an acceleration. We also have as secondary power, for slow running and silent approaches, a Ford V8 engine that can move us at up to eight knots. Declutching this engine, in order to return to the Packards and maximum revs, can, I understand, be a bit tricky in the heat of battle, especially if the main engines are crash-started."

"Being so new off the stocks, she seems to be much more up to date generally than our Fairmile 'C' boats," noted Willoughby-Brown, taking in the businesslike, uncluttered deck and functional upper works of the boat.

"Since she's short and rather broad in the beam, she does tend to wallow somewhat at low speeds, but open the throttle and she immediately comes into her own," replied Tremayne.

"John, who is over the moon about them, told me that they are among the most technically advanced MTBs and MGBs that the Navy currently possesses. Their radar and radio equipment is IFF and, apparently, her echo sounders are pretty well state of the art. I understand that some of the other Coastal Forces flotillas are now also taking delivery of these new Vospers. It was John who insisted on new pennant numbers for our boats out of any recognisable sequence with those of other flotillas – hence our 1801 and Mick's 1802."

Well clear, to the south of St Mary's and St Agnes, Tremayne asked 'Taff' Jenkins, his leading yeoman of signals – now recovered from his wound, "Yeo, make to 1802: *'Test all weapons'*."

"Aye aye, sir." As ever, the mellifluous lilt of the Valleys was obvious as Jenkins's signalling lamp began its flickering transmission.

Almost instantaneously, six-pounders, Oerlikons and the twin .303 Vickers machine guns with their rotary drum magazines, opened up with a frenetic cacophony of thumps, staccato cracks and rattles. The weather was clear but cold and the white-crested waves were churning and breaking rather than crashing wildly and, with little wind noise, the din of the guns carried over the rolling water for miles.

During the weapons test, Tremayne and Taylor put their boats through a succession of rapid, tight turns and standing-start accelerations, but found the vessels to be solid gun platforms, apart from the rapid rising and falling of the boats' bows when punching through the seas at forty knots.

The grinning First Lieutenant, who was in his element and clearly enjoying the experience, summarised the challenge of synchronising firing with changing wave motion with his customary, uninhibited imagination: "It's a modern version of the typical Nelson-era command – 'Fire on the up-roll, lads!'"

Tremayne smiled as he saw the merest suggestion of the coxswain's eyes rolling heavenwards in mock disbelief. At this point, Tremayne turned to Irvine, "Right, Cox'n, zigzag if you please. Maximum revolutions!" Then, as an aside to Willoughby-Brown, he added with a grin, "Even Nelson couldn't bloody well do *this*!"

Taylor, he saw, was following suit, astern and to starboard, his bow clear of the waves throwing up cascades of water either side of the wheelhouse as his boat swung rapidly from port to starboard and back again.

Returning his attention to his own boat and its crew, Tremayne looked for the impact upon both of firing when moving at maximum speed. The gun-layer and his loader were secure, seated inside the small, box-like, power-operated open turret of the six-pounder. The Oerlikon gunner was tightly strapped into his harness and at one with his twin 20mm automatics as he swung round, traversing the weapons, while firing. It was the marionette-like antics of the two Vickers machine-gunners – hanging on to their twin machine guns for grim death – that really caught his eye. With little or no support by which to steady themselves, they continued to fire burst after burst at imaginary targets out to sea, swinging their guns in wide arcs and covering a considerable expanse of water.

On Tremayne's command, "All guns, CEASE fire, check, check, check," the muffled roar of the powerful Packard engines was once more the main sound as they pushed further south, punching through the now increasingly swelling, leaden-grey seas of the English Channel.

After a further twenty minutes, during which neither their radar nor their echo sounders identified any close potential threats, Tremayne ordered, "Return to base — maximum revolutions."

Knowing that Captain MacPherson, Commander Enever and several of the Executive Branch, Intelligence, Supplies and Admin Branch officers would be present along New Grimsby harbour, curious to see their return, Tremayne signalled Taylor to muster hands to fall in, by duty watch, for entering harbour routine. Willoughby-Brown issued the same order to those onboard 1801. At 12.00 hours precisely — and smart as paint — with their crews at attention on the fore and aft decks, both MTBs glided into the anchorage at Braiden Rock and secured under the hypercritical eyes of MacPherson.

After saluting MacPherson at the head of the path leading up from the anchorage, Tremayne and Taylor were at once subjected to a barrage of questions — on largely irrelevant minutiae.

The point of the interrogation seemed to Tremayne to be twofold — to impress them with MacPherson's grasp of the detail of the boats and to catch them out on their own lack of knowledge of such marginally relevant specifics. Little of what MacPherson ever said was intellectually stimulating or challenging but usually took the form of a succession of verbal hammer blows. Luckily, the largely pointless grilling, with its intended ego trip, was cut short when MacPherson was called away to respond immediately to an urgent telephone call from Coastal Forces headquarters.

Sharing their obvious relief at his sudden, hurried departure, Enever and the other officers clustered round Tremayne and Taylor, keen to know how the two experienced boat captains had found the Vospers under test conditions. How much more relevant and to the point were their questions, thought Tremayne, as the lively, involved discussion continued all the way back to HMS Godolphin.

Enever dismissed all officers except Fischer and Simmonds, who joined Tremayne and Taylor for a short final briefing on the planned deception operations, now due to commence at 21.00 hours that night when the incoming tide would be in full flow.

Conscious of the palpable, but unspoken curiosity about his intention to launch a body dressed in a COPP suit close to the French shore, he addressed the issue as the first item on his agenda.

"We had to wait, gentlemen, until we could find the right sort of body – young and obviously that of a fit, strong man and, preferably, one who had been drowned at sea within the last twenty-four hours." Enever paused to take in the faces of the four boat captains sitting in front of him.

"That we now have. He was a young deckhand from a British cargo vessel, sunk in the Channel with all hands by a U-boat yesterday afternoon. He carried no identity and was not injured in the fatal attack. Fully kitted up in a COPP suit and swim fins, he is as close to the genuine article as we could hope for." Enever stopped to reach for his inevitable empty pipe.

"A white marker board, secured to his suit and suitably inscribed with fictitious and untraceable – but plausible – plottings of sea-bed contours, as well as weighted lines in one of his pouches and separate, free floating beaded lines, will be released with the body to be washed ashore along the same stretch of beach. To invest his appearance on the beach – as a corpse – with some credibility, the Royals cleverly damaged his buoyancy control to make it look as if it failed in use and led to his death by drowning."

Unrolling a large-scale map of the western coast of the Cherbourg peninsula, Enever turned to the four boat captains, pointer in hand, "Richard, you will drop off our friend, late of the Merchant Navy, half a mile offshore and approximately two miles south of Granville. Your ETA should be around 02.00 hours. Approach your target area well west of the Channel Islands – to minimise radar contact – and to the south of the Plateau des Minquiers and Les Iles Chausey. These two clusters of islands, rocks and islets are navigational hazards that you can well do without, particularly in the dark. Your final approach, naturally, will be silent running on the V8 engine at around seven knots. I leave it to you, Richard, to choose your own route back, depending upon circumstances."

Turning to Fischer and Simmonds, he said, "You'll both be depositing odds and sods, such as a floating homing beacon, half of a double paddle and another floating, partially marked-up white board. You'll be roughly between Cherbourg and Jersey – and well within radar range – so maintain station, in line astern, as close together as you possibly can and you might just fool Jerry into believing that you are one of his own E-boats that he's monitoring on his screen! Your dropping-off points, gentlemen, will be the stretches of shore immediately south of Carteret."

Enever moved his pointer across several miles of the peninsula coast.

"Stealth is the watchword for *all* of you on this operation, gentlemen. The seas around Cherbourg, St Malo and the Channel Islands could be teeming with E-boat – and other – patrols, including destroyer or corvette flotillas. Whatever you are dropping off to be washed ashore *must* look as if it came from a botched, or suddenly aborted, reconnaissance operation."

Tremayne nodded in response. "If any of us are spotted while still in enemy waters, it is essential that we give the impression that we are a predatory patrol, on the look out for some easy victims. Sooner or later, from several radar stations, Jerry will most certainly pick us up on his screens and his patrols will come looking for us, by air as well as by sea."

He turned to Taylor. "Mick, unavoidably, you are likely to be picked up by radar close to St Malo, so keep moving as if on a 'search and destroy' sweep, while you drop off your capsized cockle and one of the paddles, plus other items of COPP kit—I suggest about a mile off the coast. The incoming tide will do the rest of the job for you."

Enever began to rummage around in his uniform pockets until he found a tin of 'Blue Liner' tobacco and began to fill his pipe with it.

"Just a final word, gentlemen – as soon as you *are* able to do so, hightail it, split arse, to your RV – don't hang around. Beaufighters are on standby at RAF Bolt Head to give you air cover on your return journey. Remember to use the RAF radio frequencies that you already have. Your identification to the aircraft will be three yellow flares, fired in rapid succession." The mild grey eyes showed a degree of concern as he said, "I wish you success and a safe return home, gentlemen. By the way, you are not alone in such deception. The 'Dirty Tricks Department' in London is organising disinformation on a grand scale to keep the enemy guessing as to 'where' and 'when' the invasion will take place—from Norway round to the Cote d'Azur. Deception of this magnitude is a natural gift – and preoccupation – of the British!"

Enever withdrew from the meeting to speak by telephone with Rear Admiral Hembury and to leave Tremayne to plan the final details of the operation with his boat captains. Well before their intended ETD at 21.00 hours, Tremayne eagerly telephoned Emma to find out how she and TTB were and then took his boat captains and all First Lieutenants for a convivial, relaxed supper at the New Inn. At 20.30 hours, they joined their boats' crews for final, onboard briefings and pre-operational checks of weapons and equipment. Tremayne glanced aft at the poignant, ice-packed, tarpaulin-covered mound on the after depth-charge chute and shuddered, as a sudden cold chill momentarily engulfed him.

The indefatigable Brummies, pragmatic and down-to-earth as ever, had unhesitatingly volunteered to launch the body overboard. With even greater alacrity, they had accepted Tremayne's offer of a pre-drop tot of pusser's rum, with Watkins solemnly assuring his skipper that he would forego the opportunity to launch Nicholls over the stern at the same time. "I'll need 'im to 'elp me make the breakfasts on the way back, sir."

"Thank God, on an occasion like this, for some soul-restoring, irreverent Brummagem humour", thought Tremayne, as he smiled to himself.

With traditional naval concern for punctuality and timing, Tremayne ordered "Slip' at 21.00 hours precisely and the flotilla moved off from Braiden Rock into the velvet black night – and France.

Still in line astern, at half revolutions as they moved through The Road, Tremayne signalled: *"Arrowhead formation – twenty-seven knots"*, once they cleared St Agnes and set course, initially south-east, for a point west of the Channel Islands which was also to be their RV later the following morning. Identification at the RV, planned for 05.00 hours, was to be confirmed by a combination of one red, followed by one yellow flare – repeated at fifteen-minute intervals until other boats signalled their presence.

As usual on Tremayne's boat, those on the bridge with him were his First Lieutenant, Irvine his coxswain and a rating watchkeeper; on this occasion – as on so many others – it was Leading Seaman Nicholls.

Although it was the twenty-seventh of April, the overcast late spring night was bitterly cold and those at defence stations on deck shivered, despite their thick, polo-necked woollen submariners' jerseys and heavy duffel coats.

Checking the magnetic compass immediately in front of him and directly above the steering wheel, Irvine announced, "We're right on our correct bearing, sir, so we are, and one mile north of our estimated point of departure, sir."

"Thank you, Cox'n. Maintain twenty-seven knots until Lieutenants Fischer and Simmonds leave us, then open her up to maximum revolutions and set your course for Cap Fréhel, west of St Malo, as Lieutenant Taylor joins us."

"Aye aye, sir."

Calling Jenkins on the bridge voice tubes, Tremayne yelled to make himself heard above the pounding waves, now crashing over the Vosper's sharp, businesslike bow," Yeo, make to 1501 and 1318: *'Break now and set course for target area. Good luck!'* Make to 1802: *'Follow me, please. Maximum revolutions'*."

Within seconds of the completion of Jenkins's flickering Morse transmission, Fischer and Simmonds swung away to port, bow waves churning glowing phosphorescence in the otherwise black sea, while Tremayne and Taylor increased speed to forty knots, their bows lifting clear of the water. Keeping well to the west of the Channel Islands they raced south-east, on course for Cap Fréhel.

Well into the Golfe de St Malo and to the south-east of Les Iles Chausey, they eventually parted company, signalling each other *'good luck'*, as Tremayne's boat bore off sharply to port, heading for the beaches just to the south of Granville.

Turning to his First Lieutenant, Tremayne said, "We'll have already been picked up on enemy radar and can probably expect visitors at any time. Put the crew at action stations please, Number One."

Using the voice tube, he called to Leading Seaman Watkins: "I think some hot kye, laced with a drop of pusser's best, would be very welcome all round, Watkins, if you please."

The voice tubes added their characteristic metallic tone to Watkins's response: "Aye aye, sir. Up in a jiffy, sir."

Tremayne grinned as he spoke to Willoughby-Brown and saw the brief tightening of Irvine's face muscles:

"Wait for the early dawn chorus! Heaven alone knows what this morning's musical offering is likely to be."

"I shudder to think!"

Within seconds, speculation came to an end as a lament burst forth from the tiny galley below the wheelhouse –

'In went the lads and gave a mighty cheer,

'Cos tattooed on her arse was every town in Lancashire.

There was Oldham, Bolton, Ashton-under-Lyne –'

Any more of the Navy ballad *The Rawtenstall Annual Fair* was cut short by a sudden gasp and exclamation, "'Kin' 'ell – that was bleedin' 'ot!"

Some minutes later, cocky and irrepressible as ever, Watkins appeared on the bridge, a string of enamel mugs round his neck and a rum fanny full of hot kye, laced with the restorative amber liquor, in his right hand.

"Thank you Watkins. Just what the doctor ordered!" smiled Tremayne. "Tell me, what misadventure cut short the aria? 'Swain was most distressed."

Once more, there was an almost imperceptible twitching of the coxswain's face muscles as his eyes continued to probe the blackness ahead and regularly monitor the illuminated gyrocompass.

"I'll bet 'e was 'eartbroken, sir." Watkins's rubbery face assumed a well-rehearsed expression of solemn innocence. "I slipped when we 'it a large wave, sir, and tipped 'ot kye over me, but I'm fine now, sir." Dipping mug after mug into the lifesaving brew, Watkins handed them out in turn. "Sorry to cause you distress, 'Swain, but I 'ope the kye will 'elp," he said, with a broad wink at Nicholls. As so many times before, Watkins's progress around those at action stations on deck was accompanied by outbursts of laughter and the noisy exchange of ribald banter.

"That man's worth a guinea a minute," said Tremayne to himself as he, the First Lieutenant and Leading Seaman Nicholls constantly swept the surrounding darkness with their binoculars. Checking their bearings with Willoughby-Brown and Irvine, he said, "We must be getting close." Then, to Irvine, he ordered, "Stop all engines if you please, Cox'n, and switch to the V8. Maintain seven knots."

The declutching went smoothly as the Vosper switched to silent running and her hull settled down into the slowly rising and falling black sea, the shimmering phosphorescence of her stern and bow waves decreasing considerably.

Closed up at action stations, with a noticeable rise in tension as they approached the beaches somewhere ahead of them in the still impenetrable darkness, Tremayne ordered, "Stand by all guns! Gun crews keep your eyes peeled." Turning to Leading Seaman Nicholls, who was still watchkeeping on the bridge, he said quietly, "Go and get a tot with Leading Seaman Watkins, then make ready to launch our colleague off the stern. I will join you at the aft starboard depth-charge chute."

"Take command of the bridge, Number One. I'll be back directly."

Tremayne was met at the chute by Nicholls and Watkins who, together, lifted the tarpaulin-covered body half over the transom stern of the MTB. Tremayne said a short prayer before he signalled the two leading seamen to commit the body to the sea, with what remained of the ice also sliding over the side as the tarpaulin cover was hauled back on board.

Before returning to the bridge, Tremayne checked that the body was floating, as intended, and felt a sense of unutterable sadness as the COPP-suited corpse bobbed gently in the waves behind them, his attached white marker board floating between his outstretched arms. As he slowly fell astern when the Vosper began to pull away, Tremayne found himself thinking about their late anonymous passenger: "I wonder who he was, where he came from and who is going to feel the utter desolation of bereavement at his passing? What might he have done, or become, if he had not lost out in the hideous lottery that is war?"

He glanced at his luminous watch – it was 02.07 hours. Still close to schedule, he noted, as he turned away from the boat's stern.

Quietly thanking Nicholls and Watkins, he quickly returned to the bridge and resumed command. "Ninety degrees starboard if you please, Cox'n. We'll risk Jerry's wrath and continue, as if on an inshore predatory sweep or reconnaissance mission."

Addressing his First Lieutenant he added, "They can also put our plotted movements down to a possible search for our missing COPPist when his body turns up. A critical part of our role is to keep the bastards guessing."

After about twenty-five minutes with no sign of the Germans, Tremayne ordered a sharp turn to starboard.

"We're in the Baie du Mont St Michel. It's time to move west into the Golfe du St Malo and then, clear of the Plateau des Minquiers, we'll set course for home."

Passing north of St Malo by about eight miles at a speed of seven knots, the sky to port was suddenly lit up by three bright green flares, making the MTB immediately visible to those on shore.

"Respond in kind, Number One, with three of our green ones."

As Willoughby-Brown fired off the flares, Tremayne ordered Irvine: "'Swain, stand by to declutch and bring in the three Packards, but maintain seven knots for the moment please."

Waiting for the Germans' response felt like an eternity to those on the MTB's bridge and fore and aft gun-decks as cocking mechanisms were repeatedly checked, ready to open fire on command.

"Stand by all guns. Stand by both torpedo tubes." Tremayne instinctively checked accessibility to the torpedo firing levers to the right of the coxswain.

"What the hell is Jerry up to now?" asked Willoughby-Brown, as two further recognition flares illuminated the inky sky, casting lurid, multi-coloured reflections on the equally black sea.

"One red and one yellow this time. Do we respond with identical signals?"

"This is the tricky bit now, Number One, when we either get it right – or we give the game away. Try a green one and then another yellow flare. A red one may be a trick 'no go' signal if it comes as a reply from us."

They didn't have to wait long for an answer. Their IFF radar immediately picked up three small blips, a mile off shore, starting to head rapidly in their direction.

"Right Cox'n, declutch and bring in the Packards. It's high time we were moving. Maximum revolutions if you will."

There was a delay of several seconds while the big engines struggled to respond to the crash-start. Then, after a seemingly interminable delay, they coughed and finally broke into a muffled roar, lifting the Vosper's bows clear of the water as she quickly hit over forty knots.

"Praise be," muttered a relieved Tremayne. "As I read the situation, the three E-boats – I assume from our radar blips that that's what they are – could shortly be within range and start hitting us with their 40mm guns. Naturally, they'll be shooting in the dark – quite literally – but tracking us by radar will give them our approximate position. With three of them firing, it won't be long before they start scoring hits. Flat out, they just have the edge on us for sheer speed. They have a lot of distance to make up in order to catch us – unless they cripple us first with shellfire – but it won't be long before they get close enough to damage us. Unfortunately, our after 20mm Oerlikons have a maximum range of about six thousand yards – and that's only if we fire them with an elevation of forty-five degrees. So, maximum revolutions for home seems to be the best option for us, Number One."

Tremayne had barely finished speaking when Willoughby-Brown, who was sweeping the still invisible horizon astern, suddenly shouted, "Gun flashes astern and ten degrees to starb–" Before he could finish his sentence, a succession of explosions and splashes astern told those on the Vosper's deck that the Germans had opened fire – most likely with their 40mm weapons.

"Right, Cox'n, every last ounce out of her please and zigzag. Hard as you like!"

More flashes, explosions and shell splashes – this time from all three of the E-boats' guns – confirmed that the chase was on and that the Germans meant business.

Tremayne called down the voice tube connecting him to the wireless operator: "Sparks, RAF Bolt Head are on standby. Request air cover to deal with pursuing E-boats. Give them our position and bearing."

Moving at maximum revolutions, nine miles west by north-west of Guernsey, Tremayne received the call from the radar operator that he had anticipated, but dreaded: "Sir, two small surface craft moving at speed, on intercept course, from the east. ETA fifteen minutes, sir."

"So, Number One, it looks as if our three friends from St Malo are shortly to be joined by two more from either Guernsey or Cherbourg. Let's hope that the Beaufighters are on their way, otherwise we're going to be very busy before the night's through."

"I reckon that we have little more than ninety minutes of complete darkness, but after that we will start to become visible for target practice," confirmed Willoughby-Brown.

"Agreed, Number One. Cox'n, we'll put what added distance we can between ourselves and our new visitors. Alter course, fifteen degrees to port."

Calling down the voice tube, Tremayne spoke to the wireless operator: "Sparks, tell RAF Bolt Head we've altered course to port by fifteen degrees. Two more E-boats moving from the east on intercept course."

Within seconds, muzzle flashes, less than five thousand yards to starboard, followed by straddling explosions and splashes, confirmed the arrival of the two E-boat newcomers on the scene.

"Damn," muttered Tremayne, "the bastards may not be able to see us, but they've found our range with their first salvo."

More muzzle flashes and incoming rounds from astern created splashes ever closer to the Vosper, as the three enemy vessels continued to close on Tremayne's boat.

Behind them, the three E-boats slowly continued to whittle away the distance to their quarry in their relentless high-speed pursuit.

"Zigzag, Cox'n and let's see how long we can keep out of real trouble."

Cupping his hands around his mouth, Tremayne shouted to the gun crew manning the for'ard six-pounder, "Stand by to fire! Targets off the starboard beam. Aim just ahead of their muzzle flashes."

As if on cue, the two westerly moving E-boats fired again, using their radar to guide their gunners and, once more, straddled the MTB with exploding 40mm shells – two of which hit the Vosper's hull.

In an immediate return of fire at the rapidly closing E-boats, the British MTB's six-pounder replied with a barrage of six shells, some of which appeared to be hitting home.

A third salvo from the Germans scored several more hits to the Vosper's decking and hull above the water line. The conditioned response of a volley from Tremayne's six-pounder was followed by a sudden sheet of flame which pierced the darkness and, seconds later, a loud explosion confirmed that the E-boats were not having it all their own way. With the fire, now some thousand yards off their starboard beam, acting as a temporary target marker, the six-pounder gun crew poured more aimed rounds into the centre of the inferno. A further explosion, smaller than the first one, indicated the end of one of the enemy.

Tremayne yelled to the six-pounder gun captain, "Good shooting! Well done Towers."

Turning to Willoughby-Brown, he said, "That's better, Number One, the odds are now only four to one!"

As if to give a lie to his optimism, shells fired from astern began hitting the rear deck, destroying the companionway to the engine room and severely wounding the exposed starboard Vickers gunner who collapsed in a bloodied heap on the deck, his twin machine guns, blown off their pintle mounting, lying beside him. Whereas the Oerlikon gunner had some protection from his gun's shield and the anti-splinter 'mattresses' around the weapon's power mounting, the machine-gunners were virtually without protective cover on this particular model of the Vosper.

Even before Tremayne's order, Willoughby-Brown was off the bridge, racing to pick up the badly injured seaman with Nicholls on his heels in support. With more shells continuing to fall around them, they gently carried the wounded man below. While Nicholls applied wound dressings, the First Lieutenant injected the barely conscious man with morphine, making him as comfortable as possible before returning to Tremayne's side. Nicholls rushed over to the twin Vickers guns, relocated them onto their pintle mounting and test fired them to discover that they were still in perfect working order. He then took over the post of the starboard machine-gunner, to a grateful nod of thanks from Tremayne.

Astern of the Vosper, the three pursuing E-boats had now closed to about five thousand yards behind and Tremayne ordered the rear Oerlikon gunner to open fire: "Target their muzzle flashes, Wade — and lace the bastards."

Even with the MTB still zigzagging, the twin Oerlikons were able to maintain almost uninterrupted fire in the capable hands of Leading Seaman 'Stripey' Wade — a grizzled 'three-badge' veteran who had served in the Navy, on the Dover Patrol, during the final years of the First World War.

To starboard, the remaining E-boat was closing fast and, by her muzzle flashes, Tremayne estimated that she was now less than six hundred yards away. The Vosper's six-pounder was still firing round after round at her with its Molins auto-loader working flat out to feed the weapon. An incoming burst of 40mm shells straddled the Vosper, holing the armoured wheelhouse below those on the bridge, blowing them off their feet and choking them with acrid smoke. Coughing violently as he struggled to stand up again, Tremayne called to Irvine, "Are you OK 'Swain?"

"Aye, sir. Fine, thank you sir, so I am. Are you OK sir?"

"Thank God 'Swain, yes. Swing her round. Aim her at the E-boat on our starboard beam."

"Are we going to ram her, sir?" Willoughby-Brown was

also back on his feet and retching as he tried to clear his throat of the thick, choking smoke.

"No, Number One. We're going to *torpedo* her."

As the Vosper swung effortlessly to starboard, Tremayne waited, as he judged the closing distance between the two boats and reached for the torpedo release levers.

"Fire one. Fire two." As if commanding himself, he called out the firing sequence aloud.

With a powerful *WHOOSH*, the torpedoes leaped from the port and starboard tubes abeam of the bridge, hurling themselves into the sea at forty-five knots. For a few seconds only, those on the bridge were able to track the silvery phosphorescent wakes of the quickly disappearing torpedoes.

With smoke still swirling around them, Tremayne asked Willoughby-Brown to check the wheelhouse for damage and the vessel generally for any casualties following the E-boat's last salvo.

Peering into the darkness from the bridge, it seemed an interminable wait to Tremayne to see if the running torpedoes were on target.

"Damn, damn, I've bloody well missed the bast —" Suddenly, a mighty explosion rent the black night, followed by bright orange and gold flames framing the stricken E-boat, her back broken by the force of the explosion.

"One must have missed her, but the other certainly got her, 'Swain!"

"Aye sir. That's the bastard done for, so it is."

Shouting to the gunners on the for'ard six-pounder, he yelled through his loudhailer, "Bow gun CEASE FIRING, check, check, check!" Swinging round to face the stern, he called, "Keep those bloody Oerlikons firing, Wade."

The First Lieutenant returned to the bridge, his face blacked by smoke and dust.

With a rueful smile, he said, "I'm afraid the wheelhouse is a bit of a shambles, sir. The other wheel, plus the gyrocompass and most other instruments have been completely destroyed – as have most of the fittings and furniture. When Captain MacPherson sees that lot, we'll be as popular as a fart in a finishing school!"

Tremayne exploded with laughter. "You don't believe that he'll blame Jerry, then?"

"Not a chance, sir! There are no other casualties, thank goodness, but a hell of a lot of damage to the deck and hull."

Irvine, hands on the bridge wheel and eyes on the now barely discernible horizon, called out, "Aircraft approaching, sir, bearing red, zero two five sir, so they are."

"Thank you Cox'n. Number One, recognition flares if you please."

Shouting through his loudhailer, Tremayne yelled, "All guns, all guns, STAND BY! Aircraft approaching, red, zero two five. They should be ours but they could be Jerry's."

"Wade, keep shooting astern."

As if to reinforce his last order, another barrage of shells, fired from behind them, crashed into the sea to starboard, just where the Vosper had been only seconds before, as Irvine resumed his rapid zigzagging.

Using the boat's Very pistol, Willoughby-Brown fired off three yellow flares in rapid succession – not only identifying the MTB for the incoming aircraft but also lighting up enough of the sea for them to make out the slim, dark menacing shapes of the three pursuing E-boats.

These were now less than five hundred yards astern of Tremayne's Vosper, their bow waves cascading bright, sparkling silver in the dark sea.

On board the Vosper, tension rose as the three twin-engined aircraft roared overhead at no more than one hundred feet above sea level. Were they German Ju 88s or Messerschmidt 110s? Guns were elevated to maximum and traversed rapidly as the aircraft came in. Anxiety turned to relief – then joy – as Tremayne yelled, "All guns. HOLD YOUR FIRE – they're Beaufighters, they're OURS!"

Seconds later, the staccato roar of twelve, fuselage-mounted 20mm cannon and the whoosh of rockets signalled the aircraft's first devastating strafing run against the E-boats. The sudden, deafening noise of so many cannon and high explosive missiles, combining with the sound of the Germans' 'doorknockers' and MG42s as they returned fire and the erupting fires, explosions and smoke, appeared to those on the Vosper like a scene from hell. Tremayne yelled to Irvine, "Turn about, Cox'n, we'll give the Beaufighters support from our six-pounder and anything else that we can bring to bear," and, using his loudhailer, shouted to the gun crews fore and aft, "Right, lads, now's your chance. All guns, FIRE AS YOU BEAR!"

Racing towards what had rapidly been transformed, within seconds, from a noisy, fiery mêlée to sheer bloody carnage, the Vosper opened fire over open sights – so close was the range with, in turn, the six-pounder, the starboard twin Vickers guns and finally, her twin Oerlikons. As Tremayne turned through 180 degrees for a second run, this time giving the port Vickers gunner the opportunity to sweep decks and bridges, so the three Beaufighters regrouped for another strafing run against the luckless E-boats – all of which were dead in the water, with one already beginning to settle.

The Germans doggedly and gallantly returned fire with whatever weapons were still functioning but, with the arrival of the RAF, the battle had turned against them and it was only a matter of time before the inevitable conclusion ended the one-sided slaughter. About thirty seconds later, one of the E-boats 'brewed up' with a roar as dense smoke and flames began issuing from hatches and companionways on her deck and she, too, began to settle. To save further loss of life, the third E-boat skipper struck his colours, only one of his machine guns still capable of firing.

Tremayne called "cease fire". To the German boat captain

who had just surrendered, Tremayne signalled that he could not attend to survivors but would now withdraw to allow the Germans to effect their own rescue operations undisturbed. Willoughby-Brown had already intercepted a radio transmission for help from the E-boat, seconds before, and let Tremayne know that rescue was in hand. Standing on the bridge of the battered Vosper, Tremayne returned the solemn salute of the German boat captain before setting course, at maximum revolutions, for their RV with the other three returning Tresco flotilla boats. With Tremayne in control of the situation, the three Beaufighters withdrew, waggling their wings in salute before roaring off back to their base in South Devon.

Around forty minutes later, Willoughby-Brown pointed out one red flare, followed by one yellow one being fired into the now lightening, grey dawn sky, approximately seven miles ahead and ten degrees to port. Tremayne checked his watch. It was 05.09 hours precisely.

"That little scrap cost us some time, Number One. We're already adrift. Fire off one red and one yellow flare. At least they'll then know that we're on our way. Cox'n, set course for their flares as fast as you like, please."

Wiping the night's grime from his face, he called down the voice tube, "Watkins, are you still with us?"

"Aye aye, sir – like the poor. Would you like some kye, sir?"

"Good man! Yes please and with a drop of pusser's best in it, if you will."

"Aye aye sir."

Minutes later, accompanied by an off-key rendition of 'There are roses round my door, I'm rotten to the core...', the ever resilient Watkins appeared on deck, a string of enamel mugs around his neck and the indispensable fanny full of steaming hot, rum-laced kye in his hand.

Two minutes later, they fired off further flares which, to their relief, were immediately responded to with correct colours and in the right sequence.

As the Vosper rapidly approached the RV to rejoin the other three boats, Tremayne called to Jenkins, "Yeo, make to the others: *'Sorry to keep you. Involved with E-boats. Thank you for waiting'*."

Within seconds, back came the flickering Morse responses with Fischer's, as usual, being the most outrageous: *'Somebody had to make sure the old fellow got back home safely.'*

Drawing alongside the others, Tremayne spoke through his loudhailer, "Good to see you. Did all go according to plan?" With all responses in the affirmative, Tremayne called, "Let's go home, gentlemen. Maintain arrowhead formation. Defence stations, if you please."

As they moved off, setting their course for Tresco, it became increasingly apparent to those on the bridge that there appeared to be major fires burning to the south of Portland Bill and out into Lyme Bay, some forty or so miles to the east.

Scanning the area with his binoculars, Tremayne could

not see any vessels on the sea's surface, simply a succession of scattered red glows, just visible in the far distance in the early dawn's chill, dark grey light.

"What do you make of that, Number One?"

"It looks as if there's been a major scrap going on out there and, moments ago, I thought that I heard a muffled explosion, but with the noise of our engines – and at that distance – I can't be sure," replied Willoughby-Brown.

"Hmm, strange." Calling to Jenkins, Tremayne shouted, "Yeo, make to the others: *'Any idea what is going on to the east of us in Lyme Bay?'*."

Morse responses were generally negative, apart from Simmonds's reply, which stated: *'Have been aware of what could have been a battle as we drew closer to the RV, but no confirmed knowledge as such'*.

Puzzled and concerned, but with no mandate to take the time to investigate, Tremayne maintained course for Tresco.

With St Agnes fine on their port beam and with the tide out, Tremayne led the flotilla, now in line astern, outside the Minaltos, through the Northern Rocks and up round Shipman Head at the northern tip of Bryher. He then took the flotilla down to Braiden Rock anchorage, past the imposing stone sentinel of Cromwell's Castle, to secure at 08.43 hours.

Tremayne thanked his crew and confirmed that as soon as possible, after the inevitable boat captains' debrief, he would put them in the picture about the operation. He then told them to get ashore, clean up and have breakfast. Having radioed ahead about Able Seaman Webster, the wounded Vickers gunner, Tremayne supervised the transfer of the badly injured man from the MTB to a harbour launch on his onward journey to the hospital on St Mary's. Turning to the disembarking officers from the other three boats, Tremayne called, "Let's grab some breakfast, gentlemen, and bring one another up to speed on the operation over whatever the wardroom galley can rustle up for us."

As they were finishing off breakfast, still reviewing the events of the night and early morning, a serious-faced Enever appeared.

"Gentlemen, good morning. We'll debrief later, but right now I need to speak to the boat captains. Please join me immediately in Hut 101."

Looking somewhat surprised and puzzled, Tremayne and the other three trooped into Hut 101 behind Enever. Rarely had they seen him look so grave and tense.

"Please be seated and take some coffee." Enever indicated the five steaming cups already laid out on a tray in front of him.

"What I am going to tell you is for your ears only and is not — repeat, NOT — to be told to anyone else until further notice. I take it I have your assurance on that, gentlemen."

The universal affirmative response was immediate as the four reached for coffee and settled themselves into their seats.

Enever leaned forward, pipe in hand, "Did any of you see

or hear anything that might suggest a battle at sea in Lyme Bay earlier this morning?"

Tremayne was the first to respond.

"Well, yes sir, as a matter of fact we all did. We were just able to make out what appeared to be a series of fires at sea, south of Portland Bill and, I would estimate, at probably forty miles east of us."

Enever looked unusually concerned, "And so crew members on deck also saw the fires?"

"Yes sir, although not for long, because as the dawn sky lightened so the fires disappeared. We all checked our radar, but were obviously so out of range that we picked up nothing."

Enever nodded his thanks and leaned forward to take his cup of coffee.

"Last night, gentlemen, there was a complete disaster in Lyme Bay with serious implications for the invasion. The Americans were conducting Operation Tiger – a major dress rehearsal for their planned D-Day assault on what has been code named Utah Beach in Normandy. Because of its similarities to the French beach, the assault force – consisting principally of LCTs – was heading for Slapton Sands on the south Devon coast, west of Dartmouth."

Enever paused to take a drink. "A complete news blackout has been imposed by the Government and the Royal Navy – hence my opening comments about the need for the strictest silence. It appears that two marauding flotillas of E-boats spotted the lumbering, vulnerable LCTs on their radar and ran amok amongst them, sinking many and killing — initial estimates indicate — over seven hundred US soldiers and sailors. Reports from British Naval Intelligence are harrowing to say the least. Most of the LCTs became blazing infernos, which is what you saw as a succession of glows on the horizon, and, tragically, a lot of GIs were drowned or burned to death.

"For perfectly valid reasons — including that of an escort vessel rammed and severely holed accidentally by an LCT — the Royal Navy was not able, at that time, to provide the cover and protection needed. Communications generally were little short of chaotic and, it appears, safety and abandon-ship drills were largely unknown to the crews, who had no idea how to cope efficiently with such a sudden crisis."

Enever looked around the table at the shocked faces in front of him.

"As a result of this disastrous setback, there are serious concerns about its immediate impact upon Anglo-American relations and also on the date of the invasion itself. Our apparent lack of readiness to deal with such an attack does beg important questions about our preparedness to mount a major seaborne invasion, successfully, within the next few weeks.

"The reason that I've put you in the picture, gentlemen, is because, as I suspected, you must have already seen or heard something of this disaster at first hand as you returned from this morning's operations. Anticipating your question about explanations to the crew members who saw any evidence of fires or heard explosions, you are to tell them this — and *only* this, and then only if *they* ask — that major realistic exercises were conducted in Lyme Bay during the night and early morning as rehearsals for the planned invasion of France."

Fischer asked if this strict blackout applied to First Lieutenants and Enever replied, "Yes — to *everybody* not in this room. Sorry to play the 'heavy', gentlemen, but those orders are from the highest authorities."

After calling for and answering any questions from the group, Enever ended the impromptu meeting and said, his face softening, "Grab some sleep, you must all be exhausted. I'll see you here, together with First Lieutenants, at 15.30 hours."

Tremayne and the other boat captains returned to the breakfast table and, studiously avoiding the quizzical, expectant looks of the First Lieutenants, announced: "Commander Enever has ordered us all to get some shut-eye. We meet again for operational debriefing in 101 at 15.30 hours. Thank you again for all your hard work during the wee small hours. Let's take the SIO's order seriously and 'crash out' right now, gentlemen."

With that brief, concluding comment, Tremayne led the way out of the dining room and disappeared to his quarters...

Ten

The deception spreads

As preparation for Operation Overlord — the imminent invasion of France via Normandy — the Tresco flotilla became heavily involved in inserting more agents into eastern Brittany, raising the level of misinformation by wireless transmissions and noticeably increasing Confrèrie radio contact to the west of Cherbourg. Well aware of the Germans' ability to monitor radio traffic, British Intelligence Services increased transmissions by almost fifty per cent, of which only about one fifth were genuine encoded messages, passing vital information and operational instructions to the French Resistance. Transmitted via the BBC, these so-called *'messages*

personnels' usually consisted of either one line, or a couplet, of French verse by poets such as Verlaine, Baudelaire and Corbière.

Such *ruses de guerre*, considered as essential elements in widespread strategic deception and misinformation, were also concurrently being replicated – and further increased – in areas such as the Pas de Calais, where the Germans generally expected the main thrust of the invasion to take place.

The agents, taken over by fishing boats from Tresco, were sent to concentrate on training saboteurs and, now, engage in more frequent acts of sabotage within north-east Brittany. Imminent invasion lent urgency to the need to blow up railway lines and bridges to hamper troop movements within the region. Together with SOE, the Confrèrie had already made plans to make greater use of such trained experts deeper in Brittany, as the Allies subsequently advanced through the area.

Once the invasion was well underway and before the Allies had broken out of their beachheads, organised sabotage would take the form of paralysing telecommunications networks, interrupting power supplies and shutting off water, in addition to imposing restrictions on the Germans' ability to move around the region. Balanced against this was the need to minimise German reprisals against the civilian population.

During the following two weeks, Tremayne, Fischer and Taylor, together with their crews, made three such trips in the fishing boats over to Brittany, to deliver agents and collect up-to-date intelligence about German weapon emplacements, coastal patrol routines and troop movements. Their other task was to rescue and extract agents whose roles had been compromised and who were about to be arrested by the Gestapo.

In all cases, the latest trips involved taking ammunition and weapons – principally Stens, automatic pistols, Bren guns and grenades – to equip the growing numbers of French Resistance fighters, ready for uprisings around the area once the invasion forces had begun to move out from the landing beaches and into the interior. Plans had already been made for members of the Free French SAS to parachute into the area, to invest the Resistance members' fighting capability with some hard-edged professionalism.

As on previous occasions, the 'mystery boats' slipped away from Braiden Rock anchorage at around 24.00 hours, moved south through the darkness at maximum revolutions and then mingled with the various Breton fishing boats at dawn in order to make their deliveries and pick-ups undetected. The final stage of the operation involved seemingly casual contacts with Confrèrie-manned fishing vessels, which 'innocently' came alongside the Tresco boats to carry out the necessary transfers of personnel, weapons and documents.

At his debriefing following the flotilla's attempts to deposit evidence of increased COPP reconnaissance activity west of Cherbourg, Enever set the scene for the Tresco boats to raise their game in deceiving the Germans about 'where' and 'when' the invasion would occur.

"Over the coming weeks – in the run-up to and including D-Day – we shall be operating with less independence and increasingly as a crucial part of overall coastal forces invasion strategy," he announced to the assembled officers.

"Because of our unique location, we shall continue to concentrate our activities on the invasion and liberation of Brittany, except for D-Day when we shall be protecting COPPists and the left flank of the British invasion forces against marauding E-boats on Sword Beach. While geographically our position on the eastern flank of the invasion beaches seems pretty incongruous, the Tresco flotilla's record of success over the last two years resulted in Special Service Brigade insisting that we be in their sector, which will be Sword Beach when the balloon goes up. In particular, 45 and 41 RM Commandos stressed that we should be among the guardians of their left flank off the beaches.

"So, gentlemen, we shall be in direct support of Brigadier, the Lord Lovat and his marvellous bunch of cut-throat brigands! We shall arrive off the Normandy coast at around 02.00 hours and await the armada."

Enever looked around the group sitting in front of him, beaming with what Willoughby-Brown later described as a smile "bordering on the seraphic and sublime", before adding, "And, gentlemen, I shall be coming with you!"

Enever took time to scrape out the encrusted tobacco from his pipe before saying to Tremayne, "Thanks to Leading Seaman Watkins's culinary arts, I gather that your boat offers by far the best breakfasts in the flotilla, so I shall be travelling with you dear boy!"

With D-Day now planned for the sixth of June, in just over one week's time, the Tresco flotilla concentrated on finalising and rehearsing its part in the safeguarding of the invasion fleet's left flank. Of particular concern was the need to perfect communications and coordinated interaction with units from other flotillas and squadrons. To this end, the Tresco unit's MGBs and MTBs combined with other coastal forces flotillas for joint exercises at sea in and around Lyme Bay.

Ever mindful of the still top-secret recent disaster and appalling loss of life in the ill-fated Operation Tiger in the same area, protection of the vessels rehearsing battle coordination was considered to be of paramount importance. In addition to MTB 'guard boats', air cover was provided, on standby, by the Beaufighter squadron. While there were also LCTs and LCIs involved in these latest rehearsal exercises, communications between the different vessels and units involved had been tightened up dramatically since the catastrophe in April. Additionally, three frigates had been brought in to provide added protection, by systematically patrolling the approaches to the Lyme Bay invasion rehearsal area.

As Tremayne's flotilla was in the middle of mutual

support manoeuvres with boats from Helford River, his wireless operator came rushing up to the bridge and handed him a hastily scribbled note. "Urgent signal from Godolphin, sir."

"Thank you, Evans." Tremayne looked at the cryptic message: *'MTB1801 return immediately please — Enever'.*

Tremayne's response was equally to the point. "Acknowledge, please Evans."

Calling to his chief yeoman of signals, he said, "Yeo, make to Lieutenant Fischer: *'Please take command. Have been recalled to Godolphin. Action immediate. Good luck.'* "

"Aye aye, sir."

On the bridge, Tremayne showed his First Lieutenant the signal and ordered Irvine to return to New Grimsby harbour, with maximum revolutions.

"Starboard twenty and full ahead, if you please, Cox'n."

"I've no idea what this is about, Number One, but it sounds pretty urgent."

For a moment, Emma flashed across his mind and, momentarily, anxiety tugged at his heart.

"Let's hope that it's operational and not personal, David," he murmured, turning away from the coxswain.

With the tide still just about running in their favour as they entered Scillies' water, Irvine took the Vosper through The Road then, switching to the slow running V8 engine, passed through the Tresco Flats at six knots and onto Braiden Rock anchorage.

Leaving Willoughby-Brown to secure, Tremayne dashed up the narrow rocky path and onto the track and road leading to HMS Godolphin – and Hut 101, where an ever-welcoming Enever was waiting.

"Dear boy, sorry to drag you away from the rehearsal drills, but something urgent has come up in Brittany. It's a rescue operation and I need you to undertake it, leaving Tresco at 24.00 hours tonight."

"The Vosper needs refuelling, but that's about all – apart from provisions and drinking water. So we can be away faster if needs be. Where are we going to and what do you need us to do, John?"

"This is a fishing boat op, Richard, and *Vas-y-Voir* has been thoroughly prepared for you. She's been freshly painted – with the usual iron filings included in the paint, of course. She also carries the latest recognition tricolours painted on her bows, as demanded by the OKM, and bears pennant numbers which indicate that her base is Carantec. I must say she looks quite 'tiddly' and clearly just the part. The pick-up point is to be neighbouring Roscoff – and in broad daylight."

Enever regarded Tremayne thoughtfully before resuming. "Your guests will be a major from the SAS, Mike Black, together with one of his sergeants – 'Paddy' Nugent. Along with others, these two have been training Breton Resistance members in the use of explosives, sabotage techniques and weapons handling. Of greater immediate importance is the amount of vital intelligence which they have gathered about German coastal defences during their covert surveillance operations. They were betrayed by a double agent and subsequently taken by the Gestapo. En route to the Gestapo interrogation centre, they broke free, killed three guards, seized their weapons and then legged it. Jerry is howling for their blood and we need to get them out of France as quickly as possible. If captured, they will most certainly be tortured and then executed. "The Confrèrie have smuggled them to Roscoff through a succession of safe houses and they are now working as deckhands on a couple of lobster boats, registered at that port and crewed by members of the local Resistance."

Enever paused as one of the Communication Branch Wrens brought in fresh hot coffee.

"Many thanks, Ann. Richard, please do help yourself.

"Now. Back to *Vas-y-Voir*. Her operations boxes are replete with Brens, Lanchesters, pistols, grenades, oh – and a couple of PIAT rocket launchers – just in case you happen to come up against the *Prinz Eugen* or the *Tirpitz*!

"A fresh catch from Scilly – including some lobsters – will be put into two barrels and placed on deck and her nets give the impression of being in regular use. Because you will be right under the noses of the gendarmerie and the Germans in Roscoff harbour, mixed in with other fishing vessels – including the couple of Breton boats owned by the Confrèrie, you will need native French and Breton speakers with you.

"Your crew will therefore consist of WB and Pierre Quilghini, with Able Seamen Harberer and Dulac as deckhands-cum-engine room ratings. Are you happy with that arrangement, Richard?"

"Absolutely. WB and I can manage enough French to convince the Germans but I, certainly, would never fool any Frenchman with my accent."

"Essentially, the plot is this." Enever took a long drink from his coffee cup.

"*Vas-y-Voir* will fly an orange pennant from her mainmast, as will the two Confrèrie boats, which will be drawn up on shore for apparent necessary minor repair work. Their crews – including our two SAS friends – will be engaged, variously, in carpentry jobs, hull scraping and painting.

You will anchor opposite and close to them, in order to bring them tools, bits of wood and other paraphernalia to help them complete their tasks. The two 'safe' boats will have the major and his sergeant on board, keeping low profiles and suitably occupied above and below deck."

Enever offered Tremayne one of the warm, wedge-like conversation stoppers known as Nelson slices that had just appeared fresh from the galley.

"During the course of a couple of hours or so, keep ferrying to and from their boats in your dinghy, taking different people backwards and forwards on seemingly routine trips, in order to get repairs done and to shift tools, equipment and bodies from one boat to t'other. Is this making sense, Richard, or do I sound as if I've got at least one foot in fairyland?"

"No, not a bit, John. It all makes perfect sense to me. Presumably, those who remain on *Vas-y-Voir* can be making our own minor repairs and mending our nets, for example."

"Exactly so. Then slowly, but surely, you transport the gallant major and his formidable sergeant onto *Vas-y-Voir* and leave them there. By the way, we have collected some magnificent vintage French hand tools to add some authentic detail, including a marvellous brace and several drill and countersink bits that the Breton boats could have been 'waiting for' in order to get their repairs done. This provides you with an immediate excuse for going directly to those two boats, should you be stopped and questioned by the authorities. Amongst all the kit, there is also a most wonderful old American Millers Falls jack plane in your carpenter's toolbox. I've got my eye on that, so please make sure that you bring it back, dear boy. Carpentry happens to be one of my great passions. I have Admiral Hembury's permission — so you won't be court-martialled for misappropriating Admiralty property!"

"Aye aye, sir," grinned Tremayne.

"Presumably we pick what seems to be the optimum time to finish our joinery and net mending before we push off for home with the noisy, sociable parting of close mates and fellow fishermen?"

"Yes. You must be the judge of when is the best time to

start for home with your guests. Remember to motor slowly at first and then open up once you are clear of land. Keep radio transmissions to a minimum, but the call for supportive air cover will be a line from McCaulay's poem *How Horatius Kept the Bridge*: 'and e'en the hordes of Tuscany could scarce forbear to cheer."

"The Tresco flotilla will already be at sea, heading in your direction, awaiting your return and standing by to provide back up. I cannot stress how vital it is that you bring Major Black and Sergeant Nugent home with the information that they have collected. It represents some of the most up-to-date and thoroughly documented data that we shall have about Jerry's coastal defences and current troop dispositions."

Tremayne briefed his crew in detail and the Frenchmen were clearly revelling in the thought of fooling *les Boches* while working right under their noses.

Onboard *Vas-y-Voir*, final checks were carried out on weapons, the apparent authenticity of deck equipment and the wheelhouse – and on quarters below deck. Tremayne, anticipating possible firefights, made sure that there were ample supplies of different calibre ammunition in the operations boxes.

Recalling the phrase – typical of the aggressive commando spirit – 'When in doubt, use a grenade', he made sure that there were at least a dozen Mills '36 grenades close to hand.

A final inspection confirmed Tremayne's assessment that *Vas-y-Voir* looked exactly like what she was supposed to be –

a Breton fishing boat – and at the witching hour of midnight, he ordered "Slip".

Clear of the islands, in a glorious moonlit late May night, and with reflected silver patches on a relatively calm sea, Tremayne ordered Quilghini, now acting as coxswain, to open up to full speed ahead.

Like *Muguette* and the other 'doctored' Tresco fishing boats, *Vas-y-Voir* was constructed in the traditional Breton manner above the waterline, but with a very cleverly remodelled, streamlined underwater hull and two powerful 500hp Scott-Hall engines. Combined, these additions to standard construction gave her a maximum speed of just over thirty knots. Typical engine-room grime and grease had been deliberately allowed to accumulate around valves, joints and the suitably tarnished pipework, to give the engines the appearance of something far older, more worn and less powerful.

They pushed on, uninterrupted, across the Channel, through the now increasingly heavy seas. Tremayne and Quilghini remained on duty watch, while the other three grabbed what sleep they could with the vessel continuously rolling and riding with the waves. The decision to take a small crew was made because of the need to bring back the two SAS operatives, and a vessel the size of *Vas-y-Voir* would soon look unnecessarily – and suspiciously – overcrowded to trained eyes. An accompanying Hawker Hurricane from RAF St Mary's had provided air cover for about two-thirds of the journey and then, with a farewell waggle of its wings – shining in the moonlit sky – as a parting salute, it returned to base.

As dawn began to break, with the still clear sky becoming noticeably lighter and brighter, Tremayne ordered a speed of six knots in order to blend in with other local fishing vessels as and when they appeared looking for the early catches.

An incongruously churning bow wave and bright phosphorescent wake would give the game away immediately, both to fishermen and to the German and gendarmerie coastal protection patrols. The boat had now acquired a suitably convincing fishy smell, while nets, cordage and rigging all seemed to be in their most natural working positions.

With all the crew now awake and stood-to, Tremayne ordered defence stations all round. All weapons – apart from the quaint, but fierce looking PIATs – had been loaded, checked and briefly tested out in the Channel at around 02.30 hours.

The mood of the three Frenchmen became even more lighthearted and excited as the north Brittany coast began to appear on the horizon, initially as an indistinct blur, separating the rolling sea from the ever-brightening sky.

To port, Willoughby-Brown, scanning the eastern horizon with binoculars, spotted emerging and returning local fishing boats, both in groups and individually. Moments later, a keen-eyed Dulac, also maintaining watch with binoculars, called out, "Gentlemen. We 'ave company. Starboard beam – five thousand metres!"

Tremayne and Willoughby-Brown swung their binoculars over, following Dulac's pointing finger. Coming in fast, almost at right angles to the fishing boat, was a very purposeful looking E-boat, her sleek bows clear of the water as she approached at what Tremayne estimated to be over forty knots.

Tremayne opened one of the operations boxes and took out automatic pistols for himself, his First Lieutenant and Quilghini and placed three grenades within easy reach, but well hidden, on top of the for'ard companionway cover. He took out one of the PIATs, quickly loaded it and laid it on the winch housing with a spare fishing net draped over it. With about two hundred yards to go, the E-boat trimmed her course a few degrees to port and headed straight for the *Vas-y-Voir*.

"Look busy on deck and keep those pistols handy. Let's do all we can to avoid raising suspicion."

Through his loudhailer, the German commander called upon the *Vas-y-Voir* to cut her engine and stop immediately.

The E-boat rapidly manoeuvred alongside the fishing vessel, completely dominating her, while her crew arrogantly scrutinised the five figures on deck.

A German seaman, standing at the E-boat's bow guard rail but well clear of the field of fire of her manned, bridge-mounted machine gun, threw a securing line to Harberer. The Frenchman caught it and quickly wrapped it round a bollard on *Vas-y-Voir*'s for'ard deck. The German skipper stepped off the E-boat's squat bridge and bounded down to her spray dodgers, which were immediately above the *Vas-y-Voir*. Accompanying him were two ratings armed with MP40 machine pistols.

Tremayne could feel the cold sweat begin to trickle down his back as the tension mounted. Were the Germans going to board? Was a close, detailed search imminent? How quickly would they be able to silence the rating manning the menacing MG42, pointed directly at them, before it shredded everything – and everyone – on *Vas-y-Voir*'s deck?

Following a perfunctory exchange of greetings, the German officer asked, in quite fluent French, if they had caught any lobsters and whether they had any to spare. Quilghini was the first to respond. "Yes, of course we can give you some. How many do you want?"

"Four, if you can spare them, please."

Moving aft, to the barrel on the fishing boat's rear deck, Able Seaman Harberer began to rummage around in it and, within seconds, reappeared with four of the still very fresh-looking lobsters, caught off Tresco. He handed them across to the E-boat commander, who produced a bottle of crystal clear liquid, saying, "We are traders – not pirates. Please accept this in exchange – it is one of the best brands of German schnapps."

Turning to his First Lieutenant, who had remained on the E-boat's bridge, he called, "So Heini, tonight, thanks to these Frenchies, we shall celebrate your birthday in style!"

Willoughby-Brown quickly translated for Tremayne, who was standing close to him.

After thanking those on the fishing boat's deck, the E-boat commander ordered a ten-degree swing to starboard and then "full speed ahead". The E-boat roared away, with the officers on its low bridge grinning and saluting goodbye to the accommodating 'Frenchies'.

"A bit too close for comfort," muttered Tremayne to the others, as they continued to make a pretence of busying themselves on deck, "but thank you all for the way you handled the situation."

Turning to Willoughby-Brown, he said, "Let's get the weapons back into the operations box, we'll soon be in Roscoff."

Checking that the prescribed orange recognition pennant was flying from the masthead in the cool early morning breeze, Tremayne ordered Quilghini to bear off five degrees to port, to mingle more closely with the now increasing fishing traffic moving in and out of Roscoff and neighbouring Carantec.

Twenty minutes later, under Quilghini's expert hands, *Vas-y-Voir* gently glided into Roscoff harbour.

Dulac was the first to spot the two Breton boats flying similar orange pennants.

"There they are, almost directly ahead of us, to the left of that big blue and brown crabber from Concarneau."

Tremayne and the others began to wave at the figures painting the hulls and working on the deck gear and rigging of the two Breton boats. They quickly responded, animatedly waving back and shouting greetings. For the benefit of two gendarmes and an accompanying German guard patrolling the harbour, Quilghini moved to the foredeck, grabbed the huge hand brace and, waving it aloft, shouted, "Le voila, mes amis!"

Even one of the glum-faced gendarmes was moved to smile at the noisy Rabelaisian exchange, which flowed between Quilghini and the fishermen working on their beached boats.

"Pure theatre. Wonderful stuff!" laughed Tremayne. "Thank you, Pierre. That should have established our credentials with the guards!"

Along with Willoughby-Brown and Quilghini, Tremayne paddled ashore in *Vas-y-Voir*'s rubber dinghy to the two Breton boats, maintaining a lively exchange with the crews for the continued benefit of the patrol, who were still within earshot.

As they approached the beach, willing hands grabbed their bow painter and drew them out of the water and up onto the sandy shore. Still keeping up the pretence of being close friends and workmates, there were a succession of bear hugs, as well as handshakes and considerable laughter.

One strong hand gripped Tremayne's and a very cultivated English voice said, "I'm Mike Black, SAS. It's so good to see you. Thank you for coming over for us – that is much appreciated."

Turning to a powerful, thick-set man with black curling hair, piercing dark eyes and a piratical moustache, Black said,

"And this is Paddy Nugent, my redoubtable sergeant."

Tremayne shook hands with both and quickly outlined the plan for evacuating them.

"We'll be deliberately paddling backwards and forwards to and from our boat, ferrying different people and odd bits of kit to maintain the illusion of busy repair work on your boats — and ours.

"During those various trips we will 'lose' you both and make sure that you're safe onboard *Vas-y-Voir*. In line with the typical movement of vessels in and out of Roscoff, we will then set sail and get you to Tresco as quickly as we can. Air cover from south Devon is on standby."

"That sounds marvellous — and thank you again. Now, can Sergeant Nugent and I offer you and your two colleagues some bread, cheese and coffee? You must be starving."

"Thanks, that sounds a great idea. We're absolutely famished. First, let me introduce David Willoughby-Brown, my First Lieutenant and Lieutenant Pierre Quilghini, late of the Marine Nationale, serving pro tem with the RNVR."

Within moments, conversation took off at maximum revolutions, as Black and Nugent recounted their exploits with the French Resistance in Brittany.

After their makeshift, but very welcome breakfast, the routines of apparent repair work and dinghy trips between *Vas-y-Voir* and the shore were quickly established.

The foot patrol passed close by again, but this time they stopped by the boats and one of the gendarmes came over to speak to Tremayne, who was helping to repair a damaged 'gallows' on the larger of the Breton boats.

"Our German colleague wants to look at your boats and talk with you. We'd like to bring him over to see you."

Quilghini stepped in immediately.

"Yes, I suppose so. I'm the skipper, by the way, but why does he want to come on board and talk with us?'

Tremayne, Willoughby-Brown and the two SAS men busied themselves with various tasks, but clearly the tension around the working party had increased considerably. Tremayne was only too conscious that all the weapons – including side arms – that they possessed, were still in the operations boxes onboard *Vas-y-Voir*.

The gendarme eased his sub-machine gun further over his shoulder before replying, "He's a former fisherman from Cuxhaven on the North Sea coast and he just wants to talk fishing and fishing boats. I think he's homesick."

"Bring him over and he can come and look over our boat while we carry on – some of our work is urgent and we don't want to be held up."

While the gendarme returned to his colleagues, Quilghini quickly briefed the four Britons, directing his comments to Tremayne.

"I suggest that you and Major Black grab some tools and a piece of timber and paddle back casually to *Vas-y-Voir* while WB and Sergeant Nugent stay here. That will reduce the odds of discovery by fifty per cent."

"Agreed."

Tremayne and Black unhurriedly loaded the dinghy with pieces of kit and timber, while one of the Breton fishermen talked animatedly at them and they grunted, or nodded, in response. As the patrol returned to the boats, Tremayne acknowledged their arrival with a casual wave and nod of the head and pushed off with Black for *Vas-y-Voir.*

The German corporal obviously had a genuine interest in the Breton fishermen and their boats and, with one of the gendarmes acting as interpreter, Quilghini, along with two genuine crew members, was able to put on a rapidly improvised but convincing tour of both beached boats.

Like many people from the North Sea coast of Germany, the corporal was an affable, rather serious individual who engaged in earnest discussion with his new hosts.

Clearly, as Quilghini discovered, the man was completely authentic and as a fisherman was simply grateful to re-establish contact with his temporarily interrupted trade and escape briefly from his role of Marine Fusilier. After what seemed like an interminable visit, the German thanked Quilghini and the crew members profusely and he and the security guards resumed their wandering patrol of the harbour area.

Over a period of about two hours – and following another passing visit from the guards – Black and Nugent were eventually secure onboard *Vas-y-Voir*, having been introduced to the weapons in the operations boxes. Sergeant Nugent, a small arms specialist with the SAS, was impressed by the Lanchester – a weapon he had heard of but never seen before – and its fifty-round magazine was an immediate hit with him. His strong Omagh accent meant that much of the praise that he heaped on the weapon was largely lost on Harberer and Dulac, who dutifully smiled and just hoped that they responded in the right way, each time they grunted a somewhat bewildered "yes" or "no".

About thirty minutes after a typically prolonged French lunch hour, when there began a noticeable increase in the movement of fishing vessels in and out of Roscoff, Tremayne ordered "Slip".

Vas-y-Voir turned her bluff, sturdy bow into the churning rollers as she began heading north-west at no more than ten knots to avoid attracting attention. Her return journey was obviously going to be undertaken in broad daylight, in clear weather, with the inevitable risks of being stopped and searched once she moved north into forbidden waters. The sunny, clear blue sky was patched here and there with white, fleecy stratocumulus clouds, edged with curved golden tips.

Tremayne addressed the crew and the two SAS guests: "We'll be monitored on radar by ship, shore establishments and aircraft and it's only a matter of time before Jerry comes looking for us.

Make sure there are at least four Bren guns to hand, plus the two PIATs and some Lanchesters. No doubt Sar'nt, you'd like to try one of those!"

"That I would, sir. It looks to be a rare ould weapon," came the grinning reply.

"Give me another ten miles or so from shore and you can test one from both the shoulder and the hip. Like you, Sar'nt, we're used to being in the company of enthusiastic professionals who know what they're about," smiled Tremayne.

After a further fifty minutes at reduced revolutions, Tremayne, standing aft by the net winch, called to Quilghini: "Full ahead both engines, Cox'n. Set course for Tresco. Let's go home!"

He next spoke to Sergeant Nugent. "Select a Lanchester, if you will, Sar'nt and try it out. Check that the mag is secure – that's also a substitute for'ard grip, although this weapon has a short traditional fore-end hand-hold!"

Nugent's normally serious expression dissolved into a boyish grin. "Thank you, sir."

Nugent checked the weapon first and then let fly, firing both from the shoulder and from the hip, occasionally shifting his stance and fine tuning his grip until he was completely at home with the weapon.

Black strolled over to Tremayne. "Paddy's as happy as a pig in shit, Richard. Thank you. Just look at his face! We've never seen these at close quarters before. They are certainly well made – with clever use of standard .303 Lee-Enfield woodwork – and so well balanced."

"Mike, take one each for yourself and Paddy and grab a dozen mags. Please accept them as 'lost in action' from naval stores!"

"Richard, thank you. We'd always heard that the Navy were marvellous hosts!"

A shout from Willoughby-Brown directed their attention to a large seaplane approaching at about three hundred feet above sea level.

"Looks like a Catalina, it's –"

He was cut off in mid-sentence by Able Seaman Harberer who yelled, "No! It's a Dornier 24 air-sea rescue and reconna-issance plane."

Tremayne immediately took charge.

"Reduce speed! Both engines, half ahead. Bren guns and PIATs to hand, but keep 'em covered. Look as if you are all working on deck. Thank you Harberer – well spotted. You and Dulac start hauling in our nets – make it look real."

Addressing Willoughby-Brown, at the boat's radio in the wheelhouse, Tremayne said, "Let's see what he does and monitor his wireless transmissions. It may soon be time to indulge your arcane literary tastes, Number One, and radio Devon that 'E'en the hordes of Tuscany could scarce forbear to cheer'. Hold fire for the moment and find out what our visitor is up to."

Turning to the two SAS men he said, "Mike, look like a busy deckhand. Sarn't, disappear below please, out of sight." Within seconds, the big, elegant seaplane roared over them, its duck-egg blue undersides contrasting with its upper dark green and black splinter camouflage. Harberer waved casually to the clearly visible gunner in the plane's perspex bow turret. "He may have seen how fast we were moving before we reduced speed, but in any case it looks as if he's about to take a keen interest in us and the course we are on. If he doesn't like what he sees, he'll call up some pretty lethal support to stop us." Black nodded in reply as Tremayne joined him in apparently sorting through the day's catch on the boat's after deck.

Moments later, the Dornier was back again and, this time, she slowly circled *Vas-y-Voir*, maintaining a distance of some three hundred yards before she turned and made another low pass over the fishing boat, but at much slower speed. Tremayne slipped into the wheelhouse between Willoughby-Brown and Quilghini, who was still at the wheel monitoring the gyrocompass.

"Have you picked up anything from Jerry, David?"

"Yes. He appears to be in touch with a Luftwaffe squadron rather than the Kriegsmarine. He mentioned our apparent speed and subsequent slowing down and he's concerned to know at what point we should alter course back to Brittany. He's...Wait — he's back on air!"

Willoughby-Brown quickly adjusted his earphones and leaned forward to concentrate on the seaplane's latest transmission with its base.

Seconds later, he reported, "Our friend has rumbled us and alerted a Zerstörergeschwader* which most likely means a very destructive visit from bomb-carrying Messerschmidt 110s. These fighter-bombers are also armed with 20mm cannon and they could be with us in fifteen to twenty minutes."

"David, radio both Godolphin and RAF Bolt Head immediately and tell them about Horatius emerging from the River Tiber. Give them our position and course and please add *urgent!*"

Tremayne called action stations and deployed the versatile Harberer to the engine room, with everyone else on deck apart from Quilghini, as coxswain, at the wheel.

"Check weapons and make sure that there are plenty of mags within reach. When they do attack, they'll come in low, so aim just *ahead* of their noses, when abeam or overhead."

Calling to Quilghini, Tremayne added, "Zigzag like fury on command. First with the port engine at half revolutions and starboard one at full throttle, then reverse the process. From David's report, it seems likely that they'll send two Me 110s to deal with a boat of this size. This means that we've

* *Luftwaffe destroyer squadron*

probably got to dodge up to eight 220-pound bombs when they close on us."

Black selected both a Bren gun and a PIAT, as did Paddy Nugent, while the others kept Brens and Lanchesters to hand. *Vas-y-Voir* continued to punch her way through the rolling leaden-grey seas of the Channel at maximum revolutions, while Tremayne and his First Lieutenant constantly scoured the horizon for signs of aircraft – friendly or otherwise.

They didn't have to wait long. Willoughby-Brown's sharp ears and eyes soon picked up sight and sound of the two marauders. Coming in at not much above mast height, they were approaching their target at over three hundred miles an hour. Those on deck grabbed weapons and began to take up firing positions, finding what cover they could behind equipment, companionways and other fixtures scattered about the fishing boat's wooden-planked decking.

The leading Messerschmidt opened fire with its formidable fuselage nose armament of 20mm cannon and 7.92mm machine guns at a range of around three hundred yards.

Seconds later, the second aircraft began firing and released two bombs, as Quilghini violently zigzagged the boat, his half- and full-throttle use of the engines causing her to turn sharply and suddenly at almost ninety degrees.

Those on deck returned fire, swinging weapons as the aircraft roared overhead. Black and Nugent fired their PIATs but missed, though Tremayne and the other Bren gunners clearly registered hits on both planes. The first two bombs exploded harmlessly in the sea, drenching those firing at the two Messerschmidts.

As the aircraft rapidly flew out of range, prior to turning for a second strafing run, Black grinned ruefully at Tremayne.

"Sorry we missed, Richard, but I think that Paddy and I have cracked it. We fired the damned things too late to hit square on."

Both had already fitted fresh projectiles to the launchers and were making ready for the next attack.

Tremayne quickly checked that there were no casualties, although the fishing net winches and the 'gallows' had been shot to pieces by the heavier 20mm rounds, and part of the wheelhouse roof had also been blown away in the first burst of fire.

Tremayne managed a quick, but heartfelt, "Well done, everyone. Thank you," just as the Germans turned and began their second run against *Vas-y-Voir*. Quilghini began zigzagging again, alternating with short curving surges, at maximum revolutions, while Tremayne and the others checked magazines and lined up their weapons on the rapidly closing Messerschmidts. First to fire was Tremayne, who quickly emptied thirty rounds of .303 into the approaching aircraft. Splinters from the boat's starboard bulwark, being shredded by the incoming rounds, flew past his head before several hit and gashed his face. A shrill, agonised cry somewhere to his right, told him that someone on deck had been hit as cannon shells and bullets raked the boat from stern to stem.

Concentrating on the destruction of the two planes, he even had time to put a fresh magazine in the Bren and continued firing into the underbelly of the nearer aircraft, as the pair roared low overhead.

Three rapid explosions in the sea, one very close to *Vas-y-Voir*'s port bow, confirmed that Quilghini's boat handling and evasive tactics were still ensuring their survival.

Suddenly, there was a blinding flash of light, a loud explosion and thick black smoke which began pouring from the further of the two aircraft.

"Got him!" yelled Black. "Paddy, old son, we've got the bastard!"

Tremayne looked across at the two laughing soldiers, who were shaking hands, and shouted,

"Bloody well done, SAS. We'll make sailors of you yet!"

The stricken Messerschmidt had been hit by at least one PIAT missile and, as it exploded and broke up in mid air, its front section, containing the two-man crew, suddenly veered to the left and dived out of control into the sea.

Willoughby-Brown, who had just finished emptying his Bren magazine into the disappearing, surviving aircraft, shouted, "Our escort has arrived! Three Beaufighters coming in low on the port beam. They're —"

Quickly he broke off and yelled, his voice full of urgency, "Dulac's down," as he rushed across to the after companionway where the still, bloodied figure of the young French able seaman lay crumpled on the deck. Close to Dulac's head, a large pool of blood was slowly spreading across the scrubbed teak planks.

Tremayne waved briefly to acknowledge the Beaufighters' arrival and then, with Black and Nugent, ran over to Dulac who had now been joined by his anxious-looking compatriot, Able Seaman Harberer.

Nugent, a trained medic, was first on the scene and quickly examined Dulac's injuries.

Looking up at the gathering group, he said, "There's no head wound, but his right shoulder and upper arm are a bit of a mess. He's been hit by at least two MG rounds, both of which appear to have gone right through him. Luckily, they weren't the 20mm shells. I'll give him a shot of morphine and clean up – and dress – his wounds."

Addressing Tremayne, he said, "He'll need hospital treatment and possibly some surgery. Will you radio ahead, sir, to let them know that we have a seriously wounded casualty?"

"Of course, Sar'nt. Thank you for your prompt action in helping Dulac."

Willoughby-Brown had summarised the sergeant's diagnosis and treatment, in French, for a much relieved Harberer, whose rumbustious relationship with Dulac put Tremayne in mind of a Gallic version of the unholy partnership between Watkins and Nicholls.

Turning back to Tremayne, after he had applied a dressing to Dulac's cleaned wounds, Nugent said, "I think, sir, I ought to look at your wounds. You've got a nasty gash on your cheek."

On the point of protesting, Tremayne was cut short by Black, who said very quietly,

"Best let him have his way with you, Richard. That could turn septic and Paddy does know what he's doing."

"You're right, Mike. I'm only just beginning to acknowledge to myself that I'm not immortal!"

Grinning at Nugent, Tremayne said, "Right Sar'nt, do your worst – I won't pass out on you!"

The preoccupation with Dulac's injuries meant the surviving German fighter-bomber had been temporarily forgotten and it had been taken as a matter of course that three Beaufighters would quickly see off a Me 110 – which proved to be the case.

With Nugent's wound dressing on his face, Tremayne resumed command of the fishing boat and set course for Tresco. With both engines on 'full ahead', they made it back to Braiden Rock anchorage at around 19.20 hours. En route, they had been joined by a protective escort of Fischer and Taylor, some thirty miles south-east of Scilly. Tresco and neighbouring Bryher had rarely looked more welcomingly beautiful, mused

Tremayne, as *Vas-y-Voir* secured on what had turned out to be a glorious early summer evening.

Tremayne took Black and Nugent to Enever for immediate debriefing, prior to supper and, subsequently, their journey up to London to meet officials from SOE and SIS.

Later that same evening, Tremayne handed a wrapped brown paper parcel to Enever with a conspiratorial smile.

"One ancient Millers Falls jack plane — used, but in imm-aculate condition, sir!"

"Dear boy, how can I thank you enough?"

Like a child with a new toy, Enever lovingly ran his hands over the ancient trophy which, despite its age, was clearly still capable of being used for serious carpentry. "Although it must date from the end of the last century, the cutting edge of the iron is still as sharp as a razor. Someone has certainly looked after it and I'll maintain the same tender loving care, Richard!"

Black had brought back information about coastal defences in Normandy, above and below the sea surface, of incalculable value. He had also up-to-date intelligence of the latest deployment of German troops and armour within the areas immediately inland from the coast. Along with the inform-ation transmitted by radio by the Confrèrie, such data would prove to be vital intelligence within the next few days.

During the weeks following the invasion, as the Allies inevitably consolidated their initial foothold, bringing in continuous reinforcements, replacement ammunition and fresh equipment, knowledge of German underwater obstacles would remain a vital issue.

Operation Overlord – the invasion of France, involving the greatest armada the world had ever seen, was now scheduled to begin in just two days' time...

Eleven

Invasion!

T he Confrérie Bonaparte — and French Resistance in general — had just received the crucial message personnel, informing them that the invasion was imminent, in the shape of Verlaine's haunting couplet —

'Les sanglots longs des violons de l'automne
Blessent mon cœur d'une langueur monotone'

For many of them, too, it would now become a time for concerted activity in support of the Allied landings on the beaches of Normandy and the airborne drops just inland from the coast.

It was estimated that there were many thousands of Maquisards and Free French fighters waiting to step up their campaigns of harassment and sabotage against the Germans. Tremayne knew, from SOE reports, that in Brittany alone there were some twenty thousand such Resistance members, all of whom were armed in readiness to raise their game once the balloon went up.

The designated invasion area covered close to one hundred miles of the Normandy coast, with five code-named stretches of beach.

The so-called Omaha and Utah beaches lay to the west, where the US army would land. Next to Utah, lying immediately to the east, was Gold, where the British XXX Corps would attack; then came Juno, the beach where a combined force of Canadians and British were due to land. At the eastern edge of the invasion was Sword Beach where the British, together with Commandant Kieffer's French Commandos de la Marine, would storm ashore.

At 02.00 hours on the morning of the sixth of June 1944, Tremayne and his crew were on station off Sword Beach, protecting COPP observation teams already in the water and there to act as one of the protective lookout MTBs on the invasion armada's left flank.

The approach to the shore had been hazardous due to the many underwater obstacles and Tremayne had been guided in by the shielded blue flashlights of the COPPists. Even in the pitch blackness of the night, the menacing stakes were visible by torchlight because of the state of the tide and it required a considerable degree of careful manoeuvring by Irvine before MTB1801 was fully on station, close inshore.

Alongside Tremayne and his First Lieutenant on the bridge stood a completely absorbed Commander Enever, relishing the anticipation of forthcoming action.

Tremayne smiled to himself as he saw the unlit pipe clamped even more firmly than usual between Enever's teeth, and the binoculars around his neck as he eagerly awaited the first glimmerings of dawn to lighten the black sky. Next to Enever, imperturbable as ever, Petty Officer Irvine stood silently, one hand on the wheel, the other holding a mug of hot kye, laced with rum, brought by the ever-provident Watkins.

Leading Seaman Nicholls, watchkeeping on the bow, called out softly to Tremayne.

"Sir. Three blue flashes from the COPPist. Looks like they've finished, sir."

"Thank you Nicholls. Let's get them back on board and hear what they have to say. Lower a scrambling net and chuck 'em a line."

Tremayne spoke to Enever. "Sir, would you like to join me while I quiz our COPPists to see what they've discovered?"

"Wild horses wouldn't keep me away, dear boy!"

Sergeant Kane, the NCO COPPist, delivered a positive, detailed operator's report. Despite the rain, the strong offshore southwesterly wind and cold, black rolling sea, the prevailing water conditions confirmed a clear run in for the ungainly, flat-bottomed landing craft and the duplex-drive amphibious tanks which would provide close support for the commandos and infantry. Underwater obstacles, large enough to impede the final run-in of the beach assault, would need to be negotiated by the landing craft coxswains, but the state of tide would still make the tops of such obstructions visible.

Enever was intrigued by the technical details and keen to learn more about the COPPists' beach surveillance tactics. Tremayne withdrew, with a broad smile, back to the bridge, leaving him and Sergeant Kane locked in deep conversation – absorbed with sub-aquatic technicalities and some of the more arcane aspects of beach geology.

At around 03.00, the softening-up aerial bombardment of the beach defences began. Tremayne and the others on deck watched, fascinated, as the multiple flashes of both bombs and returning anti-aircraft fire lit up the coast from one end to the other like an enormous, but lethal firework display.

On Sword Beach alone, something like 29,000 men and their equipment were due to begin landing in just over another four hours. Across all five designated invasion beaches, close to 160,000 Allied troops would be disgorging from landing craft. It was imperative that they met with as little resistance as possible as they struggled through the water to the shore from the lowered ramps of their LCIs, weighed down with up to eighty pounds of equipment.

To create the necessary harbour installations required to maintain the flow of supplies needed by the invasion force, nearly 150 Mulberry harbour units had to be ferried across the Channel for erection on the Normandy beaches. Transporting this vast array of supporting equipment required some three thousand tugs, trawlers and other small boats.

Facing the commandos and infantry due to storm Sword Beach was the German 716th Division, commanded by Lieutenant General Wilhelm Richter. Short of top quality manpower, the German divisions defending the five Normandy beaches contained many second-rate troops, including units of former Russian prisoners who had opted to fight for Germany rather than endure the impossibly harsh conditions of the PoW camps. While such soldiers were capable of fighting well, they were also likely to surrender or desert at the first opportunity.

In anticipation of the increased visibility during the Allies' aerial attack, Tremayne had ordered Irvine to turn the MTB 'bow on' towards the shore and hold her station, in order to minimise her profile to the Germans manning the scattered coastal defence batteries and observation posts.

"Looking smart as paint, bristling with weapons and clearly up to no good, she makes an easy and ideal target for some gunner out to make a name for himself," Tremayne told Irvine.

Over the next few hours, the invasion fleet began to assemble and move into position, in readiness for the beach assaults. As the early June dawn broke and the sky noticeably lightened, Tremayne called his crew up on deck to witness the awesome spectacle of the gathering armada of warships and landing craft. In all, some 6,900 vessels were involved along the one hundred mile-front and Enever, emphasising the sheer size of the approaching warship fleet, said,

"They'll provide close support bombardment for the landing craft, which will be absolutely terrifying for Jerry. It's one thing to face field artillery, but ships' weapons are of a much greater calibre. Being on the receiving end of a sustained naval bombardment of fifteen-inch shells is a very different kettle of fish, I can tell you."

Like an enthusiastic schoolboy at the Navy's Annual Fleet Review, Enever began identifying the warships accompanying the landing craft heading for Sword Beach.

"Aha, now there's *Ramilles* – oh, and the good old *Warspite.* She was at Jutland with Jellicoe, y'know. Pretty old now, yet still impressive ships of war – they're virtually *Dreadnought*-era battleships. Heavens! The monitor *Roberts* is there too. Good Lord! Shades of colonialism and gun-boats sent up rivers to quell the locals, gentlemen!"

Raising his binoculars and placing his pipe on the parapet of the bridge, he continued.

"Off Sword Beach we have, I believe, five cruisers in support.

I can just make out *Mauritius, Arethusa, Frobisher*... and *Danai*. Ah, and one other I don't recognise... Yes! Wait one... I've got her! She's the *Dragon* — a Polish cruiser."

Willoughby-Brown grinned as he whispered conspiratorially to Tremayne, "I'll wager he was a trainspotter when he was a lad!"

In addition to the larger warships that Enever had identified, Tremayne counted at least a dozen destroyers moving in on Sword Beach in support of the landings.

At 07.25 hours, the deafening naval bombardment began and fifteen-inch, eight-inch, six-inch and four-inch shells began to tear into the German defences and coastal positions — uprooting trees, churning up the earth and wrecking bunkers. The noise and sheer impact of the thousands of high explosive shells were awesome.

"It's impossible to imagine anyone living through a bombardment like that and those that do almost have the *right* to go mad," said Willoughby-Brown, as he tightened the strap of his steel helmet.

Then, as Tremayne and the others on deck watched, the landing craft surged forward for the final beach assault. The invasion had begun.

German resistance had been seriously reduced by the naval bombardment but, seemingly against all odds, some gun emplacements remained intact and fire began to be directed onto the incoming landing craft and warships.

By 07.30 hours, the first British units were ashore on Sword Beach. These were the duplex-drive amphibious tanks of the 13th/18th Hussars, followed immediately by the infantry of the 8th Brigade. As the second wave – Brigadier, the Lord Lovat's First Special Service Brigade, consisting of various commando units, including 41 and 45 Royal Marine Commandos – began to wade ashore, they were accompanied by Lovat's own personal piper, Bill Millin, playing the stirring march, Hieland Laddie.

Suddenly, without warning, Tremayne's MTB was hit low in her hull several times. As if from nowhere, a volley of shells tore into her, holing her above and below her waterline. Some battery, lying just inland from the beach, had found 1801's range, along with those of many vessels flying anti-aircraft barrage balloons, which acted as aerial ranging markers for the German gunners. Visible, alone and yet sufficiently close to other vessels, she was a vulnerable and ready-made target.

Rapidly, the Vosper began to take in water and, within minutes, had developed a dangerous list to port. Tremayne ordered, "Abandon ship!" having ensured that the boat's dinghy and Carley floats were freed and ready for use. Using his loudhailer, Tremayne called out to his crew above the din of battle: "We'll regroup on the beach with the naval Beach Master. Good luck everyone!"

They struggled and slid off the deck, which was already awash, and scrambled either into the Carley floats or the rubber dinghy. Grabbing paddles, they began to make for the shore some two hundred yards ahead. Quickly establishing the coordinated rhythm necessary for maximum speed in the swelling, choppy sea, they paddled furiously for the shoreline. Just ahead of them, still wading through the final stretch of shallow water, were 'Shimi' Lovat's commandos, wearing their green berets rather than their steel helmets. Twenty-one-year-old Bill Millin changed the tune and began piping that fine old marching song *The Road to the Isles*.

As he struggled to paddle though the choppy surf, the tune, so familiar in Tremayne's childhood, seemed to lend rhythm and strength to his arms and he found himself very quietly singing the words his mother had taught him twenty or more years ago —

'The far Cuillins are pulling me away,

As tak' I wi' my crummack to the road.

The far Cuillins are puttin' love on me,

As step I wi' the sunlight for my load —'

Just about to hum the chorus, he was cut short by an off-key, adenoidal outburst from a grinning Watkins, paddling opposite him across the Carley float —

'With a sporran full of porridge and a caber up my kilt,

I'm in a bit of a tangle with m' piles —'

"Watkins, I'm convinced that you're a man without a soul. You've just ruined a wonderful, moving piece of music!"

"Sorry sir! But yo'm right about the lack of soul, sir — my missus often tells me that!"

Amused at the egalitarian exchange between officer and rating, the rest of the paddlers took up the tune as Piper Millin continued to pump out the rousing march at the head of the column. Quickly gaining the sandy shore, the crew of the now slowly disappearing MTB turned with Tremayne, for a moment, to salute her. Then, joining the end of Lovat's Special Service Brigade, marched up, under continuing small arms fire, to find the RN Beach Master. Miraculously, neither Lord Lovat nor his piper — both in prominent positions — had been hit, although several bodies lay still, as if sleeping, on the beach, while some of the wounded struggled to find what shelter they could.

Yards in front of them, a commando suddenly collapsed like a rag doll onto the sand, shot through the head. As Tremayne, almost simultaneously, spotted the Beach Master, an anguished cry — "Oh, NO — NOT *YOU*, mate," rang out behind him. He quickly turned to see Leading Seaman Nicholls lying on the beach, blood pouring from a wound in his chest, and a distraught Watkins bending over him, his face suddenly pale from shock. Painfully and slowly, Nicholls reached up and took Watkins's hand. "Cheers, Pablo, old mate. It's been -" Then, as the light seemed suddenly to fade from his normally lively, alert eyes, he fell silent.

Discarding the protocols of rank, Tremayne put his hand on Watkins's shoulder, who was now sobbing uncontrollably, and said quietly, "I'm so sorry, Pablo. I know what close mates you and Brummie are. Better keep moving now. I'm afraid we're making too good a target here. We'll look after Brummie for you."

Urgently, Tremayne called over a commando medic who looked closely at Nicholls, checked for any sign of a pulse and then slowly shook his head.

"I'm afraid he's a gonner, sir. I'm so sorry. There's nothing else I can do for this one, sir."

Motioning Irvine over from the shocked and silent group, Tremayne said, "Look after Watkins please, Cox'n. Get him over to the Beach Master where we'll regroup, out of that bloody sniper's line of sight."

With a tenderness that seemed incongruous with his customary tough, dour demeanour, the grizzled coxswain gently separated Nicholls and the utterly distressed Watkins. Willoughby-Brown and Leading Yeoman of Signals Jenkins, with a caring approaching reverence, carefully, but quickly, carried the dead rating towards the safety of the area ahead.

As they moved off, Tremayne, like the others, tried to come to terms with Nicholls's sudden and unexpected death. How many times during the last two years had they stood together on the bridge of an MGB or MTB? How often had he laughed at the irreverent banter and exchanges of scathing, caustic Brummagem wit as Watkins and Nicholls ribbed each other so unmercifully?

Without the unfailingly dependable Nicholls, it would be a very different boat crew, mused Tremayne.

By now, the redoubtable Millin had switched to *Blue Bonnets*. Spirits lifted somewhat and the pace sharpened, as the repetitive, insistent rhythm of the old Borders march carried across the wide stretch of beach, galvanising weary, sea-drenched legs – and now heavy hearts – into renewed action. How often, thought Tremayne, as his feet responded compulsively to the powerful beat, have Scottish and Irish pipers inspired and rallied British troops in battle? And how often has the sound of approaching pipes meant hope to the besieged and beleaguered – and terror to the enemy?

More figures in green berets dropped as snipers' bullets struck home, but the column as a whole was, at last, close to reaching the comparative safety of 'dead' ground, well out of sight of their concealed tormentors.

Ahead of them, and a few yards to the right, Tremayne could see the tall handsome figure of 'Shimi' Lovat, still striding purposefully forward, wearing his green beret and a somewhat incongruous white, roll-neck submariner's woollen jersey. In his right hand was an elegant bolt-action hunting rifle with a beautifully figured walnut stock – seemingly more suited to stalking or sniping than the sustained exchanges of a firefight.

Undoubtedly, conceded Tremayne, Lovat was an inspirational leader, whose men worshipped him and took great pride in his eccentricities. His very individualism and uniqueness made him the archetypal Special Forces leader and inspired great confidence in those under his command.

His commandos would follow him to hell and back. Brigadier, the Lord Lovat represented the very best among the élites of competence, mused Tremayne. Though very much his own man, he acknowledged the supreme value of teamwork on the field of battle.

A sudden gasp at his side, followed by a shocked, "Oh, dear boy, I've been hit," caused Tremayne to turn in anguish to see a white-faced Enever crumple slowly to the ground, his hand clutching at his left shoulder. Tremayne was immediately joined by Willoughby-Brown who took off his khaki battledress blouse, folded it and placed it carefully under Enever's head.

Tremayne immediately gave the SNIO a shot of morphine, having opened up his battledress top and gently cut it away from his wounded shoulder with his fighting knife. He next applied a wound dressing and pressed it well home to staunch the flow of blood.

"We'll soon have you in capable hands, John, and we'll get you off the beach just as quickly as we can."

"So sorry to be such a confounded nuisance, Richard," he muttered, "and only a few damn feet from safety — just as I thought I was beginning to get into the swing of things." Concerned not to provide an even more tempting static target, Willoughby-Brown called two medics over who quickly placed Enever on a stretcher. As rapidly as possible, the party began moving again with Tremayne trotting alongside Enever, talking calmly to reassure him and replace the sudden unnerving shock of the wound with some degree of normality. Enever proved to be an admirable patient, uncomplaining and accepting of his lot, despite the abrupt end to his venture on French soil. An anxious and concerned Tremayne stayed with him a few moments longer, before the medics transferred Enever to the temporary, makeshift field hospital which had so efficiently and quickly been set up by the army.

"I'll be back with you just as soon as I can, John," said Tremayne, as the burly, bear-like naval Beach Master – a commander, RN sporting an enormous black beard – called him over.

"Right, Lieutenant Commander, I want you bloody lot off this beach as soon as maybe. You're in the way here and you've been attracting sniper fire – the same as that bloody Scotsman making a noise like a vixen on heat. Who the hell are you by the way?"

"Lieutenant Commander Tremayne, Tresco flotilla comm-ander, sir. Clearly Lord Lovat views his piper rather differently from you, sir, but I'll get my men out of your way. I do have one man shot dead by sniper fire and he will need to be buried. We are a close-knit MTB team and we would want one of our own to have a proper burial, sir."

The Beach Master's craggy, lived-in features softened for a moment. "I can understand that, Tremayne. Eight hundred yards up for'ard and to the right is a small village church and cemetery. I'll talk to our own padre, who will organise things with the local priest once the area has been fully secured.

Meanwhile, the medics will look after your dead and wounded."

He paused and turned to roar at a Commando Heavy Weapons Section, struggling to drag a 125-pound, three-inch mortar up into an area of cover free from sniper fire. "You idle, bloody bootnecks, get a move on there and clear off the beach with that blasted lump of gas piping!" Returning to Tremayne, he gave a conspiratorial wink before saying, with some urgency, "At the moment, part of the column – a group of Royal Marines from 45 Commando – appears to be pinned down beyond that low ridge over there. Perhaps you and your lads could give them a bit of a hand till we get things sorted. Lord Lovat is taking the rest of the Brigade on, inland, to link up with some airborne chaps holding a bridge a few miles from here."

Pointing to a slowly increasing pile of weapons on a ground-sheet covering a small area of sand, he added, "There are some rifles and a few Thompsons and Brens – plus ammunition – collected from the dead and wounded. Grab some of those and get going."

He stopped for a moment. "Oh and Tremayne, I'll get you back in touch with your HQ by radio just as soon as I can." He held out his hand. "Good luck, lad!"

Tremayne shook the bluff yet benign Beach Master's outstretched hand and saluted him, "Thank you, sir."

Quickly returning to organise his ten remaining crew members into the temporary equivalent of a Commando Rifle Section, Tremayne saw that Willoughby-Brown had intelligently anticipated the order and had instructed the group to arm themselves. Grabbing rifles and Thompson guns, plus ammunition pouches, the MTB crew were already assembled, ready to advance to contact and join the troops ahead, fighting to open out the beachhead.

Having found the Bren gun he was looking for and a dozen magazines, Tremayne resumed command and rapidly moved up his section to place them alongside a troop from 45 Commando. Watkins, he saw, was now much more composed as he carefully checked the magazine and action of the Thompson gun he had selected. Catching Tremayne's eye, the obviously grief-stricken Watkins said quietly, "With this one, sir, I should be able to get enough of the bastards for Brummie."

The commando troop commander, a stocky major armed with a Sten gun and with his face blacked up with camouflage cream, quickly came over and shook Tremayne's hand. "Hello, thanks for joining us! Let me put you in the picture with a swift sit-rep.

"We're pinned down by a couple of mutually supporting MG posts and a rifle company, dug in along the higher ground about a hundred yards to our front. We've just received our mortar, which will help, but we need to get in much closer to those two damned MG nests. We've made several attempts already and taken rather too many casualties. Any help that you and your sailors can give us will be very welcome."

"We've all been commando trained to one degree or another,

and several of us have been in small raiding parties and had some experience of firefights," replied Tremayne.

That's a *real* bonus – I didn't expect that. I'll call my Number Two and my section commanders for a swift 'O' Group and we'll sort out a way to break the stalemate. By the way, I'm David Whitely."

"Richard Tremayne – I'm delighted to meet you. Before you hold your 'O' Group, David, just run me up to a point where I can actually see the MG bunkers and the trenches where Jerry is dug in."

"Sure. Keep your head down and follow me. Stop – and drop – when I do!"

Crawling the last few yards, they reached a low stone wall covered in lichen, sea thrift and other small seashore plants, behind which about thirty marine commandos crouched. Small apertures cut through the wall by the commandos and carefully concealed by well-draped foliage, allowed the assault party to keep the Germans under observation. Direct frontal attack, Tremayne could see, would be suicidal. There had to be another way...

Turning to Whitely, Tremayne asked, "How many Brens do you have and can your mortar put down plenty of smoke?"

"In answer to your first question – we have four, plus yours, of course. The second answer is yes -we can put down a fair volume of smoke pretty quickly."

"Good, then I think we may have a solution. Let's explore

a few ideas before you call up your people. We should work on the principle that when people expect you to come through the door and you suddenly come in through the wall, the immediate initiative is yours – but you must exploit it at once."

"Hmm, sounds intriguing! What would you see as 'the wall' here, Richard?"

"Looking at the lie of the land, I reckon that we can assault from both flanks simultaneously if we split our combined force into three and, first, put down a heavy smokescreen to our front so that Jerry thinks we are going in through that in a head-on *frontal* attack. Figuratively speaking, that is 'the door' – the *expected* route.

"We then back this up with concentrated mortar and small arms fire, directed at the MG bunkers and the rifle company positions – spiced up with plenty of rifle grenades at the latter to create shock, disorientate and to keep heads down. This should reinforce the deception."

Tremayne paused. "Making sense, David?"

"Sure."

Tremayne continued, "Thirdly, outflank their positions, taking a wide enough sweep to avoid detection and, when in a position to assault, keep their heads down with two Brens per bunker – and well-aimed rifle fire – concentrating on their firing slits. Make the final assault rapidly, in short rushes, with Thompsons and grenades – grabbing what cover we can. That, if you will, is 'the wall', the unexpected element in the fight."

Tremayne stopped briefly again, to confirm that his plan was receiving acceptance.

"At *this* stage, your mortars should concentrate solely on their rifle company, until the two sections dealing with the bunkers are free to swing round to attack them. This must be a coordinated assault, together with the section that fired, in support of the decoy smokescreen."

"Hmm. I like it: it has possibilities. Coordinating the different stages of the operation, with three sections moving in from different directions instead of the customary two in a classical flank attack, will be a challenge. Let's go with it, Richard, and get the lads in for the 'O' Group to see their reaction and what they can add."

Whitely grinned, his black camouflage cream emphasising the whiteness of his teeth. "You know – for a sailor – you'd make a bloody good marine commando!"

Lieutenant Mike Farran, Whitely's second-in-command – another short, wiry and fit-looking marine – appeared, together with a sergeant and two corporals, for the troop commander's 'O' Group.

Whitely then rapidly outlined Tremayne's proposed plan of attack on the German positions. He was concerned to gauge his marines' reaction to it before going into the detail, which he wanted them to be closely involved in working out.

The plan appealed to them. The areas of concern that they raised were that timing and coordination were paramount, that there must be sufficient smoke to hide the fact that the frontal attack was only a feint assault, and that fire aimed at the MG bunker firing slits must be accurate in order to keep the German machine-gunners' heads down.

Integrating Tremayne's blue-jacket 'infantry' into the commando troop, Whitely split the newly enlarged group into three reconstituted sections.

The largest section, armed with the mortar, would feign the major frontal attack, another would assault one MG bunker, and Tremayne's naval party – with the addition of two commandos – would eliminate the other.

On Whitely's command, the mortar crew began dropping smoke bombs to form a dense screen of thick, billowing dark grey smoke in front of the German rifle company's trench and foxhole system. Accompanying heavy small arms fire was immediately directed at the defenders, including volleys of high explosive rifle-grenades. On the left flank, Whitely led one assault group to silence the MG42, while Tremayne led his group forward to deal with the machine-gun bunker situated on sloping ground to the right.

Scrambling and crawling over the rough grass-covered terrain, the naval group were quickly in position to assault the bunker, without having so far been seen. Tremayne set up his two Bren guns and a rifle section of five men to provide covering fire and to deter the machine-gunners from raising their heads in order to sight and fire their weapons. Taking

Watkins and the two marines who had been attached to his team, he wormed his way forward, making the most of available cover, until the four of them were about ten yards from the bunker. On his signal, a devastating fire was directed to the bunker's gun apertures. The din was deafening and must have been terrifyingly disorientating for those inside. Chips of concrete were blasted off the aperture edges and sprayed around viciously within the confined space of the bunker.

Tremayne signalled those firing at the apertures to continue shooting – to maintain the noise level – but to lift their sights and fire over the bunkers to avoid hitting the assault party, now ready to move in from the flank.

"Right Watkins, now is your moment! Get down flat as soon as you've chucked your grenades in."

Accompanied by one of the marines, also carrying grenades, Watkins crawled forward the remaining few yards and raised himself up against the bunker wall, before lobbing two grenades through the nearest aperture. "For you Brummie, old mate." The marine with him quickly slipped his two grenades through the next firing slit of the bunker.

The muffled explosions, accompanied by dense black smoke pouring out of the apertures, were immediately followed by screams and then an unearthly moaning.

Tremayne rushed forward to the bunker entrance, kicked open the door – now hanging on just one hinge, and fired short bursts into each of the three bodies lying on the floor.

Having congratulated his section – and especially Watkins and the marine – he quickly reformed the group to move down to assault the rifle company's position. He looked over to Whitely's section to be greeted by a 'thumbs up' and a confident grin from the marine major, who indicated that they should attack the German line of defences simultaneously, from both directions. By now, the once thick smoke in front of the foxholes and trench was slowly beginning to dissipate. It was possible for the commandos who had been firing through the billowing grey screen to pick out the stealthy, but fast advance of both flank sections, about to join battle with the German rifle company.

Using the classical 'fire and movement' tactics, which have served infantrymen so well for generations, Whitely and Tremayne each placed Bren guns in positions to give covering fire.

On Whitely's shouted command, their respective sections charged into the trench system. Yelling wildly, they caught the occupants by surprise from both sides at once. To capitalise upon the sudden shock, they hurled both explosive and deadly phosphorous grenades into the packed trench. Bursts of automatic fire confirmed where the Thompsons were being used as 'trench brooms' and frantic, hideous screams identified where bayonets were at work in what had instantly become the desperate, bloody mêlée typical of brutal close-quarter battle.

Next, Farran's section moved up, at the charge, from the original start line and, within seconds, it was all over apart from the resolute independent actions of a few scattered, short-lived heroes. With raised hands and ashen, bewildered faces, the survivors moved off shocked, shuffling and stumbling under guard, to a small temporary stores compound surrounded by barbed wire.

"Even I can recognise that they're not speaking German," said Whitely, "who the hell are these people?"

Willoughby-Brown, who had more than a smattering of the language said, "They're Russians, sir.

"That explains why they gave up so quickly as fortunes turned in what, after all, is someone else's fight for them."

Whitely then held out his hand to Tremayne. "Richard, thank you so much – I owe you. It means we can now move on to join the rest of 'Shimi' Lovat's Brigade and head for the River Orne, where we are to relieve some airborne fellows who landed last night and are holding a vital bridge. I wish you and your sailors good luck – you are a bloody great bunch to be with!"

With Tremayne's good wishes following him, Whitely rejoined his already marching commandos at the double as they began to disappear round rising ground. Briefly he turned, smiling, to give a final salute in farewell.

Tremayne grinned as the departing marine commandos' raucous voices burst into the servicemen's own version of the tune *Colonel Bogey* from behind the grass-covered slope –

'Hitler – he only 'ad one ball

Goering 'ad two, but very small
Himmler was very similar
But poor old Goebbels
'Ad no balls at all!'

He visualised the now vanished marines swinging along with jaunty step, flushed with victory, as their irreverent refrain slowly faded from earshot –

'Bollocks – and the same to you.

Bollocks, we're gonna see it through...'

"Our casualties were remarkably light," said Willoughby-Brown, cutting across Tremayne's brief reverie. "One dead and three wounded. Able Seaman Edwards, who had just joined us from Maurice Simmonds's boat, was killed in the final assault, which is also when gun crew 'Lofty' Weeks and 'Knocker' White were wounded – but not seriously, thank goodness. Both are being looked after by the medics."

"Thanks David, I'll catch up with them in the field hospital later. First, let's gather in the flock and I will talk to them."

Tremayne addressed his significantly depleted group to thank them for the way they had fought so professionally against a well-sited and heavily armed enemy. "You all showed yourselves to good account in front of our bootneck friends – and in the sort of close-quarter battle in which they are highly-skilled specialists. You did more than was asked of you. Good as they certainly are, the Royals would not have succeeded, as quickly and completely as they did, without your courage, fighting ability and determination."

Looking at his watch, he concluded, "Dinner should be ready in about thirty minutes at the field kitchen that the Army have set up for us. It'll be more like Aggie Weston's than the Ritz, lads, but I think you'll find it very welcome. I'll be... *what* in hell's name is going on?"

Tremayne had been interrupted by a woman screaming and shouting at the Russian prisoners, dramatically waving a pistol at them as they shuffled nervously, still in shock, around the compound.

Several British junior officers working on the beach, who were remonstrating with her, were being contemptuously ignored. One, more assertive than the others and who had persisted in protesting, suddenly found himself staring down the barrel of the Makarov pistol thrust savagely into his face.

"Sod this for a game of soldiers. Enough's enough. I'll put a stop to this bloody nonsense. Come with me David – your knowledge of Russian might come in handy."

With a Thompson gun still in his hand, Tremayne strode over to the woman, whom he now saw wore some sort of uniform jacket, a dark skirt and Soviet army officers' issue, polished long leather boots.

"YOU!" Tremayne spoke harshly. "What the hell do you think you are doing?"

"Ah, more British stupidity. I am Major Elizaveta Orlova of the NKVD, national security and counter-intelligence. These are former Soviet soldiers who have acted as traitors by fighting for the Germans. They will be moved from here immediately to face trial and execution. The local Communist Resistance Group and I will take care of that."

"You will do no such bloody thing, Major. They are *my* prisoners and under *my* care – and that's how they will stay until the British Army send them to official PoW camps, which are being set up right now. Do I make myself clear?"

Orlova whipped round furiously to confront Tremayne and viciously pushed her pistol right into his face. White with anger, Tremayne deliberately dropped his Tommy gun to the ground. As the Soviet agent's eyes momentarily lowered to look at the suddenly discarded weapon, he seized the Makarov with his right hand and hit her hard across her face with the back of his left hand. With a sharp cry of pain, she fell down in a state of shock. Tremayne roughly pulled her to her feet.

"Get off this beach, Major Orlova, RIGHT NOW – or I will have you put under close arrest. The prisoners will remain under the protection of the Geneva Convention, until such time as their future is decided through proper diplomatic channels. Now MOVE, before your good luck changes."

Clearing the Makarov's magazine of live rounds, Tremayne hurled the empty pistol at the Russian officer's feet.

Orlova hesitated, as if she was going to say something, but Tremayne's eyes told her that that would *not* be a good thing to do. Now red faced and snivelling, she made a rapid and undignified exit from the beach.

"Goodness, I've never seen you so angry before, but that was exactly what was needed. Each time her arrogance and derision triumphed over reason and people deferred to her, as did those young subalterns who tried to talk with her earlier, she became even more irrational and unreasonable."

Tremayne looked at his First Lieutenant, "I've never hit a woman before, David, but having a loaded pistol literally shoved into my face made me see red. I knew that the time for discussion was well and truly over. As Edmund Burke once said, 'There is a time when forbearance ceases to be a virtue'!"

Conscious of so many people's keen interest in the events of the last five minutes — and their obvious relief at the sudden, decisive outcome, Tremayne walked over to the field kitchen with Willoughby-Brown to rejoin the others members of his boat crew.

"She is another of the Soviet NKVD political commissars that we first met eighteen months ago, if you remember. They're here to stir up Communists in France to form their own resistance groups to fight the occupying forces. That's fine, except that they refuse to collaborate with organisations like SOE, SIS, the official Free French freedom fighters' Confrèries, or the American OSS. Their motivation is essentially political and they plough their own damned furrow, to everyone else's frustration and disadvantage."

After their al fresco dinner, Tremayne sought out Enever and brought him up to speed on the day's events and the Tresco flotilla crew's part in them. Apart from some obvious discomfort and stiffness, Enever seemed largely unaware of his wound, which he described as, "clean as a whistle, according to the sawbones' diagnosis."

They sat talking for close to an hour before the indefatigable Beach Master poked his shaggy head through the field hospital entrance and boomed, "Glad to see you looking well Commander, you'll soon be back on your feet again. May I borrow young Tremayne, please?" He then added, still at a well above average decibel count, "You and your lads from Tresco did a bloody fine job today. Made quite a name for yourselves, y'did."

"Thank you sir." Tremayne flushed with embarrassment at the tannoy-volume praise, as he joined the Beach Master.

Outside the hospital tent he said, much more quietly, "We've organised your chap's funeral at that little church for 10.00 hours tomorrow. Thanks to your piratical lot – and those bloody bootnecks – the ground is now clear and secure and we've extended our beachhead considerably since this morning."

"Thank you sir – I appreciate what you've done for us, as will the lads."

Next morning's funeral took place on a clear, bright and windy day. The group were delighted and appreciative that a very pale Commander Enever had made the effort to turn up – accompanied by a military nurse in discreet attendance.

An army padre, a sensitive and perceptive man in his forties, then conducted a most moving service for 'Brummie' Nicholls. With arms reversed, the important and very appropriate naval tone was maintained. The Beach Master – who clearly had something of the resourceful acquisitive qualities of Admiral Hembury about him – had somehow managed to acquire a white ensign for the fallen sailor's coffin.

Tremayne led the firing party, of which Watkins had insisted on being a member despite his obvious continuing distress. Three volleys were fired over Nicholls's coffin and a piper, also provided as a result of the Beach Master's concern to 'do right' by his naval colleagues, played that most haunting of laments *The Flowers of the Forest.*

The touching service over, the party marched off, led by Tremayne. The piper, deliberately changing the mood – and step – played the traditional return-to-quarters march, *Black Bear.* As Tremayne well knew, the group would both give support to the bereaved Watkins – and allow him to grieve in peace when he so needed.

Later that day, the Beach Master, true to his word, established radio contact for Tremayne with HMS Godolphin.

As far as Fischer, Simmonds and Taylor were concerned, Tremayne had no idea what had befallen them in the incredible events of that historic day. Contact had been broken immediately after MTB1801 had been hit and there had been the scramble, under fire, for the shore.

The Intelligence Section at Godolphin was, understandably, most concerned to be updated on the health and strength of their much-loved leader. Tremayne was able to reassure them, on the basis of his regular first-hand contact with Enever, that the SNIO was regaining his strength and that his indefatigable spirit was, as ever, quite undiminished by his wound.

The news he received on Fischer, Taylor and Simmonds was universally good, though all the flotilla boats had sustained some damage and three of Fischer's ratings had been wounded, one of them seriously.

"Oh, sir," said the 'I' Section Wren officer, her clear voice cutting through the radio's crackling static, there is also a signal for you sir, it reads: *'Catriona sends you her love'.*"

"Who on earth is Catriona? I don't know anyone called Catriona. It must be a mistake, or... Oh! I'm a father. I'M A FATHER!! We have a *daughter*! Fanbloodytastic!!"

Tremayne could hardly contain himself as the significance of the signal registered and he stammered his confused thanks to the young Wren officer.

"That's alright sir, you're most welcome," came the very composed response, "and by the way sir, Mother is doing well and is positively radiant. She sends you *her* love, too. I thought you'd like to know that sir."

"Thank you so much. That is marvellous news. Absobloody-lutely marvellous!"

Twelve

An account settled

I t was quite ridiculous, he knew, yet Tremayne found it almost impossible not to rush up to people – strangers included – and shout, "I'm a father. I have a *daughter!*" His was a delirious combination of unbounded joy and wonder – added to an overwhelming belief that, at that moment, he was unique among men in having helped to produce a child. In private, he had also experienced tears of joy at his daughter's birth and felt, as ever, the intensity of his deep love for Emma.

An enthusiastic and competent amateur carpenter, he had already started – quite improbably, he recognised – to develop ideas for a toy rocking horse, a doll's house and a tomboy go-cart. He had, too, begun to visualise his daughter's bedroom and how it could be decorated and furnished, without developing into a series of design clichés in obligatory shades of pink.

He had been able to relay a message to Emma, but not speak directly with her. They had at least made contact with one another which, he acknowledged, was more than most of those engaged in Operation Overlord had been able to do with *their* loved ones during the last fraught and bloody forty-eight hours.

Emma had enthusiastically agreed with the suggestion in his message that John Enever, David Willoughby-Brown and his fiancée Lucy Caswell should be invited to be Catriona's godparents, along with one of Emma's closest school friends from Achiltibuie.

Enever's reaction had been so typical of the man – utter delight, a sense of rare privilege and uninhibited joy at the prospect of being a godfather, but especially so to Tremayne's child.

"Thank you, dear boy – of *course* I should delighted to be godfather to your daughter and since I was operating on the fringe of holy orders during your captivity, I feel that I've had at least *some* spiritual guidance for such a role!"

Willoughby-Brown had also felt reactions far deeper than mere flattery at being asked by Tremayne.

"This is something that I should really like to do for you and Emma – and, of course, Catriona! Lucy, I know, will be over the moon when I tell her."

With radio contact with HMS Godolphin now established, Tremayne was anxious that he and his crew became fully operational again as quickly as possible. One major temporary – but very practical – problem was that he no longer had a boat to command.

"To lose one MTB is a tragedy. To lose two is sheer carelessness – if I may parody Oscar Wilde," laughed Enever. "Talking of loss reminds me, Richard, that when that ill-intentioned brute shot me, I must have parted company with my very treasured meerschaum pipe. I know that, to most people, it's an absurd if not obscene relic, but it's one which is of huge sentimental value. I can find no trace of it anywhere and for someone clearly still in the oral stage of his psychological development, such a loss is little short of a catastrophe!"

Tremayne's smile bordered on the indulgent. "To avoid kicking our heels while we wait for new orders, I'll organise the boat crew as a beach search party to see just what we can come up with."

"On a more serious note, Richard, I'll talk with Captain MacPherson if no orders are forthcoming from him within the next twenty-four hours. As a matter of urgency, I will do my utmost to find a new command for you and to help you to become fully operational again. One thing is now for sure – unless something drastic happens and we're thrown back into the sea, our role as a Tresco flotilla is over in this area.

"The Americans have had a fearfully tough time of it on

Omaha Beach, but when they do break out from their beachhead – as I know they will – they will hot-foot it into Brittany via the Cotentin Peninsula. There will be a new major role for us there as they move westwards into territory – and Resistance contacts – that we know so well but which will be untrodden ground for the Yanks. Now, dear boy, to the pressing matter of my confounded pipe, if you will!"

Since the Beach Master was now the senior active naval officer ashore within the area, Tremayne had placed himself and his boat crew under his command and made a point of reporting to him each day. Slipping out of the beachhead's temporary casualty station, Tremayne sought out the gruff commander and tentatively raised the question of the missing meerschaum pipe, half expecting to be verbally blasted back into the sea.

"Bless m' soul, I *do* have the damned thing – would y' believe. It was brought to me off the beach by a bewildered bloody pongo who wondered if it was some sort of anti-personnel explosive device – or Byzantine booby trap." He gave Tremayne a wolfish grin. "Come with me now, lad, and I'll get it for you. We can't have the SNIO – I assume it *is* his – chewing his fingernails for want of an ounce of 'Blue Liner' baccy!"

A much-relieved Tremayne took the encrusted, semi-charred, but precious relic back to a very grateful Enever who immediately stuck it – empty and unlit, of course – between his teeth while Tremayne explained how he had managed to come by it.

"Dear boy, I'll be forever in your debt – many, many thanks. I must also remember to thank our hirsute shepherd for his part in the recovery and rescue."

Already, in the newly liberated hamlets and villages within the beachhead, the French, with customary resilience and aplomb, were beginning to re-establish the day-to-day normality of their pre-war lives, despite delayed initial counter-attacks by the Germans. Along with other armoured units, the fanatical SS Hitler-Jugend Panzer Division had moved up to the front to block the Allies' advance inland, but was being fought off and held in Tremayne's sector of Sword Beach by the British.

In his characteristically colourful manner – and reflecting his indefatigable approach to life – the Beach Master disparagingly described the SS armoured unit to Tremayne as "a tiresome bunch of ill-tempered youths from Jerry's 'gas-pipe cavalry' who need their bloody arses kicking". The wolfish grin reappeared as he added, "Our own 'donkey wallopers' are already chamfering the bastards up in good measure, well supported by the 'twelve-mile snipers' of the Royal Artillery."

In the small seaside resort of La Brèche, the bars and cafés that had operated reluctantly under the occupation, and had been stingily selective in what they had offered the Germans, now brought out their previously hidden under-the-counter wines and aperitifs. Enthusiastically, they plied their liberators with champagne, fine cognacs and armagnacs – as well as impressive arrays of wines and beers, inadvertently creating unprecedented demands on the corrective and custodial services of naval shore patrols and the Army's Red Caps.

Tremayne and his crew had discovered a small café in the hamlet recently cleared by the 1st South Lancashires, which catered admirably, in the circumstances, for the group's wide-ranging tastes in alcohol. Willoughby-Brown was positively ecstatic about the seemingly endless supply of Chateau Haut-Marbuzet – a Saint Estèphe of exquisite colour and elegant bouquet, while a still inconsolable Watkins admitted that a couple of glasses of Cognac's best "did help a bit". Petty Officer Irvine bemoaned the lack of draught Guinness or Bushmills whiskey, but – in the interest of Anglo-French relations – compromised temporarily with a reluctant, "I'll try a drop of that stuff that's brought a bit of a smile back to Pablo's face, so I will."

Tremayne's somewhat catholic tastes were certainly well catered for by *le patron*'s cellar. More than that, he recognised that the few visits that they were able to make to the café did wonders for the crew's rebonding and morale after the intensely personal experiences of D-Day and its immediate aftermath.

Strictly against the medical officer's orders, Tremayne and Willoughby-Brown – with admirable guile – managed to smuggle a heavily disguised Enever out of the sick bay for one evening's visit to the café. On that particular occasion, a talented local accordionist turned up. Unlike many of his ilk, his British song repertoire extended well beyond the tunes of the First World War and he quickly had Tremayne's group singing along to *We'll Meet Again, We're Going to Hang Out Our Washing on the Siegfried Line, The White Cliffs of Dover* and other hits of the time.

Word had obviously got around that a party of British sailors were fast becoming regulars at the café and two very enthusiastic professional ladies of the night from the casino at nearby Ouistreham arrived to join in with the singing, blatantly eyeing up the potential clientele and the prospects of new business.

"Hmm," commented Willoughby-Brown with his customary dry humour, "clearly those two won't be known around here for the strength of *their* knicker elastic."

"Quite so, dear boy, but as long as *yours* remains strong you'll be quite safe! In any case, I know that Richard has your welfare permanently at heart," laughed Enever.

"More's the pity!" Willoughby-Brown's uncharacteristic rejoinder brought surprised broad grins to both Enever and Tremayne's faces.

Turning to Tremayne, Enever said, "In the interests of *entente cordiale*, we should offer the accordionist — and the two ladies — a glass of something but I, for one, am not going to further the latter's trading opportunities with our group!"

A quick glance at Irvine's disapproving, somewhat puritanical face told Tremayne that the group had its own built-in, unofficial regulating petty officer.

"Agreed, John. You know, this is turning out to be just the sort of happy, relaxing evening that we all so desperately need. Nicholls's death has had an understandably depressing effect on such a small, tightly-knit crew."

"By the way, mentioning your crew, Richard, reminds me — I received a signal from Captain MacPherson this morning. You and your boat's company will be picked up by MTB from the main quay — or what's left of it — at Ouistreham at 10.30 hours tomorrow and transported back to HMS Godolphin."

The kindly grey eyes gave a benign twinkle, "Oh, and by the way, our revered lord and master has been promoted to full admiral and no less a person has managed to cajole some gullible soul into transferring an MTB — another Vosper, so I understand — to the Tresco flotilla. She will be your new command. Try not to lose this one, dear boy!"

Tremayne grinned. "I'll do my best! Thank you for your part in finding me a boat. I appreciate that immensely. I'm anxious to get my crew operational again and back into action. Hanging around like so many spare parts is doing none of us any good. We need to be in business again asap."

Looking quickly at his watch, Enever said, "My turn now to thank you and young WB here for the creatively clandestine way you smuggled me out of the clutches of that Amazonian nurse. Built like a brick alehouse, she puts a bloody vertical gust up me! I think I really need to sneak back in pretty soon. It's getting late and she'll never believe that I've been on the loo for over two hours!"

Before slipping away to take Enever back to the field hospital, Tremayne addressed his boat's crew and quickly briefed them on forthcoming events.

"Fall in, with kit, at the temporary MT compound, where an army three-tonner will pick us up at 09.30 hours sharp and deliver us to Ouistreham for onward transit to HMS Godolphin. Enjoy the rest of the evening lads, but not *too* well," added Tremayne with a knowing smile.

Looking in Irvine's direction, he asked, "Coming with us 'Swain or are you hanging on, hoping the accordionist will play *The Sash* for you?"

"I'll come with you, sir, so I will." Turning his baleful eyes on the rest of the crew – and the two *filles-de-joie* in particular, he said, with an air of righteousness befitting an Elder of an Antrim Kirk,

"Just yous lot behave yerselves. Anyone who's daft enough to end up with a dose of the oh-be-joyfuls will be put away for a very long time, so he will."

Tremayne complimented and warmly thanked the café patron and the accordionist and the senior group took its leave to return to the field hospital – and then quarters – for the night.

Tremayne walked with Enever, deep in conversation, but was amused to hear Willoughby-Brown and the coxswain talking behind them. His young First Lieutenant was a marvellous paradox, felt Tremayne, of urbane sophistication and yet unworldly innocence. Only an hour before, he had been engaged in a learned discussion with the café proprietor, in fluent French, about the respective merits of the wines of Margaux, Pauillac and Saint Estèphe. Now, Irvine was explaining the significance of *The Sash* to the younger man and teaching him its powerful, chauvinistic words while humming its undeniably catchy tune.

"Just listen to this, John," whispered Tremayne with a broad smile, as his Number One began to sing, albeit sotto voce, under the coxswain's tuition –

'It is old and it is beautiful,

Its colours they are fine.

It was worn at Derry, Aughrim,

Enniskillen and the Boyne.

My father wore it, when a youth,

In bygone...'

"Any more of this, 'Swain, and we'll have *you* singing *Poor Fenian Boy* with Aileen Oyler at the New Inn," interrupted a laughing Tremayne.

"Och, I'd be tarred and feathered – and drummed out of the Orange Order – so I would sir!"

It was good to see his normally dour, taciturn coxswain more relaxed and, all too rarely, to hear him laugh, thought Tremayne.

The laughter and banter quickly died down to hushed,

conspiratorial exchanges as the group approached the sick bay. While Tremayne and Willoughby-Brown engaged the duty nurse – a different one this time – in lighthearted conversation, Enever gratefully slipped away to his bed, any view of his return down the narrow corridor being blocked by Irvine's strategically placed, barrel-chested bulk.

At about the same time, 'Pablo' Watkins quietly slipped away from the group at the café and, under a clear June night sky, made his way to the tiny church where his 'townie' and close friend of so many years had just been buried. For some time he stood at the graveside, head bowed, weeping silently. Then, briefly touching the temporary wooden cross with Leading Seaman Nicholls's name so freshly painted on it, murmured, "So, long, Brummie. God bless mate. Sleep tight old friend."

The following morning, the survivors of the original boat crew, together with a beaming – but still unnaturally pale – Commander Enever, were already assembled when the three-tonner arrived, its canvas top opened up and tied back to make the most of the improving weather. To Tremayne's delight, the Beach Master appeared on the scene to bid them farewell and wish them good luck.

"God's speed, lads – I shall miss you scruffy bastards!" he roared, as the lorry pulled away.

After a short journey, they arrived at the quay in Ouist-reham, which bore the scars of the recent hard-fought battle between the Germans and Commandant Kieffer's

Commandos de la Marine, who were fighting on French soil for the first time in over four years. It was hard to believe, mused Tremayne, that all that – and so much more – had happened only five days previously. Further private thoughts were rudely cut short by a raucous voice using a loudhailer: "Trips round the 'arbour, gennelmen. Any more for the *Skylark*? Just a few places left. Hurry, hurry, take your seats please!"

"Praise be," said Enever with a grin. "Look Richard. Of all the bloody people, they've sent Hermann Fischer to pick us up!"

Within seconds, Enever, Tremayne and Willoughby-Brown surrounded a delighted, laughing Fischer and were pumping his hand as he ushered them and their boat crew up the gangway, onto the deck of his Camper & Nicholson.

"Welcome aboard everyone! Welcome aboard."

Turning to his First Lieutenant, Fischer ordered, "Number One, will you get everyone below for the moment please – except for the officers."

Looking washed out and rather frail, Enever did decide to go below and accept Fischer's provident offer of a camp bed in the boat's tiny wardroom.

"I shan't sleep, dear boy, but I will rest the weary bones," he said, as he was helped off with his tunic and settled down, as comfortably as his wound would allow, on the canvas and tubular steel Heath Robinson-style contraption. Within seconds he was fast asleep and Tremayne smiled at Fischer.

"I thought he was being a bit optimistic – that wound has most likely taken far more out of him than he realises. I wonder what outrageously creative story he spun the MO to obtain such an early release from hospital?"

With everyone onboard and allocated to the various cramped quarters typical of a motor torpedo boat, Fischer ordered "Slip" and then "All engines, slow ahead." As the MTB completed negotiating the beach area outside the harbour, he called, "All engines, full speed ahead." With a rumble that fast became a roar, the combined 2,700 horse power of the three Hall-Scott engines immediately responded and, with bows lifting clear of the sea, the big Camper & Nicholson surged forward, spray cascading over her for'ard deck with its manned six-pounder.

Above the roar of the engines, the young South African skipper yelled to Tremayne and Willoughby-Brown, "I thought you might like a quick look at the rest of Sword Beach, then Juno Beach, before we turn to starboard and set our course for Tresco. Juno is where the Canadians invaded, along with you Brits."

Looking at Sword Beach first, Tremayne was struck by the comparative order and disciplined organisation now in evidence, despite the still obvious flotsam and jetsam of war. Juno Beach presented a similar picture of well-managed busyness and controlled, well-directed activity. From seeing both beaches, he was overawed by the scale and sheer size of what Operation Overlord had been and he knew there were still another three beaches that he hadn't seen, stretching round to the Cotentin Peninsula below Cherbourg.

As they set course west by north-west for the Isles of Scilly, Tremayne became instantly aware of the vast amount of air traffic in the skies. All were Allied planes, with their broad black and white invasion force recognition markings clearly visible on their wings and around the rear of their fuselages. Immediately before – and since – the invasion, the Allies had gained complete air superiority at the Luftwaffe's expense.

As a fighting force, with the power to blow any invasion fleet out of the water, the German Air Force had all but ceased to exist. However, one to one or in small group engagements, the Luftwaffe remained a deadly foe. Accordingly, Fischer had organised air escort from the St Mary's squadron once they were north of Cherbourg and into the western approaches to the English Channel. In this area of the sea, there was also the still ever-present risk of marauding E-boats. This particular arm of the Kriegsmarine was anything but a spent force and continued to enjoy an enviable reputation with the German press and public as the one consistently successful branch of the German Navy.

Some thirty miles north-west of Cherbourg, a solitary Arado 196 floatplane appeared off their starboard beam. After apparent initial indifference to them, she all at once began to show a close interest in Fischer's MTB, circling at a height of about two hundred feet. Abruptly, she turned to port and headed straight for the Camper & Nicholson at maximum speed, assuming a threatening attacking stance.

On Fischer's command – "All guns, fire as you bear" – the first to open up were his 40mm Bofors aft and his midships twin 20mm Oerlikons. Under Tremayne's thorough and exacting tutelage, Fischer had learned the importance of doing things well first time – especially in the fields of seamanship, navigation and gunnery. Almost immediately, his crew's accurate shooting began to blow pieces off the Arado's floats and lower fuselage and she rapidly veered off to starboard to escape the heavy rounds tearing her structure to pieces. Within seconds, the Arado had disappeared out of range as quickly as she had appeared, heading for the north Brittany coast.

Tremayne left Fischer to congratulate his gun crews on their excellent shooting and then gave his own praise to the South African.

"Well done, Hermann! That was superb gunnery and fire control."

Some fifteen minutes later, three Hawker Hurricanes flying in close formation appeared, approaching almost due south and head on to the MTB. With their customary waggling of wings in recognition and greeting, they then set about establishing continuing air cover until the Scillies appeared on the horizon, bathed in afternoon sunlight.

As the MTB drew close to St Mary's and St Agnes, Tremayne looked with undiminished affection at the familiar emerald and turquoise waters surrounding the islands, with the sun adding to the glistening white wave crests. The seductive, restorative magic of the Scillies was still there.

Turning to Fischer he said, "I'll just see how John is and whether we need to radio ahead for a stretcher. When I last looked in on him about an hour ago he was asleep, but looking very pale and exhausted. He'll struggle, scrambling up that first steep rocky section of the path from Braiden Rock anchorage."

Minutes later, Tremayne returned to Fischer on the bridge.

"He insists on walking, Hermann, and clearly wants to lead us all back to Godolphin – but detail one of your petty officers to provide some physical assistance, along with my coxswain, just in case he does need a bit of help coping with those tricky rocks."

Thirty minutes later, the Camper & Nicholson, with both boat crews – including Enever – fallen in for entering harbour routine on the bridge and fore and aft decks, was cheered back to New Grimsby by officers and ship's company lining the quay.

"Always a moving experience and so very 'Navy'," mused Tremayne.

Later that day, after Enever had briefed a rather liverish Captain MacPherson and spoken at length with SOE, he called Tremayne into Hut 101.

Despite looking drawn and tired, Enever still conveyed the deceptively controlled energy that was one of the trademarks of his extreme professionalism. Tremayne noted that his eyes still twinkled merrily above his half-moon spectacles. Within seconds of Tremayne's arrival, tea appeared and Enever asked if he had managed to contact Emma since their return – and indeed how were mother and daughter?

So typical of the man, thought Tremayne. He's obviously in considerable pain and discomfort. He would be better off in bed and his desk looks overloaded with work and yet he can still show genuine, not perfunctory, concern for others – and be ready to listen to them.

Tremayne *had* spoken with Emma and was trying to come back down to earth again, to be mentally and emotionally geared up to an operations planning meeting and to switch his mind, and his heart, back fully to the pressing issues of the moment.

Enever began by congratulating Tremayne on the action on D-Day when he had led the naval detachment in the successful attack on the German machine-gun bunker and the subsequent assault on the German rifle company's positions.

"On the strength of the reports that I have received, Richard, I am recommending Able Seaman Watkins for the DCM and you for the DSO. It was a highly effective attack and you and your team played a crucial role in securing the success that was achieved."

"Thank you. At least we didn't let ourselves – or the Navy – down in front of the Royals. I'm just very sorry that so many reluctant Russians were killed in the assault. For them it was a case of 'out of the frying pan...'"

Enever moved the conversation on, to bring Tremayne up to speed on the next stage of the invasion strategy as it was likely to impact upon the Tresco flotilla – and Tremayne in particular.

"When the Yanks break out of the Omaha beachhead, they will do so in what will be known as Operation Cobra – the seizure of the Cotentin Peninsula and Cherbourg. Their intention, at this stage, is to push through Brittany as rapidly as possible to seize the naval bases of St Malo, Brest, Lorient and St Nazaire.

"If Jerry resistance in Cherbourg proves too tough a nut to crack quickly, then my guess is the Americans will seize Carentan, head for – and take – Avranches, so isolating the northern Cotentin, and then go, split arse, south and west."

Enever paused for a rare lighting of his pipe with his 'Tommy' cigarette lighter, fashioned from a First World War .303 cartridge case.

"The Confrèrie Bonaparte has a new chief – one Capitaine de Vaisseau Nicholas Mercier – code name 'Lionel'. His credentials are impeccable and he was recruited by SOE, with whom he has worked closely during the last nine months. He has also spent considerable time with Admiral Hembury and, unusually for a Frenchman, likes the British, but especially approves of our approach to espionage and the way we conduct clandestine operations! As Lionel, he has already taken up his new role as Confrèrie leader and begun to get a grip of the situation in Brittany, but he will be over here for two weeks while 'Didier' – another *nom d'espion* – his deputy, assumes temporary command.

Enever stopped for a moment and looked directly at Tremayne.

"Your reputation and standing with French Resistance are about as high as they could be. Operations that you have conducted in Brittany during the last two years, your treatment at the hands of the Gestapo and your escape from the PoW camp, all confirm you as one of the principal British contacts that the Confrèrie wants to deal with. The others are Major Mike Black of the SAS and Colonel John Farrell of the Rifle Brigade who was seconded to SOE three years ago – both of whom you know, of course. It should be a powerful advisory team, capable of giving good, sound counsel – and cutting through any nonsense. You read law at university, Farrell read politics and Mike has operated many times as a politically-sensitive honest broker in dealing with temporary civil authorities in several occupied countries."

Tremayne responded at this point.

"I like and respect both. They are highly competent professionals. There is no doubt in my mind that we will work well together."

"Lionel checked you out with SOE, as well as with agents in France, and he has asked that you work with him – and

375

the Confrèrie – once the Americans break out and sweep westwards into Brittany. What Lionel wants, I gather, is that you, Farrell and Black be attached to his 'Inner Cabinet', as he call it, for about five or six weeks. One of your tasks will be to liaise with the Americans, but representing the French view of things as seen through the eyes of highly informed specialists who have operated with the Resistance in France."

"Is he concerned that, once the Yanks begin moving into an area, their rapid pace and concern to get on with the job may, understandably, lack both subtlety and sensitivity? That – as well as their lack of our background knowledge – could mean that they perhaps fail to represent local priorities and expectations on liberation as fully as the French would naturally expect," said Tremayne.

"It is *essentially* that, Richard. We mustn't forget how the French must feel right now. Defeat and occupation have severely damaged their sense of pride. Collaboration with the Germans, or simply the passive acceptance of occupation, has given rise to guilt and shame and a chaotic interregnum will add greater frustration and helplessness. What the Confrèrie don't want is issues like the punishment of captured SS and Gestapo members and other war criminals – as well as traitors – taken out of their hands by newcomers and strangers who have not experienced the terror of occupation. Nor do they want such matters to become exaggerated or distorted and used as future political capital."

"But surely our role is not to endorse – by either omission or commission – summary punishments and executions without a proper trial and due process of law – in this case French law."

"Exactly so, Richard. As a budding barrister, you will appreciate the fundamental importance of justice, and of the fittingness of punishment in relation to a crime – and its context – given conclusive evidence of guilt or innocence. Equally, we don't want so-called 'political' issues – especially those introduced by the liberating armies – to impede or subvert the course of justice, as considered legal, as well as right and appropriate, by the French and under *French* law.

As I see the situation right now, we are faced with the potential problem of a lack of American sensitivity – and oversensitivity on the part of the French. In the current circumstances, both reactions are quite understandable."

Enever talked through Tremayne's new – and very different – role with him for another twenty minutes or so and then announced that Lionel, Farrell and Black would be meeting at SOE in London in two days' time and that he, Tremayne, was expected to be with them.

With his characteristic twinkle, he said, "You'll need to pack your gear tonight, because I've arranged for you to leave tomorrow morning so that, by train from Penzance, you'll be in London by 19.00 hours. I've taken the liberty of telling Emma, so she's expecting you, and you'll be able to take at least some time together as a family!"

An overjoyed Tremayne expressed his grateful thanks, delighted at the prospect of seeing Emma again and meeting his daughter for the first time.

"I'm afraid I can't tell you when you will take up your new post in France as that depends on how rapidly the Americans are able to break out and move into Brittany. My guess, at this stage — judging by the latest US Army reports from the battlefield — is that it will most likely start in late July or very early August."

The following evening, an excited Tremayne stepped off the train at Paddington, joining the crowd rushing to the ticket inspector and then for one of the few taxis likely to be available.

Only vaguely aware of the jostling mass of people waiting to greet passengers off the train, he handed his ticket in — just as a soft, but audible, Highland voice said, "Catriona, this is your daddy. Say hello."

Tremayne stopped, overcome with joy, to hug Emma and hold his daughter for the very first time.

"Emma, dearest Emma, I can't believe it! It really is you. You look absolutely fantastic darling and Catriona — *you* are a little winner!"

The short walk together to the taxi and the journey to Emma's apartment — courtesy of SIS, for whom she had continued to work on a part-time basis, were precious moments for Tremayne. It was difficult to reconcile the sudden new sense of completeness, of feeling part of a family, with the brutal, noisy and frightening reality of D-Day that was but a few days past.

Deliberately, Emma avoided mentioning the invasion knowing full well that, in his own time, her husband would tell her about it. She was conscious, too, of Tremayne's need to adjust to the role of a brand new father and that now they were inextricably a threesome.

For Tremayne, their time together passed so happily but, as always it seemed, all too quickly and next morning he left with a heavy sense of loss – almost one of bereavement – as he went to join Lionel, Farrell and Black at SOE in Baker Street.

Returning the salute of the sentry inside the entrance, he was met by a young captain wearing the maroon beret and insignia of the Parachute Regiment and led to a small room on the first floor. There, waiting for him with broad smiles of welcome, were Farrell and Black and a short but distinguished looking man with thick dark hair cut *en brosse* and the most penetrating, intelligent brown eyes.

"Enchanté, Richard! I am Lionel."

The animated briefing – clarification of strategy, roles and tasks for the forthcoming operations in Brittany – fully engaged each member of the group, with individuals readily building upon one another's unique contributions. Tremayne felt a sense of elation at the strength of the seductive synergy, free from unnecessary political contamination, which developed so rapidly in their discussion. Too often, he had wasted so much time at meetings where vested partisan interests had frustrated the progression of much-needed collaborative enterprise and effort. Lionel's briefing was refreshingly different – and pre-eminently productive.

"Essentially, we are a liaison team," stated Lionel, "but one with teeth – which we shall use if the need arises. We shall base ourselves close to Rennes, as soon as the Americans confirm its liberation, and will be in regular contact with the Confrèrie, monitoring the situation daily, as the Americans begin their move westwards into Brittany. With your assistance, gentlemen, I shall work closely in stepping up the sabotage of transport, communications and power supplies to impede German resistance as much as possible."

The intense brown eyes studied each of the British officers in turn, watching for reactions.

Farrell was the first to respond. "I presume, Lionel, that sabotage will be planned, systematic and geared to changing German responses and troop movements – not simply hap-hazard mayhem?"

"You presume correctly, John. To offset the risk of vindictive reprisals and to achieve maximum destructive impact, each act of sabotage will be carefully planned and directed. It is only a matter of two days since the shameless outrage of Ouradour-sur-Glane and the murder, or transportation, by SS Das Reich division of over 640 French civilians – including women and children – and so we are very aware of the constant risk of inhumanly savage retribution."

He paused, to create effect and to ensure that he had everyone's full attention.

"We are also very conscious of the need to bring a lot of people to justice for these crimes." The suddenly narrowed eyes indicated a side to his make up, seemingly so different from his usual neutral demeanour.

Following a relaxing evening together, getting to know one another socially as well as professionally, the four were taken to a secret SOE training school in the depths of Sussex for an intensive course. The purpose of the two-week course was to perfect and speed up their abilities as covert wireless Morse-code operators, polish up their cryptography and radio-intercept skills and to understand more about living under occupation day to day. Much of the training was carried out by Lionel, with the assistance of several highly professional British and French SOE operators.

At the end of what amounted to intensive operational 'sharpening' and mental honing – with the addition of some critical new knowledge and skills – the four were then taken to a Coastal Services unit based at Portsmouth, where an obviously Breton small coastal trader – *Belle de Concarneau* – waited to transport them to St Malo. Typical of her type, she was over fifty feet in length, broad of beam and carried the brick-red sails so familiar in the seaports and fishing harbours of Brittany. Her hull was black with a yellow whale; her upper works were white, with a brown timber wheelhouse.

Tremayne also noted, with a wry smile, that her paintwork had been given the iron-filings treatment – originated by the Tresco flotilla – to damp down the pristine appearance and create an appropriate impression of weathered, regular use.

The four had abandoned their uniforms, with the exception of their Service battledress blouses, and were dressed in typical Breton faded blue smocks, baggy trousers and battered blue caps.

Leaving Portsmouth at 24.00 hours, they adjusted their speed to place themselves off St Malo at around 06.30. Conscious of German radar, they had set a rather tortuous course to confirm their role as coastal trader and allay suspicion, as far as was possible.

In the expert hands of her RN coxswain, *Belle de Concarneau* busily hove to at the edge of the harbour at St Malo, deliberately under the guns of the many German coastal defence units guarding the town and its seawards-facing port installations. Bustling around on deck, apparently shifting items of cargo for onshore delivery, Tremayne and the others looked, to all intents and purposes, like a typical work-a-day trader's deckhands. All the cargo made ready for disembarkation had been carefully legitimised as necessary boat spares from Cherbourg for delivery to bona fide customers in and around St Malo or Dinard – with the necessary, cleverly forged supporting paperwork. Within minutes of their arrival, small boats' whalers were rowed out to *Belle de Concarneau* to collect the crates and parcels – and the four agents who helped to carry the equipment up and onto the quayside. Shaking hands with the four members of their reception committee, the group proceeded to enjoy a leisurely cold breakfast, under the noses of the German guards and French gendarmes.

To reinforce the unhurried and natural appearance of the group, some members of the reception committee exchanged lighthearted comments with passing gendarmes. Speaking, alternately, in Breton and French, they included Tremayne and the two British army officers in their banter who, dependent on their language skills and accents, replied, or simply gesticulated and grunted.

After about an hour, a battered old Renault *camion* appeared, convincingly wheezing its way onto the quay. The whole group pitched in to help load up the ancient lorry, with the four now ready to scramble onboard to play the role of delivery men at the various customers' drop-off points. Two gendarmes, armed with MAS38 machine pistols, came across the quay to check the delivery notes and other accompanying paperwork.

Tremayne and Farrell held their breath as one of the gendarmes nudged Black none too gently with the muzzle of his gun and, indicating one of the crates with his foot, snapped, "Open this one."

A momentary hesitation on Black's part was ended by a

quick-thinking Lionel, who handed Black a crowbar and repeated the order, pointing to the crate to be opened.

Perspiring freely, Tremayne glanced briefly across at Farrell and saw that sweat had also begun to run down *his* forehead.

As Black, now master of the situation once again, began to lever open the crate energetically, whilst still seeming relaxed, the gendarme suddenly stopped him. "That will do, that's enough. Fasten the lid back down again." Taking his cue from Lionel, Black muttered a somewhat indistinct, but suitably grateful sounding "Merci" and shook the gendarme's proffered hand as he departed to rejoin his colleague, who was leaning against the quayside lamp post looking bored out of his mind. The accompanying Germans, apparently equally bored, had moved off earlier to pastures new on the other side of the harbour.

Maintaining a front of appearing busy but relaxed, the four, along with two of the French workers, now took over the role of loading the lorry and then clambered onboard before the driver and his mate — two members of the Resistance — reversed off the quay. After a further agonising checking of papers and inspection of the crates, this time by German guards at the exit barrier of the harbour area, they set out unhurriedly for Dinan, about twenty miles south of St Malo. There, the Confrèrie had set up safe accommodation for the quartet in one of a group of five large old houses situated at the edge of the town.

Rather undistinguished buildings, they created the right degree of anonymity and dull respectability that simply did not invite undue interest and attention.

"Hmm, so respectable as to be downright vulgar!" muttered Farrell with a grin.

Tremayne and the others, including Lionel, were quickly ushered through the front door and up two flights of stairs into a large space in the attic, which was to serve as the group's sleeping quarters.

The lorry left them to make the various deliveries, so maintaining the level of normality that served as one of the Resistance members' convincing covers.

Lionel, who had used the house as a secure base twice before, showed the others the powerful radio set built into the wall of one of the bedrooms on the floor below them, concealed behind an imposing, ornately carved traditional linen cupboard.

"This wireless is our communications link to key members of the Confrèrie in northern Brittany and, of course, to SOE in England. So far, the Boches have never raided this area and the members of the Resistance who do live in the house do all they can to preserve the appearance of staid, middle-aged conservatism. The radio is used only when absolutely essential – and then briefly – to minimise the risk of roving German radio-detector vans homing in on the signals."

Lionel quickly organised food and drink for the party and then outlined his immediate strategy for introducing the British officers to the local key figures of the Resistance. Over the next two weeks, the British trio, with Lionel's constant help, built up a high degree of rapport with the Confrèrie members and an understanding of their changing role, ready for when the Americans were able to take St Lô and move west into Brittany. Delayed by the fiercely tough German resistance in and around St Lô, by the difficult *bocage* terrain of thick, high hedges and by the bad weather, the Americans, under Lieutenant General Omar Bradley, finally broke out and the delayed Operation Cobra began in earnest at the end of July.

American mobility came into its own as US forces swept westwards, seizing Rennes after a particularly savage battle, and securing vital road and rail links to the Atlantic seaports.

Tremayne, Black and Farrell quickly found themselves alternately directing and assisting in sabotage operations, designed to impede German troop movements and interrupt communications links between their different units.

St Malo proved a far tougher nut to crack and German resistance was both fanatical and, initially, tactically superior to the US attempts to take the town.

By early August, however, much of eastern Brittany had been liberated by the Americans and Lionel, along with Tremayne and his two colleagues, found themselves involved in frequent negotiations with the newly arrived US forces to ensure that those who should be brought to justice were appropriately dealt with. The British officers, especially, found the Americans to be pragmatic and very helpful in the task of seeking out Nazis guilty of war crimes within the liberated areas. Collaborators, who were usually known to the members of the Resistance, were invariably sought out and dealt with by the French themselves.

The task of restoring civil law and order out of the chaos of recent battle and the logistics of liberation were daunting. Both the Americans and regenerated French authorities varied from town to town in their organisational savvy and capacity to cope with urgently needed administration and the establishment of necessary infrastructures.

Lionel, who had experienced the loss of so many members of the Confrèrie – due to both German infiltration and exposure by traitors – before he assumed command, was particularly anxious to see justice meted out – however harsh.

He had been invited by the US senior officer establishing order, along with the French authorities in Rennes, to check a group of uniformed SS prisoners who had been captured in the fighting a few days previously. The American colonel claimed that there was 'something phoney' about several of their captives, who appeared to be unofficially protected by the others.

Asking Tremayne to accompany him, Lionel drove to Rennes in a jeep, courtesy of the US Army, and to the town hall that served as the US headquarters.

There they were met by Colonel Mark Timmins, a tall, lean, quietly spoken man who hailed from the mountains of New Hampshire. He quickly came to the point.

"We have twenty-two supposedly Waffen-SS guys and have interviewed every one of them.

Our Special Branch personnel have crawled all over 'em and, in four cases, things just don't seem to ring true. Something tells me that those guys are just not what they seem. At the moment, I'm still trying to fight a war *and* run the military administration and logistics of this town. Right now, I cannot spend any more time on this matter and I gratefully leave it to you, gentlemen – the experts – to sort it out. I've had the local Resistance – especially the Commies – baying for the blood of the Waffen-SS prisoners, whom I've locked up in the cells of the former Gestapo building close by. At the moment, I'm doing my darndest to make sure that I don't have a mass lynching on my hands."

At the mention of the Gestapo headquarters, Tremayne gave an involuntary shudder as the horrific memories of his experiences there came flooding back. All too vividly he saw, once again, the crumpled body of Petty Officer McDonald, his engineer, sagging lifeless against the execution post.

Lionel spoke first, interrupting Tremayne's thoughts.

"You would like us to interrogate the, shall we say, 'unusual' four, Colonel?"

"You betcha, Captain. I want those bastards sorted out."

"We should interrogate them individually and then, after interrogation, return them separately to new cells to await further investigation," said Tremayne.

An approving smile crossed Timmins's leathery, weather-beaten face. "Good – let's do it, gentlemen!"

Calling in two armed orderlies, Timmins led Tremayne and Lionel to an interview room that looked all too sickeningly familiar to the British officer.

"I'll have coffee sent up while you prepare yourselves and then my guys will bring in the first of these weirdo bastards to you."

He hesitated for a moment and, slowly turning to Tremayne, said, "Yours is a most unusual name, Commander, but this is the second time that I have recently come across it. I'm a keen student of military history – especially that of the American Revolutionary War. In some research that I did a couple of years ago, for *The Boston Globe,* I do recall a certain British Lieutenant of Marines – Jonathan Tremayne – featured prominently at the battles of Concord and Bunker Hill in 1775. In the reports that I read, I seem to remember that he distinguished himself by his gallantry in both encounters. Could he possibly be a relative of yours? From all accounts, he sure was one helluva guy – and a real pain in the ass to our fellas!"

"Good heavens! Yes, sir, he most certainly was. What an amazing coincidence. Before we leave, sir, please give me a contact address and I will most certainly send you copies of the information

I have on him – including letters to his wife, by all accounts a most gracious and beautiful lady – once I get back to England."

"Thank you, Commander. I'd be most grateful for that and I will send *you* copies of what I have on your illustrious ancestor."

Timmins smiled meaningfully. "Now gentlemen, let's grill those bastards and make 'em sweat real good!"

Lionel and Tremayne, who were both armed with pistols, rapidly worked out their proposed interrogation structure, drank the Americans' very welcome coffee and waited for the first prisoner.

Within a few minutes, the door opened suddenly and the first of the prisoners strode into the room. He marched in arrogantly, with an expression of studied disdain on his face, and had to be pushed into sitting in the solitary chair facing Tremayne and Lionel across the scrubbed wooden table top.

Lionel, who spoke fluent German, opened the interrogation and all his questions were met with a supercilious silence.

Tremayne, who had also remained silent while assiduously studying the prisoner's face and reactions, then spoke. Carefully choosing his words and speaking slowly in clear but simple German, he said, "I remember you. I never forget a face. You are *not* Waffen-SS – you are Gestapo. I was a prisoner here myself several months ago. You were one of the guards here. Now answer our questions."

Momentarily taken aback by Tremayne's intervention, the

former guard broke off eye contact, but reverted to his tactical arrogant silence.

Watched by an approving Lionel, and by two initially shocked American guards, Tremayne pulled out his pistol and cocked it, placing it on the table by his right hand.

"Answer our questions or I'll begin by shooting you in the balls. The next bullet will be in your belly and the third one – through your head – will come as welcome relief. TALK!"

Badly shaken, the colour draining from his face, his former arrogance evaporated totally and he began pleading his case as "only following orders".

He answered to the name of Manfred Gessler, at which point Tremayne said, "He's most certainly yours, Lionel. The number of unfortunate Frenchmen who passed through his murderous hands must run into hundreds. Over to you."

Lionel questioned him relentlessly for a further twenty minutes and then motioned the guards to remove the now pathetically grovelling prisoner, who had involuntarily soiled his trousers, and told them to take him to one of the empty cells to await further interrogation. Glancing at Tremayne as the prisoner was escorted away, Lionel said quietly, "By the end of the week, he will appear before the local French judiciary and –" Lionel left the sentence unfinished, but meaningfully drew his finger across his throat.

"Before the next one is brought in, I'm going to fire two shots, with a three-second interval between them," said

Tremayne. "These will be easily heard by the prisoners and we'll give them time to exercise their imaginations and draw whatever conclusions they like."

Tremayne pointed the 9mm Browning at the massive oak beams supporting the ceiling and fired two spaced shots into them, making sure that the bullet holes could not be seen from the other side of the table. Two more prisoners were brought in, but clearly the shots and non-appearance of their colleague in the holding cell had completely unnerved them and they readily admitted to being Gestapo interrogators. Like the first one, the second and third prisoners gave away a great deal of vital intelligence under questioning. And after each one had been taken back to his separate cell, Tremayne once again fired two rounds at three-second intervals.

The fourth and final prisoner was pushed through the door and to the chair opposite Lionel and Tremayne. Mutual recognition was instantaneous. For Tremayne, there was no forgetting the ice-cold, soulless eyes and the unnaturally pallid, expressionless face which had once so cruelly mocked and abused him and McDonald.

Wearing Waffen-SS uniform, with the somewhat incongruous insignia of an SS Oberscharführer*, Neumann was visibly shaken as he recognised the English naval officer now sitting before him – their roles now dramatically reversed from their previous encounter.

When Tremayne confirmed just who Neumann was, Lionel stood up and, pointing his finger in the German's face, said in a barely controlled voice, "So, Neumann, *you* are the one I've been waiting to meet. Indeed, there are a great many French men and women waiting to see *you* again. We have a list of crimes against French citizens — and prisoners of war — committed by you and people acting on your orders that is as long as my arm."

Pushing his face right into Neumann's, Lionel continued, "Your completely unwarranted torture and murder of Petty Officer McDonald and your obscenely cruel abuse of Lieutenant Commander Tremayne alone justify your execution as a war criminal. Add to that the torture and deaths of so many of my compatriots —" Lionel paused and took a deep breath. "You and I, Neumann, will meet again in a few days time at *your* execution — I guarantee that."

Calling to the guards, he ground out the words, "Take this scum away," and then he left, with Tremayne, to meet with Colonel Timmins.

The colonel greeted them with an enquiring expression. "Well, were my hunches right about those four guys?"

"Indeed they were, sir, and Captain Mercier and I would like to relieve you of them and let the French Judiciary take charge."

"I'll cut through the red tape to get the legal show on the

*Staff sergeant

road asap. What will you guys do with those bastards – shoot 'em?"

That question was addressed principally to Lionel.

"No, mon Colonel. Two of the henchmen will be in gaol for very long sentences but Neumann, together with the first one we interrogated, will *hang*." Lionel paused before continuing, "The case against each is irrefutable. There is just so much evidence of their collective – and individual – inhumanity. Sentences will be carried out within a matter of days, Colonel."

Hearing the Frenchman's decision about Neumann confirmed so starkly brought neither joy nor a sense of triumph to Tremayne. He had struggled for months with his emotions and the horrific memories of his incarceration and hideous treatment at Neumann's hands – and now, all at once, he felt completely devoid of emotion.

Where he had expected an overpowering sense of retribution and justifiable vengeance, there was, instead, simply a feeling of drained completeness. It did feel at long last, however, that his desperate need for justice would finally be fulfilled – and that perhaps Mac could now truly rest in peace.

Before leaving, Tremayne exchanged addresses with the American colonel, still astonished and delighted at the coincidence involving Lieutenant of Marines, Jonathan Tremayne – one of his more notable and colourful forebears.

Curiously, he recalled, the subject of his forebears had also recently come up when telephoning his father. He had reminded

Tremayne that his Uncle Harry had, for two very packed years between 1917 and 1918, been a seaplane pilot, based on Tresco, with the Royal Naval Air Service. Tremayne remembered stories of derring-do about his father's younger daredevil brother when he was a young boy. Strangely, the association with the Scillies had never really registered with Tremayne – only the tales of his uncle's bravery in action and the Russian countess he had married.

Together with Farrell and Black, Tremayne remained a further two weeks in Brittany to support the Confrèrie's need to resurrect and implement a politically uncontaminated French judiciary in the newly liberated towns, in conjunction with the rapidly advancing US forces. Just as the process of beginning to bring war criminals to justice was starting to take a more coherent form – in Rennes, at least – an urgent SOE recall brought them back to London, to prepare for further major assignments in the areas of France still controlled by the Germans.

As the Americans had finally removed the blockage of St Lô, so the British and Canadians had, at long last, overcome the fierce German resistance at Caen and were moving south and east towards Paris. Both Allied armies had now taken major steps towards the eventual liberation of the rest of occupied France.

On his return to HMS Godolphin, Tremayne was congratulated by a delighted Enever on the reports he had received from Lionel via SOE.

"To say that they are 'glowing', dear boy, is not in it — they are positively in the realm of pyrotechnics! Admiral Hembury is also cock-a-hoop and, incidentally, has approved the award of your DSO so, again, my congratulations Richard. Oh — and by the way, dear boy — the champagne is on you tonight at the New Inn!"

Removing his pipe from between his teeth, Enever said, "You have two weeks' leave due, starting tomorrow at 17.30 hours. SIS have relocated Emma — and, of course, Catriona — to a small property in a hamlet near Beaconsfield in Buckinghamshire, close to London but away from these wretched doodlebugs — flying bombs to you, Richard. While you've been away in France, these infernal things have been doing so much damage to London, until our fighter pilots developed the right tactics to begin destroying them in the air. Emma is with a small community of largely civilian intelligence operators who are doing invaluable work to support the invasion. SIS felt the move was right — it's also a lot more economical for them to maintain a few small properties out of central London. Do please give Emma and Catriona my love when you see them!"

After a riotous celebratory homecoming with Hermann Fischer and the rest of his colleagues and shipmates at the New Inn, in which he failed lamentably to negotiate the drenchings of the obligatory drinking games — The Muffin Man and Cardinal Puff, Tremayne managed to escape the party at around two in the morning. Unable — and unwilling — to avoid Aileen

Oyler's ferocious congratulatory hug, he finally tumbled exhausted, but blissfully happy, into bed after a wildly enthusiastic welcome from Bertie.

Tremayne's last day before his leave was one of tying up loose ends with members of his boat crews and exploring, with a very ebullient Enever, the likely form the next round of assignments would take within occupied Europe.

He took what he considered to be vital time out to speak with Leading Seaman Watkins and to confirm that, while still in Normandy, he had managed to write to Nicholls's widow in Birmingham. He then spent time briefing Willoughby-Brown and his coxswain before leaving to meet the liberty boat from Penzance, bringing replacement ratings – and Emma and Catriona.

They arrived on what was a fresh, but sunny evening, with the sea still a stunning palette of translucent blues and greens and white-capped crests playing along the gently rolling waves.

Aileen and Dick Oyler had prepared what was now 'their' room for them, but this time with the addition of a beautiful hand-carved oak crib, generously made by one of the Bryher boat builders. With Catriona fast asleep in her quaintly traditional new bed, Tremayne and Emma fell into each other's arms.

"Let's just forget supper, Richard."

"One of Aileen's glorious Irish breakfasts will suit me fine – as long as she includes that wonderful 'tater' bread from Kilmoganny," laughed Tremayne.

"But I agree, darling, some things are far more important than supper."

One week later, just halfway through their leave together, Catriona Mhairi Sheena Tremayne was christened at the pretty parish church of St Nicholas where, two years before, Emma Fraser and Richard Tremayne were married.

As the party, including grandparents and godparents, slowly left through the curved stone archway of the church's main door, a short, burly figure detached itself from the small crowd gathered outside and approached Tremayne and Emma with obvious diffidence.

Saluting, Able Seaman Watkins said hesitatingly, "Excuse me, sir, ma'am. Brummie's widow and my missus made this for the baby, sir. We would like her to have it as a christening present." Tremayne gently took the beautifully-made traditional rag doll with its happy smiling face and charming patchwork frock. As Tremayne earnestly thanked Watkins, Emma stepped forward and, briefly touching the seaman's arm, said, "Thank you, Pablo. This is such a wonderful, thoughtful present and one we shall treasure – that I can promise you. The needlework is absolutely exquisite – and what a lovely face she has. Catriona is going to love her. We both thank you and the ladies so very much for such a generous, touching thought."

"It was Brummie's idea too, ma'am. As soon as we heard that you were expecting – beggin' your pardon – we *both* decided this was something we'd like to do, ma'am." He hesitated a moment as the pain of recall of his lost shipmate – and best friend – almost overcame him.

As Tremayne shook Watkins's hand and returned his salute, he saw that when the redoubtable sailor turned to rejoin the waiting crowd his proud eyes were glistening – just a little more than usual...

Epilogue

3rd JULY 2000...

O n the day following the celebration of the Tresco secret
flotilla's activities during the Second World War and the
unveiling of the Special Forces' commemorative plaque
at Braiden Rock anchorage, guests of honour and former flotilla
members began to leave the Island Hotel and make their way
home.

It had been a poignant reunion and a simple, yet moving ceremony, worthy of the gallantry and courage displayed during the war on the many clandestine operations originating from Tresco. The quiet, self-effacing modesty of such brave men had added great dignity to the sense of occasion, and the comradeship engendered during those momentous years was still so very evident.

The very next morning, Tremayne made a personal pilgrimage to Braiden Rock. He stood silently, remembering the many times he and his colleagues had sailed from and to the rocky anchorage, which had been their haven, so long ago.

Later, he and Emma, together with Willoughby-Brown and Lucy, boarded the Bryher Boat Services' sturdy ferry *Firethorne*. After sailing past the stone sentinel of Cromwell's Castle, they crossed the short stretch of azure and emerald sea to the Lower Town jetty on St Martin's island. The sun shone as *Firethorne*'s bright blue hull pushed its way through the rolling white-capped waves. Her sparkling bow wave cascaded over her distinctive chine and streamed, foaming, back into the sea. Gulls – grey and black-backed – and shag skimmed the gently swelling sea, searching for prey and for outlying rocks to rest upon. All were familiar sights but with differing, as well as shared, memories for each of the four visitors.

For a nostalgic moment, as he stood before the boat's white-painted wheelhouse, Tremayne saw again, all too briefly, a young First Lieutenant and a dour Ulster coxswain standing by his side. Somewhere behind him he thought he heard snatches of the caustic — but always well-intentioned — exchanges between 'Pablo' Watkins and 'Brummie' Nicholls. Capturing their accents and turns of phrase in his mind brought a wistful smile to his face which, unbeknown to him, Emma had seen and understood.

Just for one fleeting moment, he felt the urge to order Petty Officer Irvine to increase speed to maximum revolutions as they cleared the dangerous shallows. Off the port beam, the grandeur of Men-a-Vaur looked as dramatic as ever, with successive waves crashing and breaking upon its fearsome, rocky surfaces. To distant starboard, lay the beautiful and intriguing Eastern Isles where he and Emma had sailed, swum and enjoyed their picnic on a glorious sandy beach. "Was all that really almost sixty years ago?" he mused and, sensing Emma's caring presence, he turned to see her serious, still-beautiful blue eyes watching him with anxious concern.

"I sensed that for the last five minutes you've been here, yet not *really* here," she said quietly. "I think that I understand you well enough, Richard, to know where you *have* been. I worry sometimes that such unforgettable days bring pain as well as happiness."

Tremayne touched her hand and kissed her on her cheek. "Don't worry, dearest Emma, there's far more joy than regret in my memories and your presence reminds me of the many good times we shared."

A few minutes later, *Firethorne* secured at Lower Town landing stage and April, 'Pablo' Watkins's daughter, was already waiting, her little Japanese 4x4 open, ready to transport the four of them and their luggage.

She had inherited her father's amiable grin and purposeful air and, after her warm welcome, she loaded up with the help of Tremayne and Willoughby-Brown and drove them the quarter of a mile to her guest house.

Tremayne – concerned that he had not seen Watkins for more than twenty years since his return to the mainland on the death of his wife – asked, "And how's that old reprobate of a father of yours? Is he keeping well?"

"Oh he's fine, thank you, Mr Tremayne, but he misses Mom more than he lets on – even after all these years. Dad still misses 'Brummie' Nicholls too and often talks about him. He does come back here occasionally to see his grandchildren and cause complete chaos in my kitchen. He's become very arthritic of late, but he gets down to his local and his beloved ex-Service-men's club two or three times a week."

"April, I'm really glad to hear that he's rolling along well and I'd so love to see the old devil again," grinned Tremayne.

"Rolling's the very word, Mr Tremayne. When he staggers home from the club, plaiting his legs and singing, it's a sight to behold I can tell you!"

"I miss him too," chipped in a smiling Willoughby-Brown, "particularly those glorious breakfasts of his. They were real gourmet fare, cooked so unbelievably well on that ridiculous galley stove and with that brown sauce... And oh for another mug of your father's lifesaving kye!"

Their luggage unloaded and put away, the Tremaynes and Willoughby-Browns went downstairs to join April for a welcome mid-morning cup of coffee. They then planned to walk up to Higher Town, to St Martin's post office for postcards and to see again the ever-welcoming Post-Mistress – then on to the delightful Polreath restaurant for lunch. "After that," said Tremayne, "who knows. Either a walk to The Daymark –"

"Or perhaps some Egyptian PT?" added Willoughby-Brown with a grin.

Amidst the rattle of cups and saucers, April called out, "Sit you down folks – drinks should only be a minute!"

As they sat chatting and laughing, as they had always done whenever they met over the long years, a sudden adenoidal, off-key wail came from the kitchen –

'Walk up, walk up, see the tattooed lady.

See the tattooed lady at the fair.

In went the lads and gave a mighty cheer,

'Cos tattooed on her arse was ev'ry town in Lancashire...'

"PABLO! You old rogue. I don't believe it. How bloody marvellous to see you!"

In a second, the old sailor was surrounded as he emerged with a tray of rum-laced cocoa – slapped on the back by Tremayne and Willoughby-Brown and fiercely hugged by Emma and Lucy.

"'Ere, you ladies are all the same, beggin' yer pardon. Always after me body and never me brains! By the way, ladies and gents, it's not *proper* pusser's kye but it's near enough, I suppose."

"Pablo," said Tremayne, "I believe this will be one holiday that we're *all* going to remember!"

There were tears of joy too, as well as the laughter, as the group moved outside into the welcoming sun and onto the terrace overlooking the sea, with Tresco in view across the rolling, ever-changing water...

=====O=====

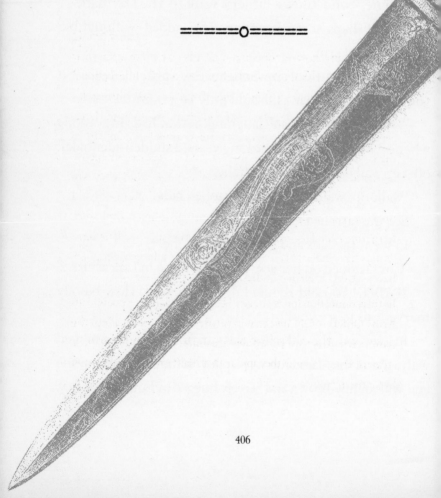

Appendix

KOMMANDOBEFEHL   **SECRET**

(Hitler's Commando Order: 18.10.42)

The Fuhrer

No. 003830/42g.Kdos. **OKW/Wst**   F.H. Qu 18.10.1942

12 copies   **Copy No. 12**

1. For a long time now our opponents have been employing in their
   conduct of the war, methods which contravene the International
   Convention of Geneva. The members of the so-called Commandos
   behave in a particularly brutal and underhand manner, and it has
   been established that those units recruit criminals not only from
   their own country but even former convicts set free in enemy
   territories. From captured orders it emerges that they are
   instructed not only to tie up prisoners, but also to kill out-of-hand
   unarmed captives who they think might prove an encumbrance
   to them, or hinder them in successfully carrying out their aims.
   Orders have indeed been found in which the killing of prisoners
   has positively been demanded of them.

2. In this connection it has already been notified in an Appendix to
   Army Orders of 7.10.1942 that in future, Germany will adopt the
   same methods against these Sabotage units of the British and their
   Allies; i.e. that, whenever they appear, they shall be ruthlessly destroyed
   by German troops.

3. I order, therefore:

   From now on all men operating against German troops in so-called Commando raids in Europe or in Africa, are to be annihilated to the last man. This is to be carried out whether they be soldiers in uniform, or saboteurs, with or without arms; and whether fighting or seeking to escape; and it is equally immaterial whether they come into action from Ships and Aircraft, or whether they land by parachute. Even if these individuals on discovery make obvious their intention of giving themselves up as prisoners, no pardon is on any account to be given. On this matter a report is to be made on each case to Headquarters for the information of Higher Command.

4. Should individual members of these Commandos, such as agents, saboteurs etc., fall into the hands of the Armed Forces through any means — as, for example, through the Police in one of the Occupied Territories — they are to be instantly handed over to the S.D.

   To hold them in military custody — for example in P.O.W. Camps, etc., even if only as a temporary measure, is strictly forbidden.

5. This order does not apply to the treatment of those enemy soldiers who are taken prisoner or give themselves up in open battle, in the course of normal operations, large scale attacks, or in major assault landings or airborne operations. Neither does it apply to those who fall into our hands after a sea fight, nor to those enemy soldiers who, after air battle, seek to save their lives by parachute.

6. I will hold all Commanders and Officers responsible under Military Law for any omission to carry out this order, whether by failure in their duty to instruct their units accordingly, or if they themselves act contrary to it.

   (Sgd) A Hitler

HEADQUARTERS OF THE ARMY (OKW)   SECRET

No. 551781/42g.k. Chefs W.F.St/Qu.   **F.H. Qu. 19/10/42**

22 Copies   Copy No. 21.

The enclosed Order from the Fuhrer is forwarded in connection with destruction of enemy Terror and Sabotage-troops.

This order is intended for Commanders only and is in no circumstances to fall into Enemy hands.

Further distribution by receiving Headquarters is to be most strictly limited.

The Headquarters mentioned in the Distribution list are responsible that all parts of the Oder, or extracts taken from it, which are issued are again withdrawn and, together with this copy, destroyed.

Chief of Staff of the Army

(Sgd) JODL

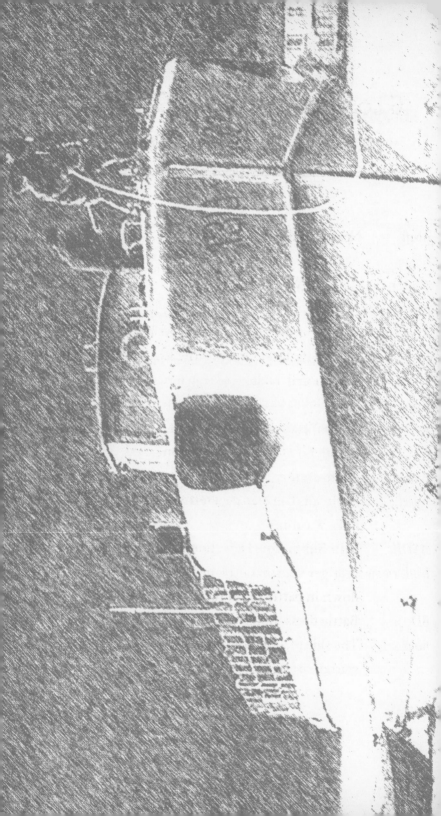

Glossary of Naval and Royal Marine terms

==

Abaft	Nearer to the stern, than…
Abeam	At right angles to the line of the ship or boat
Abwehr	German Military Intelligence
Adrift	Naval term for late
After	Behind or rear – eg, the after (rear) deck
AFO	Admiralty Fleet Orders – the Royal Navy's operational 'bible'
Aggie Weston's	Sailors' accommodation ashore, named after its founder – Dame Agnes Weston
Ammo	Ammunition
Appel	Roll-call (German) – a term used for roll-call in PoW camps
ASDIC	Anti-Submarine Detection Investigation
Battle ensign	A larger version of the normal naval ensign, flown in battle to aid recognition and identity
BD	Battle dress uniform
Beam	The side of a ship or boat – eg port (left) or starboard (right) beam

Bergen	Special Forces/Commando name for a military rucksack
Blue Liner	RN-issue cigarettes and tobacco – tins were marked with a blue line, denoting official issue, and not for sale to the general public
Bohemian Corporal	Derogatory term for Hitler, used by some German officers
Bofors	A high-angle automatic gun of Swedish origin that fires 40mm shells
Brew up	Burn fiercely then explode
Cockle	*(Mk I, or MK II)* Early Royal Marine term for Service two-man canoe
COPP	Combined Operations Pilotage Party – trained swimmer- reconnaissance operators, wearing 'dry suits', but not breathing apparatus, who reconnoitre enemy shores, prior to seaborne assaults and landings
Cox'n	Abbreviation of coxswain – the petty officer/rating who steers the boat
CTC	Commando Training Centre
Donkey wallopers	Derogatory term used to describe the cavalry and other 'horse soldiers'

E-boat/ *S-Boot*	British and German terms for German motor torpedo-boat
Egyptian PT	Period of sleep taken during the day
Ensign	Naval flag usually indicating nationality/ identity
ETA	Estimated time of arrival
ETD	Estimated time of departure
Forrard	Forward, towards the bow of the ship or boat
Gas-pipe cavalry	Unflattering term used by non-cavalry to describe modern armoured forces
Gun-layer	Crew member who feeds the weapon with ammunition
Guz	Naval slang for Plymouth/Devonport
Heads	Naval term for the loo
Horses	Horsepower (HP)
IFF	Radar equipment capable of identifying 'friend' or 'foe'
Kriegsmarine	German name for their Navy under the Nazi regime
Kye	The Navy's own hot drinking chocolate
LCT/LCI	Landing craft (tanks)/landing craft (infantry)
Make to...	The command to send a signal to someone

MAS38	French military/gendarme sub-machine gun, 1938 vintage
MG34, MG38, MG42	German machine guns of 1934, 1938 and 1942 vintage
MGB/MTB	Motor gun-boat/motor torpedo-boat
MP38/ MP40	German machine pistols of 1938 and 1940 vintage
MT	Military motor transport section
Neaters	Popular naval term for an issue of neat rum
NCO	Non-commissioned officer – eg, petty officer, corporal or sergeant
Nelson slice	A solid wedge of pastry and indeterminate fruit, topped with icing
NKVD	The People's Commissariat for Internal Affairs (former Soviet Government Intelligence Services)
Nutty ration	Chocolate/sweets (when such items were officially rationed during WW2)
Oerlikon	An automatic gun of Swiss origin that fires 20mm calibre shells
'O' Group	Orders Group – ie, a pre-operational briefing
OKM/OKW	Oberkommando Marine/Oberkommando Wehrmacht – Office of Chiefs of Staff of the German Navy (Marine) or Army (Wehrmacht)

'On parade'	Circumstances which demand that protocols of rank are maintained. In contrast, 'off parade' means that titles and rank differentiation are less important and that less formality is acceptable
OSS	Office of Strategic Services – US equivalent of British SOE
PIAT	Projectile Infantry Anti-Tank – a hand-held, infantry grenade launcher
Pongo	Naval derogatory term for a soldier
Pusser	Slang for purser, also used in the sense of 'officially' or 'properly' naval
Q-ship	Armed decoy vessel, disguised as a harmless, unarmed merchant ship
Rate	Rank
Rating	Non-commissioned sailor
Royal	A Royal Marine term for one of their own – ie, a fellow Royal Marine
Sick bay	Temporary or local military/naval hospital
SIS	British Secret Intelligence Service (more recently, MI6)
Slip	The command to let go mooring lines and move off
SNIO/SIO	Senior (Naval) Intelligence Officer
Snorker	Slang for sausage
SOE	Strategic Operations Executive – British wartime Intelligence Service

Sparks/	
Sparker	The ship's radio operator
Stone frigate	Naval shore establishment
SV	Soles vulcanised – term used to describe 'commando'-soled boots
'Swain	Alternative abbreviation for coxswain – often used as a form of address
Sweep	Systematic search for enemy mines, vessels or other targets
Three-badge veteran	Rating with twelve or more years' naval service (each 'badge' or arm stripe represents four years' service)
Tiddly	Naval term for smart, as in smart turnout or best uniform – eg, a 'tiddly suit'
Twelve-mile sniper	Naval term for members of the Royal Artillery
Wardroom	Room in a ship/shore establishment reserved for commissioned officers
WEF	With effect from...
WT	Wireless telegraphy – messages relayed by Morse code, as opposed to RT, radio telegraphy – messages relayed by voice
Yeoman	The ship's signaller (often abbreviated to Yeo when addressing the Yeoman directly)

Acknowledgements

===============================

I count myself very fortunate to have the continuing encouragement and enthusiastic backing from Thorogood Publishing's executive team. They remain an inexhaustible source of inspiration and guidance.

Their dedication, their energy and their boundless enthusiasm mark out Neil Thomas, Angela Spall and Twaambo Munjanja as consummate professionals – and pure joy to work with.

I rate the years that I have been an associate colleague of theirs among the best of a very full professional life stretching back over half a century.

On the island of Tresco, people have so generously given their time to answer my questions and to provide much helpful information, to add historical authenticity and local context to the story.

The Channel of Invasion is a fictionalised account of events, but it has its roots in real Scillonian and Special Forces history. It is the sequel to *The Secret Channel* – my first novel about the Tresco flotilla's covert wartime operations.

Those so very helpful on Tresco include:

Richard Barber, author of *The Last Piece of England* and editor of *The Tresco Times*, who has been such a willing fund of information about Tresco's clandestine operations during the Second World War, generously sharing his own extensive research.

Robin Lawson, manager of the New Inn Hotel, for his infectious enthusiasm and invaluable background information about the central role of the New Inn — and its integral shop — during the Second World War.

Isobel Nelhams, manager of The Garden Visitor Centre, for the tireless energy and professionalism that she has put into promoting *The Secret Channel* on Tresco.

On the island of St Agnes, my thanks are due to Robert Anderson, landlord of the excellent Turk's Head pub, for his help on the history and original location of the inn during the time of the novel's story.

On St Martin's, I am most grateful to former postmistress Daphne Perkins and Julia Walder, the present postmistress, for their ever generous help and readiness to answer my questions about the island of St Martin's and its place in Scillonian history.

To the late Sir Brooks Richards, author of *Secret Flotillas,* the HMSO definitive account of clandestine small boat operations between 1940 and 1944, I owe an immense debt for the time he kindly gave to answer my many questions during the research for my books.

Being a spectator in July 2000 at the moving unveiling of the commemorative plaque to the Naval Special Forces based on Tresco during the war — and meeting Sir Brooks — was an unforgettable experience and the original driving force behind both this book and the first volume of the Tresco flotilla's story.

To the Naval Club, Mayfair, of which I am a member —

and to Commander John Pritchard RN, the chief executive – I express my gratitude for the Club journal *WAVE*. This has regularly proved to be a source of relevant information on wartime Coastal Forces operations and the role of former Royal Naval Volunteer Reserve (RNVR) officers in particular.

Eight years of full-time and volunteer reserve service in first the Royal Navy (Intelligence) and secondly the Royal Marines (Special Boat Service and Commando) have provided me with a rich source of experiences and material, from which I have drawn extensively for this story.

To my fellow authors and 'scribes' in the Devizes Writers' Group, I give my unbounded thanks for their most welcome and perceptive feedback on my literary efforts. As colleagues and friends, they are an ever-stimulating source of encouragement and inspiration.

I owe so much to Brenda, my wife and my best friend, for the benefit of the breadth and depth of her experience as a talented author and poet. Her wry humour, her sensitive perceptiveness and professional acuity have been invaluable in helping me to refine my own fictional written style.

We first used our kayaks together in the waters around Scilly in 1959 – sometimes accompanied by schools of porpoise and the odd curious seal (which I was convinced were Russian naval frogmen in disguise!). Now in our seventies, we still canoe those beautiful emerald and turquoise seas…

Mike Williams